"A coming of age story recomı
deep into local history along wi.   ....g ....o ..uo
not only have each other's back, but spend the last remaining days of
their first year of high school looking over theirs, as the Dartmouth
Police Force tracks down a killer who's determined to silence what
they know."

Louise Michalos, author of *Marilla Before Anne*.

FRIENDS & CONSEQUENCES

TALES FROM THE OLD FORT - 1973

DJ WATT

Published by arrangement with Somewhat Grumpy Press Inc. Halifax, Nova Scotia, Canada. The Somewhat Grumpy Press name and Pallas' cat logo are registered trademarks.

ISBN 978-1-7380743-9-6 (paperback)

ISBN 978-1-998555-00-0 (eBook)

September 2024 v6

CONTENTS

ACKNOWLEDGMENTS

I wrote this novel with the support, assistance, patience, and knowledge of a few people in my life, and I would like to thank them:

My wife Mary, and her love of fashion and design. She reminded me of style details so prevalent in the seventies. I also thank her for her constant understanding of the hours I spent hanging over my laptop or just sitting with my thoughts.

My sister Mary Ellen, who was an excellent resource of both daily life in Dartmouth at that time as well as the thoughts and feelings of a fifteen-year-old girl of that era.

Friend and author Louise Michalos, who listened while I read my first humble scribblings and replied, "… well Doug, you're a writer!" She taught me much of how a story should be written, in terms of form and format. Thank you, Louise.

Thank you to Carolyn, Sharon, and Irene, who were the first to read my finished manuscript, suffering through the myriad of writing errors and helping it evolve into something enjoyable.

Much thanks to my editor Tim Covell, whose expertise and experience are standing behind most of the pages in this book.

Thanks to my lifelong friend Ronnie, who was the inspiration for the character Natty and whose image graces the front cover. He really did show me that there are no obstacles between true friends.

CAST OF CHARACTERS

DONALD AND FRIENDS

Donald George Langille – Grade 10 student
Robert Stephen Langille – Donald's father, a heavy machinery salesman
Jane Margaret Langille – Donald's mother
Anita Catherine Langille – Donald's sister, a university student in Toronto

FRIENDS

Peter Meijer
Andrew Francis Roche (Clip) Sean
Nathaniel Power (Natty)
Madeline Chelsea Wagner

HEIDI

Heidi Freeman Frank Freeman – Heidi's father, part-time labourer
Molly Freeman – Heidi's late mother
Mark Freeman – Heidi's brother, somewhere in Montreal?
Kevin McCrae – Heidi's uncle
Matilda Freeman – Heidi's aunt, a critical care nurse

THE LAKE WILLIAM PLANT EMPORIUM

Andreas Norberg – owner
Erik Jorgen – related to Andreas
Bradley Ferguson – Employee Paul Delaney – Employee

NE'ER-DO-WELLS

Louis Ryan – a fixer
Gerard "Jerry" LaChance – a drug wholesaler
McGregor – a fixer

POLICE

Elmer Daweson – Police Chief
Richard Rafuse – Chief Detective
Shane O'Byrne – Detective
Peter Wilson – Sergeant
Keith Fong – Corporal
Philip Hicks – Constable
Jennifer Horn – Stenographer
Jaroslaw Lukawski – sketch artist
Brian MacKay – RCMP Corporal
Ali Hassan – RCMP Constable
Trevour Harper – RCMP Constable (HARP)

PROLOGUE

SURVIVAL

Liverpool, Nova Scotia
Saturday January 13, 1973
2:30 am

Otherwise, it was a beautifully peaceful January night. Earlier in the day, the temperature was above freezing, so the top layer of snow had melted in the sunlight. This smoothed any blemishes, like footprints or tire tracks, into a million tiny hills and valleys. The evening's colder temperatures sealed this miniature landscape with a thick crust of ice. A crystal-clear moonless sky, punctuated by a billion stars, stretched from horizon to horizon.

Almost every person on Old Port Mouton Road was safely snuggled under thick blankets in cozy, warm houses. Such was the calm tranquility of the town of Liverpool, Nova Scotia.

In the basement of one ramshackle house on that road, fifteen-year-old Heidi Freeman stood at the top of the basement stairs, frantically tying one end of a rope to the doorknob and the other end around the stair handrail. She pulled with all her might to tighten the knots. There was no lock on the outward swinging door, so she prayed the rope would provide a barrier to anyone attempting to reach her. But the question of whether it held or not was moot. It was all she had for protection.

A single forty-watt bulb hung on an ancient wire from the ceiling at the top of the steps. She had pulled the chain to lighten her surroundings in the panic of a few moments ago and it swung silently, creating dancing shadows around her.

Heidi took several deep breaths to calm herself, each one a small vapour cloud lingering in the air around her. She turned and sat down on the top step, shaking uncontrollably from fear and anger. And the cold. The fire in the ancient wood furnace had long since burned to embers and was slowly dying from neglect.

Next to Heidi, on the floor, were two pieces of a hand-sized seashell. It was broken in the struggle of a few moments ago. To her it was a reminder of the best time in her life and at that moment, meant the world to her. Heidi put her ear against the door and listened. She heard nothing ... except an occasional moan from the second floor.

This was the first time in her life she had felt true fear. She had no support and no protection. She felt isolated and alone. It could have been hopeless. But she had an indomitable spirit. And one person who loved her unconditionally. And that's who she had turned to.

So now Heidi sat on the top step, clutching the rope with both hands as if it was a lifeline. She waited, listening for the sound of footsteps and whoever would be the first to arrive.

PREMONITION

Dartmouth, Nova Scotia
Saturday January 13, 1973
2:30 am

It had been a late-night broadcast. The Montreal Canadiens were playing the California Golden Seals in the Oakland Coliseum and fifteen-year-old Donnie Langille was determined to listen to the whole game. Start time on the west coast had been 8:00 pm which translated to a midnight start in Nova Scotia. His parents were in the room down the hall but, as long as he kept the volume to a minimum, they wouldn't be disturbed.

He'd been munching snacks and drinking root beer during the first two periods of play, but it was getting late, or perhaps one could say early. During the second intermission and the in-depth analysis of the game so far, he had washed up, brushed his teeth, and threw on his pyjamas. Donnie had intended to listen to the last period of the game in bed but drifted off to sleep shortly after 2:00 am, Jean Beliveau looking down on the boy from his poster on the wall. The radio-cassette player on the table by the bed continued quietly with the play by play of the hockey action until its 3-3 conclusion and beyond.

Donnie's sleep was dark and complete, as is normal for a fifteen-year-old. But it wasn't dreamless.

He was swimming in a lake, completely naked. The water was cold but not unbearable. His biggest concern was the whereabouts of his clothing. He paused to tread water while looking behind, in the direction from which he'd come, but the shoreline was shrouded in fog. An occasional treetop was sticking out of the mist as well as something else, the concrete rooftop of the Old Fort. That's strange, he thought, the Old Fort is nowhere near any lake.

He could smell the flat odour of freshwater, and the pungent scent of spruce trees all around. Except for the occasional gurgle of water, all was deathly quiet. He looked towards the opposite shore, about fifty yards away. It was sunny, bright, and clear in that direction, but the land was covered with a forest of dark evergreen trees and brush running right down to the water's edge. Which way to go?

A girl's cry leaped out of the green forest, startling him. It punched itself through the silence like a fist. A cry for help that was neither a scream nor a wail, but something in between. A voice that sounded so familiar and she was calling him by name!

"Donnie! Donnie, help me!"

He started swimming towards the sound but there was an ice-cold current pushing him sideways towards the middle of the lake. It was frustrating and Donnie re-doubled his efforts. With each stroke, he took a sideways peek at the shore and saw that he was finally making headway.

As he got within ten yards of the bright shoreline something floated into his line of sight, forcing him to splash to a stop. It was a carving knife with a ten-inch blade and a yellowed ceramic handle. Donnie had seen it before and had even used it recently, but from where and when, he could not remember. It was a large, heavy knife, and had no business floating on top of the water, but there it was, nonetheless.

The knife slowed to a stop right in front of his eyes. As it bobbed softly in the lake's waves, the blade caught the meagre sunlight, searing his eyes and he winced. He could hear the cries for help more clearly now, sounding more desperate than ever, and he knew who that voice belonged to. Heidi.

His Heidi. A rush of warmth filled his mind and body ... tempered by the obstacle in his path.

"Donnie! He's coming for me! Donnie!!" Heidi's cries turned into a scream, but try as he might, he couldn't move and was paralyzed with fear, transfixed by the blade.

Then his stomach dropped. Blood appeared around the knife and poured out of the blade, like an oil slick growing on the water. The knife turned until it pointed in his direction, and drifted closer to him. Horrified, he felt an overwhelming need to get away. Forgotten was his nakedness or his troubled friend trapped in the forest.

Donnie swam back towards the foggy shore as fast as he could, filled with loathing at his own cowardly actions. He was filled with pangs of guilt, but they were washed away by the ripples in the lake, made by the knife now skimming towards him, followed by a jagged dark red stream of blood behind.

It was another long, exhausting swim but as he arrived within twenty yards, and feeling like he couldn't swim another stroke, he saw his three best friends standing on the shoreline. Salvation! Natty, Peter, and Clip were casually talking and laughing with each other, and he knew if he could get their attention, they would help him out of the water, and the four boys could make their way to the Old Fort. And safety.

Donnie paused, treading water to catch his breath, and called out to them. But they didn't hear, turned their backs, and disappeared into the fog. Anguish tore at him as he yelled again, but only a frustrating squeak came out of his mouth. He could feel his heartbeat pounding in his ears. He turned to see how close the knife was behind him —

It flew towards his face, blade first, as if thrown. He screamed, thrashing in the water, and woke up on the floor next to the bed. How? He was sweating and swathed in bed clothes. His heart was pounding in his chest, and he was gasping for air as if he were still in the water. He held his hand out in front, trying to ward off the now non-existent knife.

Jeez, what just happened? he thought, still half-caught in the dream world. His heart thumped in his chest, but the nightmare was already fading. One thing clung to his memory: Heidi's voice crying for help. Why would he dream of his childhood friend? He hadn't seen her in six years. And even though he had barely thought of her recently, he found himself longing to see her again.

Donnie looked at his hands as the shaking subsided. *Oh man, that was bad.* Normally, his dreams were weird, obscure scenes that he barely understood, but this had been a crystal-clear nightmare, though he struggled to discern its meaning. One thing was for sure, he couldn't remember ever having fallen out of bed during a dream.

His cassette radio was still powered on, Dennis Locorriere crooning about "Sylvia's Mother." Evidently, the game had long since ended. He turned it off, took a sip of water from the glass on the table next to his bed, and dragged himself back onto the mattress.

As he fell back to sleep, part of Donnie hoped the dream would continue, because he couldn't shake the feeling that Heidi still needed his help. But it was a deep slumber and by morning most of his emotions had faded away.

It was six months before dreams became reality.

WEDNESDAY

A MINOR ERROR

Commercial Street was an important thruway in downtown Dartmouth, Nova Scotia. It wound its way from the intersection of Wyse Road and Windmill Road south along the harbour edge, past the Harbour Ferry, to the Dartmouth Marine Slips. From there, you could weave your way onto Portland Street, heading to Woodside or Prince Albert Road past Sullivan's Pond. The buildings along the street were a mix of business and commercial structures, some as much as a century old. They were quaint and rickety, but not unattractive.

Later in 1973, Commercial Street would be renamed Alderney Drive as part of a major re-vamping of the downtown area. Most of the buildings on the harbour side would be cleared but, until then, they were home to all the typical activities of a busy port city.

One of these buildings was a turn-of-the-century warehouse, which had man-doors on the east and south sides and two overhead doors at the loading docks on the western side, facing the harbour. The man-doors had windows in them, but they had been painted black and there were no other windows in the building. The overhead doors had the numbers 1 and 2 painted on them. Number 2 was open, and a plain white cargo van was backed into it. The building was one of two owned by a holding company in the Cayman Islands. This afforded the owners complete anonymity. The second building was in the Burnside Industrial Park.

Erik Jorgen stood on the edge of the number 2 loading dock; his face turned up to the midday sun, enjoying the early-summer warmth. He and his fellow employees referred to this building as the Commercial Street warehouse. He normally worked in the company's main facility, a plant nursery, The Lake William Plant Emporium, which was ten miles to the north, about a twenty-five-minute drive away.

This was one part of his job that Erik truly enjoyed. In fact, he revelled in it. Some of his co-workers called him "Delivery Boy" but he didn't care. He performed this task every Monday and Wednesday morning, and was on call for Fridays when the demand was high. He was waiting for the fertilizer shipment to arrive.

The Emporium purchased only the highest-grade for its clients, and the product had been sent across the ocean in a container that had been off-loaded yesterday evening in Saint John, New Brunswick. It was transferred to a long-haul truck this morning. The entire load of fertilizer would be off-loaded here in the Commercial Street warehouse. Depending on demand, it would then be taken to different cities around the Maritimes for processing and distribution, in smaller delivery vans like the one Erik had rented this morning. The Halifax-Dartmouth metropolitan area was by far the biggest consumer of the fertilizer, using about fifty percent of the product.

After delivering his cargo to the Emporium and before he returned the van to the rental company the next day, Erik would pay extra to have the cargo area in the rear cleaned out with a hose. This helped remove any evidence of fertilizer. A wise precaution.

The wall phone in the warehouse rang, setting Erik's pulse racing. Generally, it was only to be used if there was an emergency. He dashed over and answered it.

"Yes?"

It was his boss, Bradley Ferguson. "We're in trouble! One of the cases of fertilizer was sent on the weekend by air courier."

"Air courier? They're not supposed to do that! Why?"

"I guess people overseas are just as stupid as we are sometimes. Some new jerk who didn't know any better panicked when he realized he missed putting a box on the boat. He didn't want his bosses getting angry over an underweight shipment, so he couriered it separately. And now it's our problem! The boss says it's up to you and me to fix this, okay?"

"Okay, so do I just wait here for the courier?"

"No, no!" Bradley roared. "On top of every else, the dumb shit put the wrong address on the package!"

"Fuck! What address did they send it to?"

"283 Commercial."

"Son of a bitch," said Erik. The address of the warehouse was 238 Commercial Street. "He screwed up the numbers!"

"How soon can you get to 283?" Bradley asked.

"I can be there in a couple of minutes and wait for the courier outside. It's only a couple blocks," replied Erik.

"That won't help! I called the courier, and the fucking thing was sent out bright and early this morning. Chances are the damn thing has already been delivered and if that's the case, I don't have to tell you the kind of shit we're in if anybody opens that box."

"Yeah, no kidding! Okay, I'm leaving right now. Who's at the 283 addresses?" asked Erik.

"According to the city directory, it's just some little shithole convenience store."

"Okay, okay, I'll take care of it, don't worry." And Erik hung up.

He ran to the overhead door facing the harbour, pulled it down, and locked it. Then he grabbed his jacket and headed for the man-door at the side of the warehouse. But someone outside was already knocking on it.

DONNIE LANGILLE

1973 showed a world full of turmoil and change. The Paris peace talks, the OPEC oil crisis, Wounded Knee, runaway inflation, and Prime Minister Pierre Elliott Trudeau was nine months into a minority government. President Nixon was telling the Watergate investigators once again that he had no knowledge of the break-ins. The final moon landing was just six months prior ... and for the first time in his life, Donnie Langille needed a job. A part-time summer job, to be precise. His dad had heard of one company eager to hire students, and he suggested his son call for an interview. And when Donnie's dad suggested something, it was darn near a biblical commandment!

In two weeks, Donnie would be turning in his textbooks and saying goodbye to his grade ten teachers at Dartmouth High School. Due to the superb two terms rule introduced by the province of Nova Scotia, he had already passed his third term and was headed for grade eleven, so when Donnie asked if he could miss his afternoon classes for a job interview, the request was quickly granted.

The two terms rule stated that "any high school student who attained a minimum 85% score in any subject's first and second final term exam, would not be required to write that subject's third-term final exam and was to be passed with honours, provided he or she maintained similarly impressive marks in regularly scheduled third-term tests." Somehow, Donnie had paid enough attention in all his subjects to qualify.

So, blessed with the pope-like wave of his teacher's hand, he headed home. His dad was at work and his mom was out of town, so he made himself a ham sandwich lunch. Then he pulled off his good clothes and threw on some older ones. His dad had warned him to wear something more appropriate for working with soil. Forty-five minutes later, he jumped on a Dartmouth Transit bus heading downtown to the transfer point in front of City Hall, just off Commercial Street, for all out-of-town buses.

Donnie was a tad nervous, but one thought occurred to him. "D-

Day was exactly twenty-nine years ago today," he said to himself. "Imagine what those poor fellows had to face."

MR. MARTIN'S CORNER STORE

Donnie's destination was a plant nursery on the outskirts of town, but there was a fifteen-minute wait at the transfer point. Not a lot was happening in the ancient terminal on a Wednesday afternoon at 1:20, so, with a bus transfer in his pocket, he headed across the street to Martin's Corner Store. It was on the north-east side of the corner of Commercial and Portland streets.

The store was owned by Mr. Reginald Martin, a stocky, outgoing, and energetic gentleman in his early seventies. His store had the usual fare: canned goods, dry goods, newspapers, magazines, cigarettes, and so on, but Donnie was after a special treat that day. Mr. Martin was the patriarch of a family who specialized in the import and distribution of smoked and spiced meats, and his store had a display case chock full. A guy like Donnie, with a few quarters in his pocket, could get a tasty, nutritious snack of the best salami, pastrami, or prosciutto. Donnie rationalized his purchase as gaining valuable food energy before his important interview.

But delicious snacks notwithstanding, he loved to chat with the old fellow about his life experiences. And what a life he had! He was born in the last year of the 19th century, 1900 and had several careers from soldier to politician. And best of all, he would always leave his young friend with a fascinating historical fact to ponder.

On his last visit, Mr. Martin said, "Did you know Donnie, that most people in Halifax never saw a banana for six straight years?"

"Six years?!"

"Yessir. During the second world war, all the cargo ships were too busy contributing to the war effort to bother transporting luxuries like exotic fruit. Nobody complained much you know; we had bigger fish to fry trying to beat the Nazis and keeping England alive. When a shipload finally arrived in late 1945," he explained, "the bananas never made it to a store. Thousands of people bought cases of them right off the dock!" The man was a walking history book.

This afternoon, Donnie was looking forward to seeing his friend again and enjoying another fascinating story.

He entered the store, momentarily blinded by the gloom. He expected to see Mr. Martin behind the counter as usual, but the old fellow wasn't there. Another shopper was waiting by the cash register, so Donnie spent a few minutes perusing the magazine rack.

It was an old store and looked its part. Every surface a human hand might have touched was worn smooth. The countertop, the moulding around doors and windows, the corners of walls, the wooden magazine rack itself, and of course the floor, showed century-old age and charm. And everywhere looked clean and smelled fresh, thanks to the meticulous Mr. Martin.

Well, not quite. There was a hint of an unfamiliar smell in the air that afternoon. A sickly-sweet chemical smell, in fact. Donnie decided it was some kind of new floor cleaner, and quickly forgot about it.

After a few minutes with no sign of Mr. Martin, he wandered over to the counter and asked the other customer, "Have you seen the old guy who works here?"

"Mr. Martin?" he replied. "He had to run next door for something or other. He asked me to keep an eye on the place for a few minutes."

The stranger was mid to late thirties, a bit shorter than Donnie, with neat jeans, neat polo shirt, neat beard, and thin, straight, black, and certainly neat, hair. And he had a rolled up, light coloured jacket tucked under his arm. There was something off about the jacket, but the man was in the shadows, and Donnie only had a glance at it.

The man also had a slight case of raccoon eyes, as if he wore sunglasses a lot. Speaking of which, he had a 'Clint Eastwood' squinty stare, even though Donnie could see a pair of prescription glasses in his shirt pocket. He was fixing that stare on Donnie at that moment, but he was smiling.

You one of the Martin family?" Donnie asked.

"No, just a close family friend — Louis Ryan." He thrust his hand out.

"Donnie Langille, nice to meet you." The man's hand was the cold and clammy. "Your face has got quite the tan," he said, and noted that the hand he shook was pasty white with no tan at all. Odd.

"Florida," he said, which Donnie guessed was explanation enough. "Are you from around here?" Ryan asked.

"Dartmouth born and bred." Which wasn't technically true, but it sounded cool. "A couple of miles up Windmill Road over there." He nodded towards the north. He'd never been one to hold his cards close.

There was a moment of awkward silence. "But I see you're an ice hockey fan, correct?" Ryan asked finally. Donnie could make out a slight accent now. He was good at accents, but he couldn't quite place this one. Ryan spoke in a clipped, professional manner, like he was well rehearsed and chose every sentence before he spoke it. Donnie figured him for a Quebecois though, with the hockey reference. Besides, lots of Quebecers spent the winter months in Florida.

Donnie glanced down at front of the T-shirt he had pulled on at home. It had 'Club de Hockey Canadiens' printed on it below the team logo and a pair of crossed hockey sticks framing the emblem. "Yup, they just won another Stanley cup last month, the 4th in the past six years."

"Oh, yes?" Ryan looked puzzled. Which Donnie found odd, because he acted like he had no clue what Donnie was talking about. Every Quebecois worth their salt would have known that Montreal had won Lord Stanley's silver cup. And come to think of it, he had called it 'ice' hockey.

So definitely NOT a French Canadian. Whatever his accent and nationality, he just seemed a bit different. Yeah right, me and all my worldly experience, thought Donnie. Probably just an eccentric fellow. In any case, he felt he was in no danger. Not at that point.

"So, you're visiting from out of town?" he asked, just to kill some time.

That smarmy smile again. "Something like that," Ryan answered.

They made a few more minutes of small talk. The weather, if he was still in school, how often the Harbour Ferry next door ran, things like that. Donnie asked Ryan if he'd seen any of the Canada-Russia super summit series. To which, aside from a blank stare, Ryan offered no opinion. Finally, after a prolonged silence, he asked Ryan if he had the time.

Ryan glanced at his watch. "It's 1330 ... er 1:30."

"Okay, thanks." Donnie didn't want to be late for the bus, and still no sign of Mr. Martin, but damn if he was leaving here without his smoked meat! He started to walk around the counter, to slice off a piece of salami, when a hand, strong and unyielding, grabbed his arm.

"What are you doing?" asked Ryan. It was more an accusation than a question.

"I'm going to cut a couple slices of meat," he said. "Don't worry about it, Mr. Martin knows me, and I'll leave a couple bucks here on the counter ..." But as Donnie glanced at the cutting board next to the meat display, he noticed the big carving knife was missing. "Well damn," he murmured, "the knife's gone."

All the while, Ryan's hand was locked on his arm, and his eyes stared at the boy. They looked each other for a few seconds. The man finally smiled and released his arm.

"I can't let you go behind the counter, Donald," he said. "Mr. Martin asked me to keep an eye on this place and I don't want any trouble."

A bus rumbled past on Commercial Street, outside the front window. "That's my ride, I gotta go! Nice meeting you, say hi to Mr. Martin for me," Donnie said, all in a jumble as he walked briskly to the door. Ryan followed him closely. In fact, very closely, because as Donnie opened the door, he bumped Ryan with his elbow and was surprised to see the man almost glued to him.

Donnie was going to say sorry for hitting him, but Ryan was looking beyond Donnie, at something out in the street. Then Ryan mumbled, "Goodbye," and turned back toward the store counter.

As he dashed across the street, Donnie almost ran into a police car idling at the curb behind the out-of-town bus. The last thing he needed was to miss his bus while waiting for the cop to write him a jaywalking ticket! But he needn't have worried. The officer inside the car was on the radio and didn't notice him. As Donnie approached the bus door, the police car made a U-turn, red lights flashing, and screeched away heading north on Commercial Street at high speed, obviously on a call.

The air brakes on the bus made a loud *hissst* as Donnie stepped inside, the smell of diesel permeating the air. And it was then Donnie realized how strange Ryan had acted as he was leaving the store. A feeling of relief rolled over him like a wave, though from what, he had no idea. He also felt disappointment, as if he had somehow missed something of great importance in the last ten minutes. The hairs on the back of his neck were actually standing up. *Bizarre.*

The bus driver was someone he knew well, Earl Paris. Earl was a jolly, rotund fellow who used to drive the downtown route Donnie had used earlier. He must have switched to this more picturesque route that headed out of town. The familiar was suddenly comforting, and the strangeness of the last ten minutes almost melted away.

"How ya doin' Earl?" he asked.

"Rolling along Donnie, buckle up." Accompanied by a big chuckle. He was an odd fellow but, as Donnie's mom said, "What a boring world it would be if we were all the same."

He found a seat on the half empty bus, no seat belts to "buckle up" of course. By the time he settled into his seat, the feelings of danger and relief were passing. The bus lingered for another minute or two and Donnie kept an eye open for Mr. Martin returning from next door. He never saw him, but what he did see, as the bus pulled out, was Mr. Louis Ryan darting out the door, this time wearing his glasses, and jogging across the street and down toward the Harbour Ferry. He still had the summer jacket, hanging off his arm such that Donnie could see clearly what had bothered him in the store. The jacket was folded inside out. He could even make out the Tip Top Tailors logo on the shiny inner material.

Then he was off to his interview and had more important things to think about.

THE LAKE WILLIAM PLANT EMPORIUM

As always, the drive along the Waverley Road was picturesque. It wound its way on the edge of four lakes, Lake Banook, Lake MicMac, Lake Charles, and Lake William. The first two names were English bastardizations of Mi'kmaq words, Banook meaning First Lake and Micmac meaning … well, Mi'kmaq. The Mi'kmaq themselves were the local first-nations people of the province. The latter two lake names most likely came from English noblemen, but Donnie had never looked up which ones.

The bus glided along Waverley Road under a canopy of hardwood trees that were a spectacle to behold in the fall with their multitude of colours and shades. On this early-summer day there was a slight breeze whipping up the water, which is why the lakes on his left sparkled with the afternoon sun as if there were diamonds on top of every little wave point. This is also why he sat on the left side of the bus.

Donnie hopped off at Rocky Lake Drive, the closest stop, and walked about a quarter mile up the road, then turned down the small gravel driveway to the Lake William Plant Emporium.

The Emporium was five buildings: an office and store with a parking lot and its three-bay loading dock, three massive greenhouses behind it, and a warehouse with no windows at the far-right corner of the property. The rest of the land was used for growing trees, shrubs, and plants, and outdoor storage.

There was a fence around three sides of the Emporium, and the fourth side bordered the lake. About fifty feet from the edge of the lake shore was an old set of defunct railway tracks. Donnie remembered reading that the government kept promising to remove the tracks from this area, but they obviously hadn't yet. On the shore of the lake was a small dock with a shed on the land side.

The three-sided fence was unusual and resembled a wild-west

fort out of an old movie. There were hundreds of logs about ten feet tall fixed tightly together, and each with the top shaved to a sharp point. A large chain-link vehicle gate was in the middle of the fence, which he had passed through in the middle of these observations. He headed for the office to find out if he had the "right stuff" ... or maybe a "green thumb!"

He got the job about twenty minutes after he arrived. The head honcho at the Emporium, a guy named Norberg, went through the motions of an interview but Donnie figured he was the only person who had applied, because by the end of their session the boss grabbed and squeezed his shoulder and said, "You're strong enough, though you could use a few more pounds." Donnie couldn't help but glanced at Norberg's ample belly. "You're hired! You'll be working in one of the three greenhouses. Six days a week, $2.65 an hour. Sunday's off. You start tomorrow!"

Oh crap, Donnie thought, what did I get myself into? "Thanks so much Mr. Norberg, that's great. It's just that I'm still in school, so I won't be able to start tomorrow."

"Oh, I see. Well, come out after school and weekends till you're done."

This was going from bad to worse. "Okay, but I can't come out this weekend, I'm studying for my last exam Monday morning." Which was bullshit of course, he didn't have any exams to write during this third term at school. Donnie just wanted to spend one last full weekend with his three best friends.

"Very well then, you can start work Monday afternoon, but training can start now." He opened the door of his office and roared "Erik!" Looking at Donnie he said, "Erik will give you the tour and tell you what your duties will be. Erik! Where the hell ..."

They left Norberg's office, by the loading dock, and walked back to the main office area, arriving just as a white van drove up to the back door. Strangely, the van was dripping water on this hot sunny day.

A young fellow with bright blond hair jumped out and walked into the office. He was an inch or two taller than Donnie and skinny as a rake. And at that moment he looked like he might be sick. His face was red and sweaty, and Donnie thought he saw the fellow shaking a bit.

"There you are Erik, this is Donnie. He's starting Monday afternoon, so give him the tour!"

Erik started to protest, but Mr. Norberg cut him off with a wave of his hand.

Without so much as a hello, Erik walked Donnie around the main building mumbling the names of each area: shipping, receiving, owner's office, accountant's office, shipper's office. Emergency muster area. All said glumly with the personality of a dead toad, and when he wasn't mumbling, he wasn't saying anything. He appeared to be just going through the motions. He was still sweating, and wearing work gloves, like he'd been interrupted in the middle of a tough job.

When they were finished walking through the three greenhouse buildings, Donnie decided it was time to initiate some ground-breaking conversation.

"So, do you like working here at the greenhouses, Erik?"

"Well first off, no one who works here calls it the greenhouses, we just call the whole place the Emporium."

Donnie had meant working in the actual greenhouses, but didn't get a chance to explain as Erik continued. "And second, only assholes and customers call this place the greenhouses, and I don't see you buying anything!"

Charming fellow, Donnie thought.

FRIENDS

He just wanted to spend one last full weekend with his three best friends, before starting a six day a week summer job.

Donnie knew it sounded petty and selfish. But Natty, Peter, and Clip were special people. On the surface it probably appeared as if he and his three friends had nothing in common, like the four directions of a compass. But surfaces are often paper thin. Every now and then, that is exactly the sort of group who *do* become best friends. Because what they had below the surface, deep inside each of the four boys, such as their morality and compassion, was very compatible.

Donnie was born in New Glasgow, Nova Scotia and lived there until his father moved the family to Halifax, when he was seven years old. Their house was in the south end of the city on Edward Street, where it intersected with Jubilee Road. It was a pretty area, the streets lined with towering ancient deciduous trees, and filled with huge two and three-story houses, some a century or more old. The locals were a regular mix of residents, no better or worse than anywhere else. It should have been a pretty good place to grow up. But, for whatever reason, Donnie's friendships during that time were anything but stellar.

It seemed he was always the third wheel between any two friends and the last wheel in any group. Many times, he was ignored by these same "friends" when they made plans. "Sorry Donnie, one of us was supposed to call you." When it came time to pick teams, Donnie was always chosen last, as the unwanted kid in any sport or game.

And having an argument with any of the group was the death knell to friendship and inclusion. Inevitably, Donnie found himself on the outside looking in. The boy could not figure it out. Although shy, he knew he could make friends easily given half a chance. But, for whatever reason, these chances were few and far between with the other boys in the area.

He wasn't completely friendless in Halifax, though. He met Heidi when he was ten, and enjoyed her company for six short months. Unfortunately, when his family moved to Dartmouth in late August 1967, he lost touch with the girl and his later rudimentary efforts to find her produced one inescapable result: she and her family had vanished into thin air.

In the first week in his new home in Dartmouth, Donnie met Sean Nathaniel Power. He lived a half block away and they became instant friends. Sean's home was a side-by-side duplex around the corner, where he lived with his divorced mom and younger sister. He was four months younger than Donnie, with blond hair below his ears and a stocky, solid build. He was a natural born leader and everyone, even his family, called him "Natty."

To Donnie, his new friend seemed to be more bright, confident, and, most of all, gifted with more common sense, then he. For example, Natty was intelligent enough to have skipped grade six and smart enough to know he shouldn't have. He found school difficult after that.

One warm fall evening, after a month of friendship with Natty, he and Donnie got into what Donnie thought was a massive argument while playing on opposite teams in a game of pickup baseball with a group of kids at the local park. It started in the middle of the game, when Natty called Donnie out at second base. Everybody was an umpire in a pickup game. It quickly turned into a whole lot of shouting and insults, and culminated when Donnie stormed off the diamond, exclaiming, "there was no use playing with a bunch of cheaters." And Natty calling out after him, something to the effect, "Yeah, yeah, go home ya baby."

As Donnie walked home, his anger morphed into sadness. He had begun to flourish here and now it was all ruined. Here he was in the same old predicament in his new home. He couldn't help but compare the argument to his experience with the boys he knew in Halifax, where the simplest disagreement was the death knell of friendship. And Natty and he had had one barnburner of an argument. At least it seemed that way to Donnie.

He started second guessing himself and came to the hard conclusion that the problem had to be him. He was depressed, barely slept all night, and woke up early the next morning convinced that his life was doomed to be a lonely one.

As he moped around the kitchen getting a bowl of cereal, the phone rang. It was Natty.

"Hey man, whatcha doing?"

Donnie was speechless for a few seconds. He stumbled out the words, "Ahh ... nothing, just getting some breakfast."

"Well, eat fast 'cause me and Peter are heading up to the Dartmouth Shopping Centre. Ya got any money?"

"Er ... yeah, couple dimes and three quarters."

"Excellent! Snack cash! Meet you out front in twenty minutes. Okay?"

It was as if someone had flicked a switch and Donnie was suddenly so incredibly happy. Not just because they were still friends, but for what was happening inside his head and heart. The nature of true friendship opened up to him, and the implications of just how incredibly powerful it could be. Part of Donnie grew up in that instant, realizing that an argument was not the end of the world. With a true friend, it's something to laugh about later and never a reason to hold a grudge. A revelation — but enough of all that, he had to answer his *friend*.

"Sure! Who's Peter?" he managed to ask.

"The guy's a scream man, wait till you meet him!"

Peter was a scream, and he was also the first black friend Donnie had ever had. They had a lot in common. They both loved to read history books, were both fascinated by the police. And most important, they were both Habs fans. Natty, on the other hand, loved the Bruins and constantly ragged on his two buddies.

It was glorious.

ANOTHER FRIEND

In the fall of 1969, Donnie started grade seven at another new school, Bicentennial Junior High. It was just south of Dartmouth High School, on the other side of Thistle Street. His two close friends, Peter and Natty, were in a different school, John Martin Junior High, which was off Brule Street in the north end. The dividing line for the two districts was literally right around the corner from the Langille's house, at Elmwood Avenue.

Grade seven passed pleasantly enough for Donnie but, almost from the first day of grade eight, Donnie was experiencing something new. He was being bullied, mainly at recess and after school. The perpetrators were a chunky fellow by the name of Charlie and his three mindless idiot friends, who followed him around like nasty puppies. They were merciless to all the new kids but took a particular interest in Donnie for whatever reason.

From the very start of the bullying, Donnie did what his dad had taught him and ignored them. Every push and trip, every insult and put down, was met with the best look of derision Donnie could muster, followed up by a show of complete indifference. He acted like they weren't worth the trouble. But instead of Charlie and his friends growing bored with Donnie, they were getting more and more frustrated and decided to escalate.

Near the end of November, Donnie was walking down Green Road behind the Dartmouth Shopping Centre toward home when he got attacked. He was slugged in the back of the head and pushed down into a ditch full of muddy water. Donnie was big enough to look after himself but there were three guys his size and Charlie who was bigger and he had a lot of weight behind him, literally. The three morons pounced on Donnie, laughing and screaming while taking turns pushing his head down in the dirty water. All done while Charlie watched approvingly.

It was gross and disgusting, but it was just muddy water and Donnie figured they would rough him up a bit until he was dirty and embarrassed and then they'd let him go. But it didn't seem like it was going to end. They were getting far too much excitement out of the fact that he couldn't get his head out of the filthy water to say anything. Donnie tried to reach up and grab or hit one of them, but they had him squeezed down pretty tight.

Finally, the abuse let up. Donnie spit dirty water out of his mouth during the lull. He started to say something like, "Okay, okay, I give up," when one of them sat on his head and fixed it underwater. And now sheer panic set in. He squirmed and thrashed but that set them screaming even louder with laughter. Donnie's lungs were starting to burn ...

And suddenly he was free, gasping and gagging, and wiping the dirty water out of his eyes. Everything was quiet around him. When he could finally see, Donnie staggered to his feet and there beside him on the top of the bank was another kid. He recognized him from around the school and remembered other kids calling him Clip, for some reason. The two boys had never said so much as a single word to each other before that day. Clip was holding out a hand for him to grab, which Donnie gratefully accepted, and Clip hauled him, soaking wet and filthy, out of the ditch.

As Donnie stood there shivering, Charlie roared, "What the hell do you think yer doing, Cockroach?" He lumbered towards Clip, arms outstretched. Instead of retreating, Clip turned towards the slovenly giant and faced him. Clip stood side-on with left leg forward, his weight balanced on his right foot, left hand forward at chest level, and right hand relaxed about waist level at his side. The next few moments would forever be cemented in Donnie's memory.

Charlie may have been a chubby fellow, but he was strong as an ox, and he raised his big hands to grab Clip and pummel him. Instead, Clip effortlessly pushed Charlie's hands aside and then he somehow rolled off the massive boy, letting Charlie's own momentum carry him past. As he did, Clip gave Charlie a gentle push on the back and with his huge girth off balance, the teen pitched forward onto his belly and over the bank, face-first into the ditch.

One of Charlie's thugs, braver than the others, decided to enter the fray and came running into the fight. Clip thrust out the palm of his right hand which landed somewhere between the chest and stomach of the poor fellow, and his assailant dropped like a bag of rocks moaning and gasping, desperately trying to get his breath back.

The last two of Donnie's tormentors turned and ran.

It was the coolest thing Donnie had ever seen.

Clip surveyed the area — Charlie trying, and failing, to drag himself out of the muddy ditch, his companion just starting to get his breath back — and deeming everyone safe and no one in danger, he turned with a smile.

"Hi. You're Donnie, aren't you? I'm Andrew Roche, but my friends call me Clip." Then, after a moment's hesitation and with an even bigger grin, "You can call me Clip."

"Jeez man, I can't thank you enough. That was friggin' scary," said Donnie.

"Yeah, it sure didn't look like fun," said Clip. They both realized it could have ended badly. Then Clip surprised Donnie by saying, "Here, gimme a hand." He had reached down and taken Charlie's left hand. Donnie reluctantly grabbed Charlie's right hand, and together they pulled him out of the ditch and up to his feet.

Charlie shook them off and marched away, face red and eyes on the verge of tears. Donnie suddenly felt sorry for him. He didn't know why he felt this way, but he instinctively knew that Charlie was the kind of person who couldn't be happy and was angry at the whole world.

As they watched Charlie stalking away, Clip said, "Yeah, Charlie pisses me off. We used to be friends when we were kids, but he just got worse and worse since grade school. Always had to be in charge. You know, always had to have everything his way. He's just a jerk now."

"Why do they call you Clip? Why not Andy or something like that?" Donnie asked.

"We're from Quebec. Dad moved my mom and me and my sister down here when I was seven. My last name is Roche, R-O-C-H-E. But a lot of the local people saw the spelling and started pronouncing it roach."

Donnie was momentarily perplexed, "Yeah so, how is Clip related to roach ..." Then it dawned on him, and he burst out laughing. "Oh man."

NEVER LET A BULLY WIN

Donnie introduced Clip to Natty and Peter, and there was an instantaneous bond. It was more than just similar interests and types of humour; their values were on the same page as well. Nothing was worse than a bully.

It was because of that specific point, and no small amount of pestering by his three friends, that Clip agreed to impart his self defence knowledge to his friends. But only to a certain point. His father had taught him well and extensively, but Clip decided to pass on to his friends only a few basic self defence moves.

"This is the first thing my dad taught me. If there's a person or a group of people intent on harming you, there are two choices." He raised a finger. "Rule Number One and the preferred option is to run! RunRunRun. If there's an escape route take it. If there's a cop, or security person, or even an armed forces member run to them. Run to them and ask for help. A uniform speaks with authority, and even if they can't help you, the uniform may delay the people chasing after you. RunRunRun."

"Rule Number Two, if you're surrounded or boxed in and simply cannot run away? Strike. Immediately, without hesitation, before anyone can think or speak a word. And strike to damage. Pick the best escape route blocked by one person, the weakest preferably, and attack that person in any way you can to get them out of your way. You have to do it without mercy, and without a second thought. And then? RunRunRun!"

"Remember these people are intent on changing your life in a major way. Possibly even putting you in a wheelchair ... or worse. Think about that ... your life is ruined and so is theirs most probably when they are caught. So, end it fast. Kick him in the balls, poke him in the eye if it comes to that, fight as dirty as you need to. And then RunRunRun!"

"In summary, always use Number One unless they have you trapped. Then use Number Two."

That set Donnie to thinking about the moment when he met Clip. "When Charlie and his friends attacked me, you stood your ground and dropped them both. Don't get me wrong, I'm forever grateful, but isn't that going against Rule Number One?"

"Yeah, okay that's a good point. But you weren't in any shape to run, so I couldn't just leave you. And it's different for me. Dad's been teaching me this stuff my whole life. When I was eleven, he figured he could trust me with Amendment Two A." Clip smiled at himself. He was obviously inventing the numbering system as he went along.

"Amendment Two A?" Natty asked.

Clip's smile disappeared. "Never let a bully win."

And then he taught them the cool move he'd used to stop Charlie's friend — a solar plexus shot using the palm of his hand.

"What if we use our fist?" Natty asked.

"Your palm is all you need. It's all you should use, in fact."

After much practice, all three of his friends felt at least a little proficient with the move. The boys were already fit. Donnie and his friends, like most kids in the early seventies, were thin and wiry, but by no means were they weak. Due to their love of sports and outdoor adventure, the four boys looked after themselves, almost by default.

They lifted weights in Natty's basement, where he had built a makeshift gym. They pumped iron to the thunder of rock music, interspersed by frantic episodes of air guitar. They bicycled everywhere, disdainfully refusing offered rides by their parents in favour of riding in the rain and sometimes even snow. They played hockey all the time, including the summer. If they couldn't get a game going in a rink, they switched to ball hockey at tennis courts or empty parking lots.

They played softball. Two hand touch football. They even played soccer when they could find an empty field. Tennis, badminton, and an extremely amateurish version of basketball. Every sport including made-up variations, such as four-square volleyball and a makeshift version of lacrosse with a cut-open plastic bleach bottle taped to the end of a broom handle or broken hockey stick. Sports knows no creative boundaries. But regardless of what the activity was, they were almost always outdoors.

None of the four boys smoked, which was unusual in the early 1970s. In the outdoor area in the centre of the Dartmouth High School complex called the Quad, there were sometimes twenty or more people out for their morning smoke between periods. And half of those were teachers. In those days, high schools didn't care if a teenager smoked, as long as it was outside. As far as they were concerned, it was up to the parents to police their children if he or she had taken up such a "harmless" habit.

A BROTHER FOR EACH OTHER

Peter, Natty, Clip and Donnie. Four extremely close friends. Brothers, in fact. As Peter once pointed out, "You guys realize that none of us has an actual brother, so we have to be a brother for each other."

They were a tight-knit group of four boys, desperate to be men. They trusted each other implicitly and all of them knew they could rely on the others for back up in tight situations. They rarely got into arguments with each other and when they did, all four seemed to know when *enough was enough*, and usually they ended up laughing about it afterwards.

They were just as goofy as any other teenage boys to be sure, but they were also teetering on the edge of maturity. And whenever the four were together, they seemed to bring out the best in each other.

Donnie, Natty and Peter's meeting place for the past six years, and Clip's for the past three, was what the boy's called the Old Fort, a late nineteenth-century concrete ruin buried in the woods, on the edge of a hill overlooking Halifax Harbour. It's where every new event in each of their lives had been discussed and analyzed at length.

So, Donnie wanted *one more full weekend with his three best friends* — in a summer where he might not have another one?

Priceless!

THE DARTMOUTH POLICE STATION

Lead Detective Rick Rafuse walked around the table in the conference room of the Dartmouth Police Station. This was the only room in the station big enough in which they could place all the gathered physical evidence for examination.

"Is this everything so far?" Detective Rafuse asked.

"So far, yes. We've been trying to ID anything that might connect to Martin's store. Or anything that might just jump out at us," said Sergeant Wilson.

"Is it still hot?"

"Yup. It's been photographed and tagged, but not dusted yet. So, use the gloves over there on the side table," the sergeant scolded Rafuse.

"Yes Sergeant." Rafuse grinned at him, a nervous grin. Everyone in the station was on high alert. The Halifax Police had sent units to the long-haul bus and train stations. The Mounties were covering the airport. At this point it was a long shot since no one knew who they were looking for, but they had orders to keep a lookout for anyone acting unusual.

Rafuse sifted through the perimeter search results, which were items found adjacent to the crime location. He saw cash register receipts, soda pop cans, a house key. "That'll be interesting but probably useless," he commented.

Then something caught his eye. "What's that black paper?"

"We think it's carbon paper, part of a shipping label maybe?"

Carbon paper ... shipping label ... Rafuse looked back through the items on the table. There it was — a white piece of paper that was pretty well the same shape as the torn carbon paper. It had printing on it and some kind of colours — maybe a logo? *We'll check that out later after it's been dusted for fingerprints.* He took out his little notepad and wrote a reminder. Anything could be important. After all, this was the biggest crime to hit Dartmouth in the last forty years.

THE LANGILLE'S HOUSE

The Langilles lived in a modest two-story cape cod on Windmill Road. The wood siding was painted a flat light grey. It had a small, enclosed veranda built on the front, probably as an after-thought. They had a flat lawn in the front yard and a grassy back yard for about twenty feet. Then it sloped steeply down to the fence line and, turning into a field of bushes, continued all the way down to the harbour.

When entering the house, you walked into the living room with the kitchen behind it on the right, and a den with a dining room behind it on the left. Separating these two areas was the stairs to the second floor with three bedrooms and a bath. Donnie's dad had been keen at one time to put in an ensuite for the master bedroom, but his enthusiasm had waned recently. They weren't the richest people on the street. He had explained to his son that getting a summer job was going to help with his future college education.

Donnie strolled into the house, tired and starving. His dad, Robert, was sitting in the living room in front of the TV. His mother, Jane, was in New Brunswick visiting her sister.

Donnie shook his head. His parents wouldn't even stay in the same room with each other now, so going to the next province was no surprise. He wanted to ask why they just didn't divorce and get it over with. If nothing else, they'd stop making each other miserable.

A famous quote he read once said, "The opposite of love is not hated, it's indifference." Here was proof. When it came to each other, they just didn't care. In the past it had scared him, but he was used to it now. For the last year, Donnie spent a few minutes with his dad, then his mom, then went to his room. Three people isolated from each other, quarantined by choice.

He sat down with his dad, who was watching the six o'clock news. "How was your day?" his dad asked.

"Okay, I guess. I did alright on the interview, and got the job in about five minutes." Donnie still wasn't sure he wanted a summer job. "I start on the eleventh. I'll need bus fare till I get my first paycheque." He liked the sound of that word, but his dad had said that any paycheque money was going straight into the bank.

"Good. Good to hear," his father said, fishing out a ten-dollar bill from his wallet and handing it to him.

"Anything new on the news?" Donnie asked.

His dad made a grim face. "Mr. Martin was found dead in his downtown store this afternoon."

His dad was watching the TV and so missed the shocked look on his son's face. Donnie walked out to the kitchen and poured himself a glass of water. He couldn't let his dad see his stunned expression until he calmed down.

"How?" He managed one word.

"They haven't mentioned the cause of death, but I would imagine it was some sort of stroke or heart attack. He was around that age."

"What time?" Donnie asked, as he leaned against the kitchen door frame sipping water.

"One of Dartmouth's finest went into the store around 1:45 this afternoon, for a bite of pepperoni I suppose, and started to get worried about Martin when he didn't show up. That's when he took a look around and found him."

"Jeez Dad, I was in there at about half past one."

Mr. Langille swung away from the local news and stared at his son, "Donnie! Did you speak with him?"

"No Dad, Mr. Martin wasn't there. There was ..." He couldn't finish. Something Louis Ryan said sent a shiver down his back. *He had to run next door for something or other, he asked me to keep an eye on the place for a few minutes.*

"Did they say where they found him?" Donnie asked.

"Yes, in the back of the store out of sight from the counter. That's probably why you didn't see him."

"Inside?"

"Well of course, the back of the store would be inside, or maybe you didn't know there is no back door to his store ... Donnie, what is it?" He must have seen the shocked look on his son's face.

Donnie tried to decide what to answer. Should he tell his dad about Louis Ryan, who may have lied to him about Mr. Martin leaving the store? Why would he do that? Yes, Donnie knew there was no back door in the store. One way in, one way out. Well, there *was* a second way out — and poor Mr. Martin had taken it. In the middle of his inner debate, the phone rang.

"I'll get it," he said. Donnie had a premonition as to who was calling.

He turned and walked back the kitchen to answer the wall phone, if only to think about what to say to his dad. In the half second it took to put the receiver to his ear, he knew he had gotten himself into a very serious, and very adult, situation.

"Hello?"

"Yes, may I speak with Mr. Langille please?"

"Which one? Donald or Robert?" Donnie asked.

The all-business voice seemed to have a moment of consternation. Papers rattled, "Oh. Ahh, that would be Donald Langille, please."

"Speaking."

"Mr. Langille, this is Detective O'Byrne of the Dartmouth Police Department. We need to speak to you on a matter of some importance." A long pause on his part. "It should only take a few minutes. I'd like to send a car to pick you up and bring you down to the station."

Donnie walked to the far side of the kitchen, further out of earshot, and thought for a moment. "Okay but I'll come down to the station myself. I'll be there in twenty minutes or so."

"Sir I'd really much prefer ..." But Donnie was already hanging up.

There were alarm bells ringing all over Donnie's head and the largest, born from experience, told him to say nothing to his parents, at least not yet. His dad had turned his attention back to the news, so Donnie grabbed his coat and said, as he coasted past his father, "I'm meeting the guys." He was out the front door before his father could answer.

As much as it seemed, Donnie was not an over-confident teenager, trying to be an adult. Despite some suspicion of Louis Ryan, he really didn't think the man had done anything bad. Ryan didn't look the type. Besides, that kind of thing never happened in Dartmouth. Bad things happened elsewhere. It was sad about Mr. Martin passing away, but surely it was a heart attack after all. Just like his dad said.

So, Donnie didn't want any big fuss involving his parents. And he sure as heck didn't want any friends or neighbours seeing him being dragged off into the night in a police car. That's why he had quickly slid out the front door and was headed for the police station, for what he was sure would be a five-minute statement to clear everything up. And it would be an interesting story for the guys on Friday night when the four boys had their weekly get-together at the Old Fort. But that's not how it turned out.

THE DARTMOUTH POLICE STATION

The walk to the station took just under a half an hour. The station was a modern building off Ochterloney Street, on Wentworth. It was a two-story brick design with thousands of small blue-grey ceramic tiles under the windows, its compact size befitting a small-town police force. The front of the building had the civic coat of arms. Above were the words POLICE STATION and below, City of Dartmouth. Donnie had never been in the building before.

Dartmouth had incorporated itself as a city twelve years earlier, in 1961. The city was famous for its twenty-five lakes, the largest of which was three hundred and fifty acres, and its nickname was therefore "The City of Lakes." Dartmouth's motto written on the city crest was Amicitia Crescimus — Friendship Increases. That motto had certainly worked for Donnie since he moved there. Donnie's referring to the city as a town was simply a habit shared by half the residents.

The newly elected city council had built itself a set of all the amenities a modern city required: its own garbage collection department complete with landfill site, street and road maintenance, a first-rate fire department with stations spread strategically throughout the new city. It currently had a population of 72,000 people and was protected by the Dartmouth Police Department.

The force had a complement of about seventy regular constables, six senior officers including two detectives, two police dogs, eight police cruisers, three unmarked cars and one police patrol van. There were also five or six clerical and support workers.

When he stepped through the main door of the police station, Donnie found himself in one vast room that took up half the building. He was standing in a ten-foot waiting area in front of a countertop that ran the width of the room, save for a small swinging gate. Through that gate was the rest of the room, full of desks, in three rows perpendicular to the counter. Filing cabinets were located against the walls with no windows, and laydown tables were located where there were windows. Interspersed, seemingly at random, were assorted coat stands. A dividing wall at the far side of the big room had two features: a frosted glass door in the middle and to its right, a large clear glass window. Dark shapes would flit past the frosted glass every now and then and he could see what appeared to be a conference room through the large window.

Most of the desks were empty, except for two uniformed cops and one in plain clothes. You would think that an almost empty station would mean a relaxed atmosphere, but both uniforms were feverishly typing or writing.

Donnie had expected to see what he saw in the movies, a big sergeant behind a bigger desk, greeting him with an Irish brogue, "Well, what can I do for you laddy?" But instead, no one noticed him.

He cleared his throat a couple of times and eventually one of the uniforms looked up. "Help ya'?" he said absent-mindedly.

"Yeah, I'm Donnie … Donald Langille," he said. "I was asked to …"

When he heard the name, the plainclothes cop pushed back his chair and looked at him. "Hello, I'm Detective O'Byrne, we spoke on the …" His voice drifted off as he squinted at him. "Donald Langille? How old are you?" he asked.

"Fifteen."

"Jesus H," he replied, and sat there for a moment. Donnie wanted to say "No, my name is Donald G," but he didn't want to piss off a cop with such a stupid joke, so he stayed mum.

"Wait here please." Off O'Byrne went, disappearing through the frosted glass door.

A few minutes later, O'Bryne returned with a late thirties, salt and pepper-haired fellow of average height. He wore a wrinkled white shirt with an unbuttoned collar, sleeves rolled up, blue tie loosened at the neck, and grey polyester slacks. He had a gun on his hip, a standard issue .38 S&W Special in a little brown leather holster. In 1973, police forces were a long way from the Glock 17. And, of course, he had a Robert Redford style moustache. He approached the counter.

"Hi Donald, I'm Detective Rick Rafuse. I'd like to thank you for coming down to the station today, but I'm afraid we can't talk to you. You're a juvenile and we're not allowed to interview you without your parent or guardian present."

"Okay. What did you want to see me about?" he asked.

"I'm afraid I'm not at liberty to say at the moment. Perhaps we could call one of your parents and get them down here?" Rafuse asked.

Rafuse probably wasn't even aware he used the word juvenile. Just picked it out of the air to complete a sentence at that moment in time. But it rankled Donnie. In his mind, he was certainly not a juvenile, and the very word gave off connotations of the phrase juvenile delinquent!

As far as Donnie was concerned, he had his life in order. He was surrounded with great friends, he knew what he wanted to do in the future, he knew exactly which car he was going to be driving in a years' time, and Donnie was going to settle for only the perfect girl when and if he got married. He mentioned all these salient points to his mom once. She gave him a sad smile and a pitying look and replied, "You can make all the plans you want Donnie, but life will make all your decisions for you."

He hadn't accepted those words at the time, but in his more reflective moments, Donnie had begun to understand what she meant. Since his sister Anita had left to study at the University of Toronto, Donnie was living in a house inhabited by two people who simply didn't care about each other anymore. He knew his parents loved him. He was certainly treated well, but the indifference between them was measurable, and although unintended, it resulted in Donnie being overlooked much of the time. They obviously wanted out of the marriage. As a result, he was learning to rely on himself more and more, and when that didn't work, he had his three best buds to fall back on.

So, Donnie made the most adult decision of his life so far. *Spill the beans.* "Does this have anything to do with Mr. Martin, because if it does, I have to tell you that I was in his store about twenty minutes before you guys found him."

The proverbial pin drop. All four cops stared at the boy, but Rafuse was the only one with a blank look on his face. Donnie instinctively knew that that look could only mean one thing: *He already knew Donnie had been in the store!*

Rafuse walked over to the gate and held it open. "Come on in Donald, let's have a chat." He was brimming with excitement, like his young guest had just admitted some kind of guilt.

"Call me Donnie," he replied, following the detective across the big room and through the door with the frosted window.

THIS IS GOING TO BE INFORMAL

The back section of the police station was a main hallway starting at the frosted glass door with four plain wooden doors on the left and two on the right. There was a third door on the right side, down at the end of the hall but it was a metal door with thick rivets in it.

"What's in there?" he asked.

"The holding cells."

"Cool."

They went into first door in the hallway on the left. It was an office with two desks jammed into the space along with file cabinets, a cork board on the wall and a table on the back wall between the desks that were strewn with papers.

"Have a seat. Can I get you a drink, water, juice, pop?" Rafuse asked.

"Yeah, that'd be great, got a root beer?"

Rafuse chuckled, "I'll see what's in the fridge."

Root beer was one of God's gifts to mankind in Donnie's opinion. A root beer can be served with every meal and every type of food. Not like the swill twins, Coke and Pepsi that make every meal taste like Coke and Pepsi. Donnie noticed he seemed to be alone in that opinion, of course.

Rafuse returned after a few moments with a coffee in one hand

and tossed him a Fanta orange with the other. Donnie sighed. *Oh well, second best.* "Thanks."

The detective settled himself behind his desk. "First things first," he began. "I've decided this is going to be informal. I'm going to find out what you have to tell me. If it's not of interest to us, well, thanks for dropping by. But if it's important, I'm going to bring one or both of your folks back here for an official statement. And you'll have to tell me everything again, only this time it will be recorded." He leaned forward, "You understand?"

Donnie nodded yes. Then, before Rafuse could say another word, "Why did you guys call me in the first place? How did you already know I was in Mr. Martin's store this afternoon? Before I even said it?"

Rafuse stared at Donnie with a raised eyebrow.

"You were the only cop out there who wasn't surprised when I admitted to being in the store."

Rafuse smiled. "Fair question, Donald." And he took a swig of coffee.

"Everybody calls me Donnie."

"After Mr. Martin was found, we canvassed people in the area, and all the cab and transit drivers as well. Turns out a bus driver, ahh ..." searching through his papers on his desk, "... Earl Paris, identified you as having come out of the store, but he couldn't remember exactly when."

"Yeah, well, I went into Mr. Martin's store, after I hopped off the downtown bus."

"When was this?"

"I dunno exactly. It was after 1:00 pm."

"Why did you go to his store?"

"Salami."

"Gotcha. Did you talk to him?"

"Nope. Mr. Martin wasn't there."

"So, the store was empty?"

"No, there was a guy already in there, standing by the counter."

To Donnie it was comical and just like a movie. Rafuse choked on his coffee, stared at his desk for a few moments. Clearly his interest just jumped up another level. Then he called out, "Jen, would you come in here please."

A squeal of a chair being pushed back and a moment later into the office came Jennifer Horn, a friend of Donnie's sister. She was a little older than Anita which would make her about twenty now. Her smile lightened up the universe. "Donnie! I thought I recognized that voice. How are you?"

"Miss Horn, please stay with Mr. Langille here and record his particulars. I have to go organize some things. O'Byrne is just out front if you need him," Rafuse said. "Donald, I won't be long."

"Donnie," he replied. But the detective was already gone.

JENNIFER

Jennifer was an orphan who lived with her uncle in the Crichton Park area of Dartmouth. They had moved from the small town of Swift Current in Saskatchewan, just in time for Jennifer to start the last year of high school. She and Donnie's sister Anita instantly bonded, becoming besties and they had a reputation for being crazy wild.

The two girls had many adventures, Donnie's favourite story being the night in grade twelve when they left a party after stealing a bottle of vodka from the host's parents. They staggered around the neighbourhood, chose a back yard patio at random and finished off the bottle sitting in two Adirondack chairs, under the stars, laughing and crying in each other's arms, promising to be friends for eternity. Through one of nature's mysteries, they each made it home unscathed that night. The next day they found out the house belonged to Police Chief Daweson.

"How's your family Donnie? Everybody doing good, no troubles?"

The thought I might be in trouble jumped into Donnie's head. "No, everyone's fine. Anita's staying up in Toronto for the summer, but she might be down in August for a couple weeks before she starts her third-year courses."

Jennifer shook her head at a memory, "I never thought she was serious, you know." Donnie gave her a quizzical look. "Well, she talked about going to Toronto during the last few months of high school. That girl is a thinker. The type who would never do anything impetuous, Donnie. Nope, I never thought she would move, but she did."

"Yup. She surprised our parents for sure. Mom was the most worried because it was so sudden after her graduation from Dartmouth High," he said. "Luckily, she had a friend of Dads to stay with until she got settled. She had it all planned out." Donnie admired his sister's confidence.

"I really should go see her. Where does she live?" Jennifer asked.

"Yonge and Eglinton, right in the middle of the city!"

"And she's okay?"

Donnie nodded. "Yup. I was up to see her last summer and Toronto's changed her a bit. In a good way." He smiled. "It's her home now. I don't think she'll ever leave T.O."

Donnie remembered something else. In the last six months before Anita left Dartmouth, she and Jennifer seemed to drift apart. When Donnie asked his sister why Jennifer never came around, Anita answered, "She's hanging around with a different crowd these days. They're a little too wild for me."

Now sitting in front of him, there was nothing wild about Jennifer as far as Donnie could see. In fact, she was a straight-up professional in dress, manner, and duties. Besides, what could be wilder than singing drunk in the police chief's back yard? He hadn't seen her for a while. She was a seventies babe, for sure. Bright blond straight hair cut to curl into just below her chin on each side. She was wearing fashionable business attire for the time, sensible blouse, and a not-too-tight skirt, just below knee level, and black mid-heel shoes. Respectable pantyhose on great legs. Perfect for a civilian employee of the Police Department.

"You really have changed since the last time I saw you," she said, smiling.

"So have you," he said. They lapsed into a short silence.

"What do you do here, Jenny?" he asked finally.

"All kinds of things, stenography, shorthand, typing, filing and of course coffee for the senior people. Occasionally I'll take a turn at the radio room, but only to give a break to the dispatcher. But I won't be doing those things much longer. Between you and me, I have applied to Holland College."

"The cop course?" he asked.

She smiled. "Yes, the *cop* course. The Atlantic Police Academy. A degree from Holland College can get your foot in the door in most forces in Canada, except the Mounties of course. I might just be a policewoman here in Dartmouth. Who knows?" She was beaming. "The guys here know my plans and they are patient with me, because I ask a *lot* of questions."

"Are you planning anything this summer?" Donnie asked.

"I'd really like to go somewhere I've never been. I mean, you know, another country. For most of my life I've just been a hometown girl, but since I moved here my uncle has taken me up to our cabin in Dean. I love seeing the animals in the wild. And I love horseback riding. I even went hunting with unc last year, up in Guysborough County."

In the past Donnie had been intimidated by Jennifer, the hot blond friend of his older sister. Even just six months ago he would have said there was a great gulf between them, between adult and kid. The four-year difference in their ages seemed huge. But over the past few months, conversation came naturally with everyone. Donnie felt at ease talking with Jennifer, Rafuse, even the man named Louis Ryan.

Holy mackerel, he thought, I'm turning into an adult!

His late friend Mr. Martin said to him once, "We spend the first twenty years of our lives in a hurry to grow up, and the rest of our lives trying to slow the process!"

Jennifer and he talked some more about family, TV, and movies.

"Why is the station so empty?" Donnie finally asked, changing the subject. "And what's taking Detective Rafuse so long?"

"Most of our officers are out canvassing the downtown, looking for witnesses," she said.

"For Mr. Martin." He said it as a statement, not a question, which Jennifer confirmed with a nod.

"This is a big case, Donnie." She paused. "It's been fifty years since they had something this bad happen in Dartmouth."

Oh God, he thought, I'm right in the middle of it.

"Jennifer, my dad said he probably had a stroke, or a heart attack this afternoon ... but he didn't, did he?"

"Rick, Detective Rafuse, hasn't filled you in on what happened today?" she asked.

Donnie shook his head. "No. What happened?"

"He'll be back soon."

"Jennifer ... what happened?"

"It's better if he let Rick talk to you first ..."

"JENNIFER ..."

She could see Donnie was worried and upset, and if she wanted to be a hard-nosed cop someday, she really should keep her mouth shut. But, "Mr. Martin didn't have a heart attack, Donnie. He was stabbed in the back and, well, I think you are a suspect."

THE MEIJERS' HOUSE

Peter Meijer lived with his parents at the intersection of Brookside Drive and Rosedale Drive. Peter's father Dirk had bought the house not long after he and his wife Engele immigrated from the Netherlands. It was the second immigration of Dirk's life.

When Dirk was five years old, his parents brought the family from Aruba to the Dutch city of Rotterdam. The family had prospered there for eight years, until the Nazis razed Rotterdam to the ground. Dirk was thirteen at the time. Twelve years after the war ended, Dirk's father convinced his son to take his new wife and move to Canada.

Their new house on Brookside Drive was in a then-quaint neighbourhood, with a flower-strewn field across the street and welcoming neighbours. Well, mostly welcoming. Being the first black family to live on Brookside Avenue, a few local people took up a petition to block the sale of the house to Mr. Meijer. But most of his new neighbours ignored the petition and Dirk and Engele moved in with no fuss and plenty of people helping out. Peter was born a year after they arrived, in 1958.

Their neighbourhood was now one of the toughest parts of town. Over the past fifteen years, the Meijers had seen the empty field across the street cleared to become a shoe factory, then a bingo hall, then a vacant building. About three years later, a new developer came into town and conned the city counsellors into approving a large bar he predicted would be a huge success. It was country-music oriented and was called the Grand Ol' North.

By 1973 the bar, after several ownership changes, had degenerated into a haven for crime, and it attempted to take the rest of the neighbourhood with it. There were drug deals, armed robberies and bar fights that spilled out onto the street narrowly missing the ladies of the evening on the sidewalk. Police were often there.

Being Pentecostal Christians, Peter's parents were mortified. But their son was in his glory. As long as Donnie had known him, Peter was fascinated by the police and studied everything about the local cops. He was the tallest of the four friends at just under six feet, and lean, without an ounce of fat. He had a dark complexion and short black curly hair. An almost-afro, Natty called it. He was a mild and mannerly fellow, while being deceptively strong.

Peter had a beyond-dry sense of humour. Most people didn't get that humour, but his friends sure did. He was always sending the boys into gales of laughter. And he never cursed.

His favourite evening hobby was listening to his police scanner. Since the cops showed up at the bar across the street practically every night, he could match the radio chatter to their actions before, during, and after an incident. More often than not, the boys found their small city to be boring, but Peter's hobby provided excitement.

On this particular night, while Donnie was being entertained by Jennifer at the police station, Peter was working on his homework in his room, after supper, with the police band up and running.

"Base this is unit 8" crackled a voice. Peter's eyebrows popped up in curiosity. Unit 8 was an unmarked car used by the detectives. "Show me 10-7, 2900 block, Windmill Road." That block was near where Donnie lived. Peter would make it a point to ask Donnie tomorrow if he'd seen or heard anything.

"Roger 8."

"Base, this is Bravo 347." Peter now knew who it was. Bravo 347 was the badge number for Detective Rafuse. "Please contact the chief and inform him that I have a POI in regard to case 7319. Party is JU and I am in the process of contacting the parents for interrogation purposes."

"Roger 347, in progress."

They spoke cryptically but Peter knew it like a second language.

Rafuse had a juvenile suspect in case 7319, whatever that was, and had to get the parents in order to question the kid. *Some stupid punk who busted a window or something. Yes, another boring night. Nothing exciting ever happened in Dartmouth.*

Then, "Base, inform the chief that we will need a Sierra Whisky and a PG. Can we get that started immediately?"

"Roger 347, also in progress."

"Roger out."

Peter pondered this last call. A sierra whisky was a search warrant. He guessed the mystery kid didn't break a window after all, but what the heck did he do? Because a PG was a lie detector.

A FAMILY AFFAIR

It was going to be a hot summer. All the news outlets were predicting it. And this early-June evening was confirming that forecast. The air conditioning in Dartmouth's little police station was having a hard time keeping up with the warm muggy air.

Jennifer and Donnie had lapsed back into silence after her revelation. She pitched a weak smile in his direction, went to her office and came back with some paperwork. She sat in Rafuse's chair and began working. After a few moments she looked up at Donnie with a little smile and nodded her head. He knew what she was signalling to him. *Keep your chin up Donnie, everything's going to be fine.*

He was strangely calm at this point. It was simple as far as he could tell. Rafuse had to get a statement from him, and he wanted *everything* to go by the book. So, he was picking up his dad ... luckily just his dad. He loved both his parents but the last thing he wanted was both of them here at the station. They would probably get into an argument right here in front of everyone.

He heard doors opening and murmuring voices, then footsteps. "Right in here, sir." His father came in the door followed by Rafuse. "Have a seat next to your son, please."

Jennifer gathered up her work and, with a nod to Donnie's dad, quickly exited the room. Detective Rafuse, a little sweat on his brow, sat at his desk and wrote a few lines in a notebook.

"Sorry for the wait, Donald. As you can see, I have returned with your father so he can oversee our interview. Everything will be fine."

Not everything was fine. Mr. Langille looked at his son for a few moments, then whispered, "When I asked how your day was, you could have given me a more ... detailed answer." Donnie thought his dad was trying to sound angry and disappointed, but it seemed like he was impressed. And his eyes had a hint of humour in them. Kids learn to read their parents like a map, but Donnie was at a loss as to what to expect from his dad next. "We'll talk about this later," he said. *Ouch.*

"Okay Donald, all set?" Rafuse asked. Donnie nodded yes. The detective then turned to his dad. "Mr. Langille, I need to inform you that although this is only a witness statement, you're free to retain council for your son before we begin."

"A lawyer? No, I don't think that will be necessary. Not yet anyway."

"Okay. We're ready to proceed." He called to the open door. "Jennifer?"

Jennifer came back in with a cassette tape recorder, a pen and pad, followed by Detective O'Byrne and a uniformed policeman.

Jennifer sat in the corner and immediately began writing in the pad. Donnie figured it must be shorthand.

"This is Detective Shane O'Byrne and Constable Philip Hicks, who was first on the scene and discovered Mr. Martin's body this afternoon. I have asked them to join us in case they have any questions." Rafuse turned to Jennifer. "You ready?"

"Yes sir."

Donnie looked at Jennifer, all business-like and full of confidence. *Lady, you're going to be a great cop.*

"Donald, Jennifer has informed me that she already told you the cause of Mr. Martin's death this afternoon. And that he was stabbed to death inside his store. Is this correct?" asked Rafuse. His father never flinched at this news, so obviously Rafuse had told him on the way to the station.

Donnie didn't want Jennifer to get in trouble. "Well, yes, but I already guessed something serious had happened. She just confirmed it."

"You guessed?"

"Well, I mean obviously I wouldn't be here if it wasn't something really bad."

Rafuse jotted some notes down.

"And call me Donnie please."

Rafuse hit the record button on the cassette recorder. "Okay son, for the record, state your name, address, and phone number."

Donnie relayed that information as well as place and date of birth, religion, occupation, school and grade, and marital status. Nobody smiled at that last one.

"Okay Donald, could you please tell me where you were this afternoon. From 12:00 pm forward."

"Okay ... ahh, could you call me Donnie, please? I've always hated Donald."

Rafuse smiled. "No problem. Let's begin."

Donnie told him about the planned job interview and jumping on the number four bus. Rafuse wanted to know specifics on everything: the plant nursery company name, contact person, and the name of the bus driver. Being car-less, Donnie knew a lot of the bus driver's names including Earl, but not the name of the driver of the first bus he had taken that day. He started describing him, but Rafuse waved it off. "That's okay, we'll find out."

Donnie told him about his desperate need for salami and crossing over Portland Street to Martin's General Store.

"Did you notice anything unusual outside the store?" asked Detective O'Byrne.

"Unusual?" he asked.

"Yeah, people standing around or cars stopped with the engines running?"

"Well, there were a couple of parked cars along the street but I wasn't really paying attention so I can't say make, model or colour. I ahh ... I'm sorry guys but I was jaywalking across the street and was too busy looking out for the moving cars to take any notice of the ones that weren't!"

"We'll try not to give you a ticket son." Maybe Rafuse was warming up to him. "When you entered the store, Donnie, what did you see?"

Now he had all three cops' attention. They were leaning towards him.

"When I entered the store, there was no sign of Mr. Martin. I puttered around a bit and ..."

"Did you touch anything?" Rafuse interrupted.

"A couple magazines, a can of CBD Rav."

"CBD Rav?" asked O'Byrne.

"Chef-Boyardee Ravioli. I was thinking about lunches if I got the job."

"Did you touch any surfaces?" asked Rafuse.

"No sir. Wait yes, I touched the front counter while I was walking around it to cut myself some meat slices."

"Did you pick up the knife?" asked O'Byrne.

"You mean Mr. Martin's big knife? No, it wasn't there."

All three cops looked at each other.

Then Rafuse paused to write a few more notes. "Donnie, you

mentioned there was another person in the store this afternoon. And he was there when you entered?" asked Rafuse.

"Yup, that's right."

"And did he leave before you?"

"No."

"So, he was still there when you left?"

"Yes."

"Describe the gentleman."

He did. Exactly as Ryan looked that afternoon.

"Did you notice anything strange or unusual about the man?" asked Rafuse.

Donnie thought hard. "When he spoke, he had a weird accent, and at first I thought it was French."

"You spoke to him?" asked O'Byrne.

"Yes sir, when I first came in, I asked where Mr. Martin was, and he said Mr. Martin had to run next door and he was keeping an eye on the place for him."

"Jesus kid, you could've told us that from the start!" barked O'Byrne.

"Go on, Donnie," said Rafuse. Donnie had the feeling that the detective didn't want him getting flustered and wanted him to take his time and get everything right. Donnie also got the feeling he might no longer be the prime suspect.

"He sounded snobby? Kind of upper crust. Not in a bad way, just … you know?"

No one answered. Didn't matter, it was a rhetorical question anyway.

"I don't think he was Quebec French." Donnie continued. "He didn't know who the Montreal Canadiens were."

Rafuse tilted his head quizzically.

"I was wearing this Habs tee and with that accent I figured he'd be a fan too. But he had a blank look when he mentioned their cup win last month."

"Anything else?" asked Byrne impatiently. Donnie's parents had taught him to try not to judge people he didn't know. But Donnie couldn't help thinking that maybe O'Byrne wasn't the sharpest tool in the box.

"Well, it wasn't super bright in Mr. Martin's store, but he was squinting like he was outdoors."

"And why was that strange?" Again, O'Byrne was being impatient. Donnie noticed Rafuse flash his partner a scowl.

"Because he had a set of glasses in his shirt pocket."

"Well, there you have it, he had sunglasses and was still squinting after coming in from the outdoor glare." O'Byrne to the rescue.

"Nope, the glasses were prescription, clear glass and thick as Coke bottles. I had the feeling he was near-sighted," Donnie explained.

O'Byrne checked his watch and said, "I'm sure we have the PG set up now."

That reminded Donnie. "He had a wristwatch, so I asked the guy if he had the time."

"When was that?" asked Rafuse.

"1:20″

"What did his watch look like?"

Donnie thought for a few seconds. "It was an expensive watch. Well, looked expensive to me. Like a Bulova or something like that. Silver watch with a blue face."

"Which wrist?" Asked O'Byrne.

"Ahh ... jeez I can't ... on his right arm, I think. Yeah, the right one."

Rafuse jotted down some more notes, then closed the notebook. "Donnie we're going to have you take a test now. It's called a polygraph and by using it, we can kill two birds with one stone."

Donnie's father had been absolutely silent since the questioning began, but he leaned forward and banged his hand on Rafuse's desk. "Absolutely not, gentlemen!"

Everyone in the room, including Donnie, was shocked by the sudden outburst. But his dad didn't miss a beat. "You can ask my son any questions you want, but you will NOT hook him up to a polygraph."

"Mr. Langille, I assure you, your son is in no danger when using this machine." This from O'Byrne in a patronizing, smarmy voice. Donnie was starting to hate the guy.

"Mr. Langille, we're just trying to expedite the information we will be gathering from Donnie. Everyone is a suspect at this point, and it will help us to eliminate your son first," said Rafuse.

That sounded fine to Donnie, but his dad wasn't having any of it. "No danger? Your asinine, worthless machine just might decide to mistakenly show my son to be the prime suspect who's lying his ass off, when in reality he's just a nervous kid. You'll get some preconceived notion that he's guilty and decide to bend the facts to match your theories and," *bam,* slamming his hand down on the top of the desk again, "you've ruined his life."

Mr. Langille looked from Rafuse to O'Byrne, "And we all know it's true, you hear story after story of police getting a scenario fixed in their minds, and nothing will dissuade them. You see it every week on the news."

Donnie stared at his dad. He was being one hell of a take-charge kinda guy. And he loved it.

Robert Langille continued. "So, stop taking the easy way out and get off your asses, and start doing some serious police work!" That must have stung, thought Donnie.

Everyone stayed quietly motionless. It was almost as if no one knew what to do next. His dad filled the void by continuing in a much quieter voice. "As I said earlier, ask any question you want. Donnie will tell you the truth, with no need of a polygraph."

That evening in the police station, Donnie understood like he never had in his life how wonderful it was to have parents like his. He knew that despite what they were going through, they loved him and his sister unconditionally and would do whatever it would take to make sure they were safe. And he swore to himself, that someday he would be just as good a parent.

Rafuse looked glumly at Donnie. "Anything else?"

"After I left, and was sitting on the bus, I saw Ryan leave the store. He was wearing his *prescription* glasses." This latter part for O'Byrne.

"That must have been just after I left the scene." Hicks spoke for the first time. "Did you see which direction he went?"

"Yeah, he went toward the ferry terminal."

"Did he get on the ferry?"

"Don't know, my bus pulled out after that ... but one thing about the guy I forgot to mention, he had his jacket rolled up under his arm the whole time."

"Which arm?" asked Rafuse.

"His right arm. And it probably doesn't mean anything, but it was inside out. Is that significant?"

"Probably not, but we'll keep note of it. Anything else?"

"Yeah, back in the store Ryan actually grabbed my arm using his left hand, so maybe he's left-handed?"

"Who's Ryan?" asked Rafuse.

"Oh shit! Oh man I'm so stupid. I forgot to tell you. He said his name was Louis Ryan." Donnie's face turned three shades of purple for forgetting such an important fact.

O'Byrne looked at him like he was an idiot but surprisingly, Rafuse just smiled and nodded his head good naturedly, "Excellent Donnie. We can certainly use that. Louis Ryan, with a possible French accent." Rafuse seemed to say that last part to himself, then he looked at Donnie again, "You said he grabbed your arm? Why?"

"Remember you asked if I touched the knife earlier? And I said I started walking behind the counter to get the knife. Well, right then, Ryan grabbed my arm and told me he couldn't let go behind the counter because he was watching the place for Mr. Martin." Donnie paused and shrugged, "Didn't matter anyway. As I said earlier, the knife wasn't there."

Then he asked the cops the thing that had been bothering him since Jennifer revealed Mr. Martin's actual fate, "That knife was the murder weapon, wasn't it?"

The detectives looked at each other. "That has yet to be determined Donnie," said Rafuse quietly. "I guess that's enough for now. You can take your son home Mr. Langille." He turned to Donnie.

"Here's my card in case you remember anything else. I find a good's night sleep can sometimes bring back a lot of details."

"Actually ..." Everyone stopped dead in their tracks. "This sounds stupid ..."

"Go on," said Rafuse.

"Back in the store, when I saw my bus arrive, I said goodbye to Ryan and headed straight for the door and he followed me. Closely. In fact, he was so close to me that he literally bumped into me when I opened the door."

"What happened then?" asked O'Byrne.

"Nothing. Well, honestly, it was kind of weird. I mean his eyes seemed to be everywhere at once, looking at the door, at me, out at the street. He did a double take when he looked at the street for some reason. Anyway, then he immediately turned and went back to the counter. I mean it was just a weird moment, that's all."

"Yes, that sounds very strange, Donnie. I'll make note of it," said Rafuse. "Well, thank you gentlemen, that's enough for tonight."

"Yeah, one more question. Am I in any danger from this Ryan guy? Can I go to school tomorrow?" Donnie asked.

"Well from what you told us, he'd have to search the whole city to find your whereabouts. You weren't wearing a school jacket, or a school ring or baseball cap? Anything like that?" asked Rafuse.

"No sir."

"Ideally, we'd prefer you stay home for the next few days. But I suppose as long as you have a safe way to school, it should be no problem. We'll alert Dartmouth High School senior staff to keep an eye out for anyone matching Ryan's description, though we won't tell them why just yet. And it's best that the two of you keep this to yourselves for now. The less people who know the better. Shane, get them a ride home please."

"Good night gentlemen, and you, Jen." Robert shook hands all around and nodded to Jennifer.

"Yeah, see ya later." Donnie said to everyone and paused to smile at Jennifer. She winked at him.

O'Byrne poked his head out the door and spoke to a young

policeman. "Take an unmarked and give these people a ride home." O'Byrne paused for second. "And don't go in a straight line. A nice circuitous route, okay?"

"Yessir. Understood."

Rafuse watched the Langilles leave, then turned to the others and said, "Hicks, what did that Ryan person see out on Commercial Street, when he looked over Donnie's shoulder?"

"I would say it must have been me, on the radio in my police cruiser, Detective." Hicks shook his head. "Shit, he was right there. I'd just pulled over to go into Martin's store when I got a call. Domestic disturbance out in Shannon Park. It turned out to be nothing. A waste of everyone's time." Hicks shook his head in disgust, "Damn! If I'd just looked to my left, even for half a second, I might have seen this Ryan guy."

"Well, that part is just bad luck, Hicks, but here's the good luck. I think you being there stopped Ryan from killing a second person. I think you saved Donnie's life."

THE LANGILLE'S HOUSE

When they got home, just after 10:00 pm, his dad realized Donnie was exhausted. "Hit the sack, Buddy. Lots to talk about but we'll cover it tomorrow."

"But you're travelling for work tomorrow."

"Yes, well I was, but maybe I'll able to get out of it. Anyway, we'll see what tomorrow brings." Then he grabbed his son in a bear hug. Donnie couldn't remember the last time he'd done that and to be truthful, right then, it felt great. "You did great with the police. You acted very mature actually." He broke the embrace and held his shoulders at arm's length, "You have to stop doing that, you're making me look old."

Donnie had tears of pride in his father. "Thanks Dad, good night."

"Night son."

As Donnie drifted off to sleep, he wondered how his father could be so nonchalant about this awful situation. Little did he know that his father was on the phone right after he went to bed and was grilling the cops about his son's safety for the better part of a half hour.

Donnie slept well that night. He thought part of the reason was exhaustion and part of it was that he thought he had acquitted himself well while being questioned. But he woke up anxious and worried. He had scenario after scenario bombarding his brain as he got dressed for school. He realized he was really scared for the first time in his life, though there was also a small part of him that revelled in the significance of what he was caught up in. The sheer excitement.

Donnie also knew that, until they caught Ryan, he would pause in every doorway before he entered or exited. He would check every dark road running off the main drag on which he was walking. He would be wondering what every hang-up phone call meant. Paranoid? He didn't think so. As far as anyone knew, he was the only person besides Mr. Martin, who had seen Ryan.

And Donnie was worried that he would have a target on his back for the rest of the summer.

THURSDAY

MEETING AND MISSING

When he came down into the kitchen, his father was adamant. "Donnie, you need to just stay home from school and lock the house up."

"How long?" he asked.

"Forever," he said, almost to himself. "Donnie, I have to keep a roof over our heads. So, I must go to Toronto today, and I want you home with the doors locked."

"When are you going to tell Mom?"

"Let's just hold off on that for a while, this may well turn out to be a non-event. In fact, I'm sure this will be nothing to worry about. No need to get her upset." Donnie wondered who he was trying to convince. Then he stepped into his bedroom to get his suitcase. "And she will be home on Monday anyway."

Donnie went to the kitchen table and had a mixer bowl of Cheerios, two slices of bread and jam and an orange juice. It was his first meal since yesterday's quick lunch.

"Dad," Donnie said quietly, as he put the dishes in the sink, "I'm safer at school than I am alone here." He could feel panic rising in his gut. Just the thought of having to make a plan to keep himself safe finally hit home. He had done a good job of keeping that feeling at bay despite waking up anxious. He forced the panic back down. But it made sense. Home alone or in the middle of two thousand people. No brainer.

Donnie's father came back into the living room and hugged him tightly for the second time in twelve hours. "Yes, I suppose you are. But I'm going to give you a lift up to the shopping centre." He released Donnie and, clearing his throat, said, "Get your things, lock up and meet me in the car. I assume you're meeting up with Natty?"

"Yes, I will and yes I am."

"Okay, I'll see you tonight. I still wish I was driving you all the way to school."

"Dad you'll miss your flight and anyway there's a million people between here and the school." And if he stayed home, Donnie knew he would be dwelling on this episode all day long.

Natty was waiting for Donnie at the bottom of Green Road and looked surprised to see him getting a lift with his dad.

"When you come home tonight, get one of you friend's parents to give you a lift. Okay?"

"Sure, Dad."

Mr. Langille pulled a five out of his wallet and said "And if you can't get a lift, grab a cab. I love you, son."

"Thanks Dad, love you too." As he exited the car, his father whispered, "Don't tell Natty or anyone about this matter, okay?"

"Of course not, Dad!" he answered.

About the same time Donnie met Natty on Green Road for their walk to Dartmouth High, the Nova Scotia RCMP and Dartmouth Police Force jointly issued a public request for photos taken on the Halifax-Dartmouth ferry on Wednesday afternoon. This would be assisting the authorities in a missing person's case.

GREEN ROAD AND EVERYWHERE ELSE

A wise old sage once said you learn everything you need to know in life before the age of ten. How to curb your impatience, how to share, how turning the other cheek doesn't always work, while the ubiquitous golden rule really does. Learning to live with disappointment. Learning that hard work was its own reward. And above all other life skills, how to make and *keep* friends, one of whom Donnie was meeting at the start of Green Road, where it intersected with Wyse Road and Boland Road. It was the last dirt road in the area, and it continued uphill at a slight angle behind the Dartmouth Shopping Centre, then terminated at Nantucket Avenue, with Dartmouth High School on the other side.

Natty waved to Donnie's dad as he pulled away, then hustled over to Donnie's side. "Jeez man, I thought you were never coming. We're gonna have to boot it if we're gonna be on time." As the newbies in high school, they were fully aware of the fact that showing up late for class as freshman, even this late in the year, was not a reputation you wanted to cultivate.

"What time is it?" he asked.

Natty looked at his watch. "Crap, 7:46. Let's hoof it!"

Should I tell Natty? The cops will probably be pissed, he thought. Then again, Detective Rafuse never explicitly forbade him from telling someone. "Best you keep it to yourself," was all he had said. Semantics, of course, but Donnie was scared and needed to confide in someone and here he was walking next to his best friend. Decision made.

Donnie came to a full stop. Natty did a double take. "What are you doing man, we gotta go!"

"Natty I'm in trouble."

"Yeah? What have you got to be worried about man, you got 85% on your first two terms. You don't even have to write finals. Wish I was that lucky."

"That's not what I'm talking about, buddy. School is the least of my worries right now." And Donnie told him. Everything from the moment he walked into Mr. Martin's store until he and his dad left the police station last night.

They must have made a bad impression in high school that Thursday. They weren't just late; the two boys missed the whole morning. During the course of their three-hour conversation, Donnie and Natty walked around the entire City of Dartmouth. They journeyed up Woodland Avenue past the new Mic Mac Mall, winding their way around the rotary, up Main Street near the Kmart on Tacoma, and then turning down Woodlawn Road by Prince Andrew High School.

Dartmouth High and Prince Andrew High were natural rivals, though they shared some facilities. This past winter festival, a bunch of Dartmouth High students, including Donnie, got together and built a huge toilet out of snow in the middle of the football field beside the school and put a sign beside it that read:

FLUSH TWICE
IT'S A LONG WAY TO P.A.

From there, Donnie and Natty walked on to Mount Edward Road, back over to Portland Street, across Hawthorne and onto Ochterloney, passing Sullivan's Pond, down to King Street, and finally flipping back over to Portland Street where it intersected with Commercial Street.

And there, right in front of them across Portland Street, was the crime scene. Mr. Martin's Corner Store. The big glass windows of Dartmouth City Hall were looking right at the crime scene.

A police car and a black van were parked at the curb in front of the store entrance and the sidewalk at each end of the block on Commercial Street had been barricaded. Police officers were re-routing pedestrians to the other side of Portland Street where Donnie and Natty now stood.

The two boys stared at the store. They had stopped talking. Donnie dropped his eyes towards the sidewalk and had a moment of disbelief. Was he really in there yesterday with Mr. Martin's body just feet away, hidden from view? Natty just kept looking, probably realizing the enormity of the situation for the first time.

Finally, they silently made their way around the corner, down Commercial Street to Dillman Park, and climbed to the top. There they sat on a bench overlooking the beautiful harbour, just out of sight of Mr. Martin's store.

Natty broke the silence, "Maybe Ryan found his body but was too scared to come forward or didn't want to get involved."

"I dunno Nat, he didn't seem put out by anything. Cool as a cucumber if you know what I mean." Donnie shook his head, "Man that's creepy to think that he wasn't concerned with a dead body right next to him."

"Maybe he's a narc, undercover or some such? I mean he didn't try to ... you know, hurt you or anything, right?"

Donnie shivered thinking of Ryan coming up silently behind him as he left the store. "Maybe. Probably not though."

"Jesus." Natty was leaning forward elbows on knees, with his fingertips on each side of his forehead. Staring out at the harbour but not seeing a thing. Finally, he said, "Okay, then we have to bring the guys in on this."

"Peter and Clip? I dunno, man, I told Dad I wouldn't tell anyone else. Why tell Peter and Clip?"

"Why? Jeez buddy, I can't be there all the time. The four of us will work it out so that you're *never* alone. There'll always be one of us with you and preferably all of us. Strength in numbers man."

Donnie turned his head away to hide the tears that suddenly stung his eyes. How can you measure the value of friends like this? The relief was so overwhelming, it caught him off guard ... and his guard slipped a bit. Natty must have noticed, because he punched him in the arm.

"Hey man," he said quietly, "We can handle this, okay?"

Donnie nodded and wiped his eyes.

Natty jumped up and said with a grin, "Come on, let's see if we can at least salvage the afternoon classes!"

IN SHIT AGAIN

When Donnie and Natty finally arrived at school that afternoon, after their long walk, Donnie had no sooner sat at his desk when the loudspeaker blared. "Donald Langille report to head office please. Donald Langille." Donnie looked up at his teacher, who gave him a nod to leave.

The person sitting next to him was a fellow named Trevor, but known to all his peers as Creeper. He grinned at Donnie and said, "You in shit again Langille?"

"Aren't we all, Creeper?"

Creeper nodded and called after Donnie as he walked out the classroom door, "That's a fact man!" Everyone in class swore he was stoned 24-7, but you never smelled weed on him.

Donnie walked up to the admin area of the school, which was located just off the main foyer, a square-shaped nexus-point of the school. The biggest feature was a large staircase to the second floor. He stepped into the head office and immediately saw two uniformed policemen standing there.

"Here's Donald now," said the school secretary.

One of the cops stepped towards Donnie.

"Donald Langille? Of 2901 Windmill Road?" he asked.

He nodded nervously. Then cleared his voice and straightened up. "Yes, that's me. Er, call me Donnie."

"Okay Donnie, I'm Corporal Keith Fong, Dartmouth Police. We've been sent here to request that you accompany us down to the station."

"What's this about?"

"I didn't ask son, they just said for you to come down to the station. I should tell you that you're under no obligation to accompany us."

"No, that's okay, I'll grab my stuff from home room, and we'll go? Can I ask who wants me down there?"

"Detective O'Byrne sent us."

Oh great, Donnie thought.

Mrs. Sinclair, who was sitting behind her desk with a concerned look on her face, asked, "Is everything alright Donnie? Do you have a family emergency?"

Fong answered for him, "Nothing to worry about, Donald has to fill out a report of some type down at the station house."

MUG SHOT

Donnie was not looking forward to meeting with the charming Detective O'Byrne and was apprehensive, but his mind eased when he walked into the station and Rafuse waiting for him. That was a relief because he had visions of O'Byrne arresting him for murder. He was again ushered into the back of the station, but to a different office this time.

"How is the investigation going?" he asked.

"These things are pretty hectic in the first few hours, Donnie, and it's crucial we get as much info as possible." Rafuse continued, "Your father called us just after he dropped you off and told us you were walking to school today."

"Yeah, Dad had to go to Toronto for a three-hour meeting today. He said he'd be back late. Around nine o'clock tonight maybe. But we talked it over and I convinced him that I'm safer in a crowd than at home all alone."

"Yes, well," Rafuse moved his head side to side as if weighing the odds, "you're probably right, and it's not as if Ryan knows where you live."

Something started gnawing at Donnie's mind when Rafuse said that, but it wouldn't present itself.

"He also mentioned your mother is out of the province at this time?"

"She'll be back on Monday." Time to get to the point. "So can I ask why I'm here?" He had a sneaking suspicion they were going to try and give him a polygraph while his father wasn't available.

"Well, since you had a close-up look at Mr. Louis Ryan, we're going to get you to sit down with a sketch artist and see if you can give us an idea of what the fellow looks like."

"Sure. Sounds cool." Anything to help them find this guy.

"And after that's finished," continued Rafuse, "we're going to have you peruse some mug books. It's a long shot but you never know, maybe he'll show up."

A few minutes later the artist, Carl Lukawski, came into the room. He didn't look much older than Donnie, though he assured everyone he was twenty-six. He was a teacher at the local College of Art and Design.

"Well, I'll leave you to it," said Rafuse as he exited.

Carl and Donnie started talking, slowly and tentatively. The sketch artist told Donnie about himself. Where he'd learned his craft and how he was going to apply it now. He asked Donnie if he had any gut feelings about the guy, the mood Ryan was in, and defining features, etc. He had to explain to the boy about hairlines and nose shapes, and he had a small library of the different facial features printed on clear plastic to help Donnie along. Each time he chose a feature, he placed it on top of the previous ones to create a face.

After a few hours, that face finally began to emerge at the cost of an untold number of minor changes, and a few start overs from scratch. It ended up taking three hours to complete.

Carl passed the composite sketch to Donnie. "What do you think? Is that him?" he said.

"Yeah ... sort of."

Carl smiled. "You don't sound convinced," he said.

Donnie shrugged.

"Can you think of any way I can improve it?"

"I dunno, it's like I've been looking at this sketch for so long, I can't remember what he looked like."

"How far away was this man from you?" he asked.

"Well, he was right next to me a couple times but mostly he was between four and six feet away."

"Ah, okay!" Carl took the sketch back and walked over to the wall opposite him. "How about now?" he asked.

"I mean it's not perfect, but if you asked me what was wrong, I wouldn't be able to tell you. The hairline is maybe a quarter inch higher and the hair itself not as thick. And the beard was really close to his face."

Carl worked for several more minutes. Then held up the face of Louis Ryan for inspection. Donnie just smiled and nodded.

"Man, how long you been doing this, Mr. Lukawski?" he asked.

"Call me Carl. My first name is Jaro actually, which is short for Jaroslaw, but the fellows here started calling me Carl when I arrived. I'm available whenever they need me. There is an agreement between the local police forces and the college that gives me leave to do this whenever there is a pressing need."

Rafuse popped in. "How's it going, guys?"

"All done here!" said Jaro as he packed his gear to leave. "I'll be in touch, Detective." And he was gone.

"Donald, how close do you think this resemblance is to Ryan?" asked Rafuse.

"It's as good as I can remember," he replied. "I dunno, say 75 to 80% accurate?"

Rafuse smiled, "Yes that's pretty accurate. We couldn't have asked for more than that. Okay, we have the mug books set up in my office. Let's take a look."

There were a lot of mug books with a lot of pictures, all brought over that morning from the local RCMP headquarters. Donnie tried his best to "see the face he remembered" and ignore anything else. The pictures in the books were almost entirely black and white, very few colour photos, but he found that that actually helped. The black and white images seemed to be clearer.

By the time he was nearing his second hour, all the faces were starting to look the same. Donnie knew one thing for sure, he did not want to run into any of those faces on a deserted street.

Rafuse noted that he had yawned and rubbed his eyes a couple times. "Okay Donnie, I think that's enough for today. You go on home and get back to normal life. Listen son, do you need a note?"

"A note?"

"Yes, you know, a note for your school or teacher or whoever, because of your absence today?"

Donnie didn't think he needed a note, but it couldn't hurt, "Sure, if you don't mind."

"Okay, I'll write one up while you're getting fingerprinted."

"Fingerprinted?" asked Donnie.

"You mentioned yesterday that you touched several items and surfaces in the Martin's store, so we need to exclude your prints and maybe find the suspects."

"Yeah okay, makes sense, I guess," said Donnie.

A half hour later, off he went in the back of a police cruiser, headed for home with black fingertips and palms, and a note in his pocket. It read:

To whom it may concern:

Please excuse <u>Mr. Donnie Langille's</u> absence from class yesterday.

His assistance was required in an active police investigation.

For further information please contact <u>Detective Richard Rafuse,</u>

Dartmouth City Police 902-555-7311

FRIDAY

ROBERT HATCHES A PLAN

Donnie woke up the next morning to his dad pounding on the bedroom door. "Let's go, kid." He poked his head in the door.

"What's up?" Donnie tried to blink away the cobwebs. "Jeez, I didn't even hear you come in last night," he mumbled.

"Didn't get home till one in the morning, Donnie. I had to take the later flight. Come on, let's go, I have breakfast waiting downstairs. And I have some news."

A few minutes later, Donnie staggered downstairs into the kitchen and a full-fledged breakfast of bacon and eggs, a spoonful of baked brown beans, and toast and coffee, still hot and steaming on the kitchen table. Donnie didn't drink coffee ordinarily but decided to join his father and had a mug.

He chowed down with a typical fifteen-year-old's wild appetite. "So, what's the news?" he asked, between bites.

"First things first," his father said. "What'd you do yesterday? I understand you were with the police."

Donnie gave him a quizzical look, but of course parents know everything, so he filled his dad in on his adventures with Jaro the sketch artist and showed him his still dark fingertips.

"Then they drove me home. It was kinda cool because there seemed to be cop cars driving by the house all night. Anyway, I felt wound-up, so I decided to mow the lawn. And one of the cop cars actually stopped and parked across the street until I finished."

Robert's eyebrows shot up in an unspoken question.

"Yes, I did both the front yard and the back!" Donnie said it proudly, like he deserved a medal. "It was still light outside with lots of people around so I figured it would be safe. When I came in, I locked the house up and had a bag of chips and two Snickers bars for supper. Then I watched *Cannon* and *Sanford and Son*. And then I watched Lloyd Robertson before hitting the sack."

His father faked a shocked look. "You?! Watched the CBC National news? What is the world coming to?" They both laughed.

Robert watched Donnie finish his breakfast. Nothing makes a parent happier than seeing their child eat a hearty, wholesome meal.

"Donnie you're not going to school today and in fact you're finished for the year." He said it so casually, that at first, it didn't register with his son.

"What? Why?"

"Yesterday afternoon, I had an idea between meetings in Toronto. I'm not comfortable with you going to school every day while that murderer is on the loose. And yes, I know the police think he may have fled the province right after the incident."

Donnie tried to say something, but he held up his hand. "No, don't interrupt, hear me out. I made a few calls. First, I spoke to Principal Pembroke and made a rather unusual request, that you be excused from any further classes for the remainder of the school year. It's only two weeks anyway. And he agreed."

Then Robert looked at him, "By the way, you haven't told anyone about this, have you?"

"No, not yet." It was a lie, but Donnie didn't know where this was going. Besides, Natty wasn't just anyone.

"Good." He paused and took a sip of coffee. "Next, I called Detective Rafuse and had a long discussion on how to handle this problem. Turns out he is just as concerned about you as I am. And we came up with a plan. Yesterday, he had a city official call the Plant Emporium to inform them that you are taking a part-time summer internship course in social studies to learn civic procedures at Dartmouth City Hall. Because of the nature of this internship, the Emporium was told that you may have to leave work on short notice. And some days you may even miss the entire workday."

"What is the ...?"

"Hold on, just let me finish, Donnie. The Emporium is a pretty laid-back place. They said they were fine with this summer course as long as you notify them as to when you're leaving. Okay so far?"

"Yeah, I guess so, but why all the cloak and dagger?"

"Well as you can imagine, the last thing we want, is anyone, especially at school, finding out that you're the prime witness in a murder investigation."

Donnie started to protest but Robert held up his hand. "I'm not saying that you can't keep a secret son. But you're only human and you may inadvertently say the wrong thing at the wrong time. That kind of news, especially in high school circles, would be common knowledge in a matter of hours. That could put your life in danger. At the same time, your assistance may be needed at any time by the police, you know line ups and the sort, and therefore the need for this internship cover story. In the unlikely possibility that Ryan is still in town, the Emporium is a good safe location, well outside the city. You'll be surrounded by people at all times there. It's the best we could come up with on short notice, aside from locking you in the house until this Ryan fellow is caught. This is a serious situation, Donnie, but I think it's important not to let it rule our lives either."

Donnie knew his dad was right, this was a serious situation. Half of him was worried about going out the door at all! But he was determined to live life as normal as he could. "Yeah, okay Dad. Thanks for doing that."

"Oh yes, and we decided you'll be starting your summer job this morning."

Donnie was stunned. "What? This morning?! I'm going to be on the long bus ride to and from the Emporium every day. Doesn't *waiting around at bus stops* put me in danger too?" He paused to think. "I mean we can't afford a cab ride like that every day — and surely you can't drive me out there and back for the rest of the summer?"

"I most certainly would pay to cab you there and back. And I would certainly drop you off and pick you up myself if it came to that, but I won't have to. You see, you actually know a person who works out there, and she told Mr. Norberg that she would be thrilled to pick you up and drop you off."

"She? Who's she?"

Robert laughed, "I think you'll be pleased. It's someone you know quite well. Now get dressed, she'll be here in twenty minutes." And he watched his son mutter in panic as he raced off to the shower.

Twenty-five minutes later, Donnie finished drying his curly hair and tossed the damp towel onto an empty hook on the bathroom wall. Then he ran down the stairs, giving his dad a running goodbye, and dashed out the front door.

In their driveway, he found his dream car waiting for him: A '71 black two-door Chevelle SS with double white stripes on the hood and trunk. And the wonderful rumble of an idling 427 V8 you could feel right to the bottom of your feet. Donnie was sixteen years old in a few days and he couldn't wait to get his driver's licence. He walked over to the shiny car and got an even bigger surprise.

Inside was a friend of his who he hadn't seen in over a year. She had been an unofficial *one of the gang* until her family moved to Halifax, at the end of the last school year.

"Hi, you big hunk!" she said with a giggle. "Jump in!"

Donnie slipped into the front passenger seat, the sweet smell of leather from the light grey seats filling his nose. He lightly touched the Hurst shifter, feeling the latent power right through his body. Then he gave his friend a smile.

"Madeline! You're working at the Emporium?" From practice, Donnie pronounced her name the way she preferred, *Madeleen*.

She smiled a wide pretty smile and nodded. "This is my second summer, Donnie."

"Nice!" he said, "Man it's really good to see you again."

"You too. You look so much older now." Donnie loved hearing that. And she looked terrific. Madeline Wagner was a tall girl maybe an inch shorter than him, short black hair, intense blue eyes, and an athletic build. She was dressed for work; jeans, and a tee with the Lake William Plant Emporium logo on the front, green trees surrounding a blue lake. He couldn't help but notice that the tee was stretched impressively across her chest.

She put the gearshift into reverse, and they backed out onto Windmill Road and headed up Elmwood Avenue, eventually making their way to Woodland Avenue in the direction of the MicMac rotary.

"Where did you get the car?" Donnie asked. "It's not yours, is it?"

"That would be bloody sweet, wouldn't it!" She shook her head sadly. "But no, it's my dad's car. Ordinarily he wouldn't let me drive it, but he's out at sea. So, Mom lets me steal it to go to school and then that carried over to my summer job."

"Sweet is right! But aren't you still in school?"

"Nope, I made the two terms exemption just like I hear you did. And Halifax West will let us take the last two weeks off from school, if we have a summer job lined up. You must have the same rules at Dartmouth High."

"Yeah, pretty similar, I guess. But not all the schools do it."

It seemed like forever since he'd seen her. When you're sixteen years old, twelve months can feel like an eternity.

Madeline's father was a Fisheries Patrol officer. He served on the big boats that checked to see if foreign fishing vessels were violating our waters. Rumours were that Canada was going to unilaterally proclaim a two-hundred-mile limit next year, so he'd probably be gone even more. Mr. Wagner met Madeline's mother in England and after they married and had welcomed their new daughter, he took a

Canadian government position in Plymouth as some kind of liaison. They stayed there for eight years before moving back to Canada, settling in Dartmouth. Madeline hadn't entirely lost her English accent but a little more of it disappeared with every passing year. Her mother was a homebody who doted on their only child.

Madeline's family had lived next to Natty's on Elmwood Avenue for several years before moving to Halifax. The two children grew up together and thought of each other as little brother and big sister. They had done everything together, even Catechism at the church, which from what Donnie could gather, was like bible study for Roman Catholics.

Natty was bummed out when her family moved to Fairview last year. She was now ten miles away, on the other side of Halifax and, most importantly, in a new school district. Donnie was sad too. Whenever Madeline joined them in their shenanigans, everything was just more fun. Wait till Natty sees this car! Donnie thought.

As they sped down the Waverley Road on the way to the Emporium, the Chevelle hugging closely on every turn and bend, Donnie asked, "What's the boss like?"

"Norberg? He's a nice guy, but don't get him angry. I hear he has quite the temper if he thinks you're trying to cheat him or lie to him." Madeline paused. "I've never had a problem though."

"Is he from around here?"

"No. He and his wife Anna left Sweden and moved to Montreal when they were both about twenty-five years old. Apparently, his wife's family was loaded and if their daughter was going to follow her husband into the Canadian wilderness, then they would make sure that she at least had money."

"Did he go to college here to learn all this plant stuff?"

Madeline rolled her eyes. "Plant stuff? It's called horticulture, Donnie. And no, he didn't have to go to school here, it was the family business. And Mr. Norberg is quite the expert!"

"So, he's the brains, and she's the money."

"Something like that. Anyway, they opened a place on the

outskirts of Montreal, but competition up there was rough. They made it for ten years, but finally decided to start fresh somewhere else. Apparently, they were considering Toronto, but because of the size, they figured they'd just run into the same competition. I guess that's why they settled on the Halifax area and built the Emporium out by Lake William. And his wife Anna has a cousin in Greenwood in the Annapolis Valley, so they have a relative nearby.

"I guess a lot of people, even his family, told him that no one was going to trail all the way out to Lake William for plants and potting soil. But the local green thumbs loved the place. They liked what he grew and especially his advice on how to use it. Seeds, plants, how to pick them, how to plant them, how to cook, you name it, Mr. Norberg is a walking plant encyclopedia!"

THE LAKE WILLIAM PLANT EMPORIUM

They arrived at the Emporium twenty-five minutes after leaving Donnie's house. Madeline waved goodbye, saying, "See you in eight hours. Unless they put you in my greenhouse." She flashed him a beautiful smile and was off.

Donnie went into the main building and met Mr. Norberg again, who explained how he would be paid and that his status was temporary part-time, so there would be no benefits. But he emphasized that Donnie was entitled to collect vacation pay. After signing a few papers, he took Donnie over to a guy named Graham, who gave him a workplace introduction, and then to a guy named Bradley, who gave him a safety orientation. Donnie was given his work gloves, work boots, company tee and a blue work helmet to be used if he had to work in the shipping area, which sometimes had boxes piled fifteen feet high.

Donnie was assigned, that first day, to the potting area of Greenhouse Two. He worked at a low-standing table. Graham was with him, and it took about an hour to learn everything there was to his new job. Basically, he put the plants together. Seedlings in large multi-pot trays were done on top of the table, which was tedious. But he also potted big plants and small trees on the concrete floor, which was more interesting.

From a recipe, he had to measure out the different soil compositions and fertilizers as well as follow the precise number, depth, and spacing for each type of seed he put in each pot of the tray. This would start the seedlings in a few days. Working at the table left him bent over at an unnatural angle, and his back soon became sore.

He looked around and found a couple of old wooden boxes. He turned them upside down, cracked a lower board off one, side and fitted them together to give himself a mini platform. This raised his work area and would hopefully save his spine. It certainly made his work easier.

Easier for about an hour, until Erik strutted by. As far as Donnie could guess, Erik was Mr. Norberg's son, or maybe nephew, but whatever he was, it was obvious he was used to lording over the underlings that were the summer students.

Erik pulled up with a start behind Donnie. "Who said you could use those boxes?" he asked, attempting a commanding voice that sounded more like a squeaky door hinge.

"I did," Donnie said calmly. He could see this surprised Erik. Good. While Mr. Norberg had his respect, this guy would have to earn it. And he hadn't forgot that insult from when Erik was showing him around Wednesday.

"Put those boxes back right now," Erik commanded.

Donnie had a notion to give him a sarcastic 'Yes Drill Sergeant!' But he kept his cool. "Look they've obviously been there forever, and no one was using them, so I figured they could help ease the strain on my back."

"You've been working here three hours and already your back is bad? You shouldn't be here at all. Nobody else needs to use the boxes."

Now Donnie was getting angry, so he decided to be a jerk as well. "That's because no one else is as smart as me."

"Put the boxes back!" Erik was yelling now, his gloved hands on his hips.

"Why?" he asked.

"Because I said so."

Maybe it was the pain from bending over for hours but whatever it was, Donnie blurted out, "I don't think 'cause I said so' is worth me wrecking my back!"

"Your job isn't to think, it's to shovel shit and seeds into a box. If you can't do that, you're a retard and you're wasting my time."

"Your time? As far as I can tell you spend all your time walking around the greenhouses giving hardworking people grief!" he roared.

"I'm going to fuckin' fire you!"

"Go ahead, fire me. Right now. Do me a favour! I'm dying to leave here!"

"Alright, you're fired!"

"Bullshit! You can't fire me! I don't believe a word you say. Now get lost and let me do my job!"

"Look you little shit —" Erik was interrupted by a booming voice.

"Langille, in my office!" It was Mr. Norberg. "Right now!"

Donnie sullenly followed the boss over to his little office in the main building.

APOLOGY

Andreas Norberg was a genuinely nice guy. Which meant the scowl on his face at that moment was making Donnie nervous. And he was taking his time making the boy stew under his stare. Donnie was still angry about Erik, so he gave him stare for stare, but he couldn't maintain it and eventually looked down at his shoes, knowing that he'd screwed up on his first day.

"Kid, you trying to make me fire you three hours after I hired you?" he asked, with that same scowl on his face.

Donnie wanted to tell his boss about his sore back and his own attempt to fix it and Erik acting like a jerk, but something his dad had long ago taught him about negotiations came to mind. Never throw everything out on the table at once. And now that his temper was cooling, he began to think maybe he did fly off the handle. *Take the high road.*

"It's my fault. I've never done this kind of work before, and my back was getting sore, so I grabbed a couple of old boxes to make a platform so I could work on the plants easier. Erik said I shouldn't move any boxes and I kinda lost my temper at him."

Norberg was still staring at him but with a skeptical look on his face. "Uh huh ..."

Donnie continued. "I guess I acted like a horse's ass. I'm sorry Mr. Norberg."

"I'm sure you weren't the only one," he said, shaking his head. That comment surprised Donnie.

"Erik's not having it easy, son. He's my wife's cousin's kid. When he was younger, his father deserted Erik and his mother and is somewhere in the States now. Erik was a summer student like you and came up here from the valley to stay with us the past few years. Now he works here in the Emporium full time and sort of looks out for all you students. We're grooming him to be management, and it's always difficult when you raise someone up above their equals. He's just trying to find his way, Langille." Norberg paused. "I heard you say you were *dying to leave,* is that true?"

Oh shit. "No sir, not at all. Like I said, I was a horse's ass. My temper got the better of me."

Norberg smiled then, and shook his head. "Just like your old man." He chuckled.

"You know my dad?" Donnie was surprised.

"Yeah, I'll tell you about it some time. We almost came to blows once. Now go on back to work kid, and if Erik gives you any problems, tell him I said you could use the boxes."

"Thanks Mr. Norberg. One last question. What does Erik do around here?"

"Right now, he, Paul and Heidi work in shipping with the foreman — the guy who gave you the safety orientation, Bradley."

Donnie nodded, thanked him again and headed back to his work area.

Heidi? Hearing that name spurred a memory he had long buried. There must be dozens of girls with that name in Nova Scotia, but he only ever met one Heidi in his life, and he was sure it couldn't be her. She was a very special person to Donnie, and they were best friends when they were children, but Heidi moved away not long after his family left Halifax. And no one seemed to know where they had gone. And now memories dashed in and overpowered Donnie's thoughts.

HEIDI FREEMAN

In grade four, Heidi Freeman and Donnie Langille both attended LeMarchant Elementary School, on Watt Street in Halifax. They lived on parallel streets, off Jubilee Road near Robie Street. Both were ten years old, both had one older sibling. And there the similarity ended. At that time, Donnie was shy and introspective, Heidi was outgoing and made friends easily. When it came to dancing, she was as graceful as a ballerina, while two left feet didn't begin to describe how bad Donnie was. They were in separate grade-four classes and would never have met except that it was 1967, Canada's 100th birthday.

For the Centennial, LeMarchant School was planning a big show for faculty and parents on the 19th of April, in the school gym. It would be part of the Food, Fun and Frolics Festival, an annual event at LeMarchant. For part of the event, students would do group dances to represent all the different cultures that made up Canada. Heidi and Donnie were thrust into the dance group that would be celebrating France. Donnie was particularly concerned at the time as he was not fond of the prospect of making a fool out of himself in front of friends and family.

At their first dance practice, teachers outfitted the children in their costumes, the boys wearing a beret and a striped T-shirt, and the girls a short French skirt, and braided hair. Rumour had it that the boys were going to have painted-on moustaches when they danced for the show, but that never happened. After getting the kids to look the part, teachers announced the names of the dance partners.

Somewhere in the unending list of names, "Donald Langille and Heidi Freeman!" came over the loudspeaker.

Donnie watched as a pretty, smiling girl weaved her way through the jostle of kids and stopped in front of him. She grabbed his hand and said "Wanna dance?" Then she burst out giggling. She had a wonderful contagious laugh that sounded like bells ringing. Donnie had never said much to any girl outside of family, so they were a big mystery to him. But Heidi changed everything. They bonded instantly and were talking like best friends before the end of that first rehearsal. She did her best to help him with the steps. Instead of getting frustrated, Donnie laughed at his own clumsiness, something that impressed Heidi. When they performed their dance a few weeks later, it was a great success and he actually enjoyed himself.

Friends and family noticed a change in Donnie that summer. He had so much more confidence talking to people in general and girls in particularly. Heidi had many friends who wanted to hang around with her, but for the summer of '67 at least, she and Donnie were like toast and jam. They ended up spending the majority of their summer vacation together.

They would walk to parks, walk all over downtown, which was only a mile away, and often they would frequent the local outdoor swimming pool on the Halifax Commons. Donnie wasn't a strong swimmer, but Heidi's brother had been taking her to Red Cross swim classes the past few years and she was like a dolphin in the pool. She taught him all kinds of things, including the dog paddle, the back stroke, the breaststroke, and freestyle, though he didn't master that for another few years. She also showed him something called drownproofing.

One morning they were swimming at Black Rock beach in Point

Pleasant Park. The water was a calm sheet of glass. It was a workday, so very few people were there with them.

"This could save your life if you ever fall out of a boat or you're too far from shore. It's for when you're super tired and you feel like you can't go on. Take a deep breath and rest your body. Let you face go under water and relax everything." She demonstrated for him. "Count to ten, then push your way back up to the surface with your arms and legs and take another deep breath and go back underwater and relax and count again. Remember to keep your arms out in front of you to stay vertical. Keep doing it until you feel ready to get back to swimming."

It took a lot of confidence to try, because he wasn't comfortable with his head underwater for so long. But Donnie realized that the big breath of air you inhaled before you went underwater wouldn't let you go very deep. And after a couple panicked exits from the water, he finally got quite comfortable with the manoeuvre.

For Donnie and Heidi, it got to the point where they were together every day, all day and would have continued, except housing prices were rising in Halifax. Donnie's parents decided to sell and move to Dartmouth. His mother was less than enthusiastic but whenever questioned, his father would say, "It's going to save us a bundle, and it's just a quick flip over the bridge." And of course, it was, but there is some genetic thing in humans that makes them regard a body of water like Halifax Harbour as a natural barrier to travel, regardless of the passenger ferry and a modern suspension bridge.

The moving date would be the end of August. Donnie's sister Anita was appalled. "Dartmouth is just a patch of ground holding up the other end of the bridge! What about my friends?" she moaned. But the decision was made.

Donnie called Heidi and told her they were moving at the end of the week. During that time, he noticed that Heidi was acting differently. She was short tempered, even angry at times, and asked him more than once if he was upset. He answered yes of course he was, but there was nothing he could do.

At one point, Heidi told him, in tears, " I have a really bad feeling inside. Everything's going to be worse for me after you move away!" Donnie tried to console her saying they'd find ways to visit, and they could always phone each other. He was convinced they'd never lose touch. But he was only ten years old.

Two nights before his family's big move, Heidi and Donnie went for a walk in the Public Gardens. These are two blocks from where they lived, right in the middle of the City of Halifax. They're the oldest Victorian gardens in North America.

They walked around the pathways silently until they found themselves in the deserted north-east corner of the Gardens. It was cool, sweater weather, and the first inkling of a fall wind was rustling through the trees. The flowers were at their biggest and brightest, which meant their end was probably just weeks away. The children barely said a word.

Heidi took Donnie's hand, and they sat on one of the benches. And he was shocked to see tears in her eyes, and realized those tears must be for him. No one had ever cried for him before, and he really didn't know what to say or do. A few times he tried to speak but didn't know the right words.

Heidi stared at her best friend a few more moments, tears running down her cheek. Then she threw her arms around his shoulders and kissed him on the lips. Donnie had never kissed a girl before or been kissed, as in this case. It felt incredible, partly because of the emotion between them, but mainly because he had no idea what a real kiss felt like. Donnie's eyes were closed but he felt her tears spill onto his face and his own tears started to well up in him. Her soft lips fiercely pressed on his like they were never going to leave, and he never wanted them to.

At that age, Donnie couldn't have imagined he would ever make such an impression on someone else's life. And that person would be crying at losing him. It was a revelation. And a frustration because he had no idea how to deal with the situation. Finally, she broke off. Turning around without a word, jumped up and ran out of the gardens.

As he watched her disappear into the dusk, it dawned on Donnie that he might never see her again. It left him with a panicky feeling. And he promised himself as he walked home with the tears running down his cheeks, that he would make his way over to Halifax and visit her again as soon as possible.

Moving is never fun, and all he heard from the neighbours around them was that Dartmouth was an unwelcoming place, full of undesirable people. It was a busy time, and it was almost three weeks later, in the new house in Dartmouth, before Donnie picked up the phone and called Heidi's number. He was overjoyed with the prospect of talking to her. But the operator said that her number was no longer in service. He tried several more times over the next few weeks but still ended up with the same result. And for those first few weeks, Donnie berated himself for not calling her sooner.

A lot happens when you're ten years old and moving between cities. And though Donnie hadn't forgotten about Heidi, he was young and there are a lot of duties, interests, and distractions. New school, new friends and new activities kept him busy. It wasn't until two summers later that he made good on his promise to himself to go back over to Halifax and find his best friend ever.

On a warm Saturday in May of 1969, when he was almost twelve, Donnie, along with Peter, Natty, and Madeline, bravely walked their bikes across the mile long MacDonald bridge from Dartmouth to Halifax, where they rode around the big city. Eventually Donnie steered his friends over to his old neighbourhood.

"Come on guys, I'll show you where I used to live." He had never mentioned Heidi to any of them. He stopped on Edward Street marvelling at how the street hadn't changed a bit. They rode along and he pointed to a slightly shabby light blue Victorian home in the middle of the block. "This is my old house," he said.

"Holy cow!" said Natty, "It's double the size of the one you live in now!"

"Yes, you've really come down in the world!" laughed Madeline.

They rode over to see his old elementary school, LeMarchant, then doubled back around the corner to Henry Street.

"Just a sec' guys. I wanna see if a friend of mine is home." He walked up to Heidi's front door and rang the doorbell. He was excited and not a little nervous. He was surprised when a stranger answered. An elderly woman.

"Hi ..." he stammered "Do the Freemans still live here?"

The lady looked him over suspiciously. "And who are you?"

"Oh, sorry ma'am. My name is Donnie Langille, I used to live on the next street over, Edward Street I mean."

"Ah, I see. I'm sorry young man, the Freemans moved out a couple years ago. September month, of '67, I think it was," she said kindly.

"Okay. I don't suppose you have a forwarding address."

"No son, but if I'm remembering correctly, they left the province, or possibly the country."

Donnie was disappointed. But a long time had passed, at least for a twelve-year-old, and he rode away thinking of other things. He had a great group of friends and an unlimited future.

A FRIEND FROM THE PAST

Heidi Freeman lived in Sackville, Nova Scotia, and, appropriately enough, attended Sackville High School. She was lucky enough to have no classes at the school after 2:00 pm on Friday afternoons and she was free to go into the Emporium and work between 3:00 and 8:00 pm. About half the time she could count on a lift from Erik. Today wasn't one of those times and she had taken public transit.

She hopped off the bus at around 2:45 pm, the oily diesel fumes swirling around her as it roared away. Heidi glanced up at the hot sun in the sky above and frowned. It was giving off a mid-summer heat now, though the weatherman had promised heavy showers overnight. She walked briskly toward her workplace in the loading area, but at the last second detoured around to the back of the main building for a look inside the greenhouses. All three had their doors open. It'll be like an oven in there today, she thought, pitying the poor souls who had to work there.

As she passed Greenhouse Two, Heidi skidded to a stop. There was a new worker inside and he seemed familiar. Something about him triggered a jolt of recognition in her, something she hadn't felt for a long time. She peeked back in the door. It was much brighter outside than in, and it took a moment for her eyes to adjust.

He had his back to her. She was about to shrug and walk away when he turned back to his worktable. In the late sixties, Heidi had 'seen' Donnie every now and again for a couple of years after her family had moved to Liverpool, but it was never him, of course. That sensation faded as she tried to rebuild her life in a new home. Maybe this fellow wasn't her friend from 1967, but seeing someone so similar brought back a glow to her heart, just thinking of her childhood friend.

She was trying to decide whether to go closer and introduce herself when Erik walked up behind her and said, "What're you looking at?"

"Nothing," she said. "Well, there's a new guy in Greenhouse Two."

"So? Do you know him?"

"No, I don't think so," said Heidi. There was something menacing in Erik's voice, which was nothing new these days, plus he was sweaty and seemed nervous for some reason. So, she made a neutral comment. "I'm just surprised because I thought Mr. Norberg didn't need any more part-timers."

Erik seemed to relax a little. "Well, the boss always needs extra hands at this time of year." He pointed a gloved finger at her and said, "But you stay away from him, he's an asshole. Norbie almost fired him today."

"He did? What for?" she asked.

"I just said, because he's an asshole. Come on let's go." And off Erik went. Heidi was about to follow Erik when she saw the new guy spill some soil on the floor. To which he cursed, said "sorry" to absolutely no one, then cleaned everything up. Then he went back to work like it was his favourite job ever. All the while humming to himself.

And she knew as plain as the nose on her face. This fellow was her friend Donnie, weirdly wonderful as ever. Someone who always seemed at ease with himself. That's what she had loved most about him.

Loved? Yes. Puppy love to be sure six years ago but now, having seen him ... she felt an unexpected rush of what? Longing? Excitement? Happiness surely and something new, desire? Definitely a rush of wonderful memories.

A LITTLE PUSH

For Heidi, at age ten, it had been love-at-first sight. The quiet boy the other girls hadn't noticed was the person she wanted to meet the most. And it seemed like fate when they were paired in the Centennial dance. A point proven by the fact they were inseparable during that long, exciting summer of 1967. Mostly she and Donnie would hang out alone and Heidi loved that time — because they could just be themselves.

They went everywhere, usually with one or the other's parents. Although the two couples seemed to get along fine, Heidi noticed a distinct difference in their respective parents. Donnie's parents thought she was the cat's meow, whereas her mom and dad didn't have the time of day for Donnie. But that was a worry for later.

The evening fireworks and concert on Citadel Hill was especially memorable as it was the first time their two families had met. Before the fireworks began, she and Donnie left the others. They moved down the hill 'for a better view' and snuggled together in the cool evening air, oohing and aahing with the strangers around them as every firework exploded above them. The intimacy she felt with this boy was intense and not a little scary. Yes, they were best friends, but Heidi realized she wanted more — she wanted romance. And like in the movies, she wanted a handsome guy to kiss her. This guy right here! Her first kiss!

It didn't happen that night. Probably because there was a big crowd around them, and their parents were no doubt keeping a close eye on them. And Donnie didn't show the slightest interest in her as a girl. Their friendship was strong, and sometimes intense, but not passionate.

Heidi decided to give Donnie a little push. It was mid-August and she had waited long enough! They were alone, upstairs in Donnie's bedroom, relaxing on the bed talking about everything like they always did. It was a warm morning, and the window was open, birds singing outside. The room filled with the scent of mid-summer. There was a Beatle's Rubber Soul poster on the wall. A hand-me-down from his sister. And another poster of Expo 67. He had sports equipment, old dinky cars, a ceramic piggybank in the shape of a sneaker with a real shoelace intertwined through real eyelets. It made a depressingly small rattle when it was shaken. His room was messy, 'boy-messy', but never dirty.

There was a lull in the conversation and that didn't matter because for the first time in her life Heidi had met a person with whom there were no awkward silences. They were perfectly happy just being near each other.

Time to act. "I was talking to Kathy Rideout last week, and she said she heard you say you didn't like me all that much." She said this with a little pout.

"Kathy who?" he asked.

"C'mon tell me, did you say that?"

"I'm trying to think of all the girls named Kathy I know ... does it start with a 'K' or a 'C'?"

"Jeez, can you just answer the question?"

"What did she say he said?" he asked again.

"That you didn't like me all that much!?"

"Well, that's weird, I think you're great. Did you say her last name is Whiteout?"

"Ahh ... Rideout ... you're hopeless!"

"I'm what? Why?"

"Oh my God." Heidi exclaimed. He looked shocked to hear her swear. She walked out of the room, leaving her Donnie bewildered. Heidi knew that he was inexperienced and super shy, but he could be so stupid sometimes!

The next morning, she woke up feeling sheepish that she had tried such a foolish stunt, but Heidi was still confident that Mr. Donald Langille would come around before summer's end.

Then Donnie phoned and told her his family was moving to Dartmouth. His mom and dad had sped up the purchase process so they could move before the school year began. They didn't want their kids to have to switch schools in the middle of classes. Thus, they had not told Donnie or Anita that they were moving until the last minute in case the deal fell through. And it was five days before they were to leave.

Heidi was completely devastated. Two days later they made their last walk through the Public Gardens. And that was the last time she saw him, until today.

Just before five, quitting time, Heidi made her way over to Greenhouse Two. As if he never left, Donnie was bending over his homemade work platform, concentrating on sprinkling the right combination of fertilizers in the soil of a basil plant. Heidi came up behind him and, reaching up, tapped him on the shoulder.

Without turning around, Donnie said flatly, "Get lost!"

Heidi couldn't help but smile. He obviously thought she was someone else. Erik maybe?

The perfect reply came to her. "Wanna dance?"

THE WOODLAWN MEDICAL CLINIC

Detective Rick Rafuse sat next to his wife, listening intently to the obstetrician who had the results of several tests. The doctor was 75% sure the child would be a boy. But the only thing he really wanted to hear was that this child was healthy.

When people at work asked him if he wanted a boy or a girl he would answer "As long as the kid has ten fingers and ten toes and looks like me, I'll be happy!" The mere hint of his wife playing around on him in his reply brought forth gales of laughter from anyone who knew the Rafuses. They had been married for the past twenty years and were still crazy in love.

This pregnancy was a complete surprise. He and his wife Caroline had been very careful. They didn't want another child. Two girls were enough. He was forty-one, and his wife thirty-eight. His daughters were fifteen and thirteen and they were only ten years away from exiting the nest. Then Rafuse and his wife would be enjoying the good life when vacations were theirs alone. Well, the good life would have to wait, and truth be told the Rafuses were thrilled to be having another child. And financially, the timing couldn't be better as he would be receiving a modest raise, due to his additional assignment.

His career was on the rise. Last week the chief informed him that he was being assigned to the Nova Scotia Drug Task Force as a consultant, because of his drug squad experience. "Rick, I don't have to tell you how worried the premier is about the drug situation in the province. The number of overdoses has tripled this year. And the cocaine problem that we've seen showing up at almost every rural high school in the province is now starting to hammer the high schools here in the metropolitan area. We've got to get to the bottom of this and you're our most experienced policeman in drug related crimes." The police chief smiled, "So I volunteered you."

In a little under two months, he'd be taking delivery of the little package from heaven. And then it would begin. Sleepless nights and exhausted days. Well, life does throw curve balls, he thought. He grimaced but couldn't get upset. No, he couldn't help but be excited. A son.

Maybe he'd hire a nanny. On a cop's salary? The small raise wouldn't begin to cover it.

A nurse popped in the office door. "Detective Rafuse? There's a call for you on line three."

"Sorry Doctor, duty calls ... literally!" he smiled apologetically. The doctor handed him the handset and pressed line three.

"Rafuse."

"Detective, this is Jennifer. We think we have a hit."

Rafuse' pulse jumped. After their call for help from the public yesterday, three people had come forward with undeveloped rolls of film still in their cameras. A man from New Brunswick, a local couple and three German tourists. All films had been sent to the RCMP lab. There, a set of quick black and white prints were made first, then a set of colour prints were to be made and sent over. The black and white prints often showed more detail. As for the colour prints, their use was colour.

"Which set?" he asked.

"The German tourists, they were on the ferry that left Dartmouth at 2:04″

"Did we get the colour pictures yet?"

"Mounties say about half an hour."

"Good, I'll be back at the station by then. I want to see what we've got."

After finishing with the doctor ten minutes later, and the relief of finding out his unborn child was in perfect health, Rafuse had his wife drop him at the station. There was a lot of excitement when he arrived.

"Show me," commanded Rafuse. O'Byrne brought over a black and white photo.

"We think this is him, Rick. That Langille kid described him to a tee. Fairly muscular, 5′ 8″, dark hair, tight clipped beard, and moustache. He was sitting on the walkway side of a bench seat on the port side of the Halifax bound ferry. He was facing forward. The picture was taken at approximately 2:10 pm."

Rafuse marvelled at the spectacularly crisp, clear photo. "What kind of camera took this picture?" he asked.

Jennifer checked the notes from the lab. "It was a fancy model ... a Leicaflex SL."

"God bless German technology," Rafuse muttered.

The photo was taken from the suspect's right side and slightly from behind. He was staring straight ahead.

As he studied the picture, Rafuse whispered to himself, "Hello Louis Ryan."

CATCHING UP

When Mr. Norberg mentioned "Heidi in shipping," the memory of the little girl passed through Donnie's mind. But the Freemans had left the province and that was that. So, when he turned around, Heidi was absolutely the last person he had expected to see standing in front of him, here in the Emporium.

After the shock subsided, he was amazed how someone can look so different and yet exactly the same. There was a hell of a difference and none at all. There was no difficulty in recognizing that pretty face, the shoulder length chestnut hair, the bright thoughtful blue eyes, the light puff of freckles sprinkled around her nose and cheeks, and that smile that brightened any room she entered. As kids they were roughly the same height six years ago. Now he towered over her by a good five or six inches. She had breasts and hips, neither very prominent, but she was definitely all-woman.

Donnie realized he'd been staring and turned back toward the work bench and forced himself to be calm, despite his heart racing, took off his gloves, wiped his hands, and brushed himself off.

She was still smiling nervously as he stepped over and hugged her lightly, she responded with an equally awkward hug. After a few moments he broke the embrace but kept his hands on her shoulders.

"You saved my life," he said solemnly.

She frowned and tilted her head.

"Drownproofing," he explained, with a grin.

Heidi's look of confusion vanished and was replaced with a bright smile of understanding. Then laughter as she threw herself into his arms for a proper hug. The hug of two friends for whom time was no distance.

"Donnie! It's so crazy to see you again. Jeez you're so tall and you even have MUSCLES now!" She squeezed his arm. "And I'm so glad you still have your curls." She reached up to touch his hair but pulled her hand back at the last second.

Her voice had deepened, sounding like a young Susan St. James. Donnie loved it.

"And you're just as pretty as I remember," he said. "Jeez I can't believe it. I mean, you're a real woman now with ..." and suddenly he was tongue-tied, lost in a sea of words that wouldn't climb on board his head — so his brain picked the first thing that floated by "... all the right parts." *Oh Jesus, did I just say that?*

Her eyes widened in surprise and then she burst out laughing, "Thank you for noticing, Donnie! And look, you haven't changed a bit, you still blush at the least little thing!"

Donnie had to laugh at himself as well and she reach up and touched his red cheek for a few seconds, a gesture she made often when they were younger.

"Did you really have to use drownproofing?" she asked.

"No, not really, but I never forgot what you taught me, and I practice it every now and then."

They stood there smiling at each other, totally at ease and totally connected to each other, and suddenly it was as if six years had not passed. He had forgotten how in-sync their friendship was back then. It was an amazing five seconds that seemed wired to eternity. They each started to say something at the same time and their words ran into each other and they laughed again. There was so much to say, and nowhere to start.

Heidi's expression got serious, and she began, "Listen Donnie, there's something ..."

There was a toot out front, and he could see Madeline waiting for him in the dream car. "That's my ride, I have to go ... listen we need to get together and see what we've been up to. Where do you live? Doesn't matter, I can take a bus. How about we get together tonight, for a Coke or something?" Donnie rambled on excitedly.

Her smile disappeared, "I can't. I've got to work till eight tonight. Maybe some other time."

Madeline tooted again.

"Well, can we give you a lift home?" he asked. He didn't want this moment to end, so he had just volunteered Madeline to be a chauffeur later in the evening.

"No thanks, Donnie," she said in a strange, quiet voice. "I already have a lift."

There was a shift in her mood, he felt it rather than heard it. Donnie swore the greenhouse got colder. The wire to eternity had been unplugged.

He prided himself in being a polite guy, and ordinarily would never have intruded in anyone's private life, but Donnie had a premonition and couldn't help blurting out the question, "With who?"

Forcing a smile she answered, "Erik. Erik Jorgen. He works with me in shipping. He's a nice guy, maybe you'll meet him."

Donnie had just experienced an array of emotions, excitement, re-discovery, realizing how much he missed her, longing to be near her again, and now a new one, disappointment. But he managed to say "Yeah, I met him already, he came over and introduced himself this morning."

Then Madeline leaned on the horn loudly and called out, "Donnie sweetheart, are you in there? C'mon ya big hunk! I've got places I have to be! Don't make me come in there."

He stood there, deciding what to do next, and if it was even appropriate. *To hell with it.* He leaned in and kissed her on the cheek.

"You're going to miss your ride," Heidi said quietly.

ON THE ROAD

He sat next to Madeline for a long time while she chattered on about something or other, most of which he missed. Donnie was deep in thought, full of concern about someone he didn't really know. Heidi and he had missed the past six years of their lives. The most important years in their lives so far. Formative years. And yet for a few moments back there in the greenhouse, they were absolutely connected. He felt it, she felt it. An almost supernatural connection. Six years ago, they were so very close for that summer. They were like twins, finishing each other's sentences. *And I didn't even get her number!* Now she was dating that idiot jerk. Well, he had to assume they were dating by the way she reacted —

"DONNIE!"

He jumped in the seat, "What?"

"My God, have you heard a single word I said?" Madeline asked.

"I thought you Catholics didn't swear."

"For God's sake, of course we don't!" That's our Madeline, he thought. She continued "What is it that has you so wrapped up. You're totally spaced out! You're not even in the same car! It's like you're ..."

"Alright, alright I get it. It's nothing. I mean you know, it's none of my business ... so I shouldn't even be talking about it. I mean, I don't really know her, do I? But I can't ignore —"

Madeline interrupted him. "Well now you *have* to spill the beans to me. You can't leave a loaded question like that just hanging there between us!" She waited while Donnie composed an answer. "Well?"

He had to gather his thoughts for a few seconds, then, "What do you know about Erik?"

"In shipping? Bit of a queer duck, and a tad arrogant sometimes. Just finished grade twelve at West Kings last year. He's been down here for the past three summers, living with the Norbergs and works at the Emporium. I heard he's full time now. He doesn't say much normally, but last summer I heard him lose his cool completely with one of the truck drivers."

"What happened?" he asked.

"Well, nothing of course. After all, he's Mr. Norberg's nephew. The trucker could have squashed him like a grape, but he just took the abuse and walked away. You don't mess with the boss's relatives after all."

"Yeah maybe. What about Heidi?"

"His girl? Don't know too much. Really nice person but kind of quiet. She's from Liverpool. Came up here to finish high school. Staying with an aunt or family friend, I'm not sure which. She started working here in March doing evening shifts. I guess that's when she met Mr. Charming. She's in grade ten at Sackville High. By the way, did you ever notice how everyone at work seems to be from somewhere else?"

Donnie ignored her question. "So, are they dating?"

"Well, no one knows really. I once saw him try to kiss her at work and she pushed him away. He was none too pleased. All we know for sure is that they often drive to and from the Emporium in the same car. Wait a minute, you're not interested in her, are you?"

"I knew her back when I was a kid. And today's the first time I've seen her since '67!"

"Now Donnie, you know I'm the love of your life? Don't make me jealous!"

"Stop joking around. Besides we both know you're too old for me, right?"

"Eleven months? Men love older women!" And Madeline laughed. Her birthday was in July which would make her seventeen next month. *Seventeen!*

It was their usual banter. The two friends had been out together lots of times, but they'd never gone out on an actual date. Eleven months was a big difference at that stage in their lives, so when Donnie tried once to kiss her after seeing a movie, she laughed it off. He thought he'd screwed up a good friendship, but the next day she was affectionate with him again, which confused the hell out of Donnie. He finally decided that if anything was ever going to happen between them, she was probably waiting until he grew up a little. Well, maybe a lot!

Madeline was a pretty girl and very athletic. Built like a brick shithouse, Clip said once, but none of the four boys knew whether that phrase was a compliment or not. Madeline loved sports. She sometimes threw the baseball around with them, rock climbed, and occasionally played a game of pickup hockey and was damn good at it — but when she did, they took hitting out of the game. Mostly he liked playing tennis with her, because she wore skimpy clothes and that's when Madeline *really* looked great. She received a lot of appreciate looks from the other male players then, and in response she would act like she only had eyes for Donnie. He loved it.

A GHOST CAR

They zoomed down Windmill Road, past the old wartime prefab homes, and she dropped Donnie off at his. As he walked up the front walkway, he noticed a brown unmarked car idling by the curb, four houses up. At least he thought it was an unmarked car. The Dartmouth Police Department used standard base-level Chevy Impalas as police cruisers. Unlike police cars in Halifax, which were painted black and white, the Dartmouth Police used a blue and white colour scheme. They bulk ordered them with some sort of police package included, from General Motors, and had them painted, decaled, and outfitted right in Dartmouth at the dealership. The force's three unmarked cars were also Impalas with normal commercial metallic paint. Most of this critical data was imparted to Donnie by Peter who, of course, knew everything about the Dartmouth Police. Probably better than most of the cops did themselves.

Donnie checked from the living room window ten minutes later and the brown car was gone. Probably making sure he got home okay after his first day on the job.

THE DARTMOUTH POLICE STATION

In the Dartmouth Police Station, O'Byrne was studying the colour photos that had just been delivered by the RCMP lab. He slammed his hand on the table and exclaimed, "Yup, that Langille kid scores another ten. The guy in the picture has the same colour pants, hair, beard, shirt, and jacket." He looked across the table, "Maybe he should join you over at Holland College, Jennifer, he's got one helluva good memory and great observational skills."

"His parents didn't raise no dummy, detective," she replied.

Jennifer, along with O'Byrne and Constable Hicks joined their boss, Police Chief Elmer Daweson, as they studied the colour photo prints provided by the German tourists.

"Hicks, see if you can get Donnie Langille down for an ID of this guy in the photo," asked Rafuse.

"Or better yet, let's take the picture up to him for ID," said the chief.

"Why?" asked Jennifer.

"We want him to feel like he's part of the team, keep him involved, that sort of thing. Also, with a possible killer on the loose, we will continue the police presence in and around his neighbourhood. Show the flag gentlemen, keep the enemy at bay. At least for the short term. If the boy ID's this man as the suspect, then Rick, I want you to get a hold of the Navy and see about getting some divers into the harbour."

"You think he threw the knife off the ferry, Chief?" asked Rafuse.

"Almost certainly," replied Daweson.

Hicks had been staring at one photo in particular. "Something's not right about his eyeglasses," he said. "It's hard to see from this angle but look again at the front part of his frames around the lenses."

"Jennifer hand me the magnifying glass?" requested O'Byrne. So far, they had only used it on the black and white pictures to see details better.

He leaned closer and stared at the enlarged image. "I'll be damned" he said quietly. "The frames of his glasses are black. Look closely at the plastic around the lenses."

"I thought we decided the frames were brown." Asked Rafuse taking the magnifying glass. He studied the picture carefully. "Well, that's odd."

"What's odd?" asked Jennifer.

Handing her the glass, Rafuse said, "Ryan's eyeglass frames are black around the lenses, but the arm is brown over his right ear."

"Black and brown glasses? Two-tone?" asked Jennifer.

"No Jen, it's blood," the chief said quietly. "When blood dries, it's brown."

THE LAKE WILLIAM PLANT EMPORIUM

Heidi walked through the main building, down the passageway that led to the loading dock. There she checked her list and found all delivered items were accounted for and each van was empty. She looked over at gate three and noticed the van parked in the bay. Erik and Bradley were in the back, crouched over a box. They were talking rather loudly, about what, she had no clue. The two of them argued all the time, but she didn't think it sounded like arguing this time.

She didn't know what was in the box, but it had the standard packing label attached with red, black, and yellow stripes on it. This meant the box had arrived by the courier they used here at the Emporium. It was open, and when they heard her walking over, they stopped talking, though she thought she heard one of them say *Dartmouth High*. As in the school? she wondered.

Bradley closed up the box and packed it into the corner of the van. Then he walked over the storage room and checked that it was locked. Not for the first time she questioned why they had such security for seeds and fertilizer. Bradley returned to the van.

"Well ... what?" Erik asked, as he stood there staring at her.

"I ... I was just wondering if you were leaving now," she stammered.

"I thought you had a lift with someone else. That new guy maybe?" he replied, coldly. He turned away.

"No, I said hello to him, he's an old friend but he's gone now."

"Oh. Well," he turned and called into the van, "you need me anymore?"

Bradley's voice came out of the van. "Naw, I'm good!"

Erik turned to Heidi. "Okay, grab your stuff, I'll see you in the car."

As she walked away, he muttered something that she could have sworn was, *this should be fun.*

THE OLD FORT

The Old Fort was at the top of a gently sloping hill of small trees and brush, about two hundred feet above, and a quarter mile distant from, the harbour. Climbing to the top of the Fort's concrete walls afforded a view of Halifax Harbour and surroundings that the boys never tired of.

It was built as a brewery, at the turn of the century, by builders who made generous use of reinforcing steel in the construction, then a new technique. The strength didn't save it from being turned into ruins by the Halifax Explosion of 1917. However, two demolition companies almost went bankrupt trying to take down the remains of the structure in the 1930s. No one had tried since. Time and weather were doing the job now, but it would be another decade before the Old Fort had weakened enough for removal. The origin of the Fort was a mystery to the four friends. Its history became whatever their imaginations wanted it to be.

It wasn't raining, but a strong ozone smell was in the air, a sure sign that a thunderstorm was coming. Unusual for this coastal city, in mid-June. Normally, at this time of year, the weather was a pleasant blend of soft winds and mild temperatures. Tonight, though the strong south-west winds were warm, they howled through the trees and whistled amongst the antiquated concrete walls of the Old Fort.

Natty and Donnie navigated their way with familiar ease through the thick woods. As always, Natty was leading, through the darkening bushes and whatever lay hidden amongst them. It was still nominally light outside but that was being generous.

As the path opened up before them that night, the stark contrast of the Fort's grey walls and the deep blue of the harbour behind it, all surrounded by roiling dark storm clouds, was a sight Donnie knew he would never forget.

This was going to be a different kind of meeting his three closest friends. He and Natty needed to tell Peter and Clip the news. And even now as they waved hello to one another, he was going over the whole thing in his mind. He decided there and then to tell them everything. Outside of school, it was the first time they were all together for the past two weeks. Not unusual during exam time.

The two boys worked their way up the concrete ruins to the top of the Fort. After a short walk across the roof, carefully avoiding the disintegrating holes and their twenty-five-foot drop into darkness, they perched themselves on the harbour side, legs hanging over the edge. This is where they discussed important matters respectfully, resolved disputes gracefully, held parliament with the utmost respect, if you will.

Clip began the proceedings.

"Okay moron, why the hell are we out here in a windstorm. I've been waiting all week to see Carol's boobs!" Clip had very little use for most television, especially sitcoms. But Adrienne Barbeau, who portrayed Carol Trainor on the television show Maude, was a very good actress cursed with an impressive bosom.

Peter agreed. "Yeah man, whatever's up, I can't stay long. Dad's got me doing slave labour in the yard, and he's going to freak out, if I don't get it finished tonight. I'll be working in the dark as it is." He paused. "What's so big, it couldn't wait till tomorrow?"

"Guys!" Natty announced, "shut up and listen! Tell 'em Donnie."

Donnie cleared his throat, then immediately felt stupid. Clip was grinning at him as if he were being overly dramatic. He took a deep breath.

"You all know about Mr. Martin?" he asked.

"Yes, the old fellow with the corner store downtown? It's across from the bus station, right Clip?" asked Peter, "He had a heart attack or something yesterday, right?"

"Yeah, I heard that too. Too bad," said Clip, "I've been in his place, he's a nice old guy. But old people croak all the time. It's an epidemic. What about it?"

"Well, he didn't die yesterday, it was Wednesday. And he didn't die from a heart attack, he was stabbed to death," Donnie said quietly. Natty just stared at the grass below.

"Jeez man, how do you know that?" asked Clip. He and Peter looked at Donnie, really looked at him for the first time that evening.

Their friend looked different, as if something huge had changed in his life.

"Because" he answered, "I talked face to face with the murderer for ten minutes."

PRIME WITNESS

Donnie sat staring at the thick one-inch rusted reinforcing bars, making a lattice in the hole on the roof next to him. It was dark now, and they have to watch their steps when they made their way off the roof.

He looked up to see Clip and Peter staring at him. He could see their disbelief as they waited for him to spring the *gotcha* on them. That wasn't going to happen. He could see each of them straining for a few seconds to think and organize their thoughts into intelligent and pertinent questions.

Clip was a good friend and influence to all of them back then. His dad taught him how to be a gentleman, how to defend himself and his sister, and, most importantly, how to absorb and analyze every piece of information presented to him before he rendered any decision. And now, this last bit of fatherly advice deserted Clip completely.

"Wha ... huh ... what the HELL?"

Peter looked at Donnie, looked at Natty, looked at Clip, then stared at the harbour.

Donnie repeated his story with more detail, giving them specifics of his conversation with the man named Louis Ryan from two days earlier. They had lots of questions. Donnie felt it was like getting grilled by the cops all over again. Finally, they lapsed into silence for a few moments.

Peter, still staring at the harbour, asked, "What time did you say this all happened?"

"Wednesday between 1:15 and 1:30."

"So, I guess he did it. He killed Mr. Martin," Peter said, more an indictment then a question.

"They wouldn't say, but I think that's what the cops are assuming. They put the time of death somewhere between 12:30 and 1:30 on Wednesday," Donnie explained.

"You've seen the cops already?" asked Clip.

"Twice, Wednesday evening and for four hours yesterday. Most of it spent with a sketch artist," he answered.

"Wait a minute, why isn't this on the news. It's been two days already and everyone still thinks he had a heart attack ..." Clip shook his head. The four boys looked at each other and all wondered the same thing. How could something this big not be in the news?

Natty finally looked up, "Donnie, have you seen the news since Wednesday?"

"No."

"What'd the cops say to you?"

"Nothing, I mean they asked a shitload of questions. But they never said anything about where they were in the case. I'm just a witness, right?"

"The *prime* witness, yes," said Peter.

"Well, they told me not to tell anyone else, but I mean you guys aren't just anyone else," Donnie said. "So, we keep this between the four of us, right? Don't even tell your parents or the whole city will know about it."

"Yeah. Think about it. If we told them about this, they wouldn't let us near you," said Peter. They were silent for a moment. That was a depressing thought.

Natty continued. "On the local news yesterday, the cops were asking people who were on the ferry on Wednesday afternoon to contact them immediately. They never said why, but rumour was it had something to do with a runaway child. But now we know that's bull."

"The killer must be some rich guy's kid or cousin or something. That's the only reason they'd be going to this much trouble to cover it up," said Clip.

Peter said, "Well, they're going to have to spill the beans soon. As far as I know, they have 48 hours max before they have to notify the public of a suspicious death."

"Peter, how do you know all this legal shit?" asked Natty. It was a rhetorical question. Donnie, Natty and Clip were convinced that Peter knew *everything* about the cops.

"Yeah 'cause, you know, a knife in the gut is a bit suspicious," said Clip sarcastically.

"He wasn't stabbed in the stomach, he was stabbed in the back," Donnie said quietly.

"Yeah, well, regardless, the cops gotta warn the public 'cause this is now a matter of public safety, right? *Right?*"

They all nodded to Clip. They all had the same scenario in their minds and silence descended on them. In their grade ten history class this past year, their teachers decided that the Watergate Scandal, which had just began, was history happening before their very eyes and the school changed their curriculum to concentrate on its ongoing affairs. Thus, all four of them were self-appointed experts on the subject. Conspiracy.

And all four had read the book *Serpico*. They were excited by the announcement that a movie was being made based on the book, though it would surely be restricted. The boys looked at each other and wondered, was their local police force covering things up? Were some of them crooked like in the cops in the book?

BETTER OFF WITHOUT HIM

The ride home with Erik was depressing Heidi. She didn't want to be with him now. Erik intruded on her thoughts.

"You're really quiet. Look, we're almost to your place and you haven't said a word. It's Friday, what're we doing tonight? Jerry's got something on the go. We'll go to his place, eh?"

She glanced at Erik, but Heidi was deep in her past ...

After she said goodbye to Donnie six years ago, her parents could see how upset she was. Her Baptist Christian mother said more than a few times, "Heidi, you're just beginning your God-given life. Put your trust in the Lord. You're going to meet all kinds of people and, yes, a good Christian boy that will make you forget all about Donnie." And as time passed and the sadness healed, she supposed what her mother said would be true. She wasn't sure she liked her mother's idea of a good Christian boy however!

Her dad was less charitable or Christian. "You're going to have a hundred boys chasing you girl, and none of them will have anything to do with you if that little wimp is hanging around you."

"Charles! We're all God's children, even the unbelievers," her mother scolded her father, "but Heidi, your father's right. You wouldn't want to be friends with a homosexual now, would you? It's not natural dear."

Her father joined in. "You're damn right is not natural! A ten-year-old boy spending all summer with a ten-year-old girl. What was he doing with you up in your room, playing dolls?" Then he pointed at Heidi and said, "You'll understand someday. You're better off without him!"

PATIENT GUY

She kept staring at Erik, but into her mind came a reply for her parents, *Well I saw that little wimp today, Mom and Dad. He's every bit a man and a gentleman besides.*

Yes, she saw Donnie Langille today. And she remembered the feelings and emotions from that summer of 1967. Feelings she had felt for the first time in her life ... hope and love and forgiveness and most of all respect. And she saw in just a few moments that it was all still there. *Imagine a lifetime of that! Why the hell have I been hanging around with Erik for these past months?*

Her stare turned into a smile, and she said, "I'm tired, so I'm going to go to bed early."

Erik was silent until he pulled up to the curb in front of Aunt Tillie's house on Birch Grove Drive, just off Cobequid Road. "Listen Heid, have a rest and I'll come back at ten. The night is young."

"No Erik, I'm in for the night. And stop calling me Heid, please."

He stared at her for a long moment, like he was making his mind up "Well then, wear a sexy nightie and I'll come by even later, before your Auntie gets home."

Oh Gawd. "Good night, Erik." Out of simple habit she leaned across the car to give him a kiss — and instantly regretted it. They had been dating for nine weeks now, and he had been getting more aggressive each passing week, progressing from perfect gentleman to a professional groper during that time. But tonight, he was at another level.

Maybe the look on her face gave Erik a clue that she was going to end it. But whatever it was, he reached up and grabbed her Emporium Tee with his left hand and pulled Heidi towards him until their lips crashed into each other. Their teeth banged together but he held his grip and began grabbing her breasts with his right hand, squeezing painfully. Heidi was shocked. He'd always been a sloppy kisser, but now he started trying to French kiss her. She gagged with revulsion. And then he dropped his right hand down between her legs.

She pushed herself away, tasting salty blood from the violent kiss. Her left breast throbbed and was probably bruised from the hard squeeze he had given it. She was angry, she was furious, she wanted to claw his eyes out, and he sat there smiling at her, proud of the carnage he had created in her life.

"You ... you ..." She was sputtering at him as she pulled herself backwards out of the car. The rain had started and was falling on her, unheeded.

He ignored her indignation and began lecturing her in a monotone voice, like he was instructing a five-year-old child. "I put a lot of effort into you, Heid. I wanted you to put out sooner of course, but I was willing to wait a little longer because I'm a patient guy. Look at what I do for you. Introduce you to the beautiful people in this city, take you to the best parties, try to give a country hick like you a little culture. And what thanks do I get? I saw you with that asshole in Greenhouse Two this afternoon, fondling and smooching. What a slut you are!"

Erik shifted the car into drive and shaking his head with a huge, sickly grin, he roared, "You're such a bitch. Good luck with that faggot. That's if I don't kick the shit out of him first." He leaned over and slammed her door shut, then roared away in his borrowed blue car, with the biggest smile on his face, like he'd been waiting a very long time to say that to her.

Heidi stood there soaking wet, unable to fathom any of this. She was in a rage but totally confused. She never saw this coming; never thought him capable of such disgusting behaviour.

JUST TRY IT

Heidi was lonely and traumatized when she came to Sackville earlier this year. A few months later, shortly after starting her part-time job at the Emporium, Erik asked her to his home for dinner. She was understandably cautious and said no but he persisted. Finally, one day she relented.

Dinner at the Norbergs was enjoyable. It was a pleasant evening. Erik was witty, charming, and cute. She loved the slight Swedish accent that popped out every now and then. And he was a total gentleman and a very caring person, someone she desperately needed at that point in her life.

At his house, he showed her a picture of himself when he arrived in Nova Scotia.

"You were bigger," Heidi commented diplomatically.

"I was fat," he corrected her, and they laughed.

"How much weight did you lose? How did you do it?"

"Almost forty pounds. Hard work and good food." He patted his belly and flexed his muscles, though he wasn't blessed in that regard.

They started dating and it was pleasant, at first. He was a nice guy, said the right things, made the right moves. He worked hard at the Emporium, and she found out he volunteered as a tutor at the Junior High School downtown, two or three mornings a week. It was when she met some of his friends that the first tingle of worry appeared, as some of them were rough around the edges.

They'd been to a few parties. His friends were into drugs but just the mild ones, weed and hash. Like almost every other fifteen-year-old in 1973, she had a toke or two, but since she wasn't a smoker, she couldn't keep the smoke in her lungs and just ended up coughing. But everyone else was coughing too. Fair enough. Still not much of any "buzz" people talked about.

At one party, she once found herself sitting on a couch next to a blonde girl a few years older than her, who explained, "That'll come soon when you learn to inhale deeper. But don't feel like you have to take a toke if you don't want to." Then came the party just two weeks ago.

They were in an absolute mansion, perched right on the ocean, in St. Margaret's Bay. Around ten-thirty, someone hauled out a white powder that she suspected was cocaine. This was confirmed when people started snorting lines on the kitchen table. Erik wanted her to try it.

"Are you using this stuff?" she asked him.

"No, but it's only this one time. We'll give it a try just to see what it's like. Okay?"

She thought of the anti-drug film that had been shown to grade nine classes in Liverpool. The movie itself was cheaply made and poorly acted. But one of the scenes in the film had just become reality for her, and that was to be on the lookout for people who were saying exactly what just came out of Erik's mouth. And so, she refused. He tried several more times to get her to snort the cocaine. He was getting more and more frustrated, and she was getting angrier by the minute.

Finally, she insisted he drive her home immediately. She was fifteen years old and felt like she was getting in over her head. Erik was angry and never said a word to her, not even to say good night when he dropped her off.

The next morning, he called and apologized to her, begging her forgiveness for his having too many beers the night before and promising never to do it again.

But Heidi decided she had better things to do on her off time. She had been considering distancing herself from Erik since that infamous party. She didn't think it would be an issue with him. They didn't have much in common and there wasn't any real chemistry.

A FRIENDLY GESTURE

Well, it certainly was over now ... and Erik was thinner than ever. Was he an addict?

His aggressive demeanour with that violent grope terrified Heidi. She ran into an empty house and locked all the doors and windows. Her Aunt Matilda worked the evening shift at the Halifax Infirmary and wouldn't be home until midnight. In the fridge was the chicken casserole the two of them had whipped up when she came home from school in the early afternoon, before work. But Heidi had no appetite.

Thunder rumbled in the distance as if to match her mood. She ran upstairs still furious, seething with anger. She sat on her bed, knees up to her chin, wet hair plastered against her head with her back against the headboard. And suddenly started crying.

She had wanted this to be a new start, a new chance. After all that horrible business in Liverpool, she thought that it was all behind her. And here it was again, more violence. And right in front of the one place she felt the safest, Auntie's house.

Liverpool. Thoughts raged through her head. She never felt the love from her parents that was given to her dear brother Mark. What happened to him? Where was he now?

Anger and shame were always painting her view of herself in dark pastels. She rolled over into a fetal ball on the bed and floated in a sea of despair for what seemed like an hour. The only thing that kept her afloat was a lifeboat with the name Donnie Langille, and memories of the best time in her short life.

Six years ago, she had experienced a summer with Donnie, every moment of which was filled with mutual respect, discovery, friendship and dare she say, love?

When Heidi moved to Sackville in January, she guessed the

Langilles were still living nearby. A quick check of the phone book showed an R. Langille lived on Windmill Road in Dartmouth. Several times she wanted to go knock on the door, but she always shrugged it off. Heidi was afraid that Donnie would show indifference. If he even remembered her. She was even more afraid that Donald George Langille would have grown to be like every other male in her life ... a disappointment. Or worse, a pervert like Erik had turned out to be.

Five rushed minutes in Greenhouse Two this afternoon was all it had taken to prove he was exactly the same person she remembered from the past. She needed help, she needed friends and most of all she needed Donnie. But she had to start with getting help, and as far as she could tell there was only one option.

Madeline.

She had seen the girl talking and laughing with Erik at the Emporium several times, so she wasn't sure if she could trust her. She could be one of those hangers-on that all creeps seemed to attract. But Heidi didn't think so, because this afternoon she saw Donnie hop into Madeline's car, the two of them at ease and enjoying each other's company.

Not long after she started working after school at the Emporium, Madeline had given her phone number to Heidi. Just a friendly gesture from one female to another who had newly arrived in the city. Heidi had stuffed that piece of paper somewhere, but where?

Not in her purse, nor her wallet. If it was stashed in a jeans or pants pocket, it was lost in the wash by now. Then Heidi remembered the time of year. It was a cold, wet day in early March and she had commented to Madeline how they both were truly *Bluenosers* that morning. She checked her heavy raincoat deep in the closet and low and behold, there was the crumpled piece of paper.

She called Madeline's number.

"Hello?" An older woman with a strong British accent answered.

"Would Madeline be in please?"

"I'll check and see, who shall I say is calling?"

She took a deep breath. "Heidi from work."

"Just a moment, please."

Heidi could hear a murmur of voices, then, "Hello? Heidi?"

"Hi Madeline."

"How are you doing? This is a nice surprise," said Madeline.

"I'm sorry. If this is a bad time or or ..." Heidi stammered.

"Good God no. I'm glad you called. What's up? Are you bored and want to set the town on fire?" Madeline giggled when she said it.

Heidi didn't beat around the bush. "I need someone I can talk to and who I can trust and who can help me, because," an unwanted sob escaped her and she had to swallow, "I really, really need help."

Madeline's demeanour changed instantly, and she was all business. "You found her, Heidi. Is there anything I can do right now?"

"No, tomorrow morning is fine. I'll be up early, before six, so you can come when you want ..."

Madeline interrupted. "I'll be there at 6:15. What's the address?"

After the call, Heidi washed for bed, scrubbing a little harder than usual to get the filth of Erik off her. She put on her soft pink pyjamas and climbed into bed. She felt a little better now that she may have found someone in her corner. She was sound asleep by the time Aunt Matilda came home.

THREE OF THE VERY BEST

"Where's Donnie?" asked Natty.

"He's down there in the bushes, peeing against a rock. Probably too much root beer with his supper!" said Peter.

"Jeez that boy and his root beer. Everybody knows it's Coke or Mountain Dew that rules," said Clip.

Natty put his hands up, getting serious. "Boys we gotta keep an eye on Donnie. We gotta be with him at all times. I'm worried about him. We have to plan this right so one or all of us are with him every moment he's by himself until this thing blows over."

Clip shook his head. "Well, no offence, but isn't that the cops job? You know I'd do anything for the guy but, jeez man, the cops have guns and they're trained for this stuff."

Peter piped up. "No, that's unrealistic."

"Unrealistic?"

"Think about it, Clip. This case might go unsolved for months or maybe never. The cops can't afford a personal bodyguard for one witness," Peter explained. "Natty's right. *We* have to keep an eye on Donnie."

Clip nodded his head and muttered, "Merde." Every now and then, the Quebecois part of Clip's heritage popped out. Clip had been dating a classmate, Suzanne Mitchell, through most of this school year. She was a strawberry blond haired, blued eyed beauty who obviously liked hairy Frenchman. No one in school could figure out why she had set her cap in Clip's direction, least of all Clip. But they were pretty close, and it was working so far. Though their love life would be confined to second base for the next few years, it was never easy for them to find time to be alone.

"Jeez guys, Suzanne is going to have a fit. I can see it now. 'Sorry Suzie, I know I told you I loved you, but I love this guy more!'" Natty and Peter chuckled which of course encouraged Clip to continue. "Or when we're making out sometime, 'Don't mind Donnie at the end of the couch Suzie, but please don't kiss the wrong guy when I turn out the lights!' Yeah, sure, that'll work."

Peter and Natty laughed. "Like Natty says, we'll work it out. Donnie would do it for any one of us in a second," said Peter.

Clip watched his troubled friend climb back up to the roof rubbing his hands on some leaves and said in a quiet voice, "Yes he damn-well would ..." Then he yelled to the world at large. "Check his sneakers boys, see if he pissed all over himself!"

"What are you guys laughing at?" Donnie asked.

All three of them said it at the same time, "You of course!" Which must have been unplanned because they looked at each other and roared with laughter again.

"What a bunch of idiots!" he muttered. *God, I love my friends.*

Clip started coughing in the middle of his laugh, deep coughs.

"Okay Clip?" Natty asked.

Clip held his hand up and nodded an okay. Then took a couple blasts on his inhaler. Asthma was a bitch. But they were used to it. Clip's doctor had said he'd probably outgrow it, but that was a long time ago.

Thunder which had been rumbling in the distance was louder now and it was joined by distant flashes in the sky. Time to leave!

"Well, is that everything? If we're all done here, we should head home. It's almost friggin' ten o'clock and the rain's coming. Who's got the flashlight?" Natty asked. "What nobody? Donnie, wasn't it your turn, you were supposed to bring the light tonight?"

"Yeah, lots on my mind, sorry man," he said earnestly.

And off they went into a stormy night and an unknown future.

NE'ER-DO-WELLS NE'ER DO WELL, DO THEY?

Although Jerry LaChance lived in Toronto, he spent most of his time these days in Nova Scotia. He was in charge of sales for the east coast, and they were trying a new tactic. The cigarette industry had been doing it for years. Get a kid smoking when he or she was a teenager, and you'd have a lifelong customer. He and his group were trying to do the same thing with cocaine.

Jerry sat on his balcony, overlooking St. Margaret's Bay. He was holding a Scotch on the rocks in his right hand. It was a sweater weather night, the ocean breeze cool but bearable. There was a moon out, and it shone a phosphorous streak across the ocean that rippled in the restless waves. The light reflected off the mass of rain clouds covering the Halifax-Dartmouth area just five miles away to his left. But he had no interest in the view. He stared at the man in the chair opposite. "How many dealers have you recruited again?"

"Five. Two at QE, one at Saint Pat's, one at P.A. and one at Halifax West," Erik replied.

"And Sackville High? Dartmouth High?"

"Ahh ... not yet." Erik was beginning to sweat.

"Jesus, what's the holdup boy? I put a lot of faith in you, but I need results."

"I've had a small set back. The dealer I wanted for Sackville High ... well I couldn't get her turned ..."

They were interrupted when the patio door slid open, wafting smoke and loud music onto the balcony. A couple of giggling party goers stepped through the doorway, pausing when they saw the two men.

Jerry glared at them, which was enough to send them scurrying back inside, then he turned back to Erik.

"The skinny piece you brought to the party couple weeks back, wasn't it? I was watching you. You couldn't get it done with her? Jesus, man, there's a bunch of young bucks at my beck and call just waiting for the chance to get rich. The only reason I still got you here is you handled that courier screw up pretty well. But you're starting to disappoint me. I told you we shoulda trained your little doll my way."

Erik shuddered. He wouldn't wish Jerry's way on any girl, even Heidi. Basically, kidnapping and forced drugged addiction ... in addition to, well, God knows what else.

"It should have worked, Jerry. I kept my eyes open and ID'd her when she came to the Emporium in March. No family up here, no friends, lived with her single aunt. Lonely. I mean she was the perfect mark. She's just, I dunno, stubborn," explained Erik.

"Yeah, sometimes you get that. The lonely ones are the strong ones and the ones with all the money and friends are the ones who'll roll over for you." Jerry was a very philosophical guy. He took a slow sip of his drink.

"How much does she know?" asked Jerry quietly.

"Nothing"

Then Jerry stared into Erik's soul. "Nothing? Cause you know I don't like loose ends ..."

"Nothing. I swear." A pause. "She does know there's cocaine here, in this house. I mean, she *was* at the party."

Jerry relaxed. "God man, every narc in the country knows I have coke here." He chuckled, "I'm careful. Been searched twice by the DTF and they didn't find squat."

"DTF?" asked Erik.

"It's new. Drug Task Force. Feds and local cops put it together a couple months ago 'cause guys like me are making too much cash doing a public service. They got some smart cops in it, so we got to watch ourselves. Right now, we're doing fine, but if somebody does something stupid, like offing a pig, then they take the gloves off and we're fucked. On the other side of the coin, sometimes we got no choice, and we have to take care of one or two of them. We get guys from Montreal or Miami who can come in to do that, then disappear." He said this nonchalantly.

Erik fought off the feeling that he was in over his head. Jesus, Jerry was talking about killing a cop. But he managed to calm himself down. He wanted the big car, he wanted the gorgeous girl, he wanted to sleep on a mattress filled with cash. He would do whatever it took to get it. After all, killing wasn't so hard.

SATURDAY

AUNT TILLIE'S HOUSE

The next morning, Heidi dressed in her best bell-bottom blue jeans, pink blouse, a light brown cardigan, and finally her leather belt with the peace sign buckle and brown clogs to match. She crept down the stairs and out the front door so as not to wake her aunt, and sat on the front step waiting for her ride.

Madeline arrived at six twenty-five with bottle of Coke and cursing at being ten minutes late. "Damn squirrels!" she said.

Heidi had no idea what she was talking about. "I, ahh ..."

Madeline grinned, "I accidentally left the passenger window down a few inches last night, that's why I'm sitting on this damn towel! I hope it dries before Dad comes home! And when I opened the door this morning, a bloody squirrel jumped out of the car. I almost peed my pants! And I screamed so loudly, it woke up my mother who ran down to the front door to see what had happened. Just a grand way to start the day!"

And Madeline was right because Heidi laughed. A relaxed and genuine belly laugh like she hadn't had in a long time. It was something she needed and something that almost erased the memories of the previous night. And a great way to start a friendship.

Heidi also noticed, not for the first time, that Madeline was a very attractive girl. Much better looking than she was. And as a consequence, there was something she had to find out right away. But before she could begin, Madeline pulled the car onto the road and asked, "So, Heidi, does this have anything to do with Donnie?"

Heidi was taken aback, but rallied, "Yes. Amongst other things, it's kind of complicated, but mainly him, yes." *God that was smooth.*

"And you are not with Erik anymore, right?"

"I never really was. I mean we hung out together, but nothing ever happened. He sure wanted it to."

"Mmm, all guys do. Tell me about Erik."

And so she did. She explained everything that happened, including the horrible scene the night before.

Madeline's face clouded over, and she said, "Fuckin' wanker! I'd 'ave kicked 'im in the balls!" Then she glanced at Heidi and saw her, eyes closed, re-living last night. "Look at me, Heidi Look at me."

Heidi turned and faced her new friend.

"It's over and you won. You understand? You're the winner in all this! You hold your head up high girl because you're free from that loser. So, what has Donnie to do with any of this?"

Heidi watched the road out the front window and sighed. "This is absolutely insane and it's going to sound stupid. We knew each other when we were ten. Just kids, but I was in love with him if that's the right word. I mean the first time I saw his curly hair and those blue eyes ... my knees went week. I used to hug my pillow at night and whisper his name. Real puppy love stuff. Donnie really liked me too, but he was super shy."

Madeline stopped as an elderly lady was in the crosswalk. The pedestrian smiled and nodded to the two girls, who returned the greeting. Madeline said, "Go on Heidi."

Heidi thought about how to phrase her story, "This is going to sound overly dramatic, but he saved my sanity in the summer of '67. I was a little girl in what I can truly say was a broken home. I used to escape it at school. I made lots of friends and every evening I would try to put off going back to my house because, well, I was a nobody there. But Donnie changed everything. He was the first boy I was ever close to. Closer that any friend I ever had, and he was there every time I needed him, that whole summer. And then he was gone from my life and I all but forgot about him. Yesterday I met him for five minutes ... *five minutes*, and I can't get the feeling out of my mind, that he's the only guy in the world for me. The only person I ever truly loved. And seeing him yesterday, talking to him, being with him; it felt like an actual click in my head, like everything I had missed these past six years had dropped back into place ... and I have to see him to ..."

"To see if he feels the same." Madeline finished the thought.

Heidi looked over at Madeline. "I suppose that sounds stupid."

"No more stupid than anything else in life," Madeline answered, "and there's nothing stupid about true love."

"I mean, maybe I'll go out with him on a date, and he'll turn out to be an 'international date'?"

"A what?" asked Madeline.

"You know, he'll have Russian hands and Roman fingers?" explained Heidi.

Madeline frowned and then burst out laughing. Heidi joined her.

"No worries there, Heidi. Donnie's one of the few true gentlemen I've ever met." She stopped at a traffic light and figured it was a good time to take a swig of her Coke.

Heidi chose that moment to pop her all-important question. "I need to ask you something Madeline," Heidi began, as Madeline tipped the bottle up to her mouth and took a big gulp of soda. "Are you and Donnie dating?"

Madeline choked, then blew Coke all over the dashboard of her dad's car. "Shit!" she said. "Mother of God! Hand me those rags back there." She pulled the car quickly to the curb. Half panicked, and half laughing, she ferociously tried to clean up the sticky liquid, at the same time asking, "Why on earth would you think that?"

"Well, to anybody watching you two yesterday, it was obvious. I could see how happy the two of you were, and you did call him sweetheart."

Well damn, Madeline thought. "Don't read anything into that. We're just friends is all. He's like a little brother to me," she explained, then glared at Heidi. "Don't tell him I said that!"

"Is there anyone he's dating now, anyone important in his life?" asked Heidi.

Madeline glanced over at the hopeful expression on her face. "Yes Heidi, there is someone very important to him right now. You. You are very important to him. Hell, he has to feel the same way you do. Lord, he never stopped talking about you on the ride home last night! So, as the saying goes, *C'est l'amore!*"

Madeline couldn't make out the look on Heidi's face. She couldn't quite decide if it was a smile, a grimace, or a frown. Possibly the girl was still unsure about what might or might not be going on between her and Donnie. After all, she was new and lonely and as far as Madeline could tell, a truly genuine person.

It's so maddening, Madeline thought. She could alleviate all Heidi's concerns with one statement. She could tell her who she really was, and that Madeline would never be romantically involved with any man. But of course, she couldn't take such an enormous risk. No one knew, not her family, nor her friends, no one. Maybe someday the world will change and understand that love is wonderful in all its forms. But not today and not here in this car.

She stared out the front window, and said, "Heidi, I was serious earlier. I've known Donnie long enough that he's just like a little brother to me. And I'm so busy these days studying and working to save money for university, I have no time for romance with any man, anyway."

It was quiet for a moment, except for the idling big block. Madeline was still looking out the front window. She put her hand on the gearshift, but felt a hand on top of hers.

"Thank you for telling me that, Madeline." Heidi spoke in a quiet voice.

Madeline was surprised. Had Heidi somehow read between the

lines of what she just said? That she would never have an interest in any man? Or was Heidi genuinely thanking Madeline for trying to allay her fears?

Madeline decided that, in the end, it didn't matter. She cleared her throat and said, "Well, it only seemed fair that since you told me about the 'worst night of your life', that I should tell where my interests lie."

Heidi replied quietly. "Last night wasn't the worst night of my life, Madeline. I haven't told you about Liverpool."

THE LANGILLE'S HOUSE

Donnie woke up from a restless sleep. He had been awake most of the night thinking about one thing: he couldn't afford to wait until Monday and had to talk to Heidi immediately. His plan, hatched by his soggy brain at three in the morning, was to get up at six, call Madeline at six-thirty, (she was going to love him for that) and see if the two of them could figure out where Heidi's aunt lived.

And he damn-well woke up at a quarter to eight. "Jeez," he said to the bedroom ceiling, "the day's half gone!" He dragged himself into the bathroom and got a good hot stream going and had a power shower.

Yesterday, something clicked inside him that he never knew was there. It was spurred on by that incredible moment of seeing Heidi in person. And a feeling that the passing of six years didn't matter. And a range of other feelings: the realization of how much he truly missed her, the sheer unwavering happiness of being in her presence again, and the fact that he loved her as his best friend. And an unexpected feeling; that he should never have left her last night, that he needed to rescue her from Erik. Very presumptuous of me, thought Donnie.

And on top of it all was an astonishing discovery in the centre of his heart that he loved her far more that just as a simple friend. Maybe all these feelings were going to blow up in his face and maybe he'd be sorely disappointed before this day's end. But the ache in the pit of his stomach was going to stay there until he at least talked to her and told her how he felt.

The Martin case and even his personal safety was all but forgotten. After dressing, he raced down to the kitchen, picked up the wall phone and started dialling Madeline. And stopped after the sixth digit when the doorbell rang. Leaning around the corner, he looked out the big picture window in the living room, and there was the Chevelle parked on the curb! Madeline had come to him! She must be psychic!

Donnie could see the outline of a person through the front door's frosted glass. He grabbed his jacket and called out, "Just a minute!" Then he went to the foot of the stairs and said, "I'm going out with Madeline for a drive."

Robert called back, "Okay. Don't be long. And be careful."

Donnie was putting his jacket on, an apple clenched between his teeth, when he stopped dead in his tracks. The frosted glass in the front door that opened into the veranda had floral pattern. A distorted impression of a girl was in the glass. She must have heard him because her head shot up. She leaned forward both hands against the glass, squinting through the frosted flowers, trying to see him.

Donnie put the apple on the desk beside him, pulled off his jacket and walked over to the door. He paused for a few seconds, putting his hands where hers were on the glass and put his face against the frost as well. Donnie sensed this was going to one of those defining moments in a person's life, a moment he would never forget.

"Donnie," Heidi said softly.

He opened the door slowly.

She was shivering but it wasn't from the cold. She had puffed up rings around her eyes and dried tears on her cheeks and her nose was red. And she was the most beautiful thing he had ever seen in his life.

They stared at each other for a few seconds.

"I was coming to see you ..." he said, and stood back to let her come in.

She stepped into the entryway from the little alcove of the

veranda. "We need to talk —" she began, but never finished because he threw his arms around her. And she hugged him back fiercely, her face in his chest, her left hand grabbing his cotton shirt just below his right shoulder, as if now attained, she would never release him.

Fine with me, thought Donnie.

She raised her head and began to say something but never had the chance because Donnie gently kissed her on the side of her cheek then found her lips. He didn't think about doing it at all. He just did it. He wanted this be the kiss she had wished for, six years ago.

Their lips had barely brushed when his dad clomped down the stairs. They turned to greet him, but Donnie wouldn't let go of her.

"Donnie? I thought you were going out ... oh ...."

His dad hadn't seen Donnie in such an embrace very often — well, never. When he came closer, Heidi braved a little smile and there was a look of instant recognition on his face.

"Who? Heidi? Heidi Freeman? My goodness, how long has it been? Five years?" his dad asked.

There was genuine pleasure on Heidi's face. "Six years. Hello, Mr. Langille."

"Well, I'm happy to see you finally figured out where the bridge was! And now you've come over to visit us!"

Heidi just smiled at his dad's little joke and wiped away a tear. She pulled away from Donnie and gave his father a small hug as well.

Donnie guided her to the living room couch, then followed his dad to the door.

"How long has this been going on?" his dad whispered to Donnie. He was frowning, but Donnie thought his dad was trying to hide a smile.

"Honest to God, Dad, I just saw her yesterday for the first time in six years. She's working at the Plant Emporium!"

"Really? What a coincidence!" Robert shook his head. "Is she okay? She looks a little upset."

"I think she's fine, Dad. I'm betting neither of us got much sleep last night."

"I see." Then his face got serious. "Any problems? Anything the matter?"

"No. Everything's fine now."

"Well, look after her Donnie. I have to get to Micmac Mall and meet the maintenance staff. The new fire water pump we put in for them is acting up."

"Jeez, Dad, you have to work this early on Saturday?"

"Welcome to your future son! You two alright here for now?"

"Yeah, we'll be fine. We have a lot to talk about."

He smiled, "Yes, I imagine. Well, we'll talk about all this later, okay Sport?"

"For sure, Dad."

As he was leaving, Madeline came up to the door. "Hi Mr. Langille," she said with a big smile.

Robert grinned fondly at her. "Madeline! Thanks again, for coming to my rescue and giving Donnie a lift to the Emporium for the next while. We haven't actually seen you in — it must be over a year now. I'm running an errand right now, but I'd love to talk to you when I get back. You can tell me what your father's been up to these days."

She gave Robert a quick hug. "That would be great, Mr. Langille!"

Robert looked at Donnie and whispered, "Suddenly it's Grand Central Station here today." And he was gone.

"Do you want me to come in?" Madeline asked.

"Yes, for a little while at least."

As she squeezed past him into the living room, Donnie noticed the same brown unmarked car three houses up. It was parked, engine off this time, and no one in it. That was odd. Maybe he was wrong about it being a cop car. He shrugged, with more important matters to get to.

GRAND CENTRAL STATION

Heidi sat on the living room couch next to Donnie. She had just come back from a bathroom break a changed person. Donnie didn't know what woman's magic she used but her face was radiant, no puffed eyes, bright and clean.

Madeline sat cross legged on the living room rug just in front of the fireplace. So much had transpired for the three of teenagers in one twenty-four-hour period that they had to sit and re-group their thoughts.

"What a friggin' crazy week I've had," Donnie started. Then he realized the ladies knew nothing about his involvement in the Martin case, so he quickly amended, "A new job and friends I haven't seen in a while."

"I just had the worst evening ever last night followed by the best morning ever," said Heidi, as she took his hand.

Madeline looked back and forth between them. "Just the same old boring thing for me, thanks."

Donnie looked at Heidi. "You had a bad evening last night? What happened?" He saw Madeline and Heidi exchange quick glances. *Some kind of girl language only they speak.*

Heidi spoke. "Well, you and Madeline seemed really close, and I didn't know if you two were together —"

"Ha! He wishes!" interrupted Madeline, and she shared a giggle with Heidi. Donnie turned beet red, because it had been true at one time.

"Or if I had lost you again. I had a night where I didn't know if I'd even get to see you again," Heidi continued. At this she pulled up her legs up and tucked her feet under Donnie's right thigh on the couch. It's what they both needed at that moment, physical contact. She wrapped her arms around her knees in a relaxing crouch.

The doorbell rang. "Now who?" said Madeline, as she hopped up. "I'll get it." She peered around the corner. "It's the guys."

"All three of them?"

"Yes indeed. Would you like me to tell them to go away?"

Donnie looked at Heidi. "Is it okay if they come in for a few minutes?" He whispered in her ear, "I'd love for you to meet them."

She smiled and nodded.

Madeline opened the front door, and Donnie could hear the

surprise in Clip's voice. "Jeez. Hi Maddy! Long time no see. What are you, the doorman ... I mean the door-girl? Ha!"

"Who owns the Chevy outside? It's sweet!" Peter's voice.

"That's my dad's. He bought it a few months ago and I'm driving it this week."

"Are you kidding?" asked Natty. "You have wheels like that?"

"Only until Dad comes home next Thursday," Madeline said sadly.

The four friends turned the corner into the living room and stopped dead in their tracks. Natty, Clip and Peter looked back and forth between the two teens on the couch. Heidi rolled up in a little ball on the couch, leaning into Donnie, her left hand grabbing his right arm keeping him close. And Donnie with his right hand on her knee. An intimate and comfortable scene.

"Ahh ..." Clip began, or rather didn't know where to begin, his mouth opening and closing like a trout, as he searched for what to say next. "Ahh ... hello?"

Donnie hadn't ever had a real girlfriend like Clip or Natty. He assumed he and Peter were late bloomers or the shy type. They'd gone out with a few girls. It was nice, exciting, and a couple of the girls each boy dated, they really liked. But whatever the reason, it never went past friendship. Still, it was an important social skill. You learn important life lessons when you date in your early teens. Not the least of which is how to accept boundaries, limits, and rejection.

When his three amigos walked in the door, and they found Donnie in the unusual position of snuggling with an absolutely stunning looking stranger, he knew they needed answers, and they needed them now! They sat down and he had no sooner started a quick and a brief synopsis of the history of Donnie and Heidi when the doorbell rang once again.

The cops were here. Grand Central Station indeed!

THINKING QUICK

Donnie stood on the sidewalk in front of his house with a familiar face, Corporal Fong. Fong had brought a colour photo, which had been snapped on the ferry a mere fifteen minutes after Donnie had exited Mr. Martin's store.

"Jesus ..." Donnie muttered. He had butterflies in his stomach as again, the reality of everything that had happened crashed back down on him.

"I don't think this fellow is Jesus, Donnie," Fong said, possibly as a joke, but you never knew with Corporal Fong.

"No sir, but I can definitely say he *is* the man I was talking to in Mr. Martin's store on last Wednesday," he declared.

"That's good Donnie. Would you mind signing and dating the back of the photo, please?" asked the corporal.

He did and then Fong did the same as a witness.

"Hey, I noticed an unmarked car here on the street a couple times." Donnie looked up the street. "It's gone now. I just wanted to say thanks for keeping an eye on me."

"We'll keep you safe, Donnie. The chief has been telling us that whenever possible all units are to use Windmill Road and show ourselves here prominently. Maybe some members of the force are parking out front when they have a few minutes or eat their lunch or something," Fong said, with a smile.

"Yeah? Well, I don't mind a bit." Donnie said emphatically.

"Alright, take care Donnie. Any problems, you call us, and we'll be here in minutes, okay?" said Fong. He waved and hopped back into his cruiser.

"Thanks, Officer." As he turned to go back into the house, Donnie saw everyone standing in the windows watching him. He thought quickly on how to explain his five-minute conversation with the police. He had already decided to tell everything to Madeline when the time was right. But he was wary of doing the same for Heidi and would have to figure out when to tell her. For her own safety.

In the five seconds it took him to walk back to the house, he decided to use his father's made-up 'City of Dartmouth civic summer internship' as a cover story. Natty, Clip and Peter didn't know a thing about it. He'd have to wing it and hope they caught on. He was suddenly glad Corporal Fong had waived goodbye to him just now. It gave some credit to the story.

"What in the world was that about?" asked Madeline as he stepped through the door. The guys were behind her trying to act nonchalant.

Heidi was silent and looking at Donnie intently for an explanation. It was not lost on him that she didn't know much about him yet.

So, concoct a story, Donnie. It's Academy Award time. "Back in March I applied for the, ah," he did his best to remember what his dad had called it, "summer internship course in social studies to learn about civic procedures at Dartmouth City Hall. You know, that's the program you weren't interested in it?" He nodded towards the guys.

Peter caught on first. "Ahh yeah, that one. Nope, sounded kinda boring. And that's no way to spend your summer."

"Yeah, way to ruin a perfectly good vacation," said Clip.

Donnie looked at the ladies. "So, it works like this. On a certain day each week, I get to observe and take part in the different aspects of how the civic government works. Licensing and taxes, road works and sanitation, all that kind of stuff. And of course, that includes the police force and ah," he had to swallow because he had never lied this much in his life, "stuff like arresting and booking, foot patrol, bylaws and all that kind of stuff."

Madeline's eyes lit up. "So, what were you signing out there?"

"Huh?" Donnie was caught off guard by her question.

"One of the cops handed you a paper to sign."

"Oh that, well … I get to observe the police in their daily duties including a ride-along in a cruiser for an afternoon. But I had to sign a," he racked his brain for the correct word, "a disclaimer. A legal disclaimer. They brought it to me this morning because I forgot to sign it in class earlier." Donnie was proud of himself. He could bullshit with the best of them.

"Wouldn't your parents have to sign something like that?" Madeline queried.

"Dad already did," he clarified. "In fact the whole thing was Dad's idea." At least that part was actually true.

Madeline could read her friend like a book. She nodded her head at Donnie slowly and out of her mouth came a bald-faced lie. "Yeah, well I heard about that course too, they offered it in my school, but I wasn't interested either. Good for you, Donnie."

Madeline had lied — went right along with his story like a veteran actor ad-libbing on the Broadway stage. But her facial expression said, *Boy, you better have a damn good explanation for what the hell is going on here.*

Donnie changed the subject as fast as he could. "Anyone want some snacks?"

CATCHING UP

They got comfortable in the living room again and Clip started it off. "Heidi, I don't know where you come from or what you heard about Donnie, but he's just not in your league. And I'm telling you now, don't be hanging around this guy unless you want to get hurt."

Heidi looked confused. "You mean he'll break my heart?"

"No, I mean you'll get physically hurt. Donnie's a menace to society. For example, if you dance with the guy, he'll step all over your feet! Clumsiest human being I ever met."

Peter chimed in. "Steel toed boots and a hard hat, if you know what's good for you."

Heidi feigned shock. "And I thought you guys were his best friends?"

Clip rolled his eyes and shook his head, "Jeez no, get serious! We only hang around the guy out of pity!"

"So, what's the story with you two? When did you meet? Where did you meet? How did you meet?" asked Peter.

"We were close friends when we lived in Halifax. We were just kids then, the summer we both turned ten. Then when his family moved over here, we lost touch. And we just met again out at the Emporium yesterday," Heidi explained.

"No kidding? That's a heckuva coincidence!" said Clip.

"I think it's pretty cool," said Peter. "I mean what are the chances? Were you still here in the Halifax the whole time Heidi?"

"No, we moved to Liverpool," she answered.

"When?" he asked.

She looked at Donnie, "Not long after you moved to Dartmouth."

She was just two hours away all this time, thought Donnie. But at our age back then, it might as well have been the moon.

Natty, who had remained silent so far, turned to Donnie and asked quietly, "Heidi. She's who you were looking for, right?"

"What do you mean?" Donnie asked.

Instead of answering him, Natty turned to Heidi. "A couple of years after he moved to Dartmouth, ahh, summer of '69 it was, four of us took our bikes over to Halifax and rode around the city. At one point Donnie here takes us to his old neighbourhood and out of the blue he stops at a house on, what was it, Henry Street?" Madeline nodded yes. "Looking for an old friend. That was you, wasn't it?"

Heidi paused for a few moments and stared into Donnie's eyes, "Were you looking for me?"

"Yes," he said. "After we moved here, I called every Freeman in the phone book because I got a no longer in service message when I dialled your number. When we made that bike trip around Halifax, I went to your house, but an old lady answered the door. She told me you and your family had left the country."

Heidi closed her eyes for a few seconds and nodded, then she changed the subject. "So tell me what I missed."

The stories of the five friends came fast and furious. How they met, the things they did together, smart and stupid, and Heidi was loving every moment.

BEING BRIEFED

Donnie's father returned about half an hour after the cops left. He sat with the kids for a respectable ten minutes, then headed out to the garage to work on something.

Heidi listened to all the stories concerning the Donnie Langille she knew from the past. Despite the best efforts of Natty, Peter and Clip to belittle Donnie in every painful way, Heidi said, "You know what? He's still just the same guy he was when he was ten years old."

She was able to fill them in with a few stories of those early Halifax days, but when it came to commenting on herself, especially after her family moved to Liverpool, she would just shrug and say it was a boring place. When the boys pressed her for more details, Madeline came to her rescue.

"Liverpool? Yes, my dad once said, 'he spent a week there one night'," said Madeline, and they all laughed, including Heidi.

"It's not that bad!" she said.

"What time is it boys?" Madeline changed the subject.

It was two in the afternoon and all they'd had to eat was a bowl of cheezies with five Cokes and, of course, one root beer, at around ten.

Madeline said, "Let's go guys, we'll get lunch somewhere. We'll leave these two alone."

"You can still ditch this loser Heidi, it's not too late to come with us. Your life will be better for it!" said Natty. The guys were all laughing, but Madeline was shaking her head as if to say *what a bunch of idiots.*

"I think I'm going to stay here for a while and see what Donnie has to say about you four!" she replied.

"Ohhhhh no, we're in trouble now!" Peter said with a grimace.

"Shotgun!" roared Clip and they were off.

Before they left, Donnie grabbed Natty at the door and spoke quietly. "This is getting stupid man, you better tell Madeline everything about this whole situation, okay?"

"Everything?"

"Yes buddy, the whole thing, everything." He paused "After all, she's one of us."

Donnie came back into the living room, and Heidi walked over, reached up and put his face in her hands and on tiptoes, kissed him. A deep sensuous kiss like he had never had in his life. When she finished, she looked into his eyes and said, "I love you."

His heart swelled. He was so happy she said that.

"I love you too," he answered.

She kept her gaze on his eyes, her hands on his face and said, "So, explain why you were lying to me earlier."

Donnie took her hands off the sides of his face, but he didn't let go. He didn't know where to begin because he didn't want her in any danger. If he was lucky enough to be her boyfriend, he figured keeping her safe was his number one job. He drew her over and they sat on the couch again. He tried to think of a way to explain. She didn't seem angry or even disappointed, but she was one smart cookie and he had to be careful not to leave anything out.

Before he began, she interrupted his thoughts. "Whatever's going on, your three chums know all about it, but Madeline doesn't. She knew that whole 'summer internship' thing was a lie. Yet still, she was playing along all the same, to protect you."

God bless intuitive women. "Yes, that's true. Madeline doesn't know but is being briefed right now by Natty."

Her eyes widened and she laughed. "Being briefed? What's going on Donnie? I'm hoping you're not in any trouble with the police. But I guess I need to hear that from you first, don't I?"

"Alright, but you should know, besides the police, you'll be only one of a half-dozen people who know the truth, so don't mention it to anyone."

"You're stalling." She grimaced.

"Okay. I'm not in any trouble, not with the police anyway. I am helping them as best I can. You see, I was on the way to the Plant Emporium for my interview last Wednesday and decided to stop for salami."

"Salami?"

"Yes, salami. There's this store downtown called Martin's Corner Store ..."

Donnie told her everything that happened to him last Wednesday. They discussed his fears of being a witness and that he was very scared for his friends and family getting hurt by just being around him. And now she too might be in danger, because of his selfish need to see her, to be with her. It was a disturbing discussion to throw into the middle of their unexpected reunion day. He suggested maybe she should stay away from him until this whole thing was resolved.

But Heidi was having none of it. "You're the best friend I ever had. A piece of my life that's been missing since 1967. And I forgot, until yesterday, just how big that piece was or how much I missed you. So now that we're together, I'm not leaving you." She put her chin up with a smile, "If you want me to go, you're going to have to throw me out."

He held her hand and they were quiet. To Donnie, it felt like there were sparks arcing between their fingers. He looked into her eyes and felt like he was stuck there forever. What a beautiful girl she was — for Donnie, the most beautiful creature in the world.

"Did you really mean what you said earlier?" he asked. "That you love me?"

"I've loved you since the first moment I saw you standing there all alone in the LeMarchant gymnasium, waiting for your dance partner. For me! I felt that queer empty stomach feeling then, and I felt the same thing yesterday when I saw you again, working by yourself in Greenhouse Two." She shrugged. "We belong together, we've always belonged together, and it just felt so natural that I had to say it ... I love you."

It was the perfect moment for them to share their first truly, deeply emotional kiss. But that wasn't going to happen because God invented parents and Donnie's dad interrupted them, hollering from the garage, "Hey what do you two want for supper?"

They looked at each other and burst out laughing. "Perfect timing!" he said.

DINNER AT THE LANGILLE HOUSE

Donnie nominated himself as 'chief cook and bottle washer' for the evening and got busy making the three of them a pasta dinner. His mother was a one-woman home economics class and insisted that her two kids start learning early in life, how to cook. And he loved it. Maybe he'd make it a career one day.

He cut the veggies and sautéed them in olive oil and sun-dried tomatoes, a spoonful of pesto or two, and lots of garlic and onions. The place smelled fantastic. He was grating parmesan cheese when Heidi, sitting and watching him prepare supper from a chair at the kitchen table, stepped off in a different direction in the conversation.

"I look at you Donnie and I see such a bright light." Donnie rolled his eyes and she giggled, "No, don't let it go to your head, I just mean you're so optimistic, and you're so energetic. You don't just see the good in people, it's like you magnify it. I know so many people who are only happy when everyone around them is as miserable as they are. And you're the opposite." Donnie shook his head. Where was she getting this from?

She shook her head in return. "No don't disagree. You really are just like you were six years ago and you're going to be the same when you're a hundred, I swear." She smiled at him and continued. "And you've had the same effect on your friends as you had on me. They might never have even been friends, except that you're, I don't know, sort of at their centre. You're the glue that binds them together. They're all a little different and I don't think they have a lot in common. But it's the differences that seem to bind you all together. And you lead the way by inclusion."

Wow, Donnie thought, she's freaking me out now. "I'm not the leader at all. I'm just a big dumb goofball, who got lucky and ended up with the best buddies you could ask for, and we have a few good times." He stopped, staring at a point above the stove, "And then I got even luckier and re-connected with the greatest girl in the world." He turned to Heidi, pointing the spatula at her, "That's you, by the way!"

Heidi giggled but then got serious again. There was a salt and pepper shaker set on the kitchen table, made of wood in the shape of headstones. On one was printed *Here Lies Salt* and on the other *Here Lies Pepper*. His mom had bought them at a souvenir shop in Niagara Falls. Heidi idly picked *Salt* up and was looking at it, but she certainly wasn't seeing it. Deep in thought, she replied, "I don't think it's just luck, I mean besides the guys, look at Madeline. You're totally okay with her being the way she is. That's amazingly adult and again inclusive." She put down the shaker and looked at him. "And it's just so kind."

Wow, inclusive? Donnie was pretty sure he understood what the word meant, but the context was foreign. Heidi had a very rich vocabulary, and it occasionally poked its way out when she talked.

"Yeah? What way is that?"

"Huh?"

"You said Madeline being the way she is, what way is that?" he asked. He didn't notice the frantic look on Heidi's face. A look that said *oh my God he doesn't know!*

Maybe I am wrong about Madeline, Heidi said to herself. But I don't think so. This morning, when Madeline said 'I have no time for romance with any man', Heidi was convinced by the way she had emphatically made the statement that she was subtly trying to reveal her sexuality.

"Well, you know, sort of quirky." She quickly recovered.

"Quirky? You're wrong on that account. Madeline's probably the only sane one amongst us. She's the complete package. To be honest, I don't even know why she ever hung around with us. But I'm glad she came back today after a year. We all really missed her. She's too nice to be single and I do wish she had a guy in her life."

"I think she likes being with you guys because of the dynamic between the four of you. And the kind of bond you have with your friends." Heidi paused. "I hope I ... no, never mind."

Donnie had an intuition that she was going to say, *I hope it works out between us.* Or *I hope I can fit in with your friends too.* Something along those lines.

Which got him thinking. They had only been together about

eight hours and after the excitement of seeing each other again, was it going to last? Would they be able to live up to the expectations they had for each other, based on the experiences of two ten-year-old children, six years ago? As far as he could tell, Heidi was much more mature than him in terms of emotional health. And she was a much deeper thinker. In that regard, it was like she was a year older than him instead of two weeks younger.

The worst thing you can do is over-analyze any relationship. Something his sister Anita said to him when he was dumped by a girl he had dated. Take it a day at a time and enjoy it.

Stop analyzing and enjoy it. He was not only in love with a pretty girl, but it seemed like she was a brilliant woman as well. So, she deserved a brilliant question.

"You think I should fry-up some sausage for the sauce?"

CALLING IN A FAVOUR

When they finished supper Donnie asked the others, "Okay, I need a rating from you two, one to ten, ten being the best."

The young, beautiful judge to his left said, "Definitely a ten. That was yummy."

The crusty old judge across the table felt different, "Yes I suppose it was alright." He said grudgingly, "But I can't go any higher than six."

"Six?" Donnie exclaimed, then he shook his head, "Who taught you how to judge?"

"Who taught me?" asked Robert, who then turned to Heidi. "What about you?"

"Me?" asked Heidi.

"Yes, you're totally biased in favour of this guy!" Robert motioned towards Donnie.

"And you're just a crusty old fart!" Heidi gasped after she said it. Her eyes bulged and she put her hands over her mouth thinking she may have tried too hard to be funny and insulted Robert.

There was a pause as Donnie and his dad looked at each other and had a good laugh, then Robert said, "Well, yes I suppose she's right about that ... but it's still a six!"

Heidi and his father volunteered to do cleanup and when everything had been washed and put away, his dad could see that Heidi was exhausted. They bundled her up with a wool blanket in the back of the car and headed for her aunt's place in Bedford. The dark woods flowed past each side of their car as Robert accelerated up Magazine Hill. Donnie glanced behind him at Heidi curled up in the back seat. She was rocking gently from side to side. She appeared to be sound sleep.

They were just turning onto Cobequid Road when Donnie remembered something Mr. Norberg had said. "Dad?" He talked quietly.

"Yes Donnie?"

"Do you know Mr. Norberg at the Plant Emporium? He said he knows you."

"Yes! I had a new water pump and filtration system put in at the Emporium last summer."

"Well, he said you two almost came to blows!"

"What? Oh yes, well, on the phone perhaps. He was joking with you, I think. What happened is that he read the pricing list wrong on the final bill and thought I was gouging him. But when he called me in a rant, I calmed him down and explained the situation, including the fact that he was saving a bundle of money, and he was so grateful, he said for me to call him if I ever needed anything."

"Oh. Okay." Then Donnie realized the implication. "Oh man, wait a minute. That means I had the Emporium job before I even got there? I thought I got the job on my own."

Dad smiled at his son. "Nice sentiment Donnie, but you'll learn as you grow older that you always take the jobs that come your way, no matter how they show up. At least then, you are putting money in your pocket until a better offer comes along."

Donnie nodded his head in agreement, just a tad disappointed.

MATILDA

Early that Saturday morning, Aunt Matilda had found a note from Heidi on the refrigerator door. The note said she was going for a drive with someone named Madeline and would call later. It was almost two that afternoon before she heard from Heidi. She called from the Langille's house, told her aunt that she was fine, and she was with her friend from six years ago, Donnie. Heidi assured her she would be home later that afternoon or early evening, as she might stay for dinner. Matilda remembered the little boy Donnie well, though she had only met him the one time, back in 1967.

In the beginning, as her aunt understood it, Heidi was a popular girl in LeMarchant school, had friends and hobbies, and made an impression on just about everyone. Except her own family. Though she couldn't pinpoint why, her brother and his wife did not seem to have the time of day for their daughter. This indifference towards Heidi forced the young girl to put up barriers at home and outside, so a happy child became a more solitary child with each passing week. This worried Matilda and she would talk with Molly and especially Frank, who brushed it off as a phase. "I was a lonely kid and I turned out fine."

Heidi's older brother, Mark, was a different matter. The mother and father doted on him constantly.

As Mark grew up however, he noticed that his younger sister wasn't being treated fairly and he did his best to see that she was included in family affairs, but he could only do so much. In adult terms, Heidi was the victim of the second worse kind of child abuse, neglect.

Aunt Tillie, as Heidi affectionately called her, eventually suggested to Molly and Frank that perhaps Heidi could live with her for a while. But she was met by the response, "Don't be ridiculous! What on earth for?"

In the spring of 1967 Matilda noticed a profound difference in Heidi. She was joyous and full of life again, even when her parents were strict, to the point of being cruel, with her. When Matilda queried the parents about this newfound zest for life from their ten-year-old daughter, she was met with a blank stare. They hadn't even noticed!

Matilda was invited to supper on Heidi's tenth birthday, June 25, 1967. In the early afternoon, a few hours before supper, the young girl asked Matilda if she'd like to go for a walk up past the Camp Hill Veterans Hospital on Robie Street. As they strolled up the busy street, she noticed Heidi's head turned left and right as if looking for something, or maybe someone. The hospital was set back from the street where there was a field for the veterans to exercise. It was ringed by trees and the occasional bench. And it was at one of these benches that Heidi spied what, or rather who, she was looking for.

He seemed typical boy Heidi's age, but slightly taller than her. He had an unruly mop of brown hair blowing in every direction which made him look cute as a button, and bright shining blue eyes. They were obviously happy to see each other. Heidi ran over to him, and they had a friendly hug, though he did blush. He was looking at Matilda as she walked up and relaxed when Heidi told him who she was.

"Aunt Tillie, this is my very special friend Donnie Langille."

"Hello ma'am. It's nice to make your acquaintance."

He said it so formally and politely, and all while blushing, that she almost burst out laughing. But she managed to keep a straight face, "Nice to meet you, young man. Will you be coming to Heidi's birthday supper tonight?"

They looked at each other and the boy Donnie stammered, "I'm sorry ma'am —"

"Call me Aunt Tillie, son," she advised him.

"Yes ma'am, ah Aunt Tillie. I'm not invited."

"Really, why not?"

The two kids looked at each other again and Heidi answered. "Cause Dad says the party is only for girls."

"Oh." That's old-fashioned thinking, thought Tillie.

"I wanted to invite everyone, but Dad said it could only be girls.

But I think it's because he hates Donnie." Heidi said it in such a matter-of-fact manner that it shocked Tillie.

"Oh, I'm sure he doesn't hate Donnie sweetheart." Surely her niece was exaggerating.

"Yes ma'am ... er ... Aunt Tillie," the boy insisted. "He doesn't think we should be playing together. He's said it a bunch of times."

The boy looked so sad. *God help me, but my brother is an idiot.* But she decided to leave the matter alone. "I see you have found ways to get together after all. Well, let's make it our little secret, shall we?"

She sat on the bench and watched the kids talking and laughing for forty-five minutes. In her niece's eyes was absolute joy and not a little hero worship. In the boy's eyes she saw an innocent love for the little girl next to him. She supposed it was harmless.

Aunt Tillie looked at her watch and called out, "We better get back, honey." The kids were sitting on the grass, huddled together, looking at something. Her niece didn't seem to hear. "Heidi, time to go." Heidi stood up and turned toward her aunt, who was shocked to see the tears streaming down the girl's cheeks. Matilda walked over to investigate and found Heidi holding a beautiful seashell in her hands. It had been polished and painted with a shiny transparent lacquer. And carved into the shell was **D & H 4ever.**

Aunt Tillie was very moved by the gift. Almost as much as Heidi.

"It's so beautiful. Thank you so much." Heidi exclaimed and she leaned over and hugged Donnie who turned a bright pink but returned the hug. Tillie hid a smile. *What a sweet little boy.* Into her mind popped something her late mother had said to her when she was a teenage girl. "Matilda, always look for a man who blushes because he can never lie to you!"

As they walked home, Heidi got a paper bag at the corner store near Spring Garden and Robie, and placed her present inside, folding it over a few times to make it less conspicuous. She looked up at Aunt Tillie and said earnestly, "I have to hide this when I get to the house."

When they arrived at the Freeman home, Frank pulled his sister aside and asked her "Where did you two go? I suppose she met with that little pansy." It took everything Tillie had not to slap her brother's face. What a cruel person he had turned out to be.

In the years after Donnie moved away, Tillie would ask if Heidi had ever heard from her childhood friend. The answer was always no. Now both of them would be together again in her living room in the next few minutes.

ON THE ROAD

Louis Ryan drove his rented Chevy Impala at a steady pace up Magazine Hill. He kept the other car in sight with two cars between them. He might lose them, but it wasn't the end of the world. He knew where Donald lived now. He had watched as the girl in the Chevelle picked him up yesterday morning, presumably providing a ride to school. He followed the boy's friends the past few days and got a couple of addresses. He might have to use them as leverage if required. But a family member was always better. Right now, he was doing recon such as following this 1969 black Ford Torino. He was anonymous now, but soon enough the police would announce that the old man was murdered, and they'd be plastering his description all over the place. That wouldn't be very good at all.

Three people, including Donald, had exited the home and gotten into the Torino. The other two were a man about Ryan's age who Ryan was sure was the boy's father, and a girl with a shawl or perhaps a blanket around her shoulders. Sister, girlfriend? Doesn't matter, she'd be better leverage than one of the male friends. He smiled; he had plenty of tools to work with.

This was a different kind of work for Ryan. Normally his company sent him to the larger urban areas, all over the world, which was much better for anonymity. Because of that, he hadn't gone to the Plant Emporium yet, and would avoid doing so if possible. He had been here in Nova Scotia for the past month, meeting the others in a hotel room downtown. He explained to them that their supplier in Germany had sent him as what the business called an adviser. That is, he could advise on any unforeseen problems that might arise. And he could keep an eye on anything that might have a negative impact on his company in Germany. Just such an event, the box of product sent by courier last Wednesday, was causing amplified waves of problems even now, four days later. The guilty party in Dusseldorf had been taken care of, but the situation in Nova Scotia had yet to be resolved. *Well, that's why I'm here.*

Ryan glanced at his gloved hands on the car steering wheel. It was a warm summer night, and he was wearing a thick cotton pair. They were a nuisance, getting his hands sweaty, but at least they left no prints, and at his earliest convenience, he would get a pair of thin driving gloves.

He passed a sign that said Bedford. He was feeling good. He expected to have all this cleaned up soon.

AUNT MATILDA'S HOME

Robert pulled the car into the driveway of Aunt Tillie's home. She had a house similar in age to the Langilles, though it was one floor, split level. All the lights, exterior and interior, were turned on. It seems they were expected.

Heidi resurrected herself in the back seat with a small yawn as they exited the car.

As they came up the walk, the front door opened and a pretty, forty-something woman stepped out, arms folded at her waste. She had a beautiful, serene smile. "Hello."

Donnie could vaguely remember her from the first time they met.

"Robert Langille, nice to meet you. This is my son Donnie."

"Thank you, Robert, I'm Matilda but please call me Tillie." She turned to Donnie. "Donnie and I have met previously. Do you remember, back in 1967?"

"Yes ma'am, very nice to see you again," he said.

"I must say you certainly have grown. You're so tall, taller than me by a good bit that's for sure. You look like your dad, but I can still see a lot of the boy I met six years ago," said Aunt Tillie. "Donnie, how old are you?"

He was surprised by the question, "Er, I'm fifteen."

"He's sixteen on Monday," his father added.

"Oh yeah that's right, jeez I forgot all about it. Happy birthday to me," Donnie said with a smile, then blushed.

"Everyone, please come in and have a seat," said Tillie. She smiled again, seeing that the little boy who blushed back in 1967 hadn't changed.

Heidi, too, had a smile the likes of which she hadn't seen in a long time. And a look of contentment and relaxation she had never seen. *I hope it lasts. Life is all so simple when you're sixteen. From here on, it just keeps getting more complicated.*

Looking at Donnie and Heidi sitting next to each, it wasn't hard to see them as they were in the park that day six years ago. But something had happened to each of them in the past few months. She knew Heidi's situation, but not the boy's. And yet they both gave off the same impression of having leaped into adulthood too soon. Of having childhood taken from them forever.

"Can I get anyone a snack?" Tillie asked.

THINGS WE NEED TO DISCUSS

A half hour later, Heidi was sitting up in bed in her pyjamas and Donnie was sitting on the side of the bed. She'd been living with her aunt for five months now, but her room was still spartan. A picture of her family, taken somewhere in Liverpool, was set beside a small lamp on the table next to the bed. She was beyond exhausted, but she said, "I just don't want this day to end. I woke up this morning feeling like I didn't have a friend in the world and now I have four new friends and most of all you. I feel like everything is going to be okay from now on and I'm really excited for the first time since ... well since forever." She paused for a second, "Maybe everything that happened to me was the price I had to pay for this moment."

"What happened to you Heidi? Why did you come here to live with your aunt?"

Heidi didn't answer. She took her wristwatch off, wound it and placed it on the table. Then she smiled at him, sitting on the side of the bed. He had kept his hand on her the whole time, as if reassuring himself she was still real. On her arm, back, shoulder but never venturing anywhere provocative. He knew intimacy in this relationship would be at Heidi's discretion.

Heidi put her arms around his shoulders and kissed him gently, then leaned backwards pulling their heads down onto the pillows. They were silent for a moment, looking at the ceiling.

"I could fall asleep right now, I feel so safe," said Heidi. She turned her head and looked into Donnie's eyes. "You smell wonderful, really manly."

"Irish Spring," he explained.

She laughed and slapped his arm. "No not that, it's just ... you smell really male."

"Okay, thanks, I guess."

"I'm really tired and I'm not explaining it very well. There's something about you that makes me feel safe. Something solid. Something permanent."

"Well, that deserves a kiss," he said, and kissed her a second time, a kiss that got their hearts racing.

They turned to face each other on the bed, stayed like that for a few moments.

Heidi said, "Donnie, I can't talk about anything just yet. There are things we need to discuss, but I want to tell you in my own time, okay?"

"Sure. No one in this room is in a rush." He paused to collect his thoughts, "Heidi, I don't know where this is going, but I'm willing to do whatever I can to keep you in my life, is that okay?"

Donnie watched her slowly nod her head.

"And I won't ever lie to you again."

She smiled and nodded again.

"And I promise to protect you and take care of you whenever you need me. Now go to sleep and I'll see you tomorrow." She snuggled into his side, and he wrapped his arm around her. After a few moments her breathing changed as exhaustion caught up with her and Heidi was deep in sleep, her head on his shoulder. Donnie smiled at the beautiful girl asleep on his arm. He was surprised she lasted this long.

I wish I could do the same. I'm just too wired.

A few minutes later, he heard his dad approaching Heidi's partly open door.

Donnie called out to him in a loud whisper, "Dad, I'll be right out." After some manoeuvring, he extricated himself and replaced his shoulder with a pillow. As he pulled Heidi's door closed, his dad said, "Time to go, Sport."

Donnie stopped his dad from walking down the hall. "Dad, I've been thinking. I told Heidi about the Martin case."

Dad frowned. "I see. Was that wise?"

"Well, she's my friend as much as any of the other guys, and they all know."

"You told them too?"

"Yup. Oh, and Madeline knows as well."

"Donnie, would it be any simpler if you just told me who doesn't know about the Martin case?"

"Very funny, Dad. And since Heidi knows, I think we have to tell Aunt Tillie too."

Dad sighed. "Maybe we can take out an ad in the newspaper and tell the whole city in one shot." He shook his head. "All right, come on."

They went back to the living room and Dad said to Aunt Tillie, "Donnie and I need a few minutes of your time, Matilda. Do you have any more coffee?"

SUNDAY

DARTMOUTH POLICE STATION

The cabby let Rafuse out at the front door of the police station. Rafuse paid the driver and raced in through the main door. Nodding to the constable who was manning the front desk, he went quickly to join the others seated at the table in the conference room where the physical evidence was still stored. There was a disinfectant smell from the Saturday night cleaning.

It was a small conference room by anyone's standards. It was the size of two of the other offices nearby. It had originally been designed to be the police chief's office, but he had balked at the idea and took a smaller one further down the hall. The conference room had a small storage room at one end, and only one door to enter and exit. Along with four windows, blinds shut tight, on the exterior wall, the conference room had two inside windows, one overlooking the reception area and one in the door on the hallway side of the room.

The chief smiled sympathetically at Rafuse, as Rafuse sat down at an empty chair.

"Sorry I'm late, gentlemen." He made himself comfortable. The pieces of evidence collected at the scene were still on top of the table, and they were increasing daily as more items were found.

Also sitting at the table were Detective Shane O'Byrne, Constable Philip Hicks, Corporal Keith Fong, Stenographer Jennifer Horn, and Sergeant Mark Wilson, who were all discussing whether Ali could win back his title from Norton when the re-match occurred in the fall.

Chief Daweson said, "Alright gentlemen, to the matter at hand. You've all taken a look at the autopsy report. The first thrust in the lower portion of the front of the neck, was the fatal one. So, he was facing the murderer as he was attacked, and it severed the jugular. Then Mr. Martin pitched forward and three more thrusts in his back. A particularly gruesome way for a kind man, and a personal friend of mine, to die. Comments gentlemen?"

"We're looking for an addict, possibly. Someone desperate for money. It certainly wasn't a pro at work here. That was no way for anyone to die, let alone Mr. Martin," O'Byrne said.

"So, what was the killer after? The cash register hadn't been touched," said the chief.

"Who knows the mind of a junky? Maybe he killed him, then panicked and ran," suggested Hicks.

"Not likely," said Wilson. "A junkie's whole universe is his next hit. He'd definitely be fixated on getting any cash to support his habit."

"Well, I'm not convinced it was a junkie. Whoever it was cleaned up pretty good after he killed him. And techs say the body was moved," Fong consulted the crime scene report, "to the back, right side of the store, out of the line of sight from the cash area."

"The whole crime scene is an oxymoron," said Rafuse. "The killing of Mr. Martin was very messy. Certainly not a professional hit, and yet the cleanup afterward was definitely by a pro. It was a surgical cleanup in that it was done to remove evidence and hide the body from public view for as long as possible. This would give them a head start to get away. That's why I think they've already left the province. I am convinced we're looking at a very amateur murder which was cleaned up almost immediately by a very professional person or persons."

Everyone stopped to think about Rafuse's point.

"We had a witness who said she saw somebody putting a navy-blue or black plastic bag into the back of a van parked just around the corner on Queen Street. She couldn't say where they came from or the exact time, 'somewhere after lunch' is how she put it. Can't remember what they looked like or what they were wearing. Just dark a coat and pants. No make, no model, no year for the van and it was either metallic blue or green, or it might have been grey," said Sergeant Wilson.

"Mmm." The chief had already read all this "What did we get from evidence?"

"A whole lotta nothing," said O'Byrne. "Just the vic's blood on site. No discernably different items inside. Someone used a cleaning agent to remove visible blood from what we expect was the original crime site, next to the cash counter. We checked outside for four blocks in three directions and then in the direction of the ferry. We ID'd which of the four ferries the suspect had travelled on and after a search, came up with one excellent clue. A drop of blood near the aft portside handrail based on a ferry travelling east to west across the harbour. We talked to the skipper and he's sure he piloted the ferry in that orientation, 'cause that's what he does every day. Then he gave me a lecture on how sailing monotonously on rough seas will bring you home every time. I guess he'd rather be sailing on rough seas than a calm harbour!"

The other cops laughed.

"Oh yes, and the blood type matches Mr. Martin, so we'll be renting the navy divers, and the captain will take them on his exact route."

"Excellent work, men," said the chief. "Shane, check with the harbour traffic and see if there were any large ships that may have forced the ferry to alter course. We want to be sure we have the correct route before we put the navy divers into the water. Our illustrious ferry captain may have boasted that monotony saves lives, but it also causes people to go on autopilot, and he may just not remember changing his course."

The chief looked across the table. "Rick, would you please repeat what you were telling me yesterday?"

"Yes Chief. Some perps have been known to visit the funeral of their victims. Crazy, I know, but sometimes they do it out of a sense of guilt or remorse, and sometimes because they have a sick desire to see the agony they have inflicted on the friends and family of the victim. Either way, I recommend we draft five officers to a plain clothes assignment at the funeral. Have they set a date, Jennifer?"

"They're looking at, ahh," looking at her notes, "Monday, but the body would have to be released by the medical examiner."

"It already was last night," said the chief. "Rick, find out if Langille is going to the funeral, take him out of school if you have to, and put him between your best two street officers in plain clothes and tell him to look for anyone familiar amongst the mourners. His father Robert would be a distraction, so I'll have a word with him. Also, get some of our guys to discretely get a picture of as many mourners as they can, especially those on the outer edge."

The chief had a hunch. "And Rick, get the boy in here to look at all the evidence as soon as possible, just maybe something will stand out to him, or jar a memory loose."

Rafuse jotted everything down in his notebook. "Will do boss."

"Gentlemen, one last thing. I have the autopsy report here and, after I read it, I asked them to go back and check again."

"You think there was an error in the examination?" asked Rafuse.

"I had hoped there would be an error in the examination, but unfortunately there is not."

Chief Daweson was a bit of a showman. A police chief had to be in order to deal with the media and the public at large, but he was a straight shooter with his officers. So, he had his men's complete attention now.

He looked at O'Byrne, "And you supervised the gathering of evidence at the scene, personally?"

O'Byrne was unflappable, which meant he knew he had done a

proper job. "By the book, Chief. We were lucky Hicks was the second in the store after Langille and Ryan left, so he was able to limit access to the crime scene. Every surface possible was dusted and then swabbed. We had many sets of prints, owners' unknown, still being checked. The kid's fingerprints were right where he said they were, on the counter, by the door, and on both the magazine rack and on the most recent issue of Penthouse magazine."

"Well, he *is* fifteen!" said Hicks, to a chorus of chuckles.

"Again, excellent work. But we have a bit of a mystery." The chief continued. "The autopsy showed Mr. Martin to be in excellent health. He didn't drink as far as we know, he took no drugs prescription or otherwise, outside of Geritol and the occasional Aspirin. All these facts are backed up by the tox screen. But, and before I say this remember, no theory is too outlandish right now ... the tox screen shows that Mr. Martin had cocaine on his fingertips."

JANE

On Sunday morning, Jane Langille had risen at six to catch a ride home with her sister's neighbour from Port Elgin, New Brunswick. The sisters had been up late the night before, and Jane didn't get much sleep. She walked in the front door of her house with a suitcase in her right hand and a coat that wouldn't come off her left, and she was in no mood to be bothered by either.

The coat was caught up somehow in her watch. And, of course, that's when the wall phone in the kitchen decided to ring. She had to answer the phone with her coat hanging off one arm.

"Yes!" She answered it more brusquely that she intended, as she was shaking the coat.

"Er ... yes may I speak to Donnie or Robert Langille please."

"Whom may I say is calling?" she asked.

"This is Detective Rafuse, Dartmouth Police."

Jane felt an instant of alarm. She stopped shaking her left arm. "And what is this pertaining to?"

The doorbell rang.

"I'm afraid I cannot reveal that over the phone."

"Yes, you will, that's my husband and son we're talking about."

"Oh, you must be Mrs. Langille, Jane Margaret Langille?"

"Yes, please tell me why you're calling." She started shaking her left arm again.

"Well, I need to verify that your son will be attending the funeral tomorrow?"

The doorbell rang again. "Just a moment please!" she called out to the front door. "Funeral?" Jane felt alarm again.

"Yes ma'am, we may have to remove Donnie from school tomorrow."

"Remove him from school?!? Why, was there a fight? Is he hurt?" She was getting angry.

"He was in a fight ma'am?"

"I'm asking you!"

"No, not in a fight to my knowledge ma'am. Your son is fine, but he —"

"Well, that's good to hear, now why —" The doorbell rang again. "Oh, for Pete's sake, just a moment!" She put the phone on the kitchen table and headed for the door.

"Ma'am is there some trouble there? Ma'am!" yelled Rafuse.

Jane marched over to the front entrance, still shaking her arm. She flung the door open.

"Yes?" she blared at the pretty teenage girl at the door.

Rafuse had stayed on the line after Jane left the phone, waiting for her to return, listening intently. He heard distant voices over the phone and waved over an officer. "Get to dispatch and tell them to send a unit and do an urgent welfare check at 2901 Windmill Road. Now. GO!"

Jane looked again at the young lady, who seemed vaguely familiar.

"Mrs. Langille," said the young girl. "It's me, Heidi."

Meanwhile, Robert came down the stairs in his pyjamas and bathrobe, having heard the telephone and the doorbell. He saw the phone off the hook, picked it up and said hello, and hearing nothing, hung up.

"Heidi? From Halifax? My goodness ..." Jane was now using her right hand to try and free her coat.

Rafuse, listening intently to the phone, heard a male voice, hesitated a moment, then it went dead before he could answer. He feared the worst. He jumped up, grabbing his coat, and yelled to the officer, "Tell them to punch it! Lights and siren! Code three!" And he was out the door to find his own car.

"Come on in, Heidi, I'm in the middle of a phone call."

Matilda came up the walk behind Heidi.

"And who's this?" asked Jane.

"Oh, this is my aunt," said Heidi.

"Matilda Freeman, but please call me Tillie."

"Jane Langille. Um, I have a phone call, why don't you both come in."

Robert came up behind them, still in his bathrobe. Jane asked, "Robert, where's Donnie?"

"He's upstairs snoring. And hello to you too, Jane."

"And you and he are alright?" she asked again.

"Yes, fine why?" Then, looking past his wife he said, "Good morning, Tillie."

"Good morning, Robert."

Jane looked back and forth between them and asked, "You know each other?" She asked as she shook her arm. She still couldn't get her damn coat off! Sirens sounded in the distance, and started getting louder.

Donnie had had an exhausting and emotional Saturday, so he slept the sleep of the dead. He was unaware of the events downstairs until he heard the sirens and, half-asleep, he pulled an extra pillow over his head and drifted back to slumber land.

THE LAST TO KNOW

After Rafuse arrived and had the situation cleared up, he sent the patrol cars on their way, and everyone sat down in the living room. Introductions were made.

"Perhaps Mr. Langille I could just speak to you and your wife? This is a confidential matter after all," said Rafuse.

"Well actually, Donnie has informed Miss Freeman, ah, the younger, about the entire Martin matter," said Robert.

"He did?" asked Rafuse.

"What *is* the Martin matter?" asked Jane.

"Yes, well she's his girlfriend now, it would seem," said Robert, matter-of-factly.

"She's what?" asked his astonished mom.

"I see," said Rafuse. He turned to Matilda. "Perhaps you wouldn't mind stepping out for a little while?"

Robert responded. "I, ah, also informed Miss Freeman, the slightly older, about the Martin matter last night. Heidi is living with her aunt now, so I thought it only wise."

Jane's head whipped back and forth. She was purple in the face. Then she calmed herself down with a momentous effort, otherwise she thought she would scream.

"Everyone be quiet. This is my house and I'm talking now." She looked at the detective. "You, Rafuse is it? You're going to tell me everything I need to know about the Martin matter, whatever the hell that is." She looked at Matilda. "You're going to tell me why you and your niece are here." She looked at Robert. "And you're going to tell me why my fifteen-year-old son —"

Robert interrupted, perhaps foolishly. "He's sixteen tomorrow —"

"Yes, fine, sixteen, I have a birthday gift for him in that bag." She pointed to her un-opened suitcase by the kitchen door. "You're going to tell me how my boy has been in a relationship with a girl for the last week, who none of us has seen for almost a decade!"

"Only six years. She showed up at the door yesterday, so it hasn't been a week," said Robert.

Jane dirty-looked him into silence.

"If it's okay with everyone," said Heidi, looking at Jane, "I'm going to pop upstairs and check on Donnie."

"Sure," said Robert. "First door on the right at the top of the stairs. Better knock first."

Jane wasn't sure if she should glare at Heidi or Robert. *At least she doesn't know where his bedroom is.* She took a deep breath and tried to speak calmly. "Alright Detective, please let me know what is going on, since it seems I'm the last to know."

GOOD MORNING

Heidi skipped up the stairs, made a gentle knock on Donnie's door, and stepped in. The curtains were drawn but the window was wide open, allowing a breeze to blow them asunder. She remembered him saying six years ago that he loved to sleep in the cold, surrounded by fresh air, even in the winter.

As Heidi wandered around the room, comparisons of his bedroom in Halifax from six years ago crept in. A *Made in Japan, Deep Purple,* poster had replaced *The Beatles.* And a *Team Canada 72* poster replaced the *Expo 67* one.

Facing the foot of the bed, an almost life-size poster of Jean Beliveau, resplendent in his red, white, and blue uniform, seemed to skate out of the wall towards an unseen goalkeeper and his net.

Another new addition, a small floor model stereo, was in the corner. Its turntable was under a smoky plastic cover. Beside it was a neatly placed row of albums, some whose rock bands she had heard of, some not. Those she knew ran the gamut of popular music but at least half were hard rock. She smiled. *Boys will be boys.*

Something else that certainly wasn't in his 1967 bedroom was a five-shelf bookcase. It was about three quarters filled with hardcover and paperbacks. Their subjects and genres were as varied as his taste in music — from young-adult angst to historical fiction, historical non-fiction to current affairs, and everything in between.

Heidi scanned the titles on the spines and saw *The Drifters, My*

Side of the Mountain, Go Ask Alice, Watership Down, and *Hangman's Beach,* which she had read herself. The author was Thomas H. Raddall, a long-time resident of Liverpool who she met one day walking on the sidewalk. She saw other really good books, *The Chrysalids, The Eagle of the Ninth,* and so many more.

She was surprised and pleased. *Donnie didn't even like reading when we were friends in 1967. I wonder who finally got him to enjoy books?*

Heidi looked over at Donnie's desk. *There is the same ceramic sneaker piggybank!* She picked it up — it wasn't much different in weight from what she remembered — and gave it a little shake, resulting in an equally small rattle. She stifled a giggle. *Probably the exact same coins as well.* She put down gently, glanced over at Donnie. Smiling, she pulled all the change out of her pocket, a dime, two nickels and three pennies, and dropped them into the slot at the top of the sneaker. Then she walked over and opened the curtains.

Bright light spilled onto the bed and into Donnie's eyes. He groggily came to consciousness and perceived her loveliness leaning on the foot of the bed. Before he could say a word, she launched herself, giggling, up onto the bed next to him and they snuggled. It was a beautiful feeling. He thought about kissing her, then shoved her away and said, "Just a minute." Opening the drawer next to him, he pulled out a spearmint gum and started chewing. "Morning breath," he explained.

"Is that even a thing?" Heidi asked. She kissed him each time he tried to answer her until he gave up. Kissing her, bright and early in the morning, in his bed, was a very sexy thing to do, especially for a sixteen-year-old boy, so one can imagine what popped up. Donnie was mortified.

Heidi glanced down at the sudden tent pole pushing up the covers and asked, "Did I do that?" Then she giggled.

Being a shy fellow, Donnie was simultaneously embarrassed and excited in equal measure. But also tongue-tied, trying to think of something appropriate. Heidi whispered in his ear, "Soon, when we're ready. Besides, Aunt Tillie, your mom and the police are downstairs!" She kissed him again and left to go back to the downstairs meeting.

Donnie had to wait a few minutes before he could put his pants on and join everyone.

As Heidi walked down the stairs, she stopped halfway. A sudden wave of fear ran through her, and she gripped the handrail. She had wanted to tell Donnie last night about Liverpool and everything that happened there. But his dad was around, and this was much too personal. So, before they got too close, she was going to have to sit him down and tell him the whole thing. Heidi had no idea how he would react, and it worried her very much. Part of her wanted to keep it a secret forever but that was neither practical nor fair to Donnie.

ROUND-THE-CLOCK PROTECTION

Donnie knew his mother was a great parent, and just as devoted to him as his father. There wasn't anything she wouldn't do for Donnie and his sister, including a smack when they deserved it. As he came downstairs, his dad, Rafuse, Tillie, and Heidi were sitting in the living room, and his mother was going to bat for her son.

"Why?" asked Jane.

"Mrs. Langille," Rafuse began.

"Tell me why he won't get round-the-clock protection?"

"Mrs. Langille, I assure you everything we can do is being done. Donnie is our prime witness and number one concern. The first police cruiser this morning arrived at your residence within three minutes, and I expect better next time."

"Three minutes can be a long time," said his mother in a quiet voice. She looked over a Donnie, who had sat down next to Heidi.

"Yes," replied Rafuse, then he continued. "Every Dartmouth Police unit makes it a point of driving past this residence in order to do a visual check. The slightest leaf out of place and they're knocking at the door. All units are told to use Windmill Road whenever possible. If they normally use Wyse Road for a non-emergency call, they're to swing down past this residence. All off-duty police officers are being told to drive past this residence on their way home. RCMP constables who happen to be in the city have been told the same thing."

Jane was silent.

"Mrs. Langille the Dartmouth Police have 72,000 people to look after, some in a similar situation as Donnie. As much as we would like to, we cannot afford to provide twenty-four-hour surveillance. And it's not just the money, the cost in manpower and resources is just too great as well. You could always lock Donnie up here twenty-four hours a day. But that isn't practical for a fifteen-year-old. Moving around is far better in a situation like this."

"Sixteen tomorrow," said Heidi.

"Mom, I'm super careful. I always check before walking in and out places or turning on side streets. I've been doing this since last Wednesday, though it feels like a month. I never go anywhere now without my friends or if I'm alone, I'll only go where there are crowds of people," Donnie explained.

"And the chances that this person is still in the city are very low. He would have wanted to get out of Halifax-Dartmouth for sure," said Rafuse.

"Mom, I am never alone. There will always be somebody with me," explained Donnie.

"Hey!" Aunt Tillie interrupted, "What are those kids doing by my car?"

Everyone looked out the living room window. There was Clip and Peter leaning on Tillie's car, and Madeline and Natty leaning against Rafuse's unmarked unit. All had their arms folded staring at the house. It looked like a rock band on an album cover. Donnie thought they were a cool looking bunch!

Rafuse started for the door, but Donnie stopped him, "Detective Rafuse! They're the ones who'll make sure I'm never alone."

After further discussion, Donnie's parents agreed, his mother reluctantly, that he would attend Mr. Martin's funeral in the company of the Dartmouth Police — in plain clothes, of course. In any case, his mother knew there was no way he would miss his storied friend's interment. As for the police, the possibility of the suspect attending the event was just too strong, in the unlikely event he was still in the province. Before he left, Rafuse assured Donnie's mom that he would be just as safe with the officers around him, as he would be if he stayed at home. Which was probably true.

A BURDEN

Tillie and Jane were in the kitchen getting acquainted over a coffee. Tillie had just finished telling Mom about what had happened in Heidi's life over the past six years.

"Oh my God, the poor little thing!" said Jane. "Has anyone heard from Mark?"

"No. No one even knows where he is. He might have tried to call home but he's not exactly on speaking terms with his father," said Tillie. "It wasn't a quiet moment when the Mounties saved Heidi, I'm sure the whole neighbourhood is still buzzing about it. If Mark ever contacts any of those people, he'll find out what happened, and he may eventually get a hold of me. But for now ..." Tillie shrugged.

"I understand. What about the courts? Surely they pressed charges?"

"I talked to the Crown Prosecutor, and he said that trying to get a conviction in this case is almost guaranteed to fail. It boils down to her word against his. And he's innocent till proven otherwise." Tillie sighed. "They seemed to lose interest when there wasn't any physical evidence. But the social services people are good in this province and the court in Liverpool awarded me emergency custody of Heidi, on the condition that my brother sign no contest to the documents. I talked to him about the whole thing. He said he *was* sorry about what happened, but he *wasn't* sorry to see her go."

"Oh my God ..." Jane whispered. She had her elbows on the kitchen table and her hands on the top of her head. She looked at Tillie. "What a burden to carry. She'll be a long time letting go of it."

"I feel so incredibly guilty. I lost touch with the girl after her mother died. Before that she used to call me nearly every week. I think if I'd been less busy at work then I might had heard something in her voice, gotten some kind of clue. But," she sighed, "life interferes." Tillie stared into space. "And it's cruel."

Tillie had watched the six kids walking away a half hour ago, chattering excitedly with each other. Donnie, Heidi, and the three boys and the girl that were her new friends.

When the four young men were together, they were a world apart from what she had seen of other sixteen-year-olds. Tillie struggled for a word. Respect perhaps? It was all about the body language. Certainly, they trusted each other. But it was amazing to see that when one of them spoke, the others listened intently, not interrupting. Yes, respect and trust in themselves and each other. She had even overheard them discussing the safest route to their destination. Such maturity she thought, where did that come from? Apparently the five friends were introducing Heidi to the Old Fort. Whatever that was, Tillie was pretty sure her niece was in safe hands.

AND NOW THERE ARE SIX

Fortunately, they were all wearing blue jeans, which was their spring weather attire. Sun streaked through the cumulous clouds hovering high over the harbour heating the concrete roof on which they sat until it was too hot to touch with the bare hand.

The kids sat in the standard 'parliamentary' position of legs hanging over the harbour side of the roof. The demolition companies had long ago ripped away the wood and asphalt. But the mighty concrete had vanquished mere mortals and was still there, if cracked. They sat as they arrived, Donnie on the far left, Madeline on his right, Natty and Peter to her right, then Heidi and Clip.

Donnie and Madeline watched their four friends. Natty gestured with his hands to emphasize a point to Peter, while Peter leaned back slightly, supporting himself on his elbows, eyes closed and bathing his face in sunlight. Heidi chattered to Clip, pointing to this landmark and that, quizzing him on what the point of interest might be. And Clip was acting as a friendly tour guide. What a man!

Madeline turned to Donnie. "Remember this moment. This is magic. We've been enjoying this place, these friends, like it's going to last forever. It's not. When we're out of high school in two years, we're going to scatter like sheep. Not because of anything bad, but because we'll have more responsibilities, and we'll need to move onto new things and meet new people. And eventually the Old Fort will disappear."

"Maybe the Old Fort might be gone, but surely we'll remain friends," Donnie said.

"Friends, yes, but not like this." She gestured towards the others. "Right now, we can rely on each other to be there should any need arise. But in the future, we'll need to rely on partners, families, employers, and even government departments to be there for us. It's the way of the world Donnie, and it's coming for us."

He sat looking at the harbour, glum about that thought.

"Look at me for instance, I moved to Fairview, and we basically haven't said a word to each other in months. Almost a year, in fact! I made new friends, have new interests and responsibilities, which is no excuse I know, but it *is* a valid one. This place has been the centre of our universe for almost half our lives, and I haven't sat up here with any of you since last summer." She looked over at the others, then turned back to Donnie.

"Remember this, Donnie. Most people want the things they enjoy to never change and the things they hate, they try to change. But change comes for us in every area. It's inevitable. The world is not static, it's fluid. It's like learning evolution in school, everything changes. And you know what? Change is a good thing," said Madeline. "Don't be afraid of it, Donnie. Go to that school thousands of miles away to learn your trade, take that job in Upper Slobovia, and see the world."

Donnie chuckled. "I'm pretty sure there's no country called Upper Slobovia, Madeline."

"Whatever! The point I'm making, Donnie, is that we have to enjoy every second right now. These times are irreplaceable and will help shape us for the rest of our lives."

"You know, you're way too smart to be hanging around with a bunch of ingrates like us. But I thank God you are. And don't worry, big sister, your little brother is never going to forget any of these moments or these friends," he replied.

"One last thing Donnie. Are you and Heidi thinking of going steady?"

Donnie wasn't sure where this was going, but he said firmly "Yes. That's what I want anyway, and I think Heidi as well."

Madeline smiled slowly. "She's a beautiful person inside Donnie, not just on the outside. She's made of the right stuff. And she's smart, a real thinker. I don't know how long you guys will stay together, but things get tough in every relationship. You know?"

"Yeah, so I've heard but ... you know I haven't got a lot of experience at this stuff," he explained.

"Well, the thing is Donnie, you'll go through tough times like people do in every relationship. Just don't give up on her. I think she's a keeper. Be there for her. Try to be understanding and *never* judge her or any woman. You don't have a right to judge anybody, let alone the girl you love. Okay?"

"Okay."

"Right, well it's time to figure out who's doing what tomorrow." In a louder voice, Madeline announced, "Guys, Donnie needs your attention."

He got to his feet and walked around the Fort, looking over the sides, and checking for any souls who may have wandered within earshot. The coast was clear.

"Anyone busy tomorrow?"

"Morning or afternoon?" asked Natty.

"Eleven in the morning."

"No, the two dummies in this group have to write our third-term history exam 'cause we didn't make high enough marks for the two terms exemption," said Natty. "Do they do that at Sackville High?" he asked Heidi.

"Yes," she answered, "it's a provincial thing."

"Okay, Peter, you up for tomorrow?" Donnie asked.

"Sure, what's the plan?" he replied.

"You like funerals?"

"Yup. Any funeral except mine," he deadpanned.

"The cops have asked my parents if I could attend Mr. Martin's funeral tomorrow. I was going to go anyway. My being there will be very discreet in that I'll be walking slowly around the outside perimeter. Apparently, criminals like to survey the results of their crimes. Yeah, I know, it's sick. I'll be looking for the guy I talked to in Mr. Martin's store last week."

"And if he's there?" Natty asked.

"I'll have two cops with me and if I see him, I'm to point him out. Then they follow him as soon as he leaves, and the cops take him down when the location is safe."

"Why not take him down right there and then?" asked Natty.

Peter jumped in. "They'd want to minimize the risk of bystanders getting hurt if there's a problem."

"What kind of problem?" asked Clip.

"He might have a gun."

That shut them all up for a moment.

Donnie looked at Heidi, "You still want to be there?"

"I insist on it." It sounded like a line out of a 1940s Hollywood thriller. "Aunt Tillie is calling Sackville High tomorrow and telling them I have to go to a funeral."

"Okay. Peter, you alright with being Heidi's escort?" he asked.

"Anytime! But it looks like our first 'date' will be going to a funeral."

Everyone smiled but no one laughed. That word *gun* still had everyone rattled.

A CHILL IN THE AIR

There was a chill in the air as they returned from the Old Fort. And it existed only between Heidi and Donnie. She had stayed away from him more or less since their wonderful moment together on his bed this morning. She would barely come near him or speak to him. He wanted to ask her what was happening, but they were never alone. Now here they were in his living room and no one in sight. She on the couch, he on the chair.

Donnie had a huge drop in self-confidence wondering what he said or did that was so bad. When a man gets it into his head that he is responsible for the cold shoulder he is receiving, then outrageously stupid reasons start flowing at warp speed into his thick male skull. So, of course, Donnie asked the stupidest possible question in the worst possible way.

"So, what's up with you and Erik?" he asked. There was no trouble for him to see that he had screwed up, because she flinched a little bit at the brusqueness of the question.

"There's nothing up with Erik and me. We just hung out a bit that's all. And he gave me a ride to work," she answered coldly.

Bull in a china shop. He tried to think of something he could say to improve things.

"Thanks Jane," said Tillie, as she came out of the kitchen. "Say your goodbyes. kids."

Heidi and he had a quick hug. And Donnie kissed her cheek. And she was gone, following Jane and Tillie out the door. It felt strange. It was a cold exit and he felt like a big dumb male of the species. Which of course he was.

A LIBRARY CARD

That night, Jane and Donnie sat in their living room, and Donnie told her everything about the past five days. And again, he apologized on behalf of himself and his dad for not having called her as soon as it happened. "I'm sure he would have today, if you hadn't come back early. But we were both hoping this would be over last Thursday, then Friday, then yesterday ..."

"Mmm. How long have you and Heidi known each other?" asked mom, executing an unexpected ninety degree turn in the conversation.

"Well, you remember that we met in the spring of '67?"

Jane nodded.

"So, I suppose you could say six years or so."

Jane raised an eyebrow and repeated, "How long have you and Heidi known each other?"

Donnie thought about it. "I guess we don't know each other," he admitted. "At least not well, but we're going to find out whether it's going to work out between us. Heidi and I both consider that summer together as a great foundation. We were best friends then and that might be a great way to start out."

"Very logical and well planned. Just remember life never works out the way you think it should. Not always bad, mind you, but try not to plan too much." She looked across the room at the fireplace. "Are you going to be having sex anytime soon?"

"Jesus, Mom!"

"Stop swearing in front of me. And you don't have to tell me one way or the other, just please remember what would happen to this wonderful girl if she ever became pregnant." Spoken matter-of-factly.

"I haven't done anything with anybody, mom." And, after an awkward pause. "Well, nothing that would get anyone pregnant." He could feel his face turning beet red. "Heidi and I ... we're in no rush in that way. You know, to be intimate and all that. We may just be friends forever ... but I hope not."

His mother continued as if Donnie hadn't said a word. "Because I don't have to tell you what happens to your future, if you become a father at sixteen, do I?" She turned and stared directly at him.

Donnie had this talk with his dad when he was fourteen, but he was blushing and sweating his way through this for his mother's peace of mind. "Yes Mom. They showed us a couple films in science class last year and this year." The acting was bad, but the message was clear as a bell: if you had a baby in your teens, say goodbye to your teens.

She grabbed his face in her two hands and said, "I almost wish you'd done something wrong last Wednesday, then I could at least be angry with you for getting into this mess." Then she reached one hand up and ruffled his hair. "But you did everything just the way you were supposed to Donnie. Just the way we taught you. You're turning into a real man just like, like ... well, a real man."

"Like who, Mom?"

He had a feeling she was going to say, "your father," but Donnie would never know because his mom changed the subject again. "I always loved that little girl. She was such a great friend to you and so full of life and energy. She changed you — did you know that?"

"What do you mean?"

"I was a little worried about you in your younger years. You were an introvert, and liked playing by yourself, you didn't make friends very easily. But, starting in the winter, and by the end of the summer in '67, you were a completely different boy. You were still a bit shy — you still are, right? But even a few weeks after meeting her, you were engaging people in conversations, offering to help older people, more confident on the phone, more confident with us in sharing an opinion. And you were reading, I mean really reading. I was overjoyed to see that."

Donnie nodded.

Jane continued, "In the spring of '67, if I asked what your favourite book was, your response would be, 'I don't like reading.' By the time we moved here in August, you were a voracious reader. Anything and everything. You even went down to the Dartmouth Library on your own and got a library card, after we moved here."

"Yeah, I did. I was nervous, but I did it." He smiled at the memory.

"I always credited Heidi for these changes in you. In fact, today I thanked her for it, just before she left with Tillie, and do you know what she said?"

"What?"

"She said, 'Donnie was my first best friend. He listened to everything I said, never ignored me, never made fun of me for any idea or suggestion I made. So, thank you Mrs. Langille for bringing up such a great person.' She's a very mature, mannerly, young lady Donnie, so treat her with respect. If you really love this young lady or any other, the most valuable thing you can do is listen. Be there for her and listen."

They sat there for a few moments, in silence.

"How did she get you interested in reading? I couldn't get you to put a book down ever since that summer in '67!" Mom asked.

Donnie thought about it. "We used to go over to Citadel Hill, sometimes spend the whole day there. Heidi would have some book or other with her and she'd start reading it to me, and then she insisted I read the next chapter to her. At first, I did it just to please her, but I started to really enjoy it. Turns out we both loved being theatrical and we would read the dialogue in different voices and accents. We weren't very good, but we used to crack each other up all the time. It was during those times that I couldn't imagine my life without her. I figured we'd be friends forever. I wouldn't call it love, but everything clicked between us."

"One day she brought a radio play script called *Sorry, Wrong Number,* from the library. We not only read the thing, but we also acted out the different parts with each other. It was great fun, but after a while it got really scary, and we couldn't finish it. It just got more and more frightening." He was smiling and shaking his head at the memory.

"Yes, I know, I saw the movie," said Jane with a big grin.

"There's a movie?" Donnie asked, astonished.

"Yes, very suspenseful. It's an oldie, about twenty years ago, I think. Barbara Stanwyck is in it."

"Jeez, I hope it comes around on TV, I'd like to see it."

They were silent for a moment then Jane let out a big sigh. "Please be careful tomorrow. I know the place is going to be crawling with police. I'm told there'll be almost as many policemen as mourners at the funeral. But, please just be safe all the same."

"Yup I will. Plus, their two best street cops will be escorting me at all times. Hicks and Fong," he said confidently.

"You know their names?" She asked.

"Yeah, I met them both. Fong's been here to the house."

Mom shook her head.

"Hey, does my suit still fit me?"

WE NEED TO TALK

Just before bedtime, as Jane was turning off the lights downstairs, the phone rang in the kitchen. Donnie's brown suit, his only suit, was hanging off a hook by the back door to straighten out the wrinkles. Jane answered the phone and listened for a few seconds. "Yes, of course, sweetheart, and no, you're not disturbing anyone."

She leaned around the corner and called Donnie down from his room.

As he arrived, Jane covered the mouthpiece and whispered, "She sounds a little upset."

He didn't have to ask her who was on the other end of the line. He steeled himself for the unknown. "Hello Heidi."

Her voice sounded raw. "I needed to talk ... to explain ... to say I'm sorry the way I treated you today."

"The way you treated me? I should never have asked you that question, at least not in that way."

"You have every right to ask me about Erik, but it's more than that. I need to tell you things. Things about myself and my life. I would have already, but we need to be alone. Donnie, I'm afraid of how it will affect our friendship."

"It won't."

"You can't say that, Donnie."

"It won't, I guarantee you. But you're right, we need to talk soon. Do you want to do it now?" he asked.

"It has to be face to face. The Fort must be wonderful in the morning."

"It is. That's maybe the best time to be there," he answered.

"Okay, just a minute."

After a pause, Heidi came back. "I'll be at your place at 7:30, Donnie."

MONDAY

THE OLD FORT

A thick blanket of fog enveloped trees, old forts, and teenagers the next morning.

Aunt Tillie had arrived at 7:35, and dropped Heidi off, who brought with her a change of clothes for the funeral. They were laid out on the bed in the spare room.

Donnie had told his parents that he and Heidi were going for a walk. He promised to take the field in back of the house over to the Old Fort. His dad kept asking him why they had to go over there at this ungodly hour. But Donnie's mom had shushed her husband and waved the two kids out the door. She knew the two teenagers had important matters to discuss.

As they walked silently along a path in the woods up to the Old Fort, they passed a water pipe sticking out of the ground, on their right. Ground water was pouring out, as it had done twenty-four hours a day for as long as anyone could remember. At least two generations of kids had been drinking thousands of gallons of this water over the years and not one of them had ever been sick. It was crystal clear and tasted very good. For Donnie, it was a ritual. He cupped his hand under the cold running stream, sipping the sweet water from his fingers, not because he was thirsty but for luck. And when he was done, he usually looked out at the harbour and said *God Bless the City of Lakes*. Simply because he was so thankful to be living here.

But today Donnie didn't say it. He was apprehensive about why Heidi needed to talk. They made their way up to the roof of the Old Fort in silence. It wasn't a tense silence, but Heidi seemed nervous, as if she were impatient to begin.

They sat in the usual spot, with their legs hanging over the edge. You couldn't see the ground below because of the fog. When he looked at Heidi's profile, Donnie wished he had brought his camera. Her face was tilted up toward the fog in the sky. Any photographer will tell you that the purest light and therefore truest colours are captured in overcast, or better yet, foggy conditions. Added to the lighting was the tiniest bit of the mist condensing on her face to form a million tiny sparkles. He stared at her in awe, never wanting to forget this most beautiful of images.

But there was a flaw in that angel. Her expression was unsettling. She looked exhausted or frightened or maybe both. And now that they were sitting, she seemed hesitant to begin.

The world around them was opening up. The fog stayed thick, about twenty-five feet from the ground up, then ended roughly level with the roof of the Old Fort. Everywhere above the fog was blue sky and sunshine. It was like they were sitting on top of the clouds.

"Are you tired?" he asked. "You look like maybe you didn't sleep well."

"I didn't sleep at all." She wasn't looking at him. She was looking across the fog. "Donnie, I've been dreading this talk, up all night trying to figure out what to say and how to say it."

"Just say it." He was scared he was about to lose her, despite all that they said on the phone last night.

"First, I have to tell you about Liverpool. Starting back in 1967." She paused a moment, then began. "Our moving there was a surprise.

Nobody in the family told me we were moving there until about two weeks after you left Edward Street ..."

LIVERPOOL

Two weeks after the Langilles moved to Dartmouth, Heidi's father, Frank, quit his job with the City of Halifax. He started a new one in a pulp and paper mill in Liverpool, a town about a two-hour drive along the coast, southwest of the capital city.

Heidi had been extremely upset when Donnie's family moved to Dartmouth and unlike him, she made no attempt to contact them. Losing her best friend and then all that was familiar in her young life made her bitter. But only for a short while. Surprisingly, Liverpool was like a tonic and Heidi adjusted well to her new home. She kept in close contact with her Aunt Tillie and when they talked, courtesy of Aunt Tillie paying the long-distance charges, Heidi would tell her how she made a few new friends and enjoyed the laid-back schools and lifestyle of the quaint old Revolutionary War-era port town. During that first year, she occasionally thought of the boy she missed so much, but those thoughts eventually faded. Three years passed quickly and although her home life didn't improve, Heidi felt comfortable in Liverpool.

Heidi's brother Mark wasn't so lucky. He was in trouble in the small town, almost on a weekly basis. He was bullied in school, constantly in fights. Then in 1970 and in grade eleven, Mark was in a ferocious fight after school. He and a fellow student ended up in the hospital. While visiting his son, Frank Freeman almost came to blows with the other boy's father. Separated by hospital staff, Frank screamed, "Keep your damned son away from my boy!"

The father of the other boy stared at Mr. Freeman and said, "You don't know what happened do you? Our sons weren't fighting each other, they were trying to defend each other."

"Oh ... well, in that case, sorry I didn't realize. What happened?"

"A gang of punks attacked them because they're different. People are afraid of what they don't understand, and prejudice is usually passed down by the parents to their children," explained the man.

Frank was confused. "Prejudice? What prejudice? What reason? It's not like he's a negro or something."

The other boy's father stared at Frank for a long time and then said, "Yes, of course. Who knows why they were singled out and attacked. At least they will recover. Take your boy home, Mr. Freeman, and remember to love him no matter what."

Frank and Molly took their boy home, but promptly forgot the advice to "love their son no matter what." The gulf between Mark and his parents widened as time passed. Mark stayed away from home as much as he could, returning late in the evenings. Heidi saw less and less of her brother.

In the fall of 1970, sickness hit Molly. She and Frank had always smoked heavily but were firm believers that they would never get sick — Molly because God would protect the righteous and Frank because he had the luck of the Irish. God changed his mind apparently, but not quickly. Molly had a lot of faith in the Almighty and also in the doctors and with the help of both, she managed to live a pretty good life for the next few years. But with lung cancer, the clock on the wall ticked away.

In late June, 1972, Molly Freeman died, surrounded by her family. Heidi missed her fifteenth birthday entirely and she didn't even notice. That night, she lay in bed and glanced at the shell on her night table, Donnie's gift from six years earlier. For the first time in a long while, she wondered what he was up to and how nice it would be to see him again. Then she shook off those thoughts. He had new friends and was probably a different person now. Heidi kept her chin up and told herself, "You are strong, you'll get through this."

Two months later, almost to the day, after a huge and embarrassing fight with his father, witnessed by half a dozen families on the street, most of them peeking through curtains, Mark walked out the front door of the house and said, "I'm moving to Montreal, where I can be myself!"

Heidi ran after her brother and caught him just down the road.

"I can't stay here Heidi. I don't fit in."

"But father ..."

"Father somehow sees me as being his failure and he hates me for it!"

"Why would he think —"

Mark interrupted her. "It's not just father! It's Liverpool, it's Halifax it's everywhere in this backwoods province. I can't be who I am. I can't be," he paused, fighting back the tears. "I am a criminal, do you understand? I am a criminal for being who I am. I just can't be ...."

"You can't be with the person you love?"

Mark was surprised. "How long have you known?"

"I have eyes, Mark. I've seen your friends, your interests, your frustrations. It must be awful."

Mark was quiet for a moment, lower lip quivering. "I have to go sis. I have to go, or I'll die." He suddenly hugged his sister. "You're strong, you'll be fine." And then he left.

As Heidi watched him disappear down Old Port Mouton Road, she kept her chin up and told herself, "He's right. I am strong and I'll get through this."

On Halloween of 1972, her father got his late wife's brother a job at the pulp and paper plant. Uncle Kevin, infamous in the family for his love of rum, moved in to help with the mortgage payments. He slept in Mark's old bedroom and shared the upstairs bathroom with his niece. Not ideal, but Heidi kept her chin up and told herself, "You are strong, you'll get through this."

Sometimes her aunt would call, and Heidi would gloss things over, telling her everything was fine. Frank didn't like his do-good sister interfering, so Heidi kept the peace.

Her father, having witnessed his family destroyed in six months, took to drinking in the evenings. Kevin enthusiastically joined in. They were drunk almost every night. One night, after many whiskies, he gave a plausible though barely discernable reason for his distaste and indifference towards his only daughter. "You're not even mine. Heh, heh ... your mother screwed Reverend Patterson. Jesus it's a, hic, a joke. She fucked the preacher, he left town, and I get you to remind me every day."

Heidi didn't believe him. She couldn't afford to. She kept her chin up and told herself, "You are strong, you'll get through this."

Then in January, when the two men were in the middle of a Friday night bender at the kitchen table, Uncle Kevin grabbed Heidi as she walked past and pulled her onto his lap. He grabbed at her breasts, reach his hand between her legs, and shook her back and forth like a rag doll. She managed to squirm off his lap, swung around and hit him across the face as hard as she could. Uncle Kevin, stinking of rum, just laughed and slurred, "You're feisty!"

And her father laughed with him.

Heidi was no longer sure she could keep her chin up, and told herself, "You will call your aunt tomorrow." She should have called Matilda then and there.

About 2:00 am that Saturday morning, with her father snoring in the master bedroom downstairs, Heidi was woken by a greasy hand over her mouth, a voice urging her to "Shush, shush now, I'm going to make you feel so good." Uncle Kevin. He started fumbling with bed clothes and her pyjamas. Foul breath, body sweat, and the stink of alcohol covered her like a shroud.

She exploded into action, kicking, gouging with her fingers, trying to scream.

He got angry. "Shut up now, quiet, you little bitch."

Finally, she forced a hand free and scratched her fingernails across Uncle Kevin's eyes. He let out a squeal and rolled off her slightly, which gave Heidi enough room to bring her legs up, and in doing so her knee connected full force with Uncle Kevin's groin.

He rolled off the bed onto the floor, retching and crying. As he fell, her uncle knocked over the night table and her precious shell was broken into two pieces. Heidi grabbed the pieces of the broken gift, ran downstairs, and tried to wake her dad. He pushed her away in a drunken stupor. Terrified Uncle Kevin might come downstairs at any moment, Heidi called the only person in the world she trusted, her Aunt Tillie, for help. Tillie instructed her niece to hide somewhere in the basement until help arrived. Heidi secured herself behind the basement door using a piece of rope.

Two RCMP officers broke the front door down ten minutes later, after getting no response to their knocks. They searched for the basement door and on finding it, knocked and asked Heidi to come out. She untied her rope, tentatively opened the door a crack and, peering out, saw the telltale black hats with the yellow stripe. She threw herself in the comforting arms of the first officer she saw, crying her heart out in relief. The officer, a grizzled fifteen-year veteran of the force, was clearly moved and patted her back saying "You're safe now, little one."

And indeed, it was the first time she felt safe since her mother passed. They wrapped her in a blanket and took her to the Liverpool Detachment. In her hands were the two remnants of Donnie's seashell gift. She would not let them go.

Aunt Tillie arrived ninety minutes later.

THE OLD FORT REDUX

Donnie was surprised how calm she was as she described everything that happened. And he was shocked at himself. He felt something he never had before, burning hatred for another person. His hands kept clenching and unclenching, as if looking for something, or someone, to throttle.

But she survived unscathed, thanks to her own strength and the help of her wonderful aunt and two kick-ass Mounties. He did feel a certain amount of guilt, because during the exact same period in time, life was wonderful for him. Lifelong, carefree memories of the Canada-Russia hockey series and watching Apollo 17. Starting high school with his three best friends. Anita coming home for Christmas — it had seemed like a decade since he had seen her instead of just a year. And then in the spring, while Heidi was adjusting to the upheaval of changing high schools, he was notified that he didn't have to write his third-term exams. How could life be so easy for him, compared to what this sweet girl had had to endure.

He knew he could never be as strong as her. Donnie reached over to hug her, but she quickly pushed his hands away. He was stunned.

"No!" she said. "I'm not done."

She stared off into the last vestiges of the fog, watching it thin. "Remember yesterday, when I woke you up in your room?"

Donnie blushed a little remembering his body's reaction to her being near him, "Yeah, it was wonderful."

"Yes, it was," she said. "I ... it's ..." She was trying to decide how to say what she wanted to say.

She gathered her thoughts, stoked her courage, and worked on how she would say what had to be said. She looked across the harbour, now clear of mist. "Are you looking forward to when," she turned and looked Donnie in the eyes, "we make love for the first time?"

Donnie blushed. "What? Yes! Of course, I can't wait for our first time."

Heidi turned slightly away from Donnie, so she wasn't looking at him. "I agree," she said, "but it's only going to be your first time." Almost in a whisper.

She was still looking away from him, concentrating on the harbour at the bottom of the hill. The fog had left them during their conversation and just a thin layer was left over the distant water. Heidi didn't know how he would react, and she couldn't bear to watch him walk away in disgust or something similar.

At first, he didn't follow her, but then it hit him like a ton of bricks. Donnie knew what she was telling him. Despite what could be called a secular upbringing, Donnie was shocked. There were a couple kids in grade nine who claimed to have done it, and there were rumours in grade ten about who was with who and what they did. But by and large, if any of the kids were being intimate, they mostly, and modestly, kept it to themselves.

For a few seconds, he didn't know what to say. As far as he knew, none of his buddies had had sex yet, not even Clip, who had a steady girlfriend. He felt a pang of jealousy shoot through him. But he knew that was wrong and pushed the feeling away. Donnie searched his inexperienced mind for the right thing to say, but Heidi continued.

"I had a best friend, Joannie Swinamer. We were inseparable for the first few years in Liverpool. I think she's the first truly close girlfriend I ever had. Everything was fine till last spring. Joannie had a thing for this cool guy named Walter. He kind of looked like Erik, tall and blonde, but without the pinched face. And everything would have been fine, except Walter only had eyes for me. I didn't want anything to do with the guy at first, but soon I wondered what it would be like to be Walter's girlfriend."

"This was the time when everything was starting to get really bad. I dreaded going home after school, you know? Mom was sick, Dad and Mark arguing all the time. It was just awful."

"I'm sorry," Donnie said simply, then nodded for her to continue.

"Well, I guess Walter liked me too, because he asked me out. And I said yes, but I didn't want to hurt Joannie so I insisted that our dates would be in secret such that no one knew. For example, when we went to a movie, we'd take the bus all the way to Bridgewater so no one would see us. We went out a few times and he was a really nice guy. He wasn't too grabby or touchy, a real gentleman. My mom died during this time, and he was so kind to me then. I really appreciated his support, but I remember wishing I had someone who loved me — someone I could trust. Someone like you, Donnie."

"I'm right here for you," Donnie said, but Heidi didn't react.

"Anyway, we continued dating but we got careless. Someone saw us and told Joannie and that was the end of her friendship with me and the start of the rumours. Oh God, the rumours! Rumours that I had *done it*, and I would do it with anyone. I went from being one of the girls to being a slutty outcast in the eyes of every kid in school. I was literally propositioned and embarrassed by guys in the hallway every day, even boys I thought were my friends. I felt like I had nowhere to run. At first, I was scared and horrified but after a while I was very, very angry. You know Walter was wonderful, very supportive, but his constantly defending me was wearing him down as well.

"And ... I noticed no one was calling Walter a slut." Her eyes watered and she let out a sigh. "So last September, I called Walter and asked if we could meet in the park at around nine at night. I didn't intend anything, I just needed someone to talk to, and he was all I had. Mark had left a few weeks before. I had not only lost all my girlfriends at school, I was literally hated and ridiculed by everyone. So, I was alone at home and at school."

"We met, and I poured my soul out to Walter. He comforted me when I started crying and that's when it just sort of happened. We started kissing and I was so angry and emotional, and I thought, *alright I'll be exactly who they say I am*. I thought of my mother preaching abstinence at me and my dad threatening to throw me out in the gutter if I ever had sex before marriage and the kids at school lying about me and I just said *to hell with them all*. I decided I would give myself a late fifteenth birthday present. And truly? I just wanted someone to love me if only for a little while. Walter said it was his first time as well. The next morning, I woke up terrified that ... that I might be ... well, um ... you know."

Donnie knew. "Pregnant."

"Yes." She stared down at the rough concrete floor around them, the breeze ruffled her long brown hair. "But then the next week I realized I wasn't ... because, you know."

He nodded. He knew why. Her time of the month had returned. Thank God for older sisters because he learned a lot about the birds and the bees from Anita. Donnie felt like he should say something at this point, but Heidi wasn't finished.

"It wasn't what I expected. For one thing, it hurt a lot. Well, not all of it. And it sure didn't last long. But it did give me a small feeling of independence and even revenge against my family. And I discovered a new feeling of being a woman and being in control of my own life. I'm not sorry for doing what I did, Donnie. It is my life and my decision. But Walter seemed embarrassed to be near me after that, even when we passed each other in the hall."

After a long pause, she said, "And he ended up with Joannie after all."

Tears welled up in her eyes and she whispered, "God I miss Joannie."

They sat there in silence. In the harbour, a duty boat was arriving at the wharf near the McDonald bridge. Sailors and civilian labourers hopped on, heading to their day's work at the dockyard in Halifax.

Donnie supposed she thought he might be disapproving of her actions or considered her spoiled goods. Not at all. Being brought up by two agnostics who thought all organized religion was hogwash, it was impressed upon him that making judgments was foolishness. What worried him was that Heidi was now a sophisticated woman who had sampled the most enticing part of life while he was a little boy and not remotely in her league. And that was the reason for his silence. Fear of losing her. But he manned up and put those feelings in the trash where they belonged.

Donnie put himself in her position. If he were in the same circumstance, made a fool of at school by asinine idiots with no friends to comfort him, and no support at home from his own family, his mother dead and his sister gone, would he have felt the need for love and affection like Heidi? *God yes!*

And he thought of a quote he'd read once by a fellow Nova Scotian: *Of all the gifts we human beings have in this world, our brightest light is empathy.*

And it follows ... *Nolite iudicare ne iuducemini.* Donnie's parents may not have been religious, but when he was twelve, Donnie had read a book of inspiring bible quotes. This particular one really stuck with him. *Judge not, lest ye be judged.*

"Heidi," Donnie said. Her head tilted up slightly. "Heidi, look at me." She turned to face him.

"I *am* disappointed, Heidi," he said flatly. And at that, she sat up straight and stared him, eye to eye. Totally unapologetic and ready for whatever came next between them. Donnie could not have loved her any more than he did at that very moment. "I am disappointed, Heidi, that I wasn't your first lover." He saw her eyes widen a bit, and he continued. "But the great thing is, when we do have sex, at least one of us is gonna know what they're doing!" And he smiled at her.

And she smiled back at him, tears in her eyes. "And this time it *will* be true love," she whispered.

They fell into each other's arms, the fierce embrace of two people who had just passed a test of their love and respect for each other. *God Bless the City of Lakes.*

Was he upset, jealous, disappointed, angry? Donnie had to admit to himself yes, at least a tiny bit of all those feelings. But he remembered something his dad once said to him. *Unsuccessful people will concentrate on the one petty disappointment in a situation that successful people have long since ignored.* Well, Donnie had ignored a petty disappointment, and now he had the love of his life. He had Heidi. What more could he ask for?

WALKING UP GREEN ROAD

Two hours later, Peter met Heidi at the Langille's house and, with her changed into her finery, the two of them made their way up to Green Road. There they started the ten-minute walk up the hill to the cemetery, which was across the street from Dartmouth High School.

Heidi thoroughly enjoyed her walk and chat with Peter. She had assumed he was the quiet one of the four boys, and he was, but Peter was a thinker too and he seemed to weigh each sentence before uttering it. Regardless, he was a really cool guy.

When it came to his friendship with Donnie, it was as the saying goes, *they have as much in common as chalk and cheese.* Whereas Donnie loved the hard rock groups, the Stones, Purple, Zeppelin, James Gang, Steppenwolf and their ilk, Peter was into more progressive sounds like the Raspberries, the Moody Blues, Steely Dan, Jim Croce, and the like. Donnie and Peter connected on a different level from the other two. He told Heidi they sometimes would have deep conversations about moral, political and religious issues.

Peter's family was very religious, going to a Pentecostal church each Sunday. And at first, they did not approve of him hanging around with the other three boys. Two were papists and the third,

God forbid, never saw the inside of a church! But every now and then one or all of his best friends would impress Peter's parents with their politeness, with their generosity, and with their giving natures. Of course, all three were still *going to be cast into a lake of fire by a loving God to burn for all eternity*. But at least Peter's parents knew their son was safe with the three heathens he called friends.

"And as for me, Heidi, let me say this; I don't challenge my parents or our church on many Christian issues, but I don't believe for a second that God would ever throw anyone into a lake of fire, no matter what they did wrong," said Peter.

"So, what do you think happens to sinners when they die?" asked Heidi, with bright eyes.

"I think if they don't truly repent and become born again with Christ, their soul just ceases to exist when they die, there is no after-life for them. To me, that's the punishment a loving God would mete out. Not torture."

Heidi nodded and thought for a moment. "When you guys do discuss your religion, do they try to challenge your Christian beliefs?"

"Nope. I'm accepted just the way I am. The four of us have an agreement. I don't try to convert them, and they won't throw me in the harbour. It works well."

Heidi laughed. "Yes, I'm sure it does. Do you ever find it hard being with them?"

"They can be crude, they can curse like sailors sometimes, they pick the dumbest things to do at the worst possible time ... but of course stupid old me goes along with them."

"Dumbest things? Like what?"

"Ahh ... well, like last summer, first week of July ... the third maybe? Anyway, it was a Monday, so whatever the date was, we made the dumbest move ever and we won't make that mistake again."

"What happened?" Heidi was intrigued.

"After supper that evening, we rode our bikes down Pleasant Street past Shearwater Airbase where it changes into Main Street then all the way to the very end, a place called Hartlen Point. It's a big area of grassy fields right at the mouth of the harbour, on the

Dartmouth side. Clip said he heard of a cool place to explore down there, and we should bring our jackknives and flashlights. Turns out there was a big concrete wall built into the side of a hill which was an opening that led to a maze of underground passageways and bunkers. Part of the coastal defence system from World War Two. The opening had been bricked over when the war finished, but someone in the past thirty years had smashed the bricks away."

"I have to admit, I was excited. There's nothing so cool as exploring secret hidden places. When we arrived, we stashed our bikes in some nearby trees so no one would steal them and looked around the brick wall till we found an opening. About ten feet inside it was a steel door in steel frame, but the lower hinge was rusted right through and someone before us had wedged it open enough to crawl through."

"So that's what we did, and off we went to explore. Just the four of us with three flashlights. I never in my life imagined anything that felt so foreign, Heidi. There was no sound, absolutely no light, pitch blackness except for the light of our flashlights, and even that seemed to get swallowed up by the black."

"No one knew where we were. We hadn't told anyone. Clip found out about the place from a buddy and then looked it up on an old city map in the library. It never occurred to any of us that by hiding our bikes, it meant there was no visible sign of us anywhere. If we had run into trouble, we would have been completely screwed."

"So, what happened?"

Peter was quiet for a moment. "Well, we ran into trouble ... and I mean with a capital T!"

Heidi just stared at Peter, waiting, as they continued walking.

He shook his head, "Too long a story, we're almost to the cemetery. I'll just say we got lost, we almost drowned, two of us were bitten."

"Bitten?" Heidi was shocked.

Peter nodded, "Clip lost a fingernail. I was separated from the other fellows at one point in the pitch dark and complete silence ... and things started flying past my head!"

"Things?" Heidi gasped. "Maybe bats?"

"Don't know. Probably bats but whatever, I never want to feel that sensation again! You didn't hear them as much as you felt them." Peter shivered at the memory.

"When we finally got out, we all needed tetanus shots." Peter shivered. "Two things saved us. The fact that Donnie is a good swimmer. And the fact we had Fearless Freak with us. If we didn't have those two guys, I think one or all of us might have died."

"Swimming? In an underground bunker? Wait, who's Fearless Freak?" she asked.

"Natty. I call him Fearless Freak because, man, he's not afraid of anything. Any new rides at the fair, he's first to try. Once we were out hiking in the woods and came to an unoccupied fire tower. The three of us were a bit wary, but ZOOM, up he went. And of course, we followed. What a view it was! He's fearless and freaky. And he has an uncanny sense of direction. He can see things in three-D in his head and figure out the way things are laid out. And with our troubles at Hartlen Point, he was the key to getting us out. The guy is scary smart that way."

"I really have to hear your story. You have to promise me you'll tell me it soon, okay?" asked Heidi.

"Okay, I promise, but we'll do it at the Old Fort, that's the proper place for a story like that." Peter looked into the cemetery. "Here we are, and the funeral is just about to start."

MOUNT HERMON CEMETERY

It was a hot, sunny, June day. Too hot for the heavy old brown suit and tie Donnie was wearing. He had on one of his father's bland ties because his only tie was too psychedelic. There were four of their gang at the funeral.

Peter and Heidi were at the back of the crowd of friends and family. Peter looked cool in a lightweight blue suit, collar button open, and no tie. Heidi had on a navy-blue dress with tiny white polka dots. She had brought a suitcase and two dresses with her when her aunt dropped her off that morning. She asked them which one was appropriate. The dark green dress was the loser, too heavy, too hot. This was only the second funeral she had attended. It was Peter's first.

Madeline and her mom were in the family and friends section, as her parents were long time acquaintances with the Martins. Donnie's mother joined them.

Donnie and the officers strolled around the outskirts of the mourners.

It was a typical Nova Scotia interment. Funerals took thirty to forty minutes, depending on the church denomination. Everyone standing, except for a row of chairs set up for the elderly or infirm. Almost everyone had dressed up. Mr. Martin was a popular fellow who had many people at his store, and the news that it was a homicide by stabbing was made public yesterday, so the mourners were particularly emotional.

Donnie was doing what Rafuse had requested. Fugitives were known to wear disguises when they attended the funerals of their victims, so he was to search for aspects they can't disguise: their noses, their build, their height, mannerisms etc. To simplify, he was to look for a man with milky white hands, who was built similar to Natty but a lot older and bit shorter. Donnie saw no one even close to that description.

Donnie and the officers paused and took shelter under the shade of a huge maple tree whose lower limbs had been pruned. At this point, they were well away from the mourners, but they talked in low voices nonetheless.

"Anyone look even remotely like our guy?" Fong asked quietly.

Donnie shook his head. "Sorry."

"Nothing to apologize for Donnie, the only wasted effort is the one you don't attempt," said Fong. He continued on down the path.

Hicks let out a big sigh. Fong was getting well ahead of them He waited till the corporal looked their way, then he took the four fingers of his right hand and tapped the back of the other hand in a pattern.

Tap, tap, tap, pause. Tap, tap, tap, pause. Fong frowned and made his way back to them.

"What's the problem?"

"You're too far ahead," Hicks said. "Remember, the chief wants us to stick tight as glue to The Big Guy here." Apparently, Donnie was *The Big Guy*.

"Yes, you're right. I wanted to scan the crowd ahead for Ryan, but I went too fast," he said. "Come on, more people have arrived on the other side. Let's go around again." Fong took the lead and remained no more that ten feet in front.

Donnie quietly asked Hicks, "What's that little hand gesture you were doing?"

"Can't tell you, Donnie."

"Come on Hicks, I'm practically a cop."

He gave Donnie a *get serious* look but relented, "Alright, but you don't tell anybody, right?"

Donnie nodded.

"It's a symbol known only to those of us in the force. If one of us is ever in a serious position but can't draw attention to ourselves by asking for help, then that gesture means *officer needs assistance*. And believe me, if any of us see that gesture, the cavalry is on its way! It means whoever's making it is in immediate danger." Hicks looked at Fong. "I maybe shouldn't have used it just now, but the chief was adamant that we stay close to you at all costs."

"Yeah man, that's something else." Donnie was suddenly gripped with emotion. He was scared enough that Ryan might be around, and truly hoped he wouldn't panic or overreact if he did see him. And he was humbled to realize that these two men were risking their lives to protect him. Of course, they did that every day for the citizens of their city.

"Hey look, take this if you ever need me for anything." Hicks handed Donnie a business card, the type of which the cops often handed out to witnesses. "It's the main number and they can get a hold of me pretty quick if need be. Any time. Even if you just want to talk. And my home number is on the back."

"Thanks Hicks." Case in point.

It was cool to learn the secret hand signal, something that Peter probably didn't even know. But he wouldn't tell anyone about it, not even his friend. They rounded a bend and were in sight of the family. And Donnie stopped walking, overcome by the sight.

Mr. Martin's sons and daughter, and older people who were his siblings and friends. All crying and broken. One older woman simply left the funeral, overcome by it all. The eldest son stepped up to give a tear-filled eulogy. It wasn't just that they had lost a loved one but the manner in which he had been taken that was so inconceivable. How could one human being do this to another? What did that sweet old guy do except make people happy? Brighten their days. How horrible had his last few minutes been?

Tears ran down Donnie's cheeks as he stood and watched. Why do bad things happen to good people? Every day this kind of thing happens, and families are torn apart and had to somehow pretend that the rest of their lives would be normal again. But they would never be the same. Ever.

Donnie felt a hand on his shoulder. Not to pull him away, but in support. Fong on one side of Donnie, looking at the mourners with him. And Hicks stepped up to the other side. Donnie looked at him and wiped the tears away. Hicks said quietly, "I know man, I know." The three of them stayed a few more moments, and then they continued on their task; looking for the son of a bitch that caused this.

REGINALD MARTIN, 1900-1973

Mr. Reginald Martin, Reg to his friends and family, was gone. As a boy of ten, he survived an incident that many thought was the end of the world, Halley's Comet. It wasn't. But he was the kind of boy who felt blessed to have seen it.

In 1916, he committed the only crime of his life. He forged his birth certificate to join the Canadian Army. He was a messenger during the bloodiest battle in the bloodiest war ever recorded to that point in history, Passchendaele. He came home with no physical injuries, only to survive another attack, the great 1919 Flu Pandemic. He met and married his late wife Marjorie during the roaring twenties. Seeing the thousands of sick and dying in both the war and the pandemic set him on a new path in life, working as an orderly in hospitals and clinics, helping those in ill-health, and comforting those who were dying. Doctors and nurses began to ask for Reg to be assigned to their ward, as his reputation for kindness and efficiency, as well as his popularity with the patients, became known. Many a wheelchair he had pushed to the front door and received a hug and lifelong friendship in return. And many the hand he had held while its owner took their last breath when there were no other loved ones present.

Reg and his family then weathered the great depression, and when Hitler turned the world on its end, it wasn't surprising that he enlisted in the army as a medic at age thirty-nine, only to be sent to the navy until the war's end. He was posted to a hospital ship, HMHS Letitia, even though as he used to tell it, he would "get seasick in a bathtub." He was again known for his caring attitude towards the soldiers and sailors, Canadian, American, and German, as they came to Halifax.

He spent the last thirty years as a generous and passionate community leader, civic alderman, and the head of several charities. He helped build the city until he retired in 1968.

Reg was a *people* person however, and wanted to continue meeting and serving the people of his community. With that in mind, he purchased the little property on Commercial Street and opened his convenience store. In this way, he continued to meet friends and constituents of the city he loved. People could grab a snack, a drink, and a conversation on any topic in his store. And if people in hard circumstances couldn't afford a cup of coffee or needed bus fare to get to a homeless shelter, Reg would more often than not provide both free of charge.

"Pay me when you can," was all he would say.

One could truly say that throughout Reg's life, he was a friend to everyone he met. He was even friendly to the person who murdered him.

MOURNING

Heidi and Peter were standing next to each other, respectfully maintaining silence. It was a sad service, and the two teenagers were caught up in the seriousness of it all. Heidi had tears coming down her cheeks. She was wondering the same thing as Donnie, what kind of animal could possibly do such a thing to another person. And of course, she couldn't help but think of what might have happened to her in Liverpool. *If the worst happened to me, would anyone have come to my funeral?*

For months now, she had done her damnedest not to feel sorry for herself. Now the tears flowed down her cheeks. She pushed away the feelings and forced the tears to stop. Peter looked over at her with concern. She whispered to him, "Don't worry, I always cry at funerals." He patted her shoulder awkwardly and smiled. Looking back, she realized she hadn't cried a single tear at her mother's funeral.

The funeral proper ended. Mourners continued milling about, talking, remembering, reminiscing, hugging each other. Peter and Heidi waited under the shade of a maple tree for Donnie. The two cops she had seen him with earlier were talking to him and his mom about Lord knows what. Madeline came over to say hello, her eyes red and puffy, as well. And both started to tear up again as they hugged, then Madeline headed home with her mother.

"Man, that was so sad," Peter said. "The family was devastated over that stabbing news."

"What kind of insanity would be crawling around in your mind, for you to kill a sweet old guy like Mr. Martin?" Heidi asked. "Donnie speaks very highly of him."

"Yeah. They used to talk a lot. Donnie would use any excuse to pop in the store to get something, and they'd get to talking and he would be in there for an hour. Donnie loves history and listening to

Mr. Martin was like having a time machine." Peter smiled. "And here he comes."

"Sorry guys, the cops want me to come down to the station and take a quick look at some of the evidence they found at the scene. Just in case it 'jars any further memories'," Donnie explained. "They wanted to drive me over now, but I asked if we could have lunch first. And get a drink! It's getting really hot."

HUBCAPS

The three friends walked down to the Miss Dartmouth restaurant on Wyse Road, across from the Dartmouth Shopping Centre. On the way, Donnie asked Peter, "Hey man, do the Dartmouth Police have a brown unmarked Chevy Impala?"

"Brown? Maybe. They used to have a grey one and a blue one, a couple years ago, but since they brought in the new '73s, I haven't seen one yet, so I don't know which colours they have. Why?"

"I think there's an unmarked car keeping an eye on me, brown four door Impala," he explained.

"Well, there's one sure way to tell if it's an unmarked police car. The cops are on a tight budget, so *all* their cars are bare-bones and have small diameter stock hub caps, even the unmarked ones. Almost any other new Impala will have big, fancy, full size wheel covers," Peter explained.

"Okay, thanks. I'll check next time I see it."

When they reached the restaurant, Heidi said, "Are you sure you can't have lunch with us?"

Peter shook his head, "Mom has a big lunch ready for me. In our family, the remedy for sadness is a big meal. Actually, that the same remedy for everything! See ya soon, guys."

They said their goodbyes and Heidi surprised Donnie by hugging Peter goodbye.

As he watched his friend walk up the street, Donnie said, "Are you going to hug every no-good, two-bit thug you meet in this city?"

Heidi replied with a big smile, "Get used to it Mister, your friends are now my friends too!"

They sat down for lunch. He told her about his day with the two amigos, Fong and Hicks. Then they talked about the funeral itself.

"It was kind of cool being with the two cops and I was concentrating on trying to find Louis Ryan so much I forgot where I was for a minute or two. Then I saw Mr. Martin's family and I just lost it. I started crying. Look at me now, I'm tearing up just thinking of how sad the whole situation was ... I mean is ..."

She reached across the table and stroked the back of his hand softly. "I know, I can see it in your eyes. It *is* a horrible situation Donnie and you're right in the middle. But that's something I love about you. You don't ask anyone else what the right thing to do is. You just do it."

"Thank you, Heidi. Thank you so much for being here."

They held hands for a few moments and then heard a gruff voice.

"Can I take your order?"

WORKING TOGETHER

"They work well together but are always giving each other a hard time. I think Hicks is a bit of a hard case." Donnie took another bite, "And a joker. And Fong is so strait-laced, he doesn't get a joke half the time." Donnie was in a better mood and was finishing his story about the two cops.

He had a tuna fish sandwich, Heidi a BLT. Of course, then he needed to grab a mint at the cashier to kill his awful fish breath. This boyfriend stuff was hard work!

They walked to the police station slowly, hand in hand in a comfortable silence. If he didn't think about the past week, he'd be in heaven, but it was always intruding in his thoughts, hovering in the background of his life like the annoying static on a radio.

Heidi said, "I called Mr. Norberg up yesterday and asked him to take me out of shipping and put me into planting — hopefully in Greenhouse Two with you."

"Really? That's wonderful of course but I thought you were a star in shipping, right?"

"That's what Norberg said, but I was insistent. And he said 'What if I just refuse?' And I said 'I'll have to quit then.' And he said, 'okay, okay, I'll find you a spot over there. I suppose I can move Graham into shipping.'"

What she didn't tell Donnie was that Norberg asked her another question. Did the move have anything to do with his nephew, because Erik had been acting out of character the past few weeks. She assured him it didn't, she just needed a change.

In truth, Heidi was angry at herself because Erik had been acting a more and more strangely the past few months, not just weeks, and she didn't take the time to notice. I'm finished with Erik now, she said to herself, though I wished I'd explained everything to Norberg yesterday on the phone ...

EVIDENCE

"After you," Donnie said, holding the front door to the police station open. Inside, they were ushered through the little gate and into the back area to the conference room, which was doubling as a layout area for the evidence.

Rafuse came out of the room wearing his trademark shirt and tie. "Good morning, Miss Freeman," said Rafuse, shaking Heidi's hand.

"Good *afternoon,* sir," she said.

"Is it?" Rafuse checked his watch, "Gawd, it *is* afternoon. Time flies. Donnie, if you could step into the conference room for a few moments. Heidi, I'm sorry I'm going to have to ask you to sit in one of those chairs in my office."

Heidi sat in the first chair on the right which she pushed back, giving her a view inside the conference room through the window and open blinds. Heidi watched her boyfriend and the detective walk past the window and disappear for a few moments. When they came back into her view, she could see them walking around a large table that was out of sight, just below the window level.

Heidi got up to stretch her legs and casually glanced through the window. Rafuse was talking to Donnie and pointing at various items of evidence. Donnie was either shaking his head or empathizing a point. She was proud of Donnie because he was talking with them on an equal footing, like he belonged there. It never occurred to Heidi or Donnie that the cops were treating him that way by design, to give him a feeling of being a team member as opposed to an outsider.

Heidi returned to her seat for a few minutes, but she was getting restless. None of the other officers in the station had expressed any concerns about her walking around, so she took another stroll, this time closer to the window.

Rafuse was wearing rubber gloves, and holding two pieces of paper in front of Donnie. One was black, and the other was white with colours on it. The latter was instantly familiar, and she tried to place it, but Rafuse placed it back on the table, out of sight, before she could figure out why it was so familiar.

Donnie shook his head then they shook hands, Rafuse clapping him on the shoulder. The door opened and she heard, "So, if you can think of anything else or if something comes to mind, just call. But be aware we're going to be filing all these items away in the crime lab vault in two days' time."

She stared at the paper on the table and concentrated. Donnie came through the door, closed it, grabbed her hand, and started pulling her away saying, "Hey, maybe this afternoon we should —"

Heidi turned around, pulled her hand free, walked back to the conference room door, and knocked on the glass window. Rafuse gave her a surprised look, then walked over and opened the door.

"Miss Freeman?"

"Detective Rafuse, those two pieces of paper you were showing to Donnie? I know what they are."

"You do?"

"Yes sir, they're packing slips from DIK, a German courier service. It stands for Deutsche Internationale Kuriere. They're always sending packages to the place where I have a part-time job," Heidi explained.

Rafuse was very interested, "Yes, yes, and where is that?"

"The Lake William Plant Emporium."

D & H 4EVER

Heidi and Donnie spent the rest of the day and evening together, at the Langille house. She was a different person now, like a one-ton weight had been lifted off her shoulders. It was strange feeling for both of them, in that they had already professed their love for each other, but today was the first day they spent actually flirting with one another. The past three days had been crazy.

Three days, thought Donnie. *Oh well, ours is not to wonder why ... or how in this case. Just go with the flow.*

At around eleven that evening, Heidi went to the closet in the guest room where she had hung her dresses and retrieved her purse.

She had talked to her Aunt Tillie earlier in the day and received the okay to spend the night at the Langille house. It made some sense, as Madeline could drop Heidi off at school before she drove Donnie to work in the morning. But the biggest reason Aunt Tillie had agreed was that she was filled with joy at seeing her niece so happy. And, of course, the two kids would be chaperoned by Donnie's parents.

The Langilles had two wooden lawn chairs on a few paver stones just off the front walk. No one ever used them, so they were a bit rickety but sturdy enough. Donnie was sitting in one watching the late-night traffic go by when Heidi sat next to him with a little white giftbox in her hand.

She leaned over and kissed him. "Happy Birthday," she said, handing him the box. Donnie had already received money from his dad, and a cool pair of binoculars from his mom.

When he opened the box, there was the shell he had given her in 1967. It looked the same except for a hairline crack right down the middle. Clearly etched on the side was **D & H 4ever.**

He was speechless for a moment. "I completely forgot about this." He smiled at Heidi, "It looks like it's had a mishap?"

"Yes, I was really upset when it was broken. I thought it meant I'd never see you again," she said quietly, then brightened up. "But I managed to glue it back together all the same. Go on, pick it up," she said with a smile.

Which he did, and there was a little note under it.

Donnie, there are no words to describe how wonderful you are. Your birthday present is coming tomorrow, and I will surprise you! Welcome back into my life. Forever yours, Love Heidi

Donnie stared at the note. Then looked into Heidi's beautiful eyes and suddenly parts of a dream he had back in January filled his head. Maybe Heidi and he were connected in some special way.

"I knew I was going to see you again," he said quietly.

"You knew? What do you mean?"

"I had sort of forgotten you for the last few years. I mean, I remember all the great times and things we did back in '67, but six years is a long time and well you know ..."

"Yes, I know, same with me. But how did you know you were going to see me again?" Heidi repeated.

"Well, this'll sound strange, but back in January, I had a dream about you. Right out of the blue."

"Wow." Heidi felt a tingle. "Did I look the way I did when I was ten years old?"

"I don't remember a lot of it, but I didn't see you in my dream I only heard you."

"And you remember the sound of my voice from back then?"

"That's just it, it wasn't your voice from back then, it was deeper and more sophisticated. Kind of like you sound now."

"Really? How strange. What did I say?"

Donnie hesitated, then, "You were crying for help, and calling me by name."

A shiver rippled through Heidi's body, "Last January? Do you remember which day?"

"No. I do know it was a Friday night. I was up late, after midnight in fact ..."

Heidi threw her arms around Donnie, holding him tight. She didn't want him to see the tears that suddenly formed in her eyes and rolled down her cheeks. Then she buried her face in his sweater to dry them. She knew his dream had to have happened at the exact same moment her uncle had tried to rape her.

Donnie held her tightly, or tried his best, as they were sitting in two Adirondack chairs. He heard her sniff and knew she was sobbing gently. And then, still clinging tightly to him, she whispered in his ear, "I've never loved anyone as much as you. We truly are connected."

Donnie hugged her in return and time slowed. Everything around them blended into a dull background and the world was just he and Heidi. He'd never felt such a powerful attraction. Sure, he'd felt horny occasionally like any healthy teenage boy, but this was something different. He needed her, had to be part of her, had to be one with her. He had no idea where this feeling came from. They kissed several times, pressing their lips firmly together, passionate open mouth kisses. Then they hugged each other tightly in the chair, and Donnie continued kissing Heidi gently on the side of her head, then her ear and her neck and —

"Ahem. You two know you're getting up early tomorrow, correct?" said Donnie's dad, standing in the front doorway.

The two kids stood sheepishly and went inside. When Heidi was out of earshot Donnie said, "Dad, you interrupted me when I was making my big move."

Robert Langille gave his son a grin and said, "Go to bed, Don Juan!"

MARKED

Louis Ryan had his mark. He'd spent much of the day sitting outside the Langille house in his brown Chevy Impala. He knew which of Langille's friends to use as leverage. He'd need help in controlling the situation, but it shouldn't be any problem to convince Donald to help with getting both he and his associates out of this new 'deep shit' in which they found themselves.

DEFENCE

Half an hour later, Robert saw the light was still on in Donnie's room, so he knocked lightly on the door. "Dad here. Can I come in?"

"Sure." As Robert opened the door, Donnie added, "She's not here, if that's what you're checking."

"Hey, I trust you."

Donnie was lying in bed reading a book under the light of the small side lamp.

"How'd it go earlier today, Sport?" he asked.

"Okay, I guess." Donnie put his book down. "It was pretty tough, Dad. It didn't hit home till I saw the casket and the family, they were so upset." Tears filled his eyes.

"Yes, I can imagine it was difficult. Once again I'm sorry for missing it. Right now, I'm in a precarious position with the company and have to knuckle down and impress management. It's dog eat dog out there. Otherwise, I would have been there to support you." He paused. "And your mother, of course. I have to take another trip tomorrow, I'm afraid, around the southern loop of the province. Yarmouth, Shelburne, Annapolis, New Minas and a few others. I'll be on the road before you wake up and I won't be back till Wednesday evening."

"That's cool Dad, I'll look after things here while you're gone, okay?"

"I know you will son. Come here," Robert said.

Donnie sat up in the bed and they hugged for the third time in four days.

"Take care of yourself and your mother, okay Donnie? Watch out for the other guy," said Robert.

That last phrase was what his dad used to yell to out him, as he watched his son play hockey. But they both knew he wasn't talking hockey this time.

TUESDAY

ERIK SETS A TRAP

Donnie thought the day started out pretty funny. He and Heidi ran into each other going to the bathroom, and she was half-asleep. When she saw him, Heidi put her hand up to her face, turned away and said, "Don't look at me without my makeup!"

"You wear makeup?" he asked. He thought it was a compliment, but for some unknown reason she seemed to be a peeved at his question. *Women!*

The drive in with Madeline was a good time. The two ladies sat in the front and Donnie squeezed into the back. The three friends laughed all the way to Heidi's school, dropped her off and headed to the Emporium.

As this was only his second full workday, Donnie was proud of himself. He was getting used to the job and had set up a system for planting with the help of his homemade work stand.

Madeline was in the adjacent greenhouse, number three today, though she seemed to have various chores all over the Emporium, often in the offices, and the only time they saw each other was at noon. They chose not to go to the lunchroom, and instead ate their meal sitting on a dock leveller at an open door with their legs hanging over the side, much as they would at the Old Fort.

"You know, something's been bugging me, and I meant to ask you on Friday," Donnie said.

Madeline, her mouth full of her mac and cheese lunch, nodded for him to continue.

"Why does this place have a dock? It's not like a barge comes in here and off-loads supplies or anything like that. And that shed? What gives?"

Madeline swallowed her bite and smiled at him. "Mr. Norberg had the shed built about five years ago. It holds a few canoes and life jackets but it's mostly there for the winter storage of a twelve-foot aluminum boat and a 9.9 horsepower outboard. He's an avid fisherman and uses it often in the summer. The boat is moored there now, but you can't see it till you walk on the dock. He brought it out Victoria Day and will store it away again around Labour Day. Come on, we have to get back to work!"

The afternoon progressed uneventfully until around three. The confrontation was planned. Donnie heard his name on the PA system, and the instruction to report to shipping. He should have known.

As he entered into the main building, he stopped by the pop machine for a root beer, having worked up an enormous thirst. He drank most of it as he continued down to the end of the building and rounded the corner to shipping. There was a group of seven fellows, gathered idly in the shipping area. Two were truckers, having a smoke and waiting for the Emporium's workers to deliver the seedlings. One fellow he'd met on his first day, named Graham, gave him a quizzical look, tipping up his chin in a silent question, *why'd they call you over here?* Donnie looked at him and shrugged.

Then he knew. Erik was there grinning his wild grin, in between two friends, leaning against some racks. Bradley, who was the boss of shipping, was taping up a crate. He was giving Erik a disapproving look, but it was clear he wasn't going to interfere in whatever was about to happen.

"There he is, our new ladies' man," Erik exclaimed. He and his two chums applauded sarcastically.

"You want me for something?" Donnie asked.

"Yes. We're here to congratulate you on being the winner of the contest. You win! You're the top man in here. All the women are after you." Then he paused, and said, "Especially the slut you're with now!"

It sounded rehearsed. Donnie decided, being outnumbered, he would play it cool, let Erik ridicule him and the girl he loved, and retreat. Another axiom? Jerks aren't worth a second thought.

Donnie took a moment to gulp down the last of the root beer and set the can on some stacked pallets next to him. "Thanks, anything else?" he said, as blandly as he could.

On his left he saw movement, and casually glanced that way, but it was Graham. He'd put down the box he was carrying and moved closer. He was watching the proceedings carefully, so Donnie figured he might be able to rely on him as peacemaker, or perhaps even an ally.

The three goons just grinned at him, so he turned around and started walking back to Greenhouse Two.

"Yeah, hold on, hold on, there's one more thing,"

Donnie turned around to face him again.

Erik glanced at the guys on either side of him, as if to say *watch this*. "How does it feel to pound a retread? I mean she's totally used goods, man. I mean, I must have fucked that bitch fifty times."

The place went silent. There were seven or so people working in the loading area, and everyone had heard Erik. You could hear a pin drop. The closest men were the two truck drivers, who both dropped their cigarettes. One of them came a few steps closer.

Even Bradley's head snapped up. As far as Donnie could tell, he ran a tight ship and the last thing he needed was the boss's nephew starting a pier six brawl.

Donnie analyzed his situation. Clip's Rule Number One applied here, though in a more sedate manner. His safest move was to walk away. Just turn on his heel and head back to his work bench. He'd be called everything from a coward to a cool customer.

But damn his Scottish and French roots. He was anything but sedate and cool. Donnie's father had been his biggest influence. And into his mind popped another DADism: "Donnie, if you're ever alone and at a disadvantage, two or three against one, try to humour your way out of the situation, and if possible, get one of them on your side … it doesn't always work but it's worth a try." So, Donnie gave it a try.

He looked at the fellow to Erik's right. *Acting 101.* He started smiling at the fellow, then he guffawed a chuckle, then a full-blown laugh, and finally, pretending to get his breath back, he said, "Yeah, yeah, she told me about you …" Donnie made a few more chuckles and *worked* to get himself under control. "Yup, she told me all about you, Erik." He gave a small chuckle and shook his head. "Maybe you can take a few lessons or watch a porn film or something. Find out how a real man does it." And then Donnie stared into Erik's eyes, shaking his head and laughing to himself. *Time to exit stage right.*

Donnie's reply had surprised everyone and the guy to Erik's right burst out laughing. And pretty well everyone joined him. Erik's fury could have started a campfire, and predictably, he launched himself at Donnie, picking up the empty soda can and hurling it his way. Donnie ignored it, let it bounce off his arm, and readied himself for defence. But Bradley and one of the truckers, anticipating the escalation, had raced after Erik, grabbed him from behind, and held him back.

Donnie was seething inside, almost willing the two men to let Erik go. Normally, Donnie was very slow to anger, and he knew from experience that he had a helluva temper if you got him going. But there would be no fight this day. And Donnie honestly felt, without bravado, that Erik was lucky he had used Rule Number One.

He turned around on his heel again and left without looking back, noticing a wink from the smiling Graham. He saw the root beer can on the floor in front of him and picked it up to take with him. Why? Habit, he supposed. He liked a clean workplace.

Not only was Erik a complete asshole; he was a litterbug as well.

EVENING PLANS

After quitting time, Donnie jumped into the Chevelle with Madeline. On their way, they picked up Heidi at Sackville High. She had opted not to work that evening at the Emporium. Donnie mentioned nothing about the confrontation in front of the ladies.

"Hey guys, there's something I want to do tomorrow, so can we leave half an hour earlier in the morning?" Madeline asked.

"Sure," said Heidi, "What's up?"

"Dad's coming home in a few days, and I want to drive the car as much as I can! Can we do the Waverley highway in the morning light?"

"Sure, that'll be nice. See you then."

Heidi was looking forward to spending this evening with Donnie. Though she'd given him the shell last night, she had another gift for him. But as the two walked up the front lane, Donnie said, "Heidi, I forgot to mention I'm heading out to play hockey tonight." He played every Tuesday night, but circumstances the past week had caused it to slip his mind.

"When do you get back from the rink?" Heidi asked.

"Around nine-thirty. I'd ask you to come but there are no seats at the arena, and you'd be standing for two hours!"

"Okay. I'll be waiting for you."

He was getting dressed to head over for the hockey game when he threw his wallet onto the dresser — except he missed, and it fell on the floor. As he picked it up, he noticed a piece of white paper poking its way out of the wallet. It was Hick's business card.

As he was pushing it down into the wallet, it crossed Donnie's mind that he'd been a bit complacent in his life and he could still be in danger. As would those around him. It had only been six days since Mr. Martin's store and already he was sixteen and invincible, but it would be good to give it to someone else just in case.

A few minutes before Peter and his dad came by to pick him up, he stopped by the spare bedroom and gave Heidi Hick's card. "Just to be sure Heidi, keep it on your person at all times, not just in your purse or wallet."

"Yes, I will Donnie. But what if you need this card more than I do?"

"If I need those guys, I can always call the emergency number, 4103 for fire and ambulance and 4105 for the cops. You know that right?"

She laughed, "What? Do I look stupid?" She slipped the card into her jeans pocket.

"The important part is Constable Hick's number is on the back. He's a good person to know if you are ever in trouble. Love you!"

Donnie ran down the stairs as a car horn tooted outside. He gave his mother a kiss on the cheek and ran for the door. Jane laughed at him and called out, "Good luck, and be careful!"

A JOB

The phone was ringing in the shipper's office and Bradley trotted in to answer it. "Hello."

"I have a job tomorrow and require one of your men."

It was Ryan. Bradley tensed. "And you want me? No can do. I have to be here tomorrow."

"Well, who do you have available?"

"Erik's all I've got but, he has to go into town tomorrow morning," said Bradley.

"Yes, I'm fully aware of his duties ... and his limitations. Are you sure there's no one else?"

"Sorry man, no."

"Well, alright; it'll have to be Erik then. I trust Mr. Norberg has told you that as a representative of your premier supplying company, I am to be given your full assistance and cooperation, correct?"

Bradley sighed. "Yup."

"Good. Tell Erik I will pick him up on Rocky Lake Drive in front of the Emporium at 6:00 am. And tell him NOT to be late."

PRIORITIES

Donnie's team got their asses kicked. The Eastern Passage arena had a seating capacity for exactly zero fans. It was a utility arena, meaning instead of a thousand seats or several rows of bleachers surrounding the ice rink, there was just a three-foot-wide walkway. Just as well, as any fans would have booed Donnie's team straight out the end doors. It cost fifty dollars an hour to rent the arena, and thirty players from both teams played for two hours.

They were part of an informal league of fifteen to eighteen-year-olds. There were referees, usually somebody's dad, and the biggest rule was no body checking or fighting. Their team's sponsor, Vaughan Construction, had donated a green uniform with a white stripe; and for a crest, a highly imaginative combination of the two block letters **VC**. An unknown player on one of the other teams in the league gave their team the nickname *Charlie*. With the Vietnam war coming to a negotiated end in 1973, *Charlie* was on everyone's mind.

Natty played on right wing, Peter at centre, and Clip and Donnie on defence. Where they could, they played as one unit on their team, picking up a random left winger for each game. If any of them scored, they congratulated each other; if they were scored against, they shrugged. They had seen plenty of players on other teams who would be calling out other members of their own team for making mistakes. Players blaming each other caused hard feelings and took the fun out of it. The four friends loved playing hockey, but nothing that happened on the ice, good or bad, was worth a tinker's damn, so why make a big deal out of it? It was a great lesson in priorities. Mind you, if they were making a hundred thousand in the NHL, maybe then.

They lost 7-4, shook hands with the other team, and said "Good game" to the winners, who were sponsored by Pictou International Steel. The crest on their jerseys was **PIS**.

A PATCH OF GROUND

Heidi walked into the living room with an open bottle of Canada Dry ginger ale and sat alone on the couch, waiting for Donnie to return from his hockey game. *Boys and hockey.* She wished Donnie had skipped his game this evening. For one week he had been back in her life and now he was off with the boys. She felt a pang of irrational jealousy and tried to push it away.

This was the last night she would be staying with the Langilles, and she wanted to spend the evening with her guy. The Langilles were great people and treated her like they'd known her all her life. And now settled with her aunt, Heidi felt so full of hope for the future.

"Bored already?" Jane asked, as she came into the living room.

"At least I have my ginger ale to comfort me, Mrs. Langille," replied Heidi.

Jane smiled. "Don't feel picked on dear. Being a hockey widow is multi-generational."

"You mean you and Mr. Langille ..."

"Oh yes. By the time Donnie was born, I never saw my husband on a Saturday night. Just like his son, Robert was out playing with the boys. So? What are you going to do for the next ninety minutes?"

"I found a book in Donnie's bookshelf," said Heidi. "*Watership Down*"

"I've heard Donnie mention it, though I haven't read it," said Jane.

"I was halfway through my copy when I left Liverpool. I supposed it's still there."

They were silent for a few moments.

"Well, I'll be upstairs doing some chores, call to me if you need anything."

"Thanks, Mrs. Langille."

She watched as Donnie's mother jogged up the stairs. *A normal home with a loving mother.* She could truly say that, since January, and for the first time in several years, she was looking forward to getting up every day. In fact, she was happier than she could ever remember.

She marvelled at the life Donnie lived and again she wondered if he knew how lucky he was. Not one but three best friends, four if you count Madeline. They each seemed to have caring, tolerant parents. And each family seemed to have the same innate sense of decency and fairness about them. Before coming here in January, she could count the number of decent people she'd met in her life on one hand, and yet everyone in Donnie's circle seemed to be this way. Maybe it was Dartmouth. They all loved this city. They wouldn't live anywhere else.

Heidi took a sip of her ginger ale and thought about it. How many times when she was a little girl living across the harbour in Halifax, had she heard people say they'd rather die than live in Dartmouth? And she remembered Donnie telling her about his sister Anita, whose statement about moving to Dartmouth, *a patch of ground holding up the other end of the bridge*, summed up what those same people thought.

Yet in just one week in this *patch of ground*, she had met people of the best quality in her young life so far. Welcoming people with an inherent universal motto: *who am I to judge?* People who were not happy unless you were happy too. People with the energy and desire to create that happiness if required.

There was something she hadn't mentioned to anyone, even Donnie. As far as Heidi knew, only her aunt was aware that she was seeing a psychiatrist. It had been a condition of Aunt Tillie taking custody of her. A court ordered six-month stint for counselling after such a traumatic event in this fifteen-year-old girl's life in Liverpool.

Her psychiatrist in Bedford called it a three-strike depression, with the death of her mother, the absence of a protector in her brother, and the attempted rape, being enough to bring down the toughest person out there, let alone a girl barely into her teens. Loss, isolation and violence. Add to that the sporadic support she received at home for most of her life before that.

But her therapist had applauded her for rebounding with her aunt's help, and in acting for the most part, in an unusually adult and independent manner. That was all well and good, but she reminded

Heidi in their session last week that, now that she had this stability, she should not be afraid to seek out new friends and try trusting those friends. She had to get back to being a carefree teenager again.

Heidi wondered what her therapist would say when she told her she went from zero to five friends in about half a day! Especially Madeline. *What would I have done without Madeline?*

OLD SPICE

Peter's dad had driven them over to the rink in his station wagon. Mr. Meijer read a book while they played and then drove them home, dropping Donnie off at nine-fifteen.

When he came into the living room, Heidi was sitting on the couch. She jumped up and they greeted each other, but he stepped back from a hug. "Sorry Heidi, no showers at the rink, I'll be back in ten minutes."

When he came back down, reeking of his father's Old Spice soap, he joined her on the couch. They snuggled for a while, discussing their day. Eventually she reached over and grabbed a small bag on the coffee table. Pulling out a small, wrapped box, she gave it to him and said softly, "Happy sixteenth, Donnie."

"Wow. Thank you." He kissed her, which got a bit heated. But not too much, with his mother puttering around upstairs. Donnie unwrapped the gift and discovered a Timex box. He looked at her and they shared a laugh.

"Aren't I always on time?"

Heidi smiled. "Mostly, you are. But I gave you a watch so you will stop driving your friends crazy! Look on the back of the watch, Donnie."

Etched next to the *Made in Great Britain* stamp in tiny letters was *Love HF 1973.*

"Sweetest gift ever." Donnie loved it and put it on immediately. It was a standard, tough Timex, black face with 24-hour clock numbers, *Water Resistant* printed below the hands, and *Great Britain* printed under the numbers 6 and 18. It had a steel wristband. It was a heavy, robust watch, or as his mother would call it, substantial. He knew it was an expensive gift for someone in Heidi's position to buy.

As he admired the gift on his wrist, he started what he had planned to say. "Look Heidi, I know that you and I happened incredibly fast. It's only been three days and it feels like I've known you forever. But at the same time, I know there's a lot about each other that we haven't discovered yet. I just want you to know that I'm looking forward to getting to know everything about you. And I hope you feel the same. But you have every right to hold onto anything from the past that you consider private. As do I. I guess what I'm saying is whatever's in our past, can stay in the past."

Satisfied with his speech, he looked at her, but she was frowning.

"So, like, do you have a kid or something?" Heidi asked.

"What?" he asked. "No! I mean you know I haven't ever been ..."

"Well, you seem to want to keep me from knowing things in your past. I don't know what? Do you have a record, or are you missing your private parts?"

Heidi was saying this without humour, which scared the shit out of him. He just wanted her to know that her past was hers alone and nobody, not even Donnie, needed to know anything about it. "I'm ... just ... saying that ... no there's nothing on my side ... I was just ..."

"Good night, Donnie." Off she went to the spare room, without a hug or kiss. It was going to be another long night for him.

WEDNESDAY MORNING

THE MEIJER'S HOUSE

Of course, it was the 13th. What other date could it be?

For the second time in just four days, Donnie had made a royal mess with his brand-new girlfriend. He didn't have a lot of experience with the opposite sex but had noticed that every girl his age seemed to be so much more mature and self-confident than him. This was certainly the case with Heidi. He spent a sleepless night trying to figure out what to say to her. In trying to reassure her that her past life was no business of his, he had chosen a clumsy path for his words and now had to make amends somehow.

In the morning, to facilitate a chance to make an apology for his grievous transgressions, the exact nature of which remained a mystery to him, he suggested to Heidi that they wait on the sidewalk for their lift to arrive.

They stood quietly for a few minutes. Donnie was unsure how to begin. He heard the phone in the house ring twice. His mom must have answered. Maybe Madeline was going to be late? Or early? He'd better talk. "Heidi, I just wanted to say —"

"There's Madeline. Gosh, she's early!" said Heidi.

Madeline came racing down the street, the Chevelle's powerful rumble announcing her arrival to nearby houses. It looked like he'd have to wait till this afternoon, when Heidi arrived at work, to make his apology.

Donnie opened the front passenger door for he and Heidi and had one foot inside the car when his mom called to him from the front door of the house and asked him to wait. She walked out to the sidewalk with a message for Donnie.

"That was Mrs. Meijer on the phone. She wants to know if you can pop over to their house and help Peter and his father move some furniture they bought yesterday. She said Dirk would then drive Peter to school in his station wagon and drop you off at the Emporium."

If he'd thought about it, Donnie might have found the request strange, but he was distracted with missing his chance to apologize to Heidi.

"What? Yeah sure, of course," he stammered.

He touched Heidi's arm, and she gave him a brilliant smile, which calmed every worry in his body. Then he watched as the girls drove off.

"That's good, because I already told her you'd be right up," said his mom. "I'm going shopping soon and will probably be out for the whole day. What are the bus numbers to get to the Halifax Shopping Centre again?" Jane usually had Robert drive her.

"You'll be jumping on the Number II up at the bridge, then transferring to the Number I at the stone wall by City Hall on Barrington. It'll take you to the Halifax Shopping Centre."

"Thanks. I might be a bit late getting home, maybe even around eight. I'm going to Simpson's and the Bayers Road Shopping Centre as well, and on the way back there are things I need to get from Woolworth's in Scotia Square. Maybe you could hang around with one of your buddies, just in case."

"Already taken care of!" he replied. "Peter's coming over straight after school. When I see him in a few minutes, I'll tell him to plan on staying with us for supper, okay?"

"Of course." She ruffled his hair. "Always the planner! You better not keep the Meijers waiting."

Donnie kissed his mom's cheek, then grabbed his ten-speed bike from the back yard. As he rode down Windmill Road, then up Jamieson Street and onto the Rosedale Drive extension, Donnie was feeling happy and optimistic about the future. It was a sunny, warm day, and he had an inner voice telling him everything was going to work out between Heidi and himself.

He opened the gate on the Meijer's white picket fence, and noticed two pickets were missing. Drunks from the nearby bar were always kicking the pickets off, just for fun. Donnie rolled his bike into the yard and leaned it against the fence. As usual when arriving at Peter's house, he knocked twice at the front door, walked in, and turned into the living room. He was shoved from the side, punched in his back, and pushed down to the floor.

As he pitched forward, Donnie had a vague impression of Mr. and Mrs. Meijer sitting on the living room couch. He was falling straight for the wooden coffee table but lifted his hands at the last second, so as to shove it out of the way. Then he landed face-first on the carpeted floor. He was pushing himself up when he was kicked from the side in the ribs, and that one hurt.

"Enough!" said a voice from across the room. Donnie recognized that voice. *Louis Ryan.*

ON THE ROAD TO WORK AND SCHOOL

Waverley Road wound its way along Lake Charles in a series of curves and hundreds of small twelve-to-twenty-foot swells. Madeline's Chevelle easily navigated these, hugging the asphalt tightly. The tires barely squealed. The early morning sun shone into the car in a staccato of light, having first passed through the fresh, early-summer green leaves of the surrounding trees. As they came closer to the turnoff to Rocky Lake Drive, more and more homes and cottages dotted each side of the road, especially on the lake side.

Heidi enjoyed the drive and was sorry that next week, with

Madeline's dad back in town, she and her friends would have to find another way to their destinations. The bus, of course. *Ugghh!*

As Madeline dropped her off, Heidi smiled and remarked, "There are quicker ways to Sackville High, Madeline."

"Yes, I know, but I love that drive, especially at this time in the morning. Have a great day. I'll see you after school, Heidi."

"No, you'll see me at noon. I have no classes after eleven this morning, so I might as well come into work early and get rich."

Madeline smiled and then got serious. "Before I go, did you hear what happened yesterday in the main building? Graham called me last night. He thought you should know."

"No, what happened?"

"Erik tried to goad Donnie into fighting him," Madeline explained.

"Oh my God, poor Donnie. He never said a word last night. What did Eric do?"

Madeline paused a few seconds, "Heidi, Erik said some very unflattering things about you."

"I guess I'm not surprised. He's a pig. I suppose he called me a whore or something like that?" asked Heidi.

"Well, he apparently said you and he had sex many times and he asked Donnie how he liked his 'used goods' or something to that effect."

Heidi closed her eyes for a moment. "Jesus, how does someone that depraved even get born? What did Donnie do?"

"Apparently, he laughed in Erik's face and walked away. Don't worry about Donnie, my dear. He's a strong, solid guy and he'd probably clobber that asshole. I would be more afraid for Erik's wellbeing if they ever got in a fight." Madeline said it to reassure her friend but couldn't help feeling that Erik had turned out to be a very dangerous fellow.

"Donnie said some things to me last night. They didn't make any sense. But I think I understand now why he said them." Heidi shook her head. "I was in a bad mood last night for some silly reason. I'll talk to him, if not today at work, then definitely tonight, and straighten everything out. But it'll have to be over the phone. I miss my Auntie!"

ONE O'CLOCK DEADLINE

"Sorry Donald, for contacting you this way. But we are a bit pressed for time and I need you to act now."

Donnie was back on his feet and looking around the Meijer's living room for the first time. Peter's parents, Dirk and Engele, huddled together on the love seat. Beside them, in the big chair was Peter, looking scared but angry as well. He had a red left eye that was going to be a helluva black left eye in a little while.

In front of Donnie was Louis Ryan, pastel blue shirt open at the collar, brown cotton pants, expensive-looking tan leather shoes. He had a ring on his wedding finger, but it wasn't a wedding ring. It was gold with a black stone and a small silver star in the middle. He had a watch on his right wrist. Donnie had one on his left wrist. Ryan's was slightly more expensive.

Ryan sat on one end of the chesterfield, legs crossed with a grey automatic handgun in his left hand, a Beretta or some such, like Donnie had seen on TV. It was pointed at the floor but bobbed gently back and forth as he spoke to Donnie. And he looked different than when Donnie last saw him in Mr. Martin's store because he was wearing his thick eyeglasses and a pair of thin leather driving gloves.

Then Donnie heard a voice from behind him. "Langille? Oh man, this day just got a whole lot better!"

He knew that voice as well and confirmed its owner when he looked behind and saw that grinning freak Erik with a look of triumph on his face. He also had a pair of thin leather driving gloves on his hands, one of which had another handgun pointed straight at Donnie's head. It was Erik who gave him the shove, the punch in the back, and the kick in the ribs that hurt like hell, but right now he barely felt it.

Donnie realized Erik and Ryan were connected, and that the cops and he had completely underestimated how dangerous a situation he was in. Ryan could have killed him whenever he wanted to this past week. He despaired at how ignorant he'd been of the real danger, but tried not to show anything.

Ryan frowned at Erik's reaction and asked, "You two are acquainted?"

"This asshole just started a summer job at the Emporium," said Erik. He had dried blood at the left corner of his mouth. Evidence that someone, probably Peter, had put up a good struggle before he was subdued.

"Really?" Ryan shook his head. "This could have been so much less complicated if I had known that. But it makes no difference now." He turned to Donnie. "Let me explain Donald. I'm quite capable of looking after myself, but with this many people, I needed an associate. Hence Erik here."

Donnie turned his back on Erik to look at Ryan as he continued. "I can also see you are afraid for your friend and his parents. This is good. I really wanted to use your girlfriend. Pretty little thing, isn't she? But she has been staying at your home these past few nights, and to use a simile, your house is like Fort Knox. Every policeman in the city takes a jaunt past your residence at the most unexpected times. Amazing really. But very dangerous for me, so here we are with the Meijers."

"How did you find me?" Donnie asked.

"*You* told me where you lived, Donald. In the store when we first met, don't you remember? I asked you where you were from and you answered something to the effect of 'Dartmouth born and bred, a few miles away on Windmill Road' and you were even kind enough to point in the correct direction."

Donnie remembered telling him that. He closed his eyes for a second as it reminded him how clueless and careless he had been. He forgot to tell the police that part of their conversation in the store. *Lord Jesus, how stupid could I be*? Ryan hadn't left town at all, and he knew exactly where Donnie lived all along.

Ryan confirmed it. "All I had to do was drive up and down Windmill Road a few times. I eventually caught a glimpse of you mowing the lawn on the day after we met. After that, it was a simple matter to follow your various friends and note where they lived. I shall cut to the chase. Because of your unique relationship with the local police as their star witness, in their search for me, ironically, we need you to do a little job for us. We want you to steal two pieces of evidence from the Dartmouth Police Station concerning the case you are now involved in. Are you following?"

Donnie was barely listening; it was like a bad dream. But when Ryan used the word steal, it finally sank in and he nearly fainted. He got lightheaded and had to steady himself. "What?! Wait, that's *impossible* ... how would I even begin to do something like that?" he exclaimed.

Ryan continued as if he hadn't spoken. "You simply tell them you want to see the evidence, wait until you are alone, and steal it."

"Are you nuts? They said they were going to file it away today, no one will be able to get to it."

"They are filing it away tonight, at approximately 1930 hours, so you have the entire day. But you must come up with a believable story that will get you next to the evidence."

How does he know that? The question jumped into Donnie's head.

"Donald, people's lives are in your hands. They have a chance of life if you give this a try for us. Otherwise, we can do a lot of damage, my friend. Your other friends and their families, your mother and father. Your girlfriend and her mother."

Donnie was terrified now. The weight of the world had just smashed on top of him.

"I'm so sorry, Donnie," said Mrs. Meijer. She was crying softly.

Ryan could see what he had done to Donnie, how he had made him realize the consequences if he didn't accomplish this task.

"As I said, Donald, we need you to steal two items of evidence, and replace them with these." He nodded to Erik, who handed Donnie a small plastic bag with an exact duplicate of the DIK courier label and its carbon copy sheet which Heidi had identified amongst the items of evidence from the crime scene. They were even torn in the exact same place and manner.

Donnie had to know. "Why would I replace these two items with the exact same items?"

"Why Donald," Ryan explained, "these items don't have a thumb print on them."

A thumb print — the killer's thumb print.

"How am I supposed to do this?" he asked weakly.

"You've already been asked by the police to come back in case you remember something, so use that opportunity to see the evidence, make the switch," suggested Ryan.

How did he know that too? "What's to stop me from talking to the cops?"

"Well, my friend," Ryan began, "we will know if you do, and then someone close to you dies."

"You will know if I talk to the cops," and Donnie finally understood. "You have a policeman on your payroll."

Ryan smiled like a teacher pleased with his student. "How do you think we knew there was a fingerprint, something not released to the public?"

"Well, why can't your inside guy do it?"

"Apparently, your local police aren't the dolts most people make them out to be. They have set up an evidence chain of command and sealed the evidence away in a room with one key. The room is guarded at all times. The lights are on twenty-four hours and the room has windows so personnel can see into the room from everywhere in the squad room. Only three people are allowed in the room and anyone else must be accompanied by one of those three and they are never left alone with the evidence. They have photographs of the thumb print already stored with the RCMP in Halifax, of course, but we have that problem already covered. The pictures will soon meet with an unexpected accident."

Ryan looked at his watch. "You have until one this afternoon. If not completed, someone will die. If we hear or see any sign of the police, someone dies. And if you get caught, well ..."

"When I get the items, what do I do with them?"

"Bring them back here my boy, right here."

Donnie looked at his new Timex. *1:00 pm. Four hours.* Heidi giving him his new watch last night leaped into his thoughts. Never will a single gift figure so importantly in his life.

"Yes, check your watch, Donald," said Ryan. "As they say, the clock is ticking."

"Okay, okay." It came out of Donnie a little whiny. His mind started to swirl, and he thought he might faint there and then. But he took a huge breath, forced himself to stand up straight, and said, "Okay, I'll do it."

Ryan slapped his knee with his free hand and stood up. "Excellent!"

Donnie looked at Peter. "I'll see you soon, man. Take care of your folks."

Peter nodded back and attempted a smile.

"Goot luck Donald. Goat be wit you," said Mr. Meijer, in a thick Dutch accent.

"Shut up, you dumb fuck," growled Erik. He pointed the handgun at Peter's father with that sick grin.

Ryan walked over and pushed the gun down. "Don't ever let me see you do something like that again."

Erik turned red. Obviously he had that in common with Donnie — he was embarrassed to be talked to in such a manner in front of everyone. But he was also very scared of Ryan, that was obvious. With his ego thus bruised, he turned his attention back to Donnie.

"Come on asshole, you heard the man, time's ticking away." Erik grabbed the back of Donnie's shirt and pulled him off balance towards the door. Donnie shrugged him off and started to leave, but Erik wasn't finished, and he shoved Donnie a second time towards the door.

And Donnie had had enough of this horrible excuse for a human being. *Amendment Two A. Never let a bully win.* He stopped walking.

As Erik shoved him the third time, Donnie bent over at the waist slightly and glanced back. He saw Erik was holding the gun at his side, pointed at the floor. Staying bent over, he pivoted 180 degrees on his left heel, and threw out his right hand, palm first, straight into his adversary's solar plexus.

Erik dropped like a bag of hockey pucks on the carpet, wheezing and retching. The gun fell from his hand and landed at Donnie's feet with a ca-thunk. It was grey metal with a black handgrip and looked menacing and powerful. The panic he felt a few moments ago was now hovering at the back of his mind and he was thinking clearly, despite rage and hatred. He stared at the gun for a few moments then glanced at Louis Ryan.

Ryan was still sitting in the same position, right leg crossed over his left, arms folded, his gun held loosely in his left hand. He had watched the scene with a look of interest, almost fascination. Donnie looked down again at the Beretta at his feet. His dad had taken him shooting at the rifle range with a .303 a few times, and he knew next to nothing about handguns. But he did know one thing. Erik's gun wasn't loaded.

He knew it as sure as sunlight. Donnie thought of the carefree way Ryan had pushed the gun downwards in Erik's hand a few moments ago, and knew it *had* to be unloaded. Donnie was pretty sure he could pick up the gun at his feet and do a hula dance and Ryan wouldn't have cared. With that in mind he very slowly put his foot next to the gun and kicked it, or tried to. It was heavier than he expected, and it only travelled a foot or so. He kicked it again and sent it tumbling into the far corner of the room, as far away from the retching hulk at his feet as he could get it.

Then he looked at Ryan and mumbled quietly, "You need a better helper."

He crossed the room and was out the door. Outside, as he cooled down, the panic returned with a vengeance.

Ryan watched Donnie leave and then looked at Erik, still incapacitated on the floor. "Hmm," he said to no one in particular. Then he walked over to pick up the empty Beretta in the corner, tucked it into his belt and, turning to look at the Meijers, asked, "Anyone hungry?"

PANIC AND A PLAN

Donnie walked his bike away from the Meier's house. He didn't think he could ride it. Every step he took, his knees threatened to buckle. There were fuzzies in his eyes and he wondered if this was what high blood pressure felt like. He realized he'd better sit and try to calm down, or he was going to faint. He wanted to roll over, he wanted to sleep the day away. He had a sensation like he wasn't really there, sort of a slow-motion panic. And nausea. Donnie wanted his mother or father to come and take this horrible burden away from him. But he was on his own ... on his own ...

He sat on a grassy area attached to the curb in front of a parking lot, about a quarter mile from the Meijer's house on Rosedale Drive. Ryan's calm voice on the consequences echoed. *Your friends, family, Heidi, somebody dies.* He could feel every single tick made by his new gift, each one sinking him deeper into panic.

And suddenly, Mr. Martin's voice came to Donnie. The old fellow was talking about World War One and how, at an age not much older than Donnie, he had reacted to orders that seemed overwhelming and impossible. Bombs exploding dreadfully close, bullets passing literally through his clothes. His words echoed loudly in Donnie's mind: *Donnie, you wouldn't survive long if you panicked. When you were given a job that seemed impossible, what you had to do was divide the job into segments. Get each one done, move to the next. You don't worry about the next segment till its time comes. Forget about the fracas around you, keep your head down and just get started. And don't hurry, be steady and deliberate.*

So, he needed to break the job down into several tasks and solve or finish them one at a time. Simplify everything. Donnie focused on the steps. Get an accomplice. Get some emergency cash. Get into the police station. Switch the items. Get out. Then, if by some miracle, he managed to get back to Peter's place and hand the items over? Would Ryan keep his word? He might have believed it, if not for Erik. Someone who's word was worthless. And if instead he called Ryan to make a deal once he had the evidence? *Yeah, right, make a deal with the devil.* He was sure Ryan would cut his losses and people would die. And telling the cops? Out of the question, one of them was in Ryan's pocket. But that was all later. *Put everything else out of your mind and do the tasks, like everything in life, one step at a time.*

Back to the plan. Donnie would need an accomplice but couldn't tell them a thing. He'd have to drag that accomplice out of school somehow, or maybe not, maybe a phone call would do the trick. First, he had to go home and grab some cash. The panic faded a bit as he had focus and a purpose.

Natty or Clip, it had to be one or the other. He road his bike to Dartmouth High School. That decision was made for him as he realized he had no idea which class Natty was in, but Donnie would normally be in the same Geometry class as Clip at this very moment. Donnie walked into the back entrance off Victoria Road, through the main area to a hallway on the right and waited in front of Clip's locker for the bell to ring. Should be five minutes or so.

CALIFORNIA?

Erik sat on the chair in the kitchen, sipping a glass of water, his breath slowing returning to normal. "That fuckin' bastard!" he screeched. "He sucker punched me! The next time I see him, I'm going to waste him!"

Ryan leaned against the kitchen counter, looking at Erik and looking past him at the Meijer family. He had moved them all to the couch to keep an eye on them while he tended to Erik.

"You, my friend, can do as you like. It's a free country, but I suggest you use caution. You completely underestimated your opponent this morning and you paid a painful price. In any other circumstance you might have paid with your life. This boy Donald and his friends, I've been watching them these past few days. They are a tight-knit group. And they may have had some sort of training. He knew exactly how and where to hit you so as to incapacitate you instantly. That's an impressive skill, and it takes practice."

"You're impressed with that asshole?" Erik was angry.

"Think about it. I destroyed his whole sense of wellbeing this morning. Terrified his soul like it has never been in his young life, threatened all that he loves. Upset his world. But he recovered, dropped you to the floor and walked out with his head held high. He gained a little dignity for himself in a hopeless situation, and I can appreciate that effort in anyone. My parents were in Treblinka, you see. 1943." Ryan mused.

"Yeah? Where's that, California, or something?"

Ryan stared at Erik in disgust.

DARTMOUTH HIGH SCHOOL

Clip and Donnie were talking in the hallway next to his classroom door. All the students were supposed to be in the class now.

"Yeah, I understand everything but you're not telling me why!" said Clip.

"I can't tell you why, not yet anyway. I'm kind of desperate here man, I just need you to call the police and keep a cop busy for five minutes."

"And you don't know which cop. Man, this is so screwed up," said Clip.

Tell me about it. "I will around ten-thirty. Then I will call you and tell you how long to wait and who to call and, five minutes man, five minutes."

"Buddy, you look like death warmed over. What kind of trouble are you in?" asked Clip softly.

Donnie shrugged, his hand shaking. Clip gabbed his shoulder roughly and in a quiet voice, "I'll do whatever it takes to help."

If only it were that simple. "Thanks Clip, I've got something to do this morning and everything will be explained to everyone tonight." But who will be doing the explaining, he wondered. "Now you are already late for the next class, get going." Clip looked at him for a few moments, like he wanted to remember the face of his friend. He could sense the danger Donnie was in, but knew his friend was on his own for some reason.

PREPARATIONS

Donnie locked his bike in the backyard. Dad was well down the coast by now on his way to Shelburne and mom, believing he was safe at the Emporium, had already left on her shopping trip. His first instinct had been to get this whole thing over with, as quickly as possible. But he had until one o'clock to get back to the Meijers house, and the voice inside told him not to rush. His first priority was cash. He may only be in his mid-teens, but Donnie already knew the value of money in any situation, especially one as grave as this. *What if something goes wrong and I need a cab?*

He checked everywhere but couldn't find any money in the house. Jeez, even his ceramic sneaker piggybank was practically empty, though he did get some small change as he dumped the contents onto his bed. A quarter, three dimes, two nickels and several pennies. Enough for phone calls or taking the bus.

Donnie considered his options and decided if you need money, go to the source. He locked the house up and then made the twenty-five-minute walk out to his bank near the entrance to Shannon Park, which opened at nine-thirty. It gave him time to think about his vaunted plan. He withdrew thirty dollars, three tens, and stuffed the bills into his front jeans pocket, then murmured, "Money should be the true meaning of 'safety in numbers'!"

He found a payphone on the street near the bank. Pulling the change out of his pocket he grabbed a dime. Clearing his voice and calming down, he called the police station and asked for Rafuse.

"Sorry he's not available at the moment, can I ask who's calling?"

"My name is Donald Langille."

"Donald! My name is Constable Hall. Are you in any trouble?"

"No, no, not at all, Constable."

"That's good. What can I do for you today?"

"Detective Rafuse had mentioned that I could take another look at the evidence if I wanted to?"

"And why would you want to?"

"I think that one of the pieces of evidence, that you guys found outside. Well, it came to me last night ..."

"It came to you last night?"

"Yes, well no, not like that, I was thinking last night that maybe I saw it inside the store."

Silence.

Oh, damn he doesn't believe me. "And if I could get another look at the evidence."

Silence.

He suspects something. Donnie started sweating "Maybe, if I could just see the ..."

Then Donnie heard a faraway voice, "Just get Sergeant Wilson to sign it. He's duty officer for today." Then in a louder voice, "Sorry Donnie, didn't mean to break away there. You were going to come in and look at the evidence? Come in any time before five, O'Byrne will meet you at the door."

Oh, thank God, he was busy with someone else. "Okay thanks." His voice cracked on the word thanks. "I'll be down in an hour or so. Bye." Donnie hung up and he almost threw up — for a second there he thought that the constable was seeing right through him! *Jeez, buddy get a hold of yourself!*

Donnie left the phone booth and walked forty-five minutes downtown. Again, he could have taken the bicycle for this, or even a cab, now that he had money, but Donnie always found that a walk calmed him down and let him think clearer. He needed that time to go over everything in his head to see if there was another alternative he hadn't thought of. There wasn't.

But he did feel a glimmer of hope. Yes, Louis Ryan had him over a barrel and he was a smart guy and very professional, and he had everything meticulously planned in advance. But he got one thing wrong: he thought Aunt Tillie was Heidi's mother.

"He's not perfect," Donnie said out loud. It gave him a small victory in a day of defeats.

There was a pay phone in the main foyer at Dartmouth High, which Clip was supposed to pass by every five minutes starting at

10:45. The reason for this was simple. If a teacher or some other brass saw you standing next to a phone for half an hour, they would order you to class and you wouldn't get near that phone again. Well, it was 10:45, and Donnie was on the payphone just a block away from the cop shop.

He called the foyer number, and busy!

He waited five minutes. Called again, busy again! Was nothing going to work out today? Donnie checked his watch for the umpteenth time. Clip and he had synchronized their watches when they were together earlier. *Thanks again, Heidi.*

The third time he called, Clip picked up on the first ring. "Holy crap!" his friend said, "Mr. Farley was on the phone all this time. What's a teacher doing on the pay phone? They have their own phone in the teacher's lounge."

"Forget Farley, man. Call the police station at 11:00 this morning. No wait, on second thought make it 11:10 okay? Oh hell, you have a dime, right?"

"Jeez Donnie, you know me. I have a girl now, I always have cash on hand!"

Donnie didn't have time for levity. "Ask for Detective O'Byrne. Tell him you have important information about the Martin case. You gotta keep him on the line five minutes. Tell him you think the killer was a yeti or escaped Nazi prisoners or Lizzie Borden or whatever but I gotta have five minutes, ok?"

"Sure, sure ... look Donnie you know I'd do anything for you, but you have to give me a bone here, I have to know why I might be going to juvie for the next decade?"

Donnie thought about it, but he wasn't going to put anybody else in danger. "All I can say is, you'll know everything tonight and what I'm doing is going to help the cops, even if they don't know it yet."

"Gawd. Alright man be careful, and I'll get you the five minutes at 11:10. And it's Captain O'Brian, right?"

"Detective O'Byrne, Detective O'Byrne, okay, okay?"

"Yeah, yeah, yeah, I got it!"

"Talk soon, buddy." And Donnie hung up.

Clip stared at the phone, then he hung up as well. He was pretty sure he heard Donnie tearing up there at the end. By the good God, Clip thought, if I can't help Donnie any other way, he's going to get his five minutes, hell I'll even make it ten minutes ... now what was the cops name? O'Byrne. How to remember? O'Byrne, Byrne, Burn, Burn ... Burn victim that's how I'll remember his name, Detective Burn Victim!

RYAN CHECKS IN

Louis Ryan looked at the family sitting on the couch, under Erik's gun. *Erik!* The stupid fool still didn't know the gun wasn't loaded. Ryan could never give a moron like him any kind lethal weapon. But at least the Meijers still thought the handgun was lethal.

The Langille boy had figured out the gun had no ammunition in seconds. Perhaps he should offer him a job, he mused. He was eager to see if Donnie had followed his orders. Would the police come swarming into the neighbourhood? Or more likely would the boy come back in failure, begging for mercy? So far, two hours and neither had happened.

When he had originated this plan, Ryan originally gave Donald a 10% chance of success. He had assumed the boy would most likely be in handcuffs before the morning was over, and the police would be on their way to the Meijers house in force. But their informant at the police station was watching the events as much as possible, and no warning had been forthcoming. *Donald might just pull it off!* He closed the door to the parlour for privacy and called the Emporium to explain the situation. Bradley answered.

"Bradley, do you know a young man named Donald Langille?"

"Langille? Yeah, he just started working here last Friday."

"Yes well, he's the witness who I am using to gain access to the evidence room."

He listened as Bradley let out an exasperated breath of air. "Are you shitting me? If we had known that we could have handled everything in the Emporium quietly. What a pain in the ass!"

"Yes, the irony of him under your noses these past few days," said Ryan. "If I had checked in, just once at the Emporium. Oh well, spilt milk."

Bradley had no idea what that last phrase meant. Ryan was prone to saying the weirdest stuff.

"But," continued Ryan, "on the other hand, if you had executed the boy, he wouldn't be available now to give us a chance at grabbing the evidence."

"How's that going?" asked Bradley.

"We are holding the course at the moment, but the situation here was nearly a complete disaster!" said Ryan.

"What do you mean a disaster?" asked Bradley.

"Erik turned a simple job last Wednesday into a colossal screw up. And this morning, one week later, he has done the same thing again."

"What? How?"

"He was supposed to pull the ski mask down over his own face and then grab Langille's friend, throw a bag over his head and bundle him into the back of the van. We would then show Langille his bound and gagged friend to get his cooperation. But instead, Erik forgot to pull the ski mask down over his face, then the Meijer boy put up a huge fight and would have bested Erik if I had not interfered. Then the boy's parents got involved when they heard the commotion. We were extremely lucky there were no neighbours about, or at least, none who cared about a fight. Afterward, I had to stop Erik from pistol whipping the boy. But the result is now we have four people who can identify us," explained Ryan.

"And no sign of Langille?" asked Bradley.

"Two hours and not a stir from the police. We are using the Meijer boy's police band radio to monitor them as well and we've heard nothing on it either."

"Well, lets hope it stays that way," said Bradley. He hesitated for a moment. "So, when are you going to make all these people disappear?"

"My job is to advise and assist, Bradley. Tell you boss when you see him that he must clean up his own mess," said Ryan brusquely. "I will send Erik back to the Emporium with this family's station wagon. You will need it to tie up the loose ends. And to that point, I am sending these three hostages to the Emporium, so get one of your people here with a van immediately. I need to get my car off the street so I will park it in their garage in back of this house, while I wait for Donald's return. As far as the Langille boy is concerned, I'll take care of him myself ... if he succeeds, that is! If he doesn't, it could mean the end of your entire operation!"

"I'll tell the boss, but if this plan of yours goes south, we'll have to destroy all the evidence and any witnesses. Then hopefully it'll be a simple matter to weather the storm from the authorities till it all blows over."

"Surely, that will be hard on your boss. And his bottom line?" asked Ryan.

"If we don't clean this up, LaChance will have us drawn and quartered — and that would be *much* harder on all of us. And you too!"

Louis Ryan hung up the phone and chuckled at Bradley's last sentence. *And you too!* "As if LaChance or anyone of you could touch me ... idiots. You have no idea who you're dealing with!" Ryan said, to no one in particular.

OFFICER IN TROUBLE

Donnie was starting to hyperventilate again. He was standing ten feet from the main door of the police station. Jesus, he was about to commit robbery, conspiracy, evidence tampering, and God knows what else. "If they catch me, I won't get out of the clink until I'm sixty ... *and* I won't be able to go to any funerals, so I better not get caught." Donnie was psyching himself up. He took a huge breath and entered.

There was a cop behind the counter who said immediately, "You must be Donald Langille, I'm Constable Hall."

"Nice to meet you," Donnie said awkwardly, then added purely out of habit, "call me Donnie."

Hall didn't seem to hear. He pointed to a chair, and picked up the phone.

Now came the hard part. Donnie looked around the office area and didn't know any of the cops there. No Rafuse, no Fong, no Hicks, which was good. He prayed he had a short wait. Prayers seem to work roughly half the time, and timing was everything. Jennifer stood up from one of the desks and seemed to look right at him. But today he was in the top fifty percent because her concentration was fixed on someone else, and she did not notice him. The last thing he wanted was friendly banter.

O'Byrne strode up from the back, and leaned over the counter. "Donnie, good to see you." Donnie had assumed O'Byrne thought he was an ass, but the detective surprised him by shaking his hand and leading him to the conference room. He could see through the window that the evidence was still on the table, all in plastic bags and labelled. He glanced at his watch. 11:04 am. He had to BS for six minutes. But O'Byrne surprised him again.

"I have to say, Donald, I didn't think you were going to be much help early on." He shook his head. "You were describing the guy too well; you were going over the timeline too perfectly. And in my experience, when we get an eyewitness to a crime, they're the least reliable source. But I must say, almost everything about your descriptions, about what you saw, were right on the money."

"Well ... thanks Detective, that's a nice thing to say. And since we're being honest, that first night I met you, I thought you were the nicest guy on the planet."

O'Byrne chuckled. "Yes, I'm sure you did. So, what's up?"

"Ah, the past few nights I've been thinking that maybe I saw that piece of paper, you know the one Heidi identified as a packing slip, inside Mr. Martin's store."

"The one from the German courier?" asked O'Byrne, as he unlocked the conference room door.

"Yeah! Thing is, I just can't remember where or even when. I know this sounds stupid, but I was thinking that maybe if I had another look at it, or some of the other things you guys found, maybe I could remember something ... is it okay if I just sort of sit here for a little while and concentrate on it?"

O'Byrne shrugged. "Who knows? Sure. Take your time and give it a try. If you can put that item inside the store at the time of the crime, that might be very important."

There was a knock at the door and a cop popped his head in. "Detective, you got a second?"

O'Byrne talked to the officer in a low voice but then asked, "He mentioned the Martin case specifically?" The other cop nodded. O'Byrne turned to Donnie.

"Donnie, I have to take a call and being that this room has extremely sensitive items —"

Oh no, is he going to kick me out?

"— I'm going to have to lock you in, okay?"

A gush of relief. "Yeah sure, that's okay."

"Don't touch anything, and don't steal anything either!" said O'Byrne, possibly in jest.

Donnie gave a nervous chuckle as O'Byrne closed and locked the room. He couldn't believe he had made it even this far. *I may have to revisit this whole atheism thing.*

He could hear the officer talking to O'Byrne in the hall. "I think this guy's fairly young and as far as I could tell, it sounded like he asked for 'Detective Burnvy,' caught himself, then asked for you."

"Burnvy? Great!" muttered O'Byrne, "another crank call." The voices faded.

So far, so good. Donnie was alone and looking at the items right in front of him. He moved around to the other side of the table and sat down so he could look out the window in front of him along the hallway, and the window to his left that looked out over the office. The guys in the office were working. Those who had looked when Donnie entered the room were back at their tasks. However, the guys walking down the hall often looked in the window, and since he couldn't see them coming, they were the bigger danger.

No time to waste. He reached for the first plastic bag with the colour mailing slip and pulled it quickly down into his lap, out of sight. He reached into his pocket but realized he was sweating enough that his hands were damp. Donnie had to wipe them on his pants, then he pulled out the plastic bag from his pocket and switched the items. The thought that he was leaving fingerprints on the bag flashed through his mind, but he dismissed it just as quickly. The consequences if he failed in this task were far more concerning than any jail time. Counting to ten, breathing deep to calm himself, he placed the bag back where it belonged. He paused and waited a few moments then reached out and grabbed the second plastic bag with the piece of carbon copy paper in it, yanking it down into his lap again.

A split second after he did, a uniform cop walked past the hall window, did a double take, and stared at him. Donnie stared back, just a guy sitting with his hands in his lap. The cop tried the doorknob, found it locked and walked into the office area. Donnie watched him talk to another uniform who pointed to O'Byrne, still on the phone. O'Byrne looked up, put his hand over the phone's mouthpiece, said something. The new cop shrugged, took one last look at him. Donnie waved, the cop didn't, and then he walked out of Donnie's line of sight.

Donnie rushed to open the second plastic bag, removed the carbon copy, placed it in his pocket and replaced it with the copy Ryan had given him. Relief flooded through him. He started to close the bag and froze. He felt a presence across the table and looked up into the eyes of Detective Rafuse. He should have felt shocked or stomach sickness or some such malady, but in truth all he could see were his parents, dead at the morgue.

While Donnie had his head down switching the carbon paper, the detective had appeared on the other side of the table. It was as if he had beamed in, *Star Trek* style. Donnie stared at Rafuse for a moment, then continued closing the bag and placed it back where it was supposed to be. Donnie looked out both windows. No one was paying them any attention.

Rafuse looked furious and confused. His mouth was open as if he had forgotten what he wanted to say. He had one hand on his stomach, as if he'd been punched, and the other on the Smith & Wesson .38 on his hip. The detective was on the verge of arresting him and people were going to die. Donnie had to do something. But what?

The air was crackling with tension, but Donnie made a fist with his left hand, put his right hand on top of it and leaning his elbows on the table, supported his chin with his thumbs. A relaxed position.

He had one chance, and if Rafuse was the dirty cop he was already dead, and so was everyone else. He took it.

Donnie looked Rafuse right in the eyes, and with the four fingers of his right hand he started against the back of his left hand. Tap, tap, tap, pause. Tap, tap, tap, pause. Tap, tap, tap, pause. Rafuse tilted his head on an angle as if trying to comprehend what he was doing. His hand dropped off his pistol.

The keys rattled in the door and in walked O'Byrne, shaking his head.

"Friggin' crank calls, man oh man ..." and then he saw Rafuse and Donnie staring at each other.

Rafuse broke eye contact with Donnie and said, "Shane, would you mind stepping outside for a moment."

O'Byrne looked back and forth between Rafuse and Donnie, then shrugged. "Ahh ... yeah sure."

When the door closed, Rafuse grabbed a chair and sat next to Donnie. "Officer needs help, huh? So, you are a cop now Donnie?" Rhetorical question. "Now. I imagine you have a few things you want to say to me. Such as why are you stealing evidence, and who is the cop that needs assistance?"

Donnie's hands were shaking, his face was red, his blood was pounding in his ears, he was sweating profusely. He was a wreck but at least his voice was a tad steady.

"You are!" he exclaimed. "You got a dirty cop on the force."

"Is that right? And who told you that?"

"Louis Ryan."

Rafuse sat back in the chair like he'd been slapped.

"You talked to him?"

"7:30 this morning." he answered.

"Where?"

"Look Detective Rafuse, we can't talk anymore."

"What? Why?"

"Cause the dirty cop might be watching us right now." Donnie could tell that Rafuse wasn't buying it, though he looked out into the squad room for a moment. "You have to let me go."

"With the evidence? Not a chance! Ryan is lying to you son, he's ... just —"

"He knows you have a thumbprint on the packing slip!" Donnie blurted out.

The detective's eyes widened. "Sweet Jesus." He looked down at the table for a moment. "It could be true; we might have a bad one. But it doesn't matter, we already have photographs of the evidence including the thumbprint at the RCMP lab."

"Ryan said he already had that covered."

Absolute silence. Rafuse was astonished. Having someone in the RCMP lab with access to the evidence safe working for Ryan? That was some pretty high-level corruption. "Where is he? Is he picking the items up, or are you delivering them? Where? When do you have to get the items back to him?"

"We can't keep talking! They have to think that we're talking about evidence but if I stay too long, they might get suspicious."

"We can protect you —" Rafuse began.

"It's not just me! It's everyone. Ryan seems to know the name of everybody I love." The last part came out as a whisper, and Donnie was close to full-blown crying.

Realizing Donnie's burden, Rafuse put a hand on his shoulder but then looked out at the room of cops through the window. The wrong person might be watching. He snatched his hand back.

"Detective Rafuse, I have to go. I don't know who he's going to kill, but if they know I'm talking to you right now, they're dead already." Donnie stared at Rafuse, who looked like he finally realized the toll this was taking on the boy. "Detective, in ten minutes time I'll tell you as much as I can in Dillman Park, or better yet, at the back of the park in the old cemetery, off Park Avenue."

"By the iron gate?" Rafuse nodded his head, took a deep breath and, despite a career of not making rash decisions, made one anyway. "I'm going to get fired for this. Alright, go. Go right now."

Amid all Donnie's thoughts, all his fears, curiosity popped up unbidden. "How'd you get in here?"

"I was here when you arrived." He nodded toward the large blackboard on wheels parked in the corner. Behind it was a doorway to a tiny room Donnie hadn't noticed before.

"It's supposed to be a small storage room, but we use it as a quiet office when we want to relax. Sure as hell didn't work today. Now get going!"

Donnie walked briskly out the conference room door and nodding goodbye to O'Byrne and Hall, headed out the front entrance. Jennifer was nowhere in sight.

As he watched Donnie exit the front door, Rafuse picked up the phone. He had to make a call to someone he could trust at the RCMP lab to get duplicates made of the photo evidence and a guard put in place — but they'd have to do it without raising attention! Hopefully it was not too late. Lives depended on it.

WE'RE ON OUR OWN

The Dartmouth Public Cemetery butted up against the north-east side of Dillman Park in downtown Dartmouth. It was built on a sloping hill and had great tree cover for any group of people who wanted to have a covert meeting.

With no time to plan anything that might arouse the suspicions of their crooked cop, Rafuse had contacted the two guys he felt he could trust. The same two cops he knew Donnie *would* trust. It was Hick's day off but he was to pick up Fong at the station and the two would arrive here in a few minutes.

When Rafuse arrived in the cemetery, he found a terrified but determined teenager. Donnie was shivering.

"You okay, son?" asked Rafuse.

"I'm fine, I'm fine," said the boy, verging on tears.

Rafuse grabbed his shoulders and said, "Nice deep breaths." And after a few moments the shivering seemed to subside. "Where's Ryan?" asked the detective.

"2012 Rosedale, the extension part that angles up to Victoria Road. That's Peter's home."

"The Meijer's Place? He's holding one of the Meijers?"

Donnie nodded, "He's holding all of them. He and another guy named Erik."

"Erik? Erik who?"

"I can't remember his last name, but he works at the Emporium. He's the boss's nephew."

The Emporium again, thought Rafuse.

"And Ryan doesn't trust him, he gave Erik an unloaded pistol," Donnie continued.

"How do you know it was unloaded?"

"It was just ... he ... Ryan... I just know, okay. I'll explain later." Donnie was getting frustrated. "I have to get these things back to Ryan."

"Absolutely not. We can't intentionally put you in harms way, Donnie, we have to bring your parents into this. You're still classed as a minor. Is your mother home?"

"No, she went shopping over in Halifax today."

"Well, where does your father work?"

"You can't get him either, he's on a sales trip somewhere in Shelburne." Donnie's voice started to rise. "Look, you have to let me go or they're dead." And a sob wracked out of the boy, he couldn't help it.

"Who? The Meijers?" asked Rafuse.

"Like I told you, Ryan rattled off the names of all the people who matter to me —" He stopped when he saw Rafuse look to the street.

A nondescript 1971 two-door Chevy Nova pulled up on Park Lane. Fong jumped out with three police-issue portable radios, followed closely by Hicks.

"What's up, Rick?" asked Fong.

Rafuse quickly explained the situation. There was a moment of shocked silence as they took it all in. Hicks said finally, "But surely we aren't considering letting Donnie go in there alone?"

"You have to. What are you going to do, save me and have three or four others killed under your nose?" Donnie asked. "We know he has three at least people, how do we know he hasn't got anyone else?"

"And you say he's not alone. This Erik, can you remember a last name?" asked Hicks.

"No but he is some kind of relation to our boss at the Emporium, Mr. Norberg."

"Son? Nephew?"

"Sorry, I just can't remember. It's been a shit of a day." *Understatement of the century.*

"We'll figure it out," said Rafuse.

"The big point here is, we can't trust anyone else," Fong said, shaking his head in disbelief.

"Look guys, it's almost one o'clock, I just want to get this over with, okay?" Donnie said plaintively.

"Out of the mouth of babes ... I'm going to get fired for this. Did I mention that?" Rafuse paused to take a deep breath. "Do you know which vehicle is theirs?"

Donnie shook his head.

"Well, they must have one, and if they put the four of you in a car, we'll follow them and find out what their destination is. Hopefully, it's their home base. *But,* if at any time something looks wrong, we're coming in to get you." Rafuse shook his head, "Damn I wish we had time for a wire. And giving Donnie a radio is out of the question." He put his hand on the boy's shoulder, "We'll be a couple hundred feet away beside Notting Park School son and we'll be there in seconds if need be." Rafuse thought for a moment, "Donnie, what kind of car do the Meijers have?"

"A big green Pontiac station wagon. I gotta go." He took a deep breath to calm himself, shook the hands of the three cops, and off he went.

Fong, shaking his head, watched Donnie walk towards the unknown. "You sure he's only sixteen?"

When the boy was out of earshot, Hicks turned to Rafuse. "Boss, there's three of us, all armed. If I can get around the back of the house, I could cause a distraction to bring them towards me, meanwhile you and Fong hit the front."

"We can't risk it. We're not experts in this kind of thing, and from what Donnie has said, this situation is knee-deep in high-level corruption, right up to RCMP headquarters. We have to take this one step at a time."

"In other words, guys," said Fong, looking back and forth between Rafuse and Hicks, "we're on our own."

RYAN MAKES A PROMISE

Donnie opened the gate of the white picket fence, knocked twice on the door, and entered, as per his usual habit for Peter's house. Ryan was sitting in the same spot on the couch, in the same position, legs crossed, gun held loosely in his gloved left hand, looking like he had never moved. But he was alone.

"So, Donald, success or failure?" Ryan asked.

"Where is everybody?"

Ryan looked angry for a split second. Then he sighed and said, "Why not? They're in a safe location, very much alive. But I would prefer you answer the question now or I will call Erik and tell him to kill the one of his choice. Would you like that?"

The coldness of the statement felt like a punch in the gut. Donnie reached into his pocket and brought forth the two scraps of paper in the plastic bag, throwing it on the living room coffee table.

"Excellent. Would you mind sitting on the other end couch?

Good, now bring you knees to your chest with your feet on the couch. Good, now grab your ankles with your hands. Very good."

He pointed the gun at Donnie, looked him in the eyes, then picked up the two scraps of paper without looking at them. As a hockey player, Donnie appreciated someone who had good peripheral vision.

Ryan stepped over to the kitchen's bright light, pushed the gun under his belt in front, and pulled out a tiny magnifying glass from his pocket. "By the way, if you take either hand off an ankle, I'll kill you where you sit." He studied the carbon copy paper. "Yes that's the one." Donnie thought he'd be satisfied seeing the thumbprint, but then he pulled up the multi-coloured packing slip and examined it as well. "You did an excellent job, Donald. One more duty."

Unlike most of the four boys' parents, Peter's folks didn't smoke and in fact wouldn't allow it in their home. So, Ryan brought a fry pan in from the kitchen and placed it on the coffee table. Then he pulled out a lighter, grabbed the two pieces of paper, and burned them, dropping them in the pan. Apparently just to be sure, he then went to the little two-piece bathroom under the stairs and, while keeping an eye on Donnie holding his ankles, flushed the black cinders down the toilet. He came back and smiled. "Who knows what criminal science would have found in those black shards, mmm?"

Donnie shrugged. He was a weird mobster in that he had a friendly demeanour and was damn near likeable, but at the same time, he left no doubt in his resolve to kill if necessary. Donnie couldn't wrap his head around it. For reasons he didn't understand, he wondered what Ryan's parents were like.

"Alright, time to leave. Come along."

"You're not letting me go?"

"Sorry Donald, that was never part of the agreement. Come along, we're going for a ride."

Donnie couldn't make his feet move. "No" he said, "I will not."

He looked at Donnie and let a big sigh. "You're a brave boy Donald, but I have limited patience."

"If you're going to kill me, do it now. I'm not going to help you again." Donnie was in a weird world. He'd never felt this way before. He was terrified and he felt extreme sadness, but never in his life had everything around him been so clear. Every sound was crisp, every smell was strong, every colour was more brilliant. And for some unknown reason he wasn't shaking. Very weird.

After a long pause, "Yes, Donald I have killed people. But I give you my word you will not be one of them and I will do my best to make sure your friends are released alive as well, okay?"

"Your word? The word of the guy who killed Mr. Martin?"

"I didn't kill Mr. Martin, Donald. I merely cleaned up the crime scene."

No one in their right mind would have believed Louis Ryan, but Donnie clung to his words. At that point it's all he had. And after a moment's hesitation, he walked out the back door.

As they made their way across the backyard to the garage, Donnie's realized that if the three cops were by Notting Park School, they wouldn't be able to see the garage. Mr. Meijer had built the garage in the far corner of the lot, away from Brookside Drive because the land was flatter. As Donnie waited for Ryan to unlock the side door of the building, he pondered the notion of running out onto the street where the cops would see him. But that ugly grey Beretta in Ryan's pocket dissuaded him.

Ryan motioned for him to go into the garage. Inside was a brown Chevy Impala. Donnie noticed the hub caps were big, fancy, and full size. *I wish I'd known about the hub caps earlier.*

"What happened to Mr. Meijers car?" he blurted out.

Ryan ignored his question, "I'm afraid I'll have to ask you to get into the trunk, Donald. Can't have your friends in the police seeing you in the car with me now, can I?"

Donnie started to protest, but Ryan held up a hand and continued. "No, no, don't bother with any denials. You and I both know your chances of success were minimal at best. And I foresaw a possibility that the police might be assisting you currently. I *am* surprised that they gave you the actual evidence though. Well regardless, into the trunk. They no doubt intend on following me so we shall have to frustrate them a bit."

Donnie crawled into the trunk. But something else was on his mind. Who killed Mr. Martin?

FOLLOW THAT CAR

After the they arrived, the three policemen watched Donnie enter the front door of the Meijer's house. There were no vehicles anywhere in sight.

"Maybe Donnie will find the house deserted," suggested Fong.

"Hard to say," said Rafuse checking his watch. "They might be parked down the road. Either way, we'll take them as soon as they leave."

A few minutes passed.

Hicks was watching the house and quickly pulled the binoculars from his eyes. "Oh hell! Car's pulling out from behind the house." He studied the car for a few seconds. "Brown Chevy, one occupant and no sign of Langille. Or anyone else."

"Alright, Hicks, give me the keys, I'm going to follow that car," said Rafuse. As he jumped into the Nova, he said to Hicks and Fong, "You two, check out the house and garage. There's a very good chance that the Meijer family are in there with Donnie and being held hostage by a third party named Erik something, who may or may not be armed with a pistol that may or may not be loaded. Set your radios to channel three so we can communicate privately, but if you need to call for backup, switch back to the station standard." He took a deep breath. "Once I figure out where he's going, I'll radio it in." *I have a pretty good idea where that will be.*

He paused, weighing the responsibility of his next decision, but better to look like a fool than to fool around with lives. "Keith, see the chief in person. We're going to have to risk it and let him know what's going on, and get him to call Inspector Dumas at HARP, tell him he may have to put his unit on standby."

As his men ran over to investigate the Meijer's residence, Rafuse roared down Brookside Avenue in the direction of Windmill Road. He was guessing that the brown Impala had turned right at the fast-approaching intersection. He pulled the radio out of his coat pocket and laid it on the seat next to him.

Rafuse had no idea what would happen next, there were a million variables and unknowns, but he wished he'd kissed his wife when he left for his shift early that morning.

WEDNESDAY AFTERNOON

BURNSIDE INDUSTRIAL PARK

When the Impala first pulled onto the street, Donnie could sense that they made a right turn down Brookside Avenue. He thought maybe he could guesstimate where they were going. But all his attention was spent on surviving the trip. Ryan was driving at speed and, due to Donnie's body-size, he was jammed across the trunk, not front to back. He was bracing his feet and hands against the walls of the trunk to protect his head and prevent him from crashing around loosely in the hot, suffocating space. There were also exhaust fumes which were making him woozy. It seemed to go on for hours but was probably no more than fifteen minutes.

Eventually the car pulled into what Donnie thought was a driveway. He heard the car door open and, a few seconds later, the sound of an overhead door being raised. The car door closed, the car moved about twenty feet, and then the closing of the same overhead door by a chain ratchet system. So, it wasn't a small car garage but a bigger building. They hadn't driven far enough for Bedford or Sackville, so they were some ways along Windmill Road. Maybe two or three miles up the same road on which he lived. His guess was somewhere in the Burnside Industrial Park.

The trunk flew open. "There, that wasn't so bad, was it?" asked Ryan.

Donnie was in a bad way. He grimaced as he pulled himself out of the trunk and Ryan grabbed his arm to steady him. Once again, Donnie was struck by the disconnect of it all. A polite, concerned man who was apparently also a ruthless killer.

Donnie had secretly hoped that Ryan might be undercover for some agency or other. If he was, he was a long way from home. While he had a slight unknown accent, there was a definite European vibe about him, which he had missed other times. Kind of like Clip's mom. But his actions didn't warrant hope that he might be one of the good guys.

"I'm a bit sore but okay," he answered.

"My apologies. I'm fairly certain we were not followed, though."

"Look, I told you I took those pieces of paper, and no one saw me!"

Ryan stared at him, then chuckled. "Never be a politician, you're not made from that mould."

They were in a small warehouse, not much more than an oversized garage. There were two other vehicles, but the space was mostly empty. The building was dark as the lights were off. Donnie guessed the size at about ninety feet by sixty feet with an eighteen-foot-high ceiling. There were four windows near the ceiling and evenly spaced on each of the two long walls. There was a small back room, probably a lunchroom or office.

Ryan guided Donnie there, at gunpoint of course. It was about twenty feet by fifteen feet, but the walls were only ten feet high, and the ceiling of the room was made out of chicken wire and steel angle bars. The walls were smooth, white-painted concrete block. One of the four windows was directly above the room, about five feet higher, out of reach, closed, and locked he assumed. But it was letting in natural light. There was a small eating table with two chairs and an old six-foot couch on one wall.

"What is this place?" Donnie asked. "Some kind of garage or something?"

"It's a utility building owned by the Emporium. I'm using it to hide things that I don't want to be seen or heard. It's quite soundproof. You'll be staying here a few hours. There's a bathroom through that door at the back. And in the cupboard over there are a few snacks and in the small fridge are some soft drinks. Root beer if I heard correctly." *How the hell did he know that?* "Hopefully, I will be the one to come and get you again but if not, I wish you all the best Donald."

"Wait, who killed Mr. Martin?" Donnie demanded.

Ryan paused, looking at the floor, then murmured, "A fool."

He had so many more questions, not the least of which was *Why are you dumping me here? What's going to happen to me?* But Ryan quickly closed the door, locked it, and left. As dangerous as Ryan was, he was smart and polite, and so far, had more or less kept his word. Now that he was gone, a known danger was replaced by the more dangerous unknown.

He heard an engine start. Not the Impala, a smaller car, maybe a four cylinder. The overhead door opened, the car exited, and the big door closed. That was the last thing Donnie heard for the next few hours, except for the pop of a soda bottle or two.

PURSUIT

"Damn. Damn. Damn." Rafuse cursed under his breath. He had caught sight of the brown Chevy Impala in the traffic a few blocks ahead of him, as he raced down Windmill Road. With several leads pointing to the Lake William Plant Emporium, he had assumed Ryan was heading there. But he was surprised to see the car make a right turn onto Wright Avenue, into the Burnside Industrial Park.

The right turn lane opened up in front of him and he hit the gas pedal in the Nova to make up some distance to the Impala. Suddenly an eighteen-wheeler, hauling gas, pulled out of a Texaco station in front of him. He slammed on the brakes and hit the horn, which of course didn't work, so he waved his arm out the window in frustration. The truck driver just gave him the finger; then he stopped the truck and began backing back into the parking lot. Apparently, he was just repositioning the big rig.

By the time Rafuse made the right turn onto Wright, and had driven up and down the street twice, looking down every side street and into every parking lot, it was obvious he had lost the Impala. He had no idea where it could be. He did have one tidbit. As the car moved out of sight beyond the big rig, he was sure he had seen the left turn signal come on. That meant the Impala could have turned into any of the businesses along Wright — or into McCurdy or Borden or even further up, Fielding. He'd done a cursory look at all four possibilities, but there was no sign of the Impala.

He radioed Hicks and Fong, using the pre-arranged channel three, and explained his situation. "What about the house?" asked Rafuse.

"The house and the garage in back are both empty. But we found blood stains in the living room," said Fong.

"A lot?" asked Rafuse.

"Nope, hardly any. You want forensics on it?"

"No, we can't risk the snitch at the station finding out that we're on to them. We'll have to hold off for now. Hicks, grab a cab to Burnside and start canvassing door to door on Wright and its side streets for the brown Impala. All the way up to and including Fielding. Fong, get back to the station and tell the chief as we discussed earlier. Keep an eye on things — and remember, you may be being watched!"

"What are you going to do?" asked Fong.

"I'm heading out to Rocky Lake Drive. We've had our eye on the Emporium since the Freeman girl identified it as a possible source of the courier waybill."

Hicks chimed in. "Okay. Good luck boss, and keep that radio close by."

THE NEXT SILAS

There was no TV in the room, of course. There was not much of anything. He was trying to figure out a way of signalling someone. Outside of the little bathroom, there was no light switch in the room, so he couldn't use Morse code to signal the outside world using the little window fifteen feet up. Besides, outside of SOS, he didn't know Morse code and neither did anyone else in 1973.

For the first time in his life, he had a sense of what prison time was like. He paced around the little room like a caged lab rat, shaking, thinking, worrying. What did Ryan mean when he said that he hoped it would be him who came back to pick him up? Who else might come?

Eventually, he lay down on the ratty old couch to try and relax. He took stock of his overall situation and his possible fate. Mr. Martin was the first person Donnie had known personally who had passed away. Before that, he had no real experience with death ... except for last summer.

Donnie had volunteered at a local animal shelter, mainly cleaning cages and walking the dogs. To their credit, the shelter did as much as possible to save the stray pets, but they had only so much money and space. And so it was, that once or twice a week, they would have to pick an animal or animals to euthanize. He didn't know much about it at the time, but he thought it callous and quite frankly cowardly for these people to kill the animals and not try harder to place them. His disdain for their methods became known.

The vet, Dr. Kellough, decided to have a little talk with him. He found Donnie cleaning the cage of a sweet old beagle named Silas. "Donald, I'm hearing rumblings. Maybe you're disapproving of our policy of euthanizing the animals?" He was an older veterinarian, looking more like a farmer than a doctor. He was in his sixties, with a full head of bushy white hair, glasses, and a bit of a belly.

"It just seems like we're giving up too easy. I just think, well, there's got to be a whole bunch of people looking for a dog or cat and we're not trying hard enough to connect with them."

"It's a nice idea, Donald, but it flies in the face of reality, I'm afraid. For example, you volunteer here on these Sunday mornings, am I correct?" asked the vet.

"Yup, and sometimes I volunteer on a weeknight when you guys get in a bind."

"And believe me when I say, we're very grateful for your help. But we could use you every night. And all weekend if we could get you."

"Oh." Donnie was surprised.

"Donald, almost every one of the people associated with the shelter is a volunteer."

"What about you?" he asked.

Doc smiled. "Especially me, and I have my own practice. In that office we're extremely busy, sometimes with frivolous requests by pet owners. I wish they could see the beautiful animals in this shelter. But they'd rather spend five hundred dollars for a purebred animal with papers. And it turns out that many of those are so in-bred, the poor things have genetic deformities." He shrugged. "It pays the bills. But I put in about five to ten hours a week volunteering, Donald, and just to let you know, I've cleaned my fair share of cages as well. But I have to ask, are you willing to accept an animal from the shelter?"

"Well, if I could convince my parents, sure."

"Excellent. So, what about next month?"

"Next month?"

"Oh yes, my young friend. We would need you, and many other people, to accept an animal every month just to keep up with those that have been abandoned," said Kellough. "Oh, and I'll need your four-year university tuition just to keep this place going for the next month."

"Okay, okay, doc, I get it. Man, it's so jeezily frustrating."

The doctor smiled again. "Tell me about it! Just make sure you keep telling people, spay and neuter, spay and neuter — it really is the kindest thing you can do for the pet population. Can I call you Donnie?"

He smiled back. "For sure. I prefer it."

"Well Donnie, I'm afraid we have to put down Silas today. He's just too old, too arthritic, in constant pain, and has more or less stopped eating. I'd like you to be there when we do it."

"Me! I'm not sure ..." Donnie didn't know if he wanted to watch that.

"I think at a time like this, old Silas would be happy to have all the people who love him nearby."

Donnie agreed, and at the appointed time he went into the lab, and watched as they placed Silas onto an examination table. Everyone, himself included, gave the old dog a scratch behind his ears and on his head. He feebly wagged his tail. For some reason, the old dog pushed himself up into a sitting position. Maybe he sensed something and wanted one last show of dignity.

They put an IV into his right foreleg, with a tube leading up to a bottle of clear fluid. The tube had a little valve on it. A lab tech came over to Silas and wrapped his arms around the old guy hugging him and kissing him on the head, and Donnie could hear him whispering gently to the dog. Maybe saying "Everything's going to be fine boy, just go to sleep." Something like that. The doctor opened the valve. After half a minute, Silas slowly slipped back down into a lying position, then onto his side, and then he was gone.

Donnie was saddened, but was impressed with the care and respect shown, and he had a new appreciation for the people who volunteered with him.

Now, Donnie couldn't help but wonder, when Ryan or whoever came through that door again, would he be another Silas? He tried to think of something else.

He was scared, and also exhausted. Exhausted from fear. Call it meditation or the power of positive thinking or whatever, but he lay on the dirty couch and simply decided that the cops were going to save him. He didn't know who or when, but he did know the next person through that locked door was going to be a cop. It had to be ... it just had to be ...

Cops. Depending on a person's outlook they were the last line of defence against the criminal hoards, or the ruination of a perfectly viable criminal career. They were the good and the bad and the ugly all rolled into one. Donnie thought that all the cops he met in the Dartmouth Police were decent guys. Even O'Byrne. Donnie's opinion that he was a jerk was only coloured by their first meeting last Wednesday. The other few times he met him, O'Byrne was a pretty stand-up fellow. He couldn't complain about any of them. But one of them was a bad egg, a barren seed, a spoiled piece of fruit which had to be plucked out before it spread its rot to others. Hopefully, that wouldn't be the cop who arrived. Donnie almost smiled. It was like the *Serpico* story except in reverse, in that the title character was one honest cop in a sea of dishonesty, while in his situation, the Dartmouth cops were a group of honest hardworking people ... with one exception.

THE LAKE WILLIAM PLANT EMPORIUM

Rafuse pulled the Nova into the angled parking on the side of the Emporium's main building. He sat for a moment to collect himself and prepare for his visit. When he was ready, he turned the radio off and hid it under the front seat.

He left the Nova, went around to the back to the main door of the office, and let himself in. There were three people working at the half-dozen desks in the main office area. He walked up to one of them and showed his badge. "Detective Rafuse, Dartmouth Police. I'd like to see Mr. Norberg please."

"Just a moment, sir," said the worker, who then trotted around the corner into the main warehouse. After a few moments, in walked a man in his fifties, overweight, with a white shirt, black pants, and no tie. White hair surrounded a pink face, and he was smoking a cigarette furiously.

"Mr. Norberg, good to meet you."

"A pleasure, Detective Rafuse. Always willing to help where I can. So, what brings you out to our little business?"

"Just in need of some information."

"We'll go to my office, it's air conditioned."

Norberg's office wasn't in the main office area. The owner of the company had chosen a windowless cubbyhole overlooking the truck loading bays. When they were seated, Rafuse started pleasantly. "I wouldn't call your business little. Yours is one of the biggest plant nurseries in the Maritimes."

"Yes, that's true —" began Norberg.

"You're quite magnanimous as well, sir," said Rafuse, laying on the respect. "You have singlehandedly given your time, your product, and even your money to several other nurseries in need all over the east. Most businessmen would be busy destroying the competition."

"Detective, I learned a long time ago that competition makes everyone stronger. And I have a philosophy that the busier we all are, the stronger our industry will be as a whole. I had to go without money a few times in my life and luckily there was always someone there to help me. No one is successful on their own. I'm just giving back."

"Well said, Mr. Norberg." *And well rehearsed too.* "Would you mind giving me the five-minute history of your company?"

"Not at all Detective, but may I ask why?"

"Yes, of course. We're involved in a case regarding irregularities in shipping charges, involving some of the larger courier companies," explained Rafuse.

"So, you aren't working on the high-profile murder of that poor fellow in your hometown? I would have thought that would been your priority."

Rafuse frowned at Norberg.

"Sorry Detective, I saw the interview you gave to CBC on the weekend."

"Ahh, yes well, we're a small department Mr. Norberg, just two detectives. And one crime doesn't wait for the other to finish. Now just a small history, if you don't mind."

"Certainly. My wife and I first came to Quebec City in 1952 ..." He continued for considerably more than five minutes, and had coffees and a Danish for himself, and his guest, delivered during his history lesson. "... in all three Atlantic provinces." Norberg finished his story at last.

"I'm very impressed Mr. Norberg," said Rafuse. He was. Norberg had not just carved out a life for himself and his wife, he was a definite boon to the community. "And you supply New Brunswick and Prince Edward Island as well? How do you transport the plants inter-provincially?"

"Same as locally, we rent trucks."

"That seems expensive."

"Well, the shipping department decided about three years ago to sell the company vans and work out long-term leasing with the rental companies. Means we don't tie up capital in purchases, and we don't need a garage, or mechanics or van parts storage. On the whole, it's worked out quite well."

"I don't suppose you have time to give me a tour?" asked Rafuse.

"Well, time is money, but how can I say no to one of the very people who protects my business?"

"I understand your nephew works here, an Erik Norberg?" asked Rafuse.

Without missing a beat, Norberg said, "Erik Jorgen, actually, and yes, he does. To be more precise, he's my wife's second cousin but, for all intents and purposes, yes, he's my nephew. Why do you ask?"

"I have a few questions for him on a separate matter."

Norberg frowned. "Concerning?"

"I'm afraid I'm not at liberty to say. It's a confidential matter."

"I see. Well at the moment, I'm afraid I can't help you. He was here all morning but left on a run somewhere, either delivering product or picking up supplies," said Norberg. "I tell you what, let's have a little tour and during it, I'll check his ETA."

"That sounds good."

"Excellent. Let's start with the three greenhouses. Literally nothing happens at the Emporium without them."

Meanwhile, Heidi had arrived at work just before noon, and been working for a while, potting plants as requested, in Greenhouse One. She was wiping soil off her hands with an old towel when the main door swung open and through it walked Detective Rafuse, his eyes exploring every bit of the greenhouse.

Heidi threw the cloth onto the table next to her and started towards the detective with a warm smile. As she neared him, she saw Rafuse's eyes widen in alarm. Mr. Norberg was coming in the door behind him. Rafuse gave a slight shake of his head, and she realized the detective was asking her for anonymity. She said, "Mr. Norberg, if I had known you had guests coming in today, I would have cleaned up around my work area."

"Just a small tour for a new friend, my dear. Heidi Freeman. this is Detective Rafuse, Dartmouth Police."

"Pleased to meet you, Miss Freeman."

"You too, sir. Enjoy your tour." And off the two men went.

Now that's strange, Heidi thought. Rafuse seemed to want to keep their acquaintance private. And speaking of strange, Donnie hadn't come from the other greenhouse to say hello yet. She trotted over to Greenhouse Two but there was no sign of him. His bench hadn't been worked on and his jacket wasn't hanging on the hook behind it. She skipped over to the pay phone in the main building and called Donnie's home number. No answer. *Rafuse being here can't be a coincidence.*

IN THE LOADING DOCK

Total blackness. He could hear someone talking, far away. It was a feeling of being at the bottom of the lake in darkness, so he pushed his way up. It was a struggle, but he wanted to know what the hell had happened and where he was. The last thing he remembered was that he was in the Emporium, walking back to the shipping area with that guy who runs the place ... whatever his name ... *can't remember it.* He was desperate to go back to sleep, but he knew he shouldn't. He soldiered on, trying to see where he was.

His eyes. It was like trying to push open your eyelids after they were stuck shut with glue. He concentrated hard and got his right eye, then his left, opened a crack. It took a few seconds; everything was blurry but eventually he could make out his two hands. One looked normal, the other had polish on the fingernails. He watched stupidly as his hand with the red fingernails started moving of its own volition. Why can't I feel my hand moving, he thought? The hand disappeared above his eyes, he felt a tickle on his head, and suddenly everything got brighter. I think I just pushed hair out of my eyes. Who's hair? Mine of course.

He felt the need to shake his head but when he tried to just lift it there was a blinding white pain, so he relaxed. Everything was coming back in a rush now. He was in the Emporium, walking back into the shipping area from ... somewhere. It was a hot humid place. The greenhouses, of course. He'd been with that rotund fellow ... Norberg. And there was something to his right in one of the offices next to his host's. He had glanced in and saw ... something. Something that shocked him. Right to the core.

And that was when he felt an explosion take place in his head. He saw a million sparks in front of his eyes, and in his ears was a deafening buzz. Then a second, far away, bang. Then darkness until now.

What was it he had seen? Whatever it was, it had explained something that had been eluding him recently, something big. Whatever he saw was right there, just through a flimsy little lace curtain in front of his brain.

He could make out three people at some distance away. The pretty hand that he thought might have been his for a second or two was gone. He could tell he was lying on his side. There was dirty rough plywood against his cheek. Rafuse forced himself up onto his hands even as he cringed at the pain in his head. There was a large pool of blood on the floor where his head had been, so he propped himself on one elbow and felt the back of his head. There was a bloody wound just behind the crown. *Thank God they hit me on the head and not anywhere important.* Then he actually smiled at himself — *at least I still have a sense of humour.*

"How are yew feelink, Detekteef Rafuse?" asked Mr. Meijer. "I vould like to haf rendered assistance, but as you can zee day haf toid us up quite toit."

Wow, thought Rafuse, *here for twenty-five years and they still have a tik Dutch occent. This must be the Meijer family in that house on the corner.*

"I'm a bit the worse for it, I'm afraid. How long have I been here?" His words were slurred, but understandable at least.

"I don't know, ven did day hit you?" asked Meijer.

Okay, let's try this again. "When did they drag me in here?" asked Rafuse.

"Twenty minutes ago. You probably have a pretty serious concussion, and you could be making it worse. Just stay there and relax." The young fellow, obviously Donnie's friend Peter, had said that.

"Am I not tied up like you?"

"No, you're not. I guess these guys figure you're in no shape to go over and beat them all up."

Rafuse let out a big sigh. "Point taken. I think I'll just relax here for a few days."

He pulled himself over to the wall at right angle to the three Meijers, and drew himself up into a sitting position, with his back to the wall. When the pain in his head subsided, he opened his eyes and turned his head gingerly to the right, so all four people were looking in the same direction ... and now he understood. They were in the back of a van, with the two pale overhead lights shining down on them and the back door rolled up. There were several people milling about, but one of them was looking at the back of the van. He threw down his cigarette and walked over to the open door of the shipping office.

"He's awake."

Out of the office came Bradley, who Rafuse didn't know, and someone he did know from his dealings with the DTF, Jerry LaChance, who was not trying to hide himself from Rick. And that was very bad news indeed.

LAST SUMMER

Donnie was still reflecting on life. He was lying on the small six-foot-long couch trying to take his mind off his predicament. Thinking about happier times, like last summer with his sister Anita.

In August, he had taken a plane to Toronto, his first flight ever, as well as his first experience in the big city of two and a half million people. His sister borrowed her boyfriend's car and met him at the airport, and it took Donnie a second to recognize her. When Anita left for Toronto two years earlier, she looked like the sister he had known for fourteen years. The lady who walked though the airport the morning looked like Carly Simon. She was beautifully dressed, with fashionable bell bottoms and a silky light blue blouse. And Carly's long wavy brown hair. *Wow, what a difference.*

They spent a week bombing around the big city, seeing the sights of the GTA. High Park. Niagara Falls. The Scarborough Bluffs. The Ontario Science Centre. The Toronto Islands. The Royal Ontario Museum. The TD bank building that stood fifty-six floors in the air! While on the top floor in the observation deck, Anita pointed out a huge roped-off area half mile away to the south-west.

"That is where they're building a super high tower, Donnie, one hundred-eighty stories high," she said. He couldn't believe it. One hundred and twenty-four stories higher than where he was then standing. "It should be finished by the time you're eighteen!"

They ate the best Italian and Greek food on the planet. She took him to the outdoor markets on Spadina, where he could sample all sorts of new foods and drinks. He spent a couple days riding the red rockets in the underground to go to the extreme ends of Toronto including all the way north to York Mills! Downtown, there was shopping and eating in Chinatown. It was a great time.

Donnie met her boyfriend, Bill. The two had been together for a few months. Anita met him at a University of Toronto volleyball game. His company, Sports-ON, was a supplier of equipment for sports teams.

Bill was twenty-nine and, to Donnie, it seemed that the nine-year difference between him and Anita was too much. But while she was at her summer job, Bill took some time off from his work to hang around with Donnie. They went 9 hole-par 3 golfing, visited Old Fort York, and he even took Donnie to his company's corporate box at the CNE stadium where they watched a Toronto Argonauts football game. Donnie was delighted when Bill snuck him a couple beers when no one was looking, though Donnie discovered that it was one and a half beers too many for a rookie like him! *Bill was a pretty good guy.*

At the end of his week, Anita and he flew back together to Dartmouth and had a grand time for another week until she had to return to her new city. His summer of 1972 was wonderful.

His sore thigh brought him back to the present. A half hour earlier, he had put the six-foot couch on end and climbed up onto it. He was trying to bend any part of the chicken wire ceiling in his little prison cell. Ryan had left the lights off, so the little window fifteen feet up was the only illumination he had. Unfortunately, the couch became unstable and collapsed under his weight. He came crashing down, left thigh first onto the arm of the couch. At least it was padded. But *Ouuuucchhhh.* There was already a bruise forming there. Still, he would try again soon. He had to.

As his leg began to feel better or at least usable, he heard *thump-thump-thump.* He wondered what it could be — the front door! Someone was pounding on the front door! Donnie limped over to the door of his little cage and, yelling as loud as he could, pounded on it, but it was no use. Whoever it was, they were already gone.

HURTS LIKE A BITCH

Not good news at all. LaChance stared at him for a long while. Rafuse tried to give back stare for stare, but his headache only got worse, and he eventually had to close his eyes and lower his head.

"It hurts like a bitch, don't it, Rick? Even with a skull as thick as yours, you caught a helluva double-bash. Now I can see you wanna ask, 'Why aren't I tied up like the others', right? That's what you want to know, right?"

"I already know," said Rafuse quietly.

"And I don't have to worry about the cavalry, do I? I figured you wouldn't have told anybody you were coming out here. You always were a lone wolf. If they do come looking for you, they won't find you here. It's okay though, they'll find you somewhere. Eventually." LaChance chuckled and walked away.

"Why aren't you tied up? What do you already know?" asked Peter.

Rafuse pondered what to say to the young fellow but there was no way to sugar coat this. "These guys here know that if you kill a cop, police forces around the world *will not stop* till they find you. So, their best bet is to stage an accident, and it won't help when you do that if the victim has rope marks on his wrist."

"But what about us? Our hands are tied," said Peter.

"Hopefully, that means they're going to let you folks go." Rafuse knew he didn't sound very convincing.

Peter stared at the plywood floor of the van. Old scrapes and stains covered it. It was uncomfortable but that was the least of their worries. The back door of the van had been closed earlier when he and his parents heard some kind of confrontation. Then the back door flew up and two men dragged an unconscious Detective Rafuse in next to them. He thought of the woman he had seen earlier who came in and played with Rafuse's hair. Someone called her Jennifer. He knew there was a Jennifer who worked at the police station, but had never seen her. Donnie mentioned her when the four boys met at the Old Fort last Friday evening, saying she had blond hair, just like this one.

LOOKING FOR THE BROWN IMPALA

Hicks had covered all three side streets, and even part of Isnor Drive. He checked the main drag, Wright Avenue, but there was no sign of the brown Impala. He had gone door to door to every business on the main street, checking the parking areas and warehouses, but still no sign of the car or the boy. All he had left were two buildings. They were locked up tight. One on Borden Avenue and one on McCurdy Avenue. Hicks had pounded on the doors of each building earlier but had gotten no response.

Since he could not enter or see inside either building from the ground floor, Hicks needed to get higher in the world and as such, had managed to borrow a sixteen-foot extension ladder from a nearby company.

He made a quick radio call to Fong at the station who checked the ownership of the two premises. The one on McCurdy was owned in the past by a now bankrupt company. The one on Borden Avenue was owned by a numbered holding company in the Cayman Islands. The interesting thing was this same company owned a second building downtown on Commercial Street.

He was nearest to the building on McCurdy and would start with there. A tattered legal notice of bankruptcy was attached to the front door. There was also an overhead door and next to it, a four-foot square air grill which was closed and locked, and he could therefore not see inside the building through it. The place was built like a concrete block vault. There were no windows anywhere, so he was going to use the ladder to get up on top of the roof. There he hoped to see down through any vents or equipment. *I've done crazier things.*

MY MIND IS CLEARER NOW

It was coming back. Rafuse remembered walking with Norberg back down the hall from the office towards shipping, with Norberg, after his tour of the greenhouses.

"And I met Heidi there. Yes, that's right," he said to himself, and he pieced the past few hours together.

He'd seen Jerry LaChance sitting in the shipping office next to Norberg's. And, judging by their interactions, he also saw someone who must be his girlfriend. A pretty blonde girl who Rafuse had known for the past year. And now he knew the dirty Dartmouth cop wasn't a cop at all. Jennifer Horn.

There was a big grin on LaChance's face and Rafuse headed straight for him. There was a cacophony of yelling voices, and someone tried to grab him from behind. But he shrugged off those hands. Then the almighty explosion that put him here in the back of the van.

"She was the one who brushed the hair out of my eyes as I was waking up," he said, to no one in particular. "Nice red nail polish."

"Her name's Jennifer, isn't it?" asked the boy named Peter.

Rafuse nodded, but before he could answer, Mr. Meijer said, "You mean da blonde girl. Yays, eet vas her. Vat happeens next, Deetektif Rayfoose?"

He looked at those three scared faces, sweating and uncomfortable in the back of the van. They didn't deserve any of this. They had nothing to do with any of it. *How many innocent people fall prey every day to assholes like these?*

"Hopefully they'll just stick us someplace where we can't contact anyone until they all leave town."

Meijer shook his head. "Da troot, Mister Rayfoose. Da troot bleale."

Rafuse looked at the Meijers, then looked away.

Meijer nodded his head in understanding, pulling himself closer to his wife. Peter, sitting next to his mother, put his face into his folded knees. He was either praying or crying. Either was the correct response in this situation, thought Rafuse.

IS JENNIFER BACK?

Chief Daweson was sitting at his desk in stunned silence, trying to process what Fong had just told him. They had a crooked cop on the force, a family missing, and a young man kidnapped. Evidence stolen out of right out of the station, with the help of the lead detective by that same young man. One thing for sure, his career as chief was over. He would be lucky if they let him retire quietly.

Fong was thinking along the same lines. He'd worked hard for his promotion to corporal. And with Sergeant Wilson's imminent retirement in the next few years, Fong figured he would at least get a nice hard look from the brass. Now? A security guard at Kmart was probably in his future.

It was a testament to both these men that those thoughts were fleeting and easily pushed aside by the dedication of two career police officers. They had made a solemn commitment to protect the people of Dartmouth. And right now, Daweson and Fong were going to save Donnie Langille and catch the bastard that threatened his loved ones, whatever the personal cost.

"And you say the last contact we had from Rick was he was headed for the Emporium?"

"Yes sir. There was a piece of evidence from the Martin case that was identified as being associated to that business," replied Fong.

"The courier waybill?" asked the chief.

"It's flimsy, but maybe the detective just wanted to tie up loose ends?"

"I've known Detective Rafuse his whole life, Keith and believe me when I say he has more than a hunch something's not kosher out there. Get a unit to run by the Emporium and see if there's any commotion."

"Will do, Chief," said Fong.

"I'll call the RCMP as a courtesy to tell them we'll stepping on their toes a tiny bit."

Chief Daweson seemed to weigh his next decision. "And Keith? We're going to need more people we can trust. Maybe someone who's not in uniform. Is Jennifer back yet?" She had taken a few hours off for an appointment of some sort just before noon.

"She's just back now, sir, from an extended lunch. She said she'll be staying late tonight to make up the time."

"Good. I'm going to bring her up to speed on all of this. I want her sticking to me like glue in case I need a set of eyes and ears, okay? And Keith?"

"Sir?"

"Let's try spreading a little misinformation to help flush out our crooked cop. If anyone here asks about Rafuse, tell them you checked with me and I said not to waste your time, he'll turn up tomorrow."

"Hmm. That's worth a try, Chief!"

"And by the way, Keith, the divers found the knife."

"What? Really?" Fong was incredulous.

"Yes, I know, a one in a million chance, but everyone from the divers to the ferry pilot to the weatherman did their jobs way above their pay grades on this one."

"Are they sure it's the right knife? I imagine there could be many —"

The chief held up his hand, "No, no, it's been identified as being Reggie's knife by his son Scott. It's in the lab right now being dusted for prints, though they're not hopeful." The chief stared at the desk in front of him. Reggie was a close friend and Chief Daweson had taken this very personally. He'd been able to hide his emotion thus far but seeing that knife this afternoon ...

"Yessir, and HARP?" Fong was asking about the Hostage Assault and Rescue Program. An early attempt at SWAT, it was brand new. It was run in Nova Scotia by the RCMP, and led by a former army major, now Inspector, Dumas. He had been with a famous Canadian regiment, the Royal 22nd, 'the Vandoos', before becoming a Mountie.

"On standby mode, ready to move as soon as we know where the Langille boy or the Miejers might be."

Fong picked up his portable radio. "Bravo 378 to Bravo 347, over. Bravo 378 to Bravo 347, over." Nothing. Fong had been trying for an hour to contact Rafuse. "Bravo 378 to Bravo 391, over." "Bravo 378 to Bravo 391, over." And now he couldn't get a hold of Hicks, either.

THE FEDS ARRIVE

What the hell, Hicks mumbled to himself. Now what? Someone on the ground was yelling up to him. He'd climbed to the roof of the first building of the two he had to check, the concrete block vault. It had been tough. The roof's parapet was eighteen inches above the last rung of the ladder, but also projected about nine inches out past the wall, so he'd had to stand precariously on the second last rung, reaching up and out and pull himself up and over onto the roof. In doing so however, he had inadvertently knocked the radio out of his pocket. The twenty-foot drop onto the concrete below had finished off the poor thing.

Poor me. Chief will probably take it out of my pay. And how am I going to get down? Feel around with my feet?

Hicks had managed to remove an air vent from the roof with a Swiss army knife. It should have been almost impossible to do, but the roofing and sealing compound was in terrible shape and he was able to cut through it with the blade of the knife. When he first poked his head in, it was difficult to see anything. But as his eyes adjusted, the meagre light streaming through the opening was enough to let him see most of the garage and there was no sign of any cars at all. The place was barren. He had replaced the vent, was fixing the last screw in place, and was reminding himself to inform the chief of his official vandalism when he heard, "Hey! Up on the roof. Show yourself."

He walked over to the edge and looked down. Two RCMP officers were looking up at him. An older early-forties guy and a young whippersnapper next to him. *He looks like he just got off the train from Saskatoon.*

"Hi guys. I'm blue, I'm on the job. Dartmouth, Constable Philip Hicks, badge 391."

"Yeah, sure okay, why don't you come on down," said the older fellow.

"Yeah, okay, but I'm armed."

"Yeah? What's your setup?"

"Police Special in a shoulder holster."

"Alright come on down ... slowly."

Hicks swung himself gingerly over the parapet, feeling with his feet for the ladder, his arms burning as they held all his weight. The young Mountie below called up. "A little to your right." Hicks felt with his feet and eventually hooked onto the ladder and got comfortable. He noticed the young fellow was steadying the ladder below.

When he reached the concrete ground below, the older Mountie said, "Hands up." Hicks put his hands behind his head and interlocked his fingers.

"Where's your badge?" the older Mountie asked, as he removed Hicks's firearm.

"I have a badge wallet, back pocket," said Hicks.

The older Mountie nodded to the younger. "Go get it."

"Yeah," added Hicks, "don't stay down there too long, okay?" He and older cop shared a grin.

The younger Mountie shook his head. "All the glamorous jobs. Yes, here it is, Dartmouth Police, 391."

The senior Mountie relaxed. "I'm Constable Brian MacKay and this is the newest member of the Sackville Detachment, Constable Ali Hassan. We just finished some business here in the industrial park and were headed back when we saw your ladder and thought we'd take a look-see."

"Nice to meet you guys. Can we speed this up? I'm in a hell of a hurry!" said Hicks.

"That yours?" Hassan nodded toward the broken radio.

"Yeah, it *was*."

"First thing's first. Ali, get on the radio, ask the detachment to call the Dartmouth station and make sure Hicks here checks out. Who's the sergeant down there?" MacKay knew exactly who the sergeant was.

"Wilson's on duty today, but when they call, can you tell them to ask for Corporal Fong or Chief Daweson?"

MacKay turned to his partner. "Ali, tell them to get hold of Corporal Fong." And to Hicks, "I know him, Fong's a good man." He gave Hicks his badge back. "Now, what's the story?"

"The Martin murder." MacKay nodded for him to continue. "In a nutshell, our prime witness has just been kidnapped by the prime suspect. And we've got a dirty cop in the force, so we don't know who of our own people to trust."

MacKay whistled. "Mother of God ..." he muttered. "Go on ..."

"First, can you guys spare a few minutes for a fellow officer in need? Just help me with the other building so I can tie off all the possible locations of the suspect's car. Derby Twins and couple of draft is on me, if you can."

"Sounds great. Let's you and I see if we can squeeze that ladder in the car trunk somewhere." The men dropped the ladder down to its smallest size, and carried it over to the car. MacKay opened the trunk, and re-arranged some items. Then they tried to put it into the trunk, but more than half of it hung out.

"This isn't going to work," said MacKay. "Let's see if we can lash it to the roof." He found some rope in the trunk, and opened the rear doors.

Hassan got out of the car. "They got hold of Fong. He was concerned as to why Hicks hadn't radioed, and I explained that the radio was broken. So, Fong said Hicks should phone him. This is all very strange, but Hicks checks out. Are you trying to put the ladder on the car? Where are we taking it?"

"There's one more building on Borden I need to check," said Hicks.

"I'll just carry it down there," said Hassan, who threw the ladder on his shoulder. "Up on Borden Avenue?"

"Yeah, third building in on the right," said Hicks. Hassan walked off. After a moment, Hicks turned to MacKay and asked, "Where did you guys find him?"

"Parents immigrated here from Lebanon when he was in high school. They must grow them right over there."

"No kidding." Then Hicks told MacKay everything he knew.

RESCUED

The second building was on Borden Avenue and was different from the one on McCurdy in that it was a plain-Jane industrial style, about sixty feet by a hundred feet and maybe twenty-five feet tall. It had grey aluminum siding and a set of four small windows on the front wall and the back wall, about three quarters of the way up. They no doubt let in a semblance of natural light. There was no company sign on the building but maybe it was just rented out to whichever business needed offsite or extra storage.

Hassan already had the ladder in place when the two men arrived. Hicks climbed up to the top rungs that would allow him to look in one of the small windows in the second and final building. As he pulled himself up to the window, the brown Impala was the very first thing he saw.

"Well, I'll be damned!" exclaimed Hicks.

The two constables below looked at each other. "What do you see in there?"

"I see the car. Hold on now, there's a little room in the back."

Hicks scampered down the ladder. "The suspect kidnap vehicle is in there. But there's also a small room in the back. The door is closed so I can't see in, but it has no ceiling so I should be able to see down into it from a window on the other side of the building. Quick, help me carry the ladder round the back."

Mackay looked at Hassan with a big grin. "You heard the man."

Inside, Donnie sat on the couch, still daydreaming and refusing to have his thoughts controlled by this situation that was out of his control. He thought of Heidi and the improbability of them ever having re-connected —

BAM BAM BAM!

Donnie was so startled he fell right out of his daydream and right off the couch. He staggered to his feet, the bruise on his side throbbing like thunder. The pounding had come from behind him. And above! He forgot all about the pain when he looked up to see that big, ugly, beautiful face of Hicks smiling down at him from the window!

CLEAR OUT EVERYONE

Mr. Norberg had left the Emporium but would be back sometime in the next hour. And Bradley was starting to worry.

After the Meijers arrived at the Emporium and then Rafuse had been knocked unconscious, Bradley had sent anyone in the main building, who wasn't part of his inner circle, home for the day. Luckily, none of them had seen either incident. Bradley used the pretext of a surprise Department of Agriculture inspection. The greenhouse staff could remain on the job as long as they stayed where they were. But they were not to access the main building.

At the same time, Jerry sent some of his own people to the Emporium. The kind of people who take orders and don't ask questions. And a few of those were armed. But things were moving too quickly, and he should never have told the people in the greenhouses that they could work late. Too much danger that someone might see something.

Bradley waved over his two best men. "Check the greenhouses and the grounds and tell anyone who's still working that they have to leave now. They'll be paid full shift even though it's only five-thirty. Tell them the government inspectors want everyone off the property."

"Right away boss."

BATHROOM BREAK

It was a warm afternoon. Heidi had asked her workmate, a gal named Grace, if she could leave the door to their greenhouse open. As a consequence, she had seen quite a bit of activity around the main building. Cars and people, vans especially, had been coming and going more frequently than usual, especially as the afternoon progressed. She recognized some of them, but most were new to her.

Erik had arrived in a green station wagon at the same time she arrived, shortly before noon. He was always borrowing somebody's car. He parked it at the side of the building and ran into the office. An hour later and the green car was gone.

Heidi had a gnawing worry in the back of her mind. It had nettled her more as her day progressed. The least Donnie could have done was call the Emporium and let her know he wouldn't make it into work today. When Detective Rafuse showed up at the Emporium, around one-thirty, she feared that there might have been an incident involving Donnie. But his signal to her for anonymity seemed to mean that he was here for another reason. She told herself to stop worrying, Donnie would tell her tonight what it was all about. He's such adorable dork, she thought to herself with a smile, thinking of his clumsiness last night. Well, that's okay, her aunt said to her once, *the best men are the ones you have to train yourself.*

During her lunch, she saw a Mercedes car pull up. A swarthy man jumped out of the driver's side … good God. It was Erik's friend Jerry. He walked around the car and opened the passenger door. A blonde girl stepped out. Heidi had seen her at his parties, but they had never met. He had his arm on the small of her back, his girlfriend she assumed. She wasn't as dolled up today as she was at those parties. From some instinct she didn't recognize, Heidi ducked behind the door so she wouldn't be noticed. *What are they doing here?*

Mr. Norberg had sent everyone who worked in the main building home for the day, not long after she saw Rafuse. There was some sort of inspection. People like Heidi, who worked in the greenhouses, could stay if they wished. Madeline was working on office tasks, and so was sent home early. Heidi declined when Madeline asked if she wanted a ride home. She would stay on and get a lift from someone else or get a cab home. When she started this job, Mr. Norberg had said that since this was the busiest time for the Emporium, Heidi could work until eight at night any day she wanted. That was very good, because Aunt Tillie wasn't made of money and Heidi wanted to do her part with the finances.

Later, around two-thirty, she noticed the Chevy Nova she had assumed belonged to Detective Rafuse was gone. She wondered whether he had found something here to investigate but it looked like that wasn't the case. No doubt her clue about the courier slip had brought him out to the Emporium in the first place. One thing for sure, she had felt safer knowing a policeman was here. Now that he had departed, she was wary. She definitely did not want to run into Erik while she was here by herself.

A couple of hours later, another curiosity. A Dartmouth Police car parked by the office. Two uniformed officers went inside for about ten minutes, then departed. *What was that all about?*

Now it was about five-thirty. Things were quiet, and she'd completed a lot of work. She was ready for a short break, and needed to pee. That's what got her in trouble, and also saved her. The washroom she normally used was in the office area, but the building was off limits for the afternoon because of the inspection. "Grace, I'm going over to Greenhouse Two for a few minutes." Her co-worker, in the middle of something murmured, "mmm-hmm."

She walked over to Greenhouse Two, where Donnie normally worked. The lights were on, but there wasn't a soul there. That was unusual but not unheard of. Not everyone was keen to stay late.

After a few minutes in the washroom, Heidi stepped out and was surprised to see that all the lights had been turned off in the greenhouse. And someone had closed the one-way locking door. She could still exit the building using the push bar, but she wouldn't be able to get back in. *Just don't drink anymore,* she chuckled to herself.

Walking back to her work, she could see the door to Greenhouse One had been closed and locked as well. She looked in the door window. No Grace, and no lights. Someone had shut and locked all the greenhouses while she'd been doing her business. She'd have to get someone in the main building to let her back into Greenhouse One. Mr. Norberg was still there. She recognized his car, a 1972 Volvo 144. He had bought it new last year and he probably spent nearly three thousand for it, according to Graham. Jeez, no car is worth that, she thought. There were two other cars in the lot she didn't recognize but the cars she saw every day were gone. Erik's borrowed green car wasn't there and neither was Jerry's Mercedes.

Heidi knocked, waited, then opened the door to the office. None of the daily staff were at their desks and the lights were off here as well. Even this late in the day, there were usually a couple of office staff here catching up on something. These mysterious meetings had apparently sent everyone home.

As she walked through the dark office, the unusual silence and darkness gave her goose bumps. Heidi's work boots made a ca-thunk sound with each step, and she found herself trying to step as gently as possible to minimize that noise. She slowed down, picking her way quietly between the desks, and peeked around the corner down the hallway to the loading dock. The lights were on in the loading area, and she heard muffled voices, so someone was definitely there, but the eeriness of the office made her cautious.

Instinct told her there was something wrong with what she saw a split second before her brain figured it out. There, just eighty feet away, was a van backed into one of the loading bays. Its vertical sliding back door was open, its cargo lights were on, and in the yellow glow were three people sitting down with their hands behind their backs, tied obviously, and to the left of them was Detective Rafuse, covered in blood. Out of Bradley's office stepped two men she didn't recognize. And one had a handgun!

Heidi gasped and she backed around the corner into the office, overwhelmed with questions and panic. Had anyone seen or heard her? What the hell happened? Who were those two guys milling about next to the van? Was Erik mixed up in this? And — she risked another peek — something was familiar about one of the three tied up on the floor. What was it? His hair, an almost-afro. *Oh my God, that's Peter.*

The urge to run straight out the office door was huge. But Heidi was a smart girl, and cautious. She was in the middle of whatever this was. And now was not the time for panic. She had a horrible thought. *Did they have Donnie too?* She had to get help, find someone in the Emporium she could trust. Where was Mr. Norberg? She had to find him, she had to call someone, she had to call the cops.

She started towards the nearest desk with a phone when she heard heavy footsteps coming up the hallway from the loading dock. Looking for cover, she ran quietly over to the middle desk of three by the windows and, pushing the chair aside, fitted herself into the little space between the drawers. *Thank God I'm small!* As she pulled herself into the cubbyhole in the desk, she heard another vehicle arrive in the parking lot. It sounded like one of the vans.

Someone walked across the clean office floor in heavy work boots and opened the office main door. Then she heard voices. Heidi was flooded with relief. It was Mr. Norberg talking with Bradley.

She couldn't hear what they were saying, but these were two people she could trust. She tried to pull herself out from her hiding space, but as much as she wanted to jump up and call to them, her body wouldn't budge. Bradley had come from the direction of the loading bay. Surely, he had seen something wrong there? A voice inside her warned her to stay put. She had ignored that little voice last year in Liverpool to disastrous results and she had promised herself she would never ignore it again.

The two men came closer. "How did it go?" It was Bradley asking.

"The job is done. I have found a buyer and made arrangements for our product to be transferred to new suppliers. They'll give us seventy on the dollar. I argued, but they have us over a barrel, so we'll have to live with the loss. Unfortunately, they insist we move it to the Commercial warehouse till midnight or maybe one in the morning, when they say they will pick it up. Then they'll use our vans and transport the product."

"Good. We already moved most of it down. Erik and Paul just left with the final load."

The two men continued walking across the office. She could see their legs. They stopped at the same place Heidi had stopped a minute earlier. Apparently, Mr. Norberg could see clearly down the hallway into the back of the van with the hostages as well. "What the hell?" roared Mr. Norberg, and before Bradley could answer, he demanded, "Why are they still alive?"

IN A MOUNTIE CAR

There were tears running down Donnie's cheeks as they pried the door open with the crowbar stored in the RCMP car's trunk, though the Mounties called it a pry bar for some reason. The cops were pretty emotional themselves.

Donnie had spent the whole afternoon in this little room, escaping from reality, so he wouldn't have to think about who it might be that came back for him, though he was hoping it would be cops. He was delighted it was Hicks, with two Mounties in tow. Donnie's relief was measured in the number of times he had to wipe away the tears. After thanking everyone profusely, the feeling of freedom and sheer relief for Donnie was intoxicating. He offered to take the ladder back to the company down the street.

"Not a chance kid. You aren't leaving my sight till you're home," pledged Hicks.

After the ladder had been returned by Hassan, MacKay drove everyone in the cruiser down to a pay phone at an Esso station on Windmill Road. To ensure privacy, Hicks phoned the station as opposed to using radios. He came back to the RCMP cruiser with bad news. No one had heard from Rafuse since he'd radioed Fong hours earlier.

"The Emporium, like Bedford and Sackville, is RCMP territory. Which means the chief had to contact your main detachment to inform them that we would be checking a location in their jurisdiction. We got the all clear and the chief sent a car out to the Emporium to check on Rafuse's whereabouts, but there was no sign of him or my car. It's a Chevy Nova. They talked to a guy named Bradley Ferguson on site, who said that Rafuse had a chat with the boss, Mr. Norberg, got taken on a twenty-minute tour and then, when he finished, he hopped in his car, turned left and headed down Rocky Lake Drive toward Bedford."

"Did your chief want us to take a look in the Waverley or Bedford area?" asked MacKay.

Hicks answered, "Not at the moment. Fong said to stay put. The chief is contacting your watch commander at RCMP HQ to ask for assistance."

MacKay asked, "What do we do about Donnie here?"

"The station has been trying to contact Donnie's parents but there's been no response. So, the chief suggested dropping Donnie off at home and stationing a unit outside," answered Hicks. "But in the end, we decided not to as we still have that major problem."

"What problem?" asked Hassan.

"They have a crooked cop, Ali, a snitch, but we're not sure who they are or what they're capable of," explained MacKay. "It could be anyone on the force, even the fellow they put out front to protect Donnie and his family. That's why we're not sending Donnie home just yet and also the reason we're not using the radio."

Hassan shook his head in disbelief.

"I'm a lot safer sticking with you guys and three guns in the car, then I am at home anyway," suggested Donnie.

"Don't forget the shotgun in the trunk," said MacKay, with a grin.

"Oh man, really? That's too cool!"

"Where are your parents, Donnie?" asked Hassan.

"Mom's shopping. On days like this she's sometimes at the Halifax Shopping Centre till it closes at six. She and Dad love the Red Fox Tavern so Mom's probably grabbing supper there till 7:30 or so. And Dad's in Shelburne, probably just starting the drive back home."

"Alright then, it's decided. We're going to keep this young gentleman with us for the time being."

Hassan was looking at Donnie, "I bet you haven't eaten all day, right?"

"No sir, I wasn't hungry before, but now I'm starved!"

"Alright. Let's go grab a coffee at the Chicken Burger and await instructions." MacKay put the car in gear and off they went to the Chicken Burger for a coffee, and of course, in Donnie's case, a chicken burger. Or two.

A FIXER

Heidi didn't understand for a few moments. *Why are they still alive?* Why are *who* still alive? Surely Mr. Norberg wasn't talking about the people in the van? That would mean he was not only aware of what was happening, he was wrapped up in the whole thing as well. Maybe even in charge.

"Didn't you tell me that Jerry's crew could take care of things like this? So, why are they still alive, Bradley?" Norberg repeated.

"Because none of the guys here is willing to waste a cop. I trust these guys, Mr. Norberg, but they are workers, not cleanup men. And that cop in the back of the van has them really spooked. When those two Dartmouth cops showed up earlier this afternoon looking for their detective, I managed to play dummy and send them on their way. But it scared the shit out of Jerry's guys even more, and anyone who might have taken the job earlier isn't interested now. Killing a cop is a big step. Even if you are offering to pay five large, these guys don't want that kind of trouble!" explained Bradley.

"God Almighty. What is this world coming to?" Norberg lamented, "Nobody wants to do an honest day's work anymore." Bradley nodded in agreement.

The two men weren't moving, and Heidi stayed still in her cubbyhole, listening and trying to figure out what was going on.

"Well, what is Jerry going to do about it?" Norberg demanded.

"I phoned him and explained our problem. He said he would call in a big gun from Vancouver."

"Vancouver?" asked Norberg.

"Yeah. Well, the guy's home base is Vancouver but he's in Moncton right now on other business. Just got off the phone with him and Jerry said he should be here between eight and eight-thirty."

"Excellent. Can he get it all finished tonight?" asked Norberg.

"Barring anything unforeseen, yes. That's how he put it, anyway."

"Good! I want all this cleaned up tonight. We're bound to come under suspicion after this unholy mess, and we'll have to make sure we have a tight ship. Did the fellow introduce himself?"

"No, but Jerry mentioned the name McGregor. Ever hear of him?" asked Bradley.

Norberg's face went white. "Never met him, but I've heard things about him. Not the kind of person you want on your bad side. Anything else?"

"Yeah, Ryan called a little while go. I suggested maybe he could get rid of these hostages, but he said that wasn't his job."

"No, it isn't," answered Norberg curtly. "Did he say anything else?"

"He wanted you to know that the evidence with the thumbprint on it has been destroyed."

"Excellent. How did he do it?"

"He used the Langille kid, Donnie, to make the switch, then he burned it," said Bradley. "And he wanted you to know he took care of Donnie, and you won't have to worry about him anymore," Bradley added, matter-of-factly.

"Alright, good," said Norberg. "Shame though, he was a nice kid."

WEDNESDAY EVENING

DEVASTATION

Norberg and Bradley walked away into the shipping area. Heidi had a perfect chance to escape but stayed where she was, frozen in place, her emotions exploding in every direction.

Donnie dead? Her Donnie? That Ryan fellow had found him? She couldn't believe what she just heard. When Donnie told her what was happening to him this past week, it sounded exciting and unreal. Now the implications virtually slapped her in the face, and she suddenly had to cover her mouth to keep from wailing. Was it somehow her fault? Had they all taken it too lightly? How unfeeling she had been toward him last night! Was that on his mind and had it made him careless? Unbidden thoughts coursed through her mind.

She was shaking and sobbing silently. Her brain was in overtime analyzing every thought swirling through her mind, but instead of falling apart, Heidi pulled herself together. *You are strong, you'll get through this.* And she had so far in her life, but Heidi suddenly realized something else, that Donnie had *always* been there for her these past years, even when they were apart. Now he was gone. She started sorting things out in her head, point by point. Her last moment with Donnie in the open door of Madeline's car this morning, he had smiled and squeezed her arm, and she had smiled back. He knew she loved him.

She heard his mother call out that the Meijers needed help with something, and that is where he had obviously gone this morning. Now the Meijers were here as prisoners, which suggested Ryan had been waiting for Donnie at their house. Even if she or any of his friends had inadvertently led Ryan to Donnie, there was only one guilty party in this whole narrative, and that was Louis Ryan, nobody else.

Heidi felt an enormous amount of pain and shock at her loss. But maybe that was selfish. Donnie was her loss? She thought of Anita, Jane and Robert, Madeline, Natty, Clip and who knows who else. Compared to her, their loss would be almost insurmountable. And now Peter and his parents might be the next victims.

And the coldness that exuded from Mr. Norberg and Bradley's conversation was shocking. Discussing killing like everyday shop talk.

She made herself into a little ball under the desk, knees up to her chest, arms crossed on top of her knees, her head buried in her arms. She had to think. Heidi had never been one to fly off the handle, *to run off half-cocked*. And most important, Heidi realized *she was it*. She was the only one, the only hope. It was up to her to get help. *You are strong, you'll get through this*.

She prepared herself for an escape. Heidi's sweater was locked in the greenhouse, and although it was fairly warm outside by early-summer standards, it might not be warm enough for what she planned to do. Walking out the front door next to the loading dock would be as good as delivering herself into these awful peoples' hands. Which meant, at the first opportunity, she would race through the office, out the back door, run down to the dock, and make her way along the lake shore, which was full of slippery boulders. Then she would pull herself around the big wooden fence and push through the thick brush and trees until she made it to Rocky Lake Road.

Then she had to find a house or business. If she went left on Rocky Lake Road, it would mean walking past the entrance of the small access road to the Emporium. If she went right, there was a convenience store on the corner of Rocky Lake and Waverley Road, but it was a much further walk. Either way *should* get her to safety, so she would decide on a direction when the time came.

And once she called the cops, who next? Her aunt? She would come at a moment's notice, but she was a critical care nurse. And there were people whose lives were literally in her hands. And she was further away in the south end of Halifax, at the hospital. So, she would call a friend. Madeline of course. Pray to God she was home tonight. She would have to tell her about Donnie — *I hope he didn't suffer.* The thought came like a punch in the stomach, but she drove it out her mind. She had to get help for Peter and the others. Everything depended on her getting away.

Heidi had work boots on her feet, though they had no steel toe. And a heavy work T-shirt supplied by the Emporium, with the company logo just above the breast pocket. Neither was going to be very warm if they got wet. The lake hadn't had a chance to warm up much and the water was still spring-time cool. It was already just sixty-five degrees out and it was supposed to drop even more as the night came on.

Heidi risked a peek out the back windows. Two of the unknown men were standing by the office back door chatting, and nervously smoking cigarettes. Regardless of their demeanour, she would have to wait for them to leave. She glanced around the office. There was a phone two desks over, but she could not get near it without being seen. And her wrist was conscious of every single tick of her watch as valuable time slipped by. She tried not to think of Donnie.

THE GANG

Madeline pulled up to the curb, parking in front of Peter's place. Her dad was back in town on Friday, so this was her second last day with the car. Damn. Donnie hadn't come into work today, and after she left work and changed, she drove over to the Langille's home but there was no answer when she knocked there. Madeline took a chance that maybe he'd spent the whole day with the Meijers.

She got out, went through the gate at the white picket fence, did the traditional two knocks, then tried to open the door. Locked. She thought for a moment, then went down to through the backyard to the garage and peered in the window. Well, I guess they've gone somewhere, she thought. No car and no Donnie.

She walked back up towards her car, then detoured to the back door of the house at the last the second and tried the knob. The door swung open. She went to the kitchen and picked up the phone. *I'm sure they won't mind, it's not like it's a long-distance call or anything.* Madeline paused. There was a smell in the air. Not offensive exactly, and very faint but definitely a smell that didn't belong. She couldn't place it.

She dialled Natty. His mom answered and called him to the phone. He didn't even say hello. "Have you talked to Clip today?"

"What? No, I haven't."

"Something big is happening today involving Donnie," said Natty. "Don't know what or where! But I'll tell you this, he might need our help. We have to get together, maybe at the Langille's place and be ready to roll if the call comes. Clip and I have to fill you in on what happened this morning. And Heidi and Peter too, but I haven't been able to reach either of them." Natty's rushed words showed his concern.

"I'm standing in Peter's living room. The family is not here, no one. I looked in the garage and the car's also gone."

"That's weird," said Natty.

"And Heidi's at work. She's staying late, till eight."

"Okay. Clip is here already, come on over and pick us up. We'll go over to the Langilles."

"I was already there. Nobody's home, and their car is gone," said Madeline.

"What the hell is going on?" Natty was worried. "Pick us up and we'll figure out what to do."

"Will do."

As Madeline hung up the phone, she considered calling the Emporium but decided to do it later. She would do it closer to the time she would be picking Heidi up, so the girl wouldn't have to call a cab. After all, Heidi was perfectly safe at the Emporium. Yes, they had sent everyone in the office home, but there were always a couple people working overtime in the greenhouses and even if there wasn't, Mr. Norberg would still be there until closing. Heidi was safe.

Madeline walked across the living room floor towards the front door but stopped when something caught her eye. A stain on the tan-coloured chair in the living room. Dark brown and not one but two dots, one was an inch in diameter and one about a quarter inch. She stepped back and looked around. The Meijer's carpet looked like spaghetti factory. It had a burgundy base and with multi-coloured paisley pattern all through it, but she saw an even bigger blood stain next to the chair. Yes, blood. She was sure of it. She played sports and she had shed enough blood to know what it looked like when it dried. Besides Madeline hoped to be a forensic investigator some day and she'd be a piss-poor one if she couldn't recognize blood when she saw it!

As she unlocked and opened the front door her mind finally recognized the source of the smell, she noticed earlier. Burned paper. She shrugged and left.

Madeline arrived at Natty's home on Elmwood Avenue at just after six. She was concerned and confused in equal measure. As she headed up the front walk to the little duplex, Natty and Clip came out to meet her.

"Hi Maddie. So, what do we do?" asked Clip, straight to the point as usual.

"Maybe go to the police and ask them if they know where Donnie is?" suggested Natty. "I mean from what you said, that's where he was headed this morning."

"No, like I said, Donnie wanted me to keep that O'Br ... ah, that cop, busy for a few minutes. It was obvious there was something wrong with the cops, or at least some of them," explained Clip.

"Yes, they might be the problem," said Madeline. "And Donnie could be hiding from them right now."

"And you said there's nobody at Peter's house? Weird!" said Clip.

Natty wasn't convinced. "Maybe we're getting all riled up for no reason. Look, it's just two families, nobody home, no cars in the driveway and it's a workday. There's nothing too scary about that."

"Guys, there were spots of blood on the chair and carpet in Peter's place, and the car's gone from the garage."

The two boys looked at each other. "Somebody got hurt and they went to the hospital?" asked Clip.

Madeline shook her head. Natty shrugged his shoulders.

"Okay Clip, one more time, tell us exactly what happened today with Donnie," said Natty.

Madeline interrupted. "Let's do it in the house, Natty. We should make some phone calls."

Madeline started by calling her mother. "Hi Mom, it's me. Yes, I will, but I have a favour to ask of you. If Donnie calls for me, could you take a message? Yes. Yes, but there's more. Could you call Mrs. Power and tell her to do the same thing? Yes, Natty's mom. Yes. It's because she'll get the message to me, okay? That's great mom. Yes, Love you too. Ta." Madeline's call to her mother had gone easier than she thought it would.

"I guess my mother is finally accepting how truly weird I am!" she said to Natty.

"Well yeah, the rest of us already have." He grinned. He passed on what Clip had done for Donnie earlier, while Clip called his mom.

Clip spent almost ten minutes on the phone, trying to give his mom the same message as Madeline had. She had many more questions, but it was done and finally they were ready to leave. They still weren't sure where to look for Donnie, but it was late enough to go pick up Heidi, and she might have heard from him.

Madeline dialled the nursery, and waited a good seven rings.

"Hello, Lake William Plant Emporium. I'm sorry, we're currently closed." It was Mr. Norberg himself.

"Mr. Norberg, it's me Madeline."

"Madeline? Yes, what is it?"

Sounds like Norberg's having a bad day, the surprise inspection must not have gone well. "Yes sir, I was wondering if you could tell Heidi Freeman that I'll be picking her up at eight."

"What? No. No she's not here. We sent everyone else home around five-thirty. The ah, surprise inspection by the Department of Agriculture is still ongoing tonight."

"Tonight?" *Government employees working past five?* Madeline had never heard of such a thing.

"Is there anything else, Madeline?"

"No."

"Well, have a nice evening, good night." Click.

Wow, thought Madeline, that was strange, and he sounded so preoccupied. She called Aunt Tillie's twice. Then called Donnie's house and still had no answer at either one. Madeline turned to her friends. "Heidi's boss says she already went home, but she's not there, and something odd is going on at the Emporium. Let's check that out."

As they climbed into the Chevelle, Clip hunched in the back, Natty in front. He held something up.

"A walkie-talkie?"

"That's right. Donnie will most likely call me first if he needs us. So, my mom is going to radio us ... if we're within range. Where are we going to be?" asked Natty

"First stop is Lake William, to confirm Heidi's not there."

"Hmm. We might get a signal, but I'm betting we'll have to drive in a little closer to town."

THE CHICKEN BURGER

The taste never gets old. Donnie could eat at the Chicken Burger in Bedford every day for a week, and he would still be back on the eighth day. The sandwich was simple: steamed chicken meat in a plain, white bun. Sometimes simplicity is the best flavour!

"The way I figure it, we go downtown and take a look at that second building on Commercial Street," said Hicks.

"Well, why are we sitting here eating?" asked Hassan.

"Chain of command. The chief's getting a warrant for us to start looking but we have to wait. Don't want to screw up the Crown Prosecutor's office with a bad search."

"That could take hours or even till tomorrow. Surely the emergency clause would take precedent in that case?" asked MacKay.

"Yes, but we'd have to prove we are aware of an emergency situation. So, it'd be thrown out. We don't dare have a cop even walking past that warehouse," replied Hicks. "Breaking into the building in Burnside to rescue Donnie was a whole different ballgame, as we had prior knowledge of a criminal abduction and a victim in imminent danger.

"There's something else we've been keeping to ourselves," said Hicks. "We found evidence of cocaine at the murder scene. On the victim's fingertips."

"Coke? You mean the old fella might have been mixed up in something bigger?" asked MacKay.

"No, there's no indication of anything like that," said Hicks. "We're thinking it's exterior to the store, brought in by the perp. There was a struggle at some point, and we're thinking maybe incidental transfer of the substance."

Donnie was following along. "You mean he got it when fighting with the killer?"

Hicks looked at Donnie in surprise, as if he had forgotten the boy was with them. Then he shrugged. "More or less, yes, Donnie."

In the emotional roller-coaster that was his incarceration and subsequent rescue, Donnie had forgotten about the main reason they were all here. The thought of Mr. Martin having to fight for his life sent a seething shaft of hatred shooting through his veins. He put his chicken burger down, his appetite suddenly gone.

Hicks continued, "We still can't find Rafuse or the car he was driving." *My car.* "Chief Daweson is getting worried. His fear is that

Rick saw something he shouldn't have and now someone has him captive somewhere. I asked him about the last place he'd been, but the chief said there's no reason to suspect the Emporium just yet. We already had officers drop by earlier, and everything seemed fine. Chief suggested we could check out the Commercial warehouse, but only when we get a warrant. Without positive confirmation of the Detective's whereabouts, no cop is going near the place without a warrant."

"Yeah, I suppose you're right," said Hassan. Everyone took another bite of their delicious burgers.

Donnie was listening to the conversation, and couldn't help picturing the detective bound and gagged somewhere in the city, maybe even in the warehouse downtown. Again, he was overwhelmed by the sheer bravery of these men.

"I could do it," he said.

"Do what?" asked Hicks.

"I could take a look in as I walk past the Commercial warehouse. And if I see anything, I could officially report it to the police."

The three cops looked at each other, then looked back at Donnie.

"Jesus, kid, I just saved your butt out in Burnside and now you want to throw it in the sling again?" said Hicks.

"I'm just walking past and using my eyes, nothing else," explained Donnie. "If I see something then, I'm just a concerned citizen."

"I could sit the car on Shore Road or Geary Street. Or we could even hide in the bushes next to the warehouse just make sure Donnie here is okay," said Hassan.

"It might screw the case if the Crown gets picky ... but it may be worth a try. You sure you're comfortable doing this, Donnie?" asked Hicks.

"You bet!"

MacKay made the decision. "Eat up boys, let's go downtown."

THE COMMERCIAL WAREHOUSE

They double timed it, eating and driving. Exiting the Chicken Burger parking lot to the right and heading up Magazine Hill resulted in a straight-line drive right to the warehouse. Just shy of arriving, Hassan made a right down Mott Street and a left onto Shore Road, coming to a stop across from Geary Street. They were two hundred feet away and on the harbour side of the warehouse. The Mounties stayed in the car, as Hicks and Donnie trotted down the train tracks past the warehouse — just a couple of guys speed walking towards the Harbour Ferry terminal.

There were three buildings that were probably warehouses, but the first one they walked past had no company name on it, unlike the other two. And there was a white van backed up to one of the loading bay doors facing the harbour.

"Hey, that's the same kind of van the Emporium uses," said Donnie. "That's got to be the building."

"No windows in the building except in that man-door and they're blacked out," noted Hicks.

The overhead door was about two feet wider than the van, which meant a one-foot open gap on each side. Fortunately, this would allow a nosy someone to look inside the warehouse if they were close enough. Even at this distance Hicks and Donnie could see a figure or two, flitting back and forth between the back of the van and the warehouse. Loading or unloading.

They walked up, hidden by the building next door.

"I wish it was darker out," Donnie said. "It'll be harder to see in that little sliver as I walk by."

Hicks stared at Donnie for a few moments like he was debating the pros and cons, and Donnie's safety. "Okay, give it a try, and watch yourself."

Donnie took a deep breath and walked on a diagonal across the parking lot of the Commercial Street warehouse. It was not dusk yet, but to Donnie it felt like high noon, the sun making him visible to everything and everyone. He was wondering how many eyes were looking at him through the open gap. In truth, the sun was setting low in the west which shone in through the gaps between the transport van and the overhead door. This aided him greatly in seeing into the warehouse. He walked past the front bumper of the van but slowed down when he looked at the other side. He could see clearly into the warehouse and there were two men inside, their backs were to him. They were wrestling with a shipping crate.

Donnie made a split-second decision. He knew he was about to give the watching cops a heart attack, but he changed course, ran quietly over to the gap and peered inside. While the men were busy, he looked as far as he could to the left. It was just a shell warehouse with no inner rooms or offices, and no sign of Rafuse. There were large boxes and crates full of gardening supplies and equipment on that end of the building. Some of them had the DIK red and yellow labels on them. Donnie turned his attention back to the two men and caught a profile view of the taller one.

Erik. Erik and some other guy. He might be one of Erik's friends who were with him at the almost fight yesterday in the Emporium. *Was that really just yesterday?*

Donnie had to figure out what they were doing. They had placed a large wooden shipping crate on the floor in front of them. The top was pried open. On the concrete floor in front of the shipping crate was a cardboard box about a foot and a half on all sides. He watched the two men until he saw a pattern.

They would pull a new box out the shipping crate, open it, do something he couldn't see from his angle. Then they'd close it up, put it back in the crate and pull out another shoe box and repeat the actions. What the hell were they doing?

Donnie *had* to find out. He figured he would have a better angle to see what they were up to if he reversed course, slipped back over to the right side of the van, and looked through that gap. Of course, that could mean it might be easier for the men inside to see him. Well, he always had the cops.

Donnie silently ran around the front of the van over to the other side and, crouching, again peered in. They were starting the next box. Donnie took the opportunity to explore the other side of the warehouse. Same situation. No rooms, no Meijers, no Rafuse. He turned his attention back to the two men.

Erik's companion bent the box top open, but not too far. He was wearing rubber gloves and an air mask. He reached in and pulled up the top side of a plastic bag. There was some kind of sealing mechanism affixed to it which he undid. He grabbed what looked like a metal scoop.

At the same time, Erik pulled a small glass bottle out of the paper bag and twisted the cover open. His friend put the scoop into the plastic bag and a dug out a heaping scoop-full of some kind of white powder, which he poured into the bottle. He continued until the bottle was full, then Erik screwed the cover back on the bottle, and placed it gently into a paper bag.

Cocaine. Probably the from the same source as the killer had possibly snorted.

Finally, Erik's partner re-sealed the plastic bag and pushed it back down very carefully back into the box. Then Erik placed the box back into the shipping crate. The two criminals seem to relax as Erik re-taped the shipping crate.

"Whew, glad that's over! Fifty-fifty, right? Four bottles for you and four for me," said Erik, as he finished taping. "Now push that crate back where it belongs, and I'll put our share in the cab of the van." He picked up the paper bag and started heading for the vehicle. Donnie made ready to run.

"Forget it," said his friend. "That bag doesn't leave my sight."

"Jesus Christ," said Erik, but he didn't push the issue. "I'll just be over here. And get yourself cleaned up."

Obviously, it's true, there is no honour amongst thieves. Donnie said to himself. Nobody trusted nobody.

Without warning, Erik headed straight towards the truck, and Donnie, who ducked down out of view. He was hidden by the overhang of the dock leveller below the door. He heard Erik trying to pull down the truck's rear rolling door with one hand. Erik cursed and set the paper bag gently down right in front of the gap on the loading dock floor! Apparently, he needed two hands to pull the door down.

Donnie had to think quick. He couldn't take a bottle with him now; they'd know right away someone was on to them. So, he came up with plan B, get a sample.

He risked a look and Erik was still cursing with the door, staring up into its inner workings. Donnie reached his hand through the gap, into the bag, grabbing the top bottle. He did his best to loosen the cover with one hand. Without seeing it, he had to clench onto the glass bottle between his baby finger and ring finger and then used his thumb and index finger to try and unscrew the metal cover.

Erik gave it an almighty yank and the door finally started sliding down. Donnie hadn't been able to get the sample, but he pulled his hand free and out of sight. Had he been seen?

Erik kicked the van's now closed cargo door and muttered under his breath, "Fuck's sake!" He reached down, grabbed the bag, yanked it up — and white powder exploded out the top. "Fuck's sake!" Erik screamed it this time. "Get a goddamn broom or something."

"Fuckin' hell, what did you do?" asked his friend. "Can't you do anything right?" A rhetorical question. "You mark that bottle, 'cause I'm not settling for less because of your fuckup!"

"Just shut the hell up and find a broom!" And Erik joined him looking for something to clean up their lost plunder.

Donnie peered in through the gap and spotted a generous clump of white power within reach. He pinched it between his thumb and index finger and placed the powder on a ten-dollar bill he had pulled out of his pocket. He was holding his breath so he wouldn't accidentally blow the evidence away as he folded the dollar bill up to safeguard the powder.

Then, checking that the coast was still clear, he took off sprinting over to and then through the small wooded are beside Geary Street, and literally ran right into the Mounties.

Hicks arrived a few seconds later and Donnie said, as he breathed heavily from the run, "No sign of Rafuse or anyone else. The place is basically one big room. But I did get a sample of some white powder. I think they're stealing it from their boss."

MacKay put the tip of his little finger into the white powder, then gently rubbed it on the inside of his lower lip. The older white-haired cop grimaced, then smiled and nodded his head affirmatively. And spit three times.

COMPANY ORIGINS

Norberg was worried. He had maybe another hour to wait until the people in the van were taken care of. *What a mess!* One small decision by an ignoramus in Hamburg to courier a box of product had set in motion a colossal catastrophe that threatened six years of work. The business had operated with complete anonymity until today. And today ... *mother of God!* First, the whole Meijer family had been kidnapped and brought here for God's sake! *Here!* Bad decision by Louis Ryan. Then Rafuse showed up.

Norberg was thrown for a loop when Rafuse had mentioned Erik. His nephew had an unfortunate propensity to juvenile behaviour when he was stressed. Then LaChance arrived on a lunch date, with his girlfriend no less, at the exact time that cop was finishing his tour. All hell broke loose.

Bradley had shut down the Emporium office, under the guise of a Department of Agriculture surprise inspection, and sent the employees home. *Good move.* Meanwhile, Jerry had sent some of his people to the Emporium for the day.

There was some other good news. Jerry had called his inside connection in the Dartmouth Police Station. No one knew anything about a matter involving Erik, so that was just a case of the detective trying to rattle him. As for Rafuse, no one at the station knew where he was, but he wasn't missed as he was a loner and was known to be gone for a whole day on occasion. Still, the Emporium had decided to send everyone home, and remove all product from the premises, just in case any more cops came here snooping about.

Jerry's men were helping move all the product out to a safer location, the Commercial Street warehouse, but for how long? Hopefully long enough until his buyer took possession of the product. Erik had taken the last load down and would be back here soon. His only worry was that the deal might fall through.

The recent call from Madeline was strange, but Norberg wasn't too concerned. The men had searched the plant and all the workers, including Heidi, were already gone. *Or were they?* If one of his staff had witnessed anything of what was going on today ... well, McGregor was coming to take care of any problems that might arise. Norberg just hoped he wasn't blamed for anything that had gone wrong.

Norberg sat back in his chair and sadly inspected his tiny office. He had chosen this modest space overlooking the shipping area because anything bigger would be an insult to his spartan nature. Everything in the room was business oriented except for a small protruding wall cabinet with a glass door. In it were several local awards and trophies, from the Better Business Bureau, the local merchants' association, the horticultural society and others. Next to them were the many charities with which the Emporium had a good name: the Nova Scotia Society for the Poor, the Christmas Elf Foundation, and several more. The Lake William Plant Emporium was well known across the country as a solid, stable business that gave back to the local community. And a single box from Europe was about to destroy it all.

When he moved to Montreal in 1952, he thought the money his wife's parents had given them would be enough to start his business, but he had underestimated how expensive the big city would be. Still, he seemed to be doing okay, making a tiny profit or at least breaking even each year.

A local entrepreneur named Rejean LaChance offered financial backing to grow his business. Other businessmen in the area warned Norberg to steer clear of LaChance, due to his shady reputation. So, he said no, which led to a string of unprofitable years. Ultimately, he decided to try Toronto, but if he was to start again in the big city, he'd have to accept LaChance as a prime investor. At their first meeting, Rejean surprised him by saying, "I'll give you the cash for everything you need. But you have to open up your greenhouses in Nova Scotia or New Brunswick. Exactly where is up to you, but I need you there. And I guarantee you'll make a tidy profit every year."

Norberg had made a deal with the devil and gotten rich. With success came a lifelong commitment to LaChance, whose son, Jerry, now lorded over him.

O'BYRNE AND JANE

After a fruitful day of shopping, Jane Langille walked in the door expecting to find a couple of starving teenagers and found an empty house instead. She called the police, frantic to know where her son was. The officer that answered didn't know but transferred her to Detective O'Byrne, who informed Mrs. Langille that her son was completely safe and in the capable hands of Detective Rafuse. They were doing field work involving some of the evidence for the case, and he assumed they would be finished soon.

Mrs. Langille wanted to know why she wasn't informed about all this. O'Byrne told her they had called several times, with no answer. Then Mrs. Langille wanted to know how long they would be. The detective replied that it could be as much as another hour.

"Alright, but I want you to know I'm not pleased with this situation at all. Dragging my young boy around to help you with this case. Honestly!" said Jane.

"The thing is ma'am; your son actually came to us with this concern. He said he remembered something extremely important to the case."

There was a long pause, then Jane sighed, "Yes that's my Donnie, determined to give his mother a heart attack before her time."

"Yes ma'am, they're like that, trying to grow up too fast. If you like, I could send a car and you can wait here at the station. I'm sure they'll be calling in shortly."

"No, not right now but I might take you up on that offer later if I don't hear from him soon. It's a bit lonely here."

"Your husband isn't home, Mrs. Langille?"

"No, he's in the south of the province, in Shelburne today, and won't be home for a few more hours."

"Would you like me to send a unit to sit outside your home, Mrs. Langille?"

"No that's alright, Detective. I have the phone and I have my husband's .303 rifle if I need it."

O'Byrne chuckled. "Well, that's comforting but I'll still make sure a car passes by your house every now and then just to be sure. And again, call anytime if you need me, Mrs. Langille."

"That's very kind, Detective. Thank you, and please call me Jane."

"I will, if you promise to call me by my first name."

"Which is?"

"Shane."

She laughed. *Shane and Jane.* "I'll do that, Shane."

PLANNING FOR THE FUTURE

"Come on Paulie, hurry up and stop fucking around and help me get this mess cleaned up. I don't want to miss meeting the new guy. He could be a good connection for our future."

Almost from the first day Paul began working at the Emporium, the other workers called he and Erik "The Twins." They were both the same height, both thin as rakes, and they each had long blond hair. And, for some reason, management always teamed them up for assignments. It bothered Delaney immensely, as he was *not* a friend of Erik's in any way. He couldn't stand the fellow. Erik loved giving orders and acting as if he were always in charge, but with Erik being the boss's nephew, there was nothing Paul could do about it. Maybe soon, though.

Something else bothered Paul. Erik couldn't call anybody by their name. He had to make up stupid nicknames. To Erik, Norberg was Norbie, Graham was Gray, and he even called his girlfriend Heidi, Heid. What a dickhead! From what the guys were saying she was now his ex-girlfriend. He must be out of his mind angry that a damn kid has pushed him out of the way and was now with that Freeman girl. *Fuck, I'd love to have seen it when that Donnie fellow made an ass out of Erik on the loading dock yesterday.* Paul smiled at the thought.

He wasn't alone in his thinking. Paul had heard through the grapevine that The Big Guy was running out of patience with Erik. So, this was no time to be stealing cash right out of the boss's pocket. But hey, he'd be an idiot not to go along with Erik's plan. It was a kilo each. Fifty grand, maybe even seventy-five in the US.

They were going to the States tomorrow, just skipping out of town. Planning to leave maybe three in the morning, a four-hour drive, then they're into Maine and heading their separate ways. The blow would go a long way to getting them each a head start. And if the chance arose, he was going to take Erik out and then he'd have double the coke on which to get started.

"Yeah, keep your shirt on. I'm cleaning up *your* mess, you ass." *Jesus Erik, you're acting like a ten-year-old Hitler.*

He threw the dustpan and the dirt, including the powder, into a garbage bag and tied it off. He tied another bag around the brush head of the broom. They'd have to take the garbage bags with them and throw it all out into the woods somewhere along the Waverley Road.

"Why the big rush? Who's coming to the Emporium? Who's this new guy?" asked Paul.

"I hear they're bringing in McGregor to make that cop and the others disappear."

Paul shuddered. Everyone in the drug business heard of McGregor. If you needed a person to disappear, he was your man. Paul finished cleaning up any trace of powder by hosing down that area of the loading dock floor, letting the water run down into the parking area outside.

"Alright, let's get in the van," said Erik.

They shut down the building, turned off the lights, locked the doors and headed out.

THE CAVALRY

The Crown Prosecutor's office, the Chief of the Dartmouth Police, and the Chief Inspector of the RCMP in Nova Scotia all agreed to send the HARP unit to the vicinity of the Lake William Plant Emporium as a precaution while a select group of Dartmouth Police were to investigate the site. They would all arrive there in approximately forty-five minutes.

Chief Daweson also sent a special request to the Halifax Police for four to six additional police officers. When they arrived at the Emporium, he would explain their special assignment, which would be to keep an eye open for any unusual activity amongst their brother police officers from Dartmouth. He informed Jennifer Horn that she would be accompanying him and Fong to the Lake William Plant Emporium. She would remain in the car on the perimeter until summoned. She would also be carrying a portable radio, to maintain constant communication with various members of the force. Jennifer said she was looking forward to her first field assignment.

Meanwhile, MacKay, Hassan, Hicks, and Donnie were already there. They had driven to a spot near the Emporium after dropping off the powder sample at Bedford RCMP detachment where the guys ran a quick test and determined it was indeed cocaine. Which had set everything into action.

Hicks was in constant communication with the chief and Fong, but it was cumbersome. They relayed radio messages through the RCMP, who called Dartmouth Police by phone. They had decided to bring in another person to help them and since Ryan implied that the snitch was a cop, they chose Jennifer. Good choice, Donnie thought.

They were parked up a curved dirt road adjacent to the Emporium but well hidden from Rocky Lake Drive. The presence of a civilian in the car dictated some measure of safety was required. The two Mounties were getting ready to leave. They had been ordered to head down on foot and set up a preliminary position to the west of the Emporium's driveway, on Rocky Lake Road. They would be hidden in the woods to the left of big wooden gates, ready to assist the HARP team when they arrived. Hicks and Donnie were to stay in the car. The Mounties went to the trunk, and dropped their hats with the big yellow stripe into the trunk. MacKay grabbed the shotgun. And as they left, MacKay leaned into the window of the car, pointed at Hicks, and said, "Derby Twins, don't forget!"

CRAMPED

Heidi was cramped in every way possible. She had been crouched in one position for hours, and her legs were sore. At one time she had stretched her legs in front of her for relief. But doing it resulted in a nasty cramp in her calf muscle, which she had to massage with both hands until it went away. She had taken her boots off, so at least she could wiggle her toes and flex her ankles.

Two idiots outside had been talking and smoking for ages, and Heidi had heard everything they said. They weren't sure who was who but were told that they were to follow Mr. Norberg's orders. And then one of them mentioned how for this job, they were both carrying. Guns, she assumed, and it scared the hell out of her. It made her even more desperate to get to the authorities because she knew she was the only hope that the Meijers and Rafuse had. But she'd be of no use to anyone if she got caught.

A little after eight, she was massaging her leg when a loud male voice came from directly above her hiding spot. "Nope, don't see him."

She almost screamed; she was within a hair's breadth of it, but she didn't. She even managed to muffle her gasp somehow. Fear, she supposed. Whoever it was had walked right over to her desk with making a sound. Then she heard the heavy food steps of work boots.

"What'd ya say?" It was Bradley coming down the hall.

"I said, I don't see him," said the person above her, who was apparently leaning on her desk looking out the window, an old sneaker and dirty grey sock visible on the floor next to her hiding place.

Bradley cursed under his breath and he and his unknown companion headed for the office door. He leaned out and summoned the two men.

"Where the hell is he?"

"Who? Erik? Don't know. He's not back from downtown yet."

LOOSE ENDS

Bradley was pissed. Erik was at least a half hour late, and he had reminded him before he left to get back fast, as they needed him to drive the witnesses to a new location. There were to be two accidents, and to make them believable, Jerry had secured the services of that fellow McGregor, who was a legend in all the worst circles. They had Rafuse's car and the Meijer's station wagon stashed at an old quarry in Enfield and their plan was to make sure that car and their occupants disappeared, figuratively of course. The final decision on how this would happen belonged to this McGregor fellow.

Bradley was looking forward to seeing how he would pull it off. Maybe stage a crash *between* the two cars. That would be the way to do it, get rid of them all in one fell swoop.

Norberg came down the hall. "Bradley, I've been looking for you two. Where's the other van, where's Erik? McGregor will be here momentarily. The police must be getting worried about their detective and may return for a second look."

Bradley just shrugged his shoulders. "Erik was doing a last run to the downtown warehouse. Paul's with him. Maybe they stopped for a burger?"

Norberg shook his head. He cursed the day, two years ago, when Erik had accidentally met Jerry LaChance. Erik had jumped at the opportunity to be a member of LaChance's group of hoodlums. The boy was just too sloppy. And he never tied up any loose end or doubled checked any job in his life.

Loose ends. Perhaps the Freeman girl was still here? Hiding somewhere. They couldn't take a chance. Norberg turned his attention to the man standing next to Bradley, "What's your name?"

"Gonzalez," answered the swarthy young man.

"Alright Gonzalez, do a check of the entire site. Greenhouses, warehouse — even here, upstairs in the storage loft, okay? Make sure no one is hiding. Bradley, get him a set of keys."

"Boss, we cleared everyone out at five-thirty. You wanna do it again?" complained Bradley.

"Yes please ... indulge me."

Lights appeared at the front gates to the Emporium. Norberg stepped over to the window and looked to the left. If he had looked to the right, he would have noticed Heidi's feet under the desk. But he didn't.

"It's Erik," he said. "Finally."

A CLEAN GETAWAY

Jennifer Horn hurried out the front door of the police station, a piece of paper tucked in her coat pocket.

About ten minutes earlier, when it was obvious that her cover was about to be blown, she went from person to person in the stationhouse, jotting down snack requests from her co-workers. "I'm heading to the Wentworth Street Café and will be back in soon," she had called out lightly to the men in the office.

Once outside, she crumpled and tossed the piece of paper into a waste bin attached to a lamp pole on the sidewalk.

Her 'uncle' was in his Buick Century, idling at the curb on Wentworth Street. She jumped into the front seat of the vehicle, giving the man a look of total devastation, her eyes on the verge of tears. He understood what Jennifer was feeling.

She had invested her whole life into the last three years. And yet she had been ordered to abandon her assignment when the lives of five people, two of whom she considered as close as family, were still in jeopardy. And as the car sped away, Jennifer was filled with guilt. Because it was she who had put them there.

Back in the station, the officers had been preparing to head for Lake William. With everything ready, they waited for Jennifer to return.

"Where is she again?" asked the chief.

"She ran over to the café down the street to grab some coffee and snacks," said Constable Hall.

"And when was that?"

"Twenty minutes ago, give or take. What's wrong, Chief?"

Chief Daweson didn't answer. He was running things over in his head. Jennifer took an extended lunch of two hours this afternoon around the same time Rafuse had vanished. *Could it really be her?*

"Hall, get your ass over to the café and see if she's stuck in a lineup."

As his surprised constable hurried out the door, the chief already knew the answer.

ERIK RETURNS

As Erik backed the van into loading bay three, Paul complained.

"I dunno why we had to come back here. We could be halfway to Boston by now and no one would have a clue where we went!"

"Jerry's crowd have people everywhere. We wouldn't get far," said Erik. "But if you and I just happen to ask for a couple days off starting tomorrow, no one will be the wiser and no one would be wondering where we were for days. Besides, I have to meet McGregor."

"For fucks sake, why?"

"You don't get it, do you man. I've already got experience in this stuff. He and I have a lot in common," boasted Erik.

"Like what?"

Erik had heard stories over the past few years, told by the older fellows working for Jerry, and they said this McGregor guy was a legend. And that's exactly what Erik wanted to be. A fixer. Not the two-bit type of fixer that Louis Ryan was, a real fixer. The kind that commanded respect and the biggest salary. The kind who could save a whole organization, which would then be in his debt. Hot women, hot wheels, and respect. Erik had no doubt he could do it. He thought of himself as tough and ruthless now. Especially after last Wednesday.

He gave Paul an evil grin, "Let's just say, after last week, I've already been blooded."

Paul grabbed his coat and backpack, and paused as he opened the passenger door, "Blooded huh? Yeah, whatever. I've had enough. Tell the boss I went home early." He paused, then said, "If you need me, give me a call and I'll come get ya." Then he walked around the corner of the main building, hopped in his Datsun, and headed for Fall River and home.

HOW IT ALL WENT DOWN ONE WEEK AGO

After Bradley's call explaining the disastrous courier shipment, Erik had wanted to run down to Martin's store and get the package immediately. But Louis Ryan, who had arrived to monitor the new shipment of cocaine, convinced him that they should drive over in the van together. Ryan grabbed a large white case out of the trunk of his car and the two of them drove the three blocks to the store.

When they arrived, Erik parked the van on the next side street facing the harbour and ferry terminal a block to the right. Ryan wanted to go into the store and get the box, but Erik said that the boss wanted him to do it, and he could handle it. Against his better judgment, Ryan acquiesced and stood outside, after having placed a Metro Pest Removal sign on the front door. He would be able to divert people from entering the store.

Inside Martin's Corner Store, Erik began talking to the owner. During the conversation, he noted that the courier box in question was directly behind the counter. The clock was ticking. Erik had to get the old guy out of the way for a minute. Then he had an idea, and thought about a less well-known cigarette brand. He checked the racks, so he knew what to say. "Anyway, I'm here for a pack of Peter Jackson, king size please."

"Hmm," said Mr. Martin. "I don't have any out here. Let me check in back."

As soon as he was out of sight, Erik came around the counter. *Damn, the box has been opened.* When he bent down to look, he was in shock. The old bugger had even opened a plastic bag. *Son of a bitch.* He quickly folded over the top of the plastic bag, then four-folded the top of the cardboard box. He was hoisting the package when the old guy came around the corner.

"What do you think you're doing?" he yelled. "Get out here, you thief. Leave my package alone."

"It's not your package," Erik explained over his shoulder. "There was a mistake and they sent it to the wrong — " Erik felt a nasty pinching pain in his back. He dropped the box and turned around. The old guy was holding a knife. The bastard had poked him!

He was holding the knife in two hands. Erik reached for the weapon and Martin lunged at him, cutting his little finger. That did it! Erik was lost in rage. When Martin lunged at him again, trying to drive him away from the counter, Erik grabbed his hands, twisting the knife free, then slashed at him with it. It tore across the left side of his neck, and as he pitched forward, Erik stabbed him several times in the back, in a blind fury. He wasn't sure how many. Then he went into a panic, running to the door and summoning Louis Ryan, who came inside and closed and locked the door.

Louis surveyed the damage and the mess, then leaned over to check for a pulse.

"Can't remove the body, not from this place, and in any case, and there's no time," said Ryan. "There's blood all down the front of your shirt. Take it off, then zip up your jacket. There's only a small spot on it. Put your shirt inside the box, close the top and carry it out to the van. Come back here with the white case."

Erik did as he was told. When he rounded the corner with the courier box, he shifted it to one hand so he could open the van's side door. In doing so, he ripped the courier waybill and the carbon paper under it in half, where the wind took it back to Commercial Street. It's always windy in a harbour town.

He went back with the white case and gave it to Ryan.

"Right. Now wait in the van," said Ryan, which Erik did. You didn't argue with a fixer who was cleaning up your mess.

After ten minutes, Ryan returned to the van, placing the pest control sign, a large black plastic bag, and the white case in the back. "Drive out to the landfill and dump that black bag. Then go to the car wash and clean the van, inside and out. When you are finished, you can then drive back to the Emporium."

"What about the main shipment?" asked Erik.

"I've already called the Emporium; the big delivery truck from Saint John is backed into the downtown warehouse. They will wait until the Emporium sends two more workers out in another van, one to supervise the product off-loading and the other to return my car to the rental agency. As I said, you are to drive back to the Emporium."

"What are you going to do?" asked Erik.

"I am going to do a last-minute check, then I have business elsewhere."

"Suit yourself," said Erik, trying to sound calm, which he was anything but, and then he drove off.

Ryan went back into the store, checked the scene from various angles, and decided it was the best he could do. He'd also decided something else. The knife hadn't gone into the white case with the other evidence. Ryan had put it in a plastic bag and kept it in the store. He wrapped the bagged knife in his jacket. He wasn't sure whether he could use it to incriminate someone else or not. He was a wary man, and liked to keep an insurance policy against clients who decided he might know too much and need to be eliminated. It had happened to him twice before in his career and both times, just such a bargaining chip had worked.

He turned to go and glanced at a mirror above the door. There was a dark spot on the side of his glasses. He took them off and saw blood on the frame from the cleanup. The door opened and a young gentleman with curly hair entered, so he pushed the glasses into his shirt pocket.

Later, after his conversation with the Langille boy, he rode the ferry ride across the harbour and considered what to do with the knife wrapped in his coat. The first and obvious choice was to pin this murder on the Langille boy. Donald's fingerprints were freshly scattered inside the store and the timing was prefect. But something inside him nettled at pursuing that course of action. Perhaps I'm growing a conscience, he thought.

After a few more moments, and at a good distance offshore, he leaned over the rail of the boat admiring the scenery ... and discretely dropped the knife into the water. He had reached a decision. This cleanup was his last job for this client and when he was finished here in Dartmouth, he would recommend to the managers of his company that they should cut ties with the Emporium. Until then, he'd have to keep an eye on this Langille boy. And maybe he would be forced to do something about him.

MCGREGOR

The rental car drove up Rocky Lake Drive and passed the entrance to the dirt road leading to the Emporium. It braked, backed up, and pulled onto the little dirt road. The car passed through the wooden fence gates and parked neatly into one of the diagonal spots along the side of the main building. The man who stepped out of the car was absolutely normal. He was five-eleven, with brown hair — not too long and not too short, blue eyes, a fit but not bulky athletic build, and unremarkable clothing. He could walk down the street with everyone staring at him and they would never be able to describe him without using words such as average and normal. Which, for the man named McGregor, was by design and often a matter of life and death. Hiding in plain sight.

He'd been told he would meet his client in an office in the loading bay area at the front of the building. He calmly walked toward the steps that lead to the upper level of the loading dock. One of the men holding a handgun at his side quickly came over said "Who are you? What do you want?"

"I am here to see Mr. Norberg, at the request of Mr. LaChance," he replied coolly.

Realizing who he must be talking to, the fellow quickly tucked the gun into the back of his belt and said, "Okay. Stay here, I'll tell him."

McGregor walked up the steps, wandered over to a van and looked in the back. Three people at the back looking tired and terrified, and one along the side wall who seemed like he could faint at any second, but looked steadily back at McGregor and said, "You the hired help?"

"And you must be the detective?" he asked, then looked at the family. "And you're the Meijers?"

"Yes. We need water. We've had nothing since noon," said the detective.

"Really?" asked McGregor.

"And a bathroom break would be nice, too," said the youngest of the Meijers.

McGregor motioned to the two nearest henchmen. "Take this fellow and let him have a bathroom break, then get him a glass of water. And do the same for the others."

The two men looked at each other. "Who the hell are you? You're not our boss."

"I'm not ordering you boys, but I suggest you do it. And I think it'll be in your best interest to do what I ask."

When they still didn't move, McGregor turned to glare at the two men, who looked at each other.

"Do what he says!" roared Norberg as he trotted over to the dock.

"What's the point?" asked one of the men.

McGregor pulled the two men out of earshot of the van. "Because you don't have to degrade a man when you're sending him to his grave," he whispered.

They shrugged and quickly went to the back of the van, grabbed Rafuse, and dragged him to the bathroom in the office.

McGregor roared after them. "What the hell are you doing? Can't you see he's injured? Treat him with a little respect!" Then McGregor swung around, all smiles. "Mr. Norberg, I assume?"

"Mr. McGregor, nice to meet you also. Let's talk in this office. We're on a tight schedule as you can imagine, and we have a couple ideas."

"Ok, if it's feasible, I'll see if I can do it immediately."

"Just a minute!" Everyone stopped, and turned to see Erik walking over towards McGregor. "You're not McGregor. You don't look anything like him."

Everyone stared at Erik like he was a madman. And maybe he was. He certainly looked disappointed and disillusioned. "McGregor is the toughest, meanest, and classiest man who ever lived. Everybody in this place knows about him. The best enforcer and fixer there ever was. Everyone knows McGregor always dresses in a thousand-dollar suit; he's red Irish and he always wears a plaid tie. And look at you. You look like a fucking hardware salesman. Or maybe, just maybe, you're a cop pretending to be McGregor?" suggested Erik.

"So, lad. You know him then? Did you ever meet him?" asked McGregor coolly.

"I don't have to! He's a legend and you don't look anything like a legend. You're a fucking imposter." Erik pulled out his gun and pointed it at McGregor's chest. "Or a narc!"

There was a collective gasp, then everyone was yelling at once, some agreeing, but most telling Erik to lower the gun. Mr. Norberg freaked out. "Jesus Christ, Erik, what are you doing? Are you mad? We don't have time for this —"

McGregor held up his hand to hush the group of men. Everyone stopped. He was standing with his back to the open van back door.

Rafuse, clutched between the two men returning him from the washroom, watched as McGregor moved slowly to his left, Erik and his gun shifting in place to follow him. *Why is he doing that?*

It was absolutely silent. McGregor stopped moving and stared Erik in the eyes, then walked toward him until his chest was inches from the handgun. The only noise, his footsteps.

"Listen boy. I *have* a thousand-dollar suit, four of them in fact. I *have* plaid ties to match. My hair *is* red and in fact curly, not like this!" He grabbed a patch of his straight brown hair. "Have any of you here ever met or even seen me before?" He addressed himself to the others but never took his eyes off Erik.

No one said a word.

"No, of course you haven't, and that's by design." Still inches from the gun, McGregor looked at the others, gesturing towards Erik. "This little farty whisp, what's the name, Erik? He isn't the only chump to accuse me of being a cop or an imposter. And I take that as a compliment. Of all the people who've met me in the last ten years, every one of them would give a different description. And that," he paused, looking around at everyone, then turned to face Erik again, "is my style!"

And then he did it. He turned sideways so Erik's gun wasn't pointed at his chest anymore. He reached his hands up to the Beretta faster than Erik could blink, grabbed and steadied the gun with his left hand. At the same time, he plunged his right index finger in-between the trigger and the handgrip, stopping Erik from squeezing off a round. He put his shoulder into Erik's chest, sending the boy flying backwards onto the hard concrete floor, leaving McGregor holding Erik's weapon. It took all of two seconds and most of that was the time it took for Erik to fall on his ass.

McGregor stood with the gun pointed down at Erik. Then released the magazine out the bottom of the gun, and kicked it down into the parking area next to the van. Finally, he ejected the round in the chamber, catching it deftly in his left hand.

Bradley watched the scene, leaning on the door frame of his office. He was wishing Erik would get his ass kicked now. Nobody really liked him. Something caught his attention — one of the phone line lights was on. But he ignored it to watch Erik's humiliation.

"Get up," McGregor said to Erik, then he handed him the empty gun. He held out his hand with the bullet in the palm.

"See this bullet, Erik? If you still think I'm an imposter, you can have this bullet right now. If you're still sure I'm a fucking cop, you go on and take that bullet. That'll be your one chance to end me, and you'll be the big hero. But if you do take that bullet right now, you'll make an enemy of me and that's your death warrant. I may even make sure you're dead before I leave here tonight. Your choice."

Erik was angry and red-faced. Embarrassed, but also terrified. He turned around and walked away from McGregor, and down the stairs to the parking lot level to retrieve his magazine.

McGregor watched him carefully, but figured the boy had learned his lesson. He turned to Norberg and handed him the bullet. "We've wasted enough time. After you, Mr. Norberg?"

Everyone relaxed. Surely this *was* the real McGregor!

"Yes, I have a map for you," Norberg explained, as the walked to his office. "The location we're thinking of is an old rock quarry off Oldham Road in Enfield. That's about thirteen miles north of here. There's a string of large boulders lining the roadside —"

"Hey, who's on line three?" yelled Bradley.

Erik had climbed the stairs back up to the loading dock and rounded the corner to the hallway when heard Bradley. He had an open view straight to the desks in the office area. And he saw her. Erik Jorgen knew who was on line three, and he started to run. "Girl!" he screamed.

LINE THREE

Heidi had heard the commotion and shouting when Erik confronted McGregor. That was her chance. The men near the office area and the hallway had vacated to see what was going on in the shipping area. Two others were still outside checking the warehouse, the three greenhouses and the general area for lost souls such as herself. It was getting dark very quickly and Greenhouse Two was lit up. They must be in there searching for people. *Maybe they are looking for me.*

Heidi stood up, barely noticing how stiff she was. With no one around, she could make a call before leaving, to get help sooner, and with McGregor here, help was needed fast. In her sock feet, she crept over to a phone on a desk next to the back door. She chose it because it gave her a view in all directions. Putting her boots on the floor, she picked up the phone receiver and hit line three. If someone were looking at a phone right now, she'd be dead, because the light for line three would be lit on every phone in the building. She dialled 4105.

"Police Emergency. How can I help?" A male voice.

Heidi whispered. "I'm at the Lake William Plant Emporium. There are four people here who have been —"

"Excuse me ma'am, could you speak up? I'm having trouble hearing you."

"I'm at the Lake William Plant Emporium on Rocky Lake Road.

There are four people here who have been kidnapped. They're tied up. One is a Dartmouth policeman. I believe they're going to be killed very soon if you don't get here fast." Heidi was sweating, staring at the hall as she spoke, hoping no one came down.

"You are saying four people kidnapped, including a police officer and are being held hostage at the Emporium?"

"Yes, yes sir, you have to hurry," whispered Heidi fiercely.

"I got it ma'am, what is your name?"

"Heidi Freeman —"

"Hey who's on line three?" A dark figure appeared at the corner from the shipping area with a gun in his hand. The silhouette started running towards her and screamed, "Girl!"

Heidi screamed "Help!" into the receiver, dropped it on the desk, and ran like a rabbit out the door, streaking down to the lake. Her boots were still on the floor by the desk.

AS REAL AS IT GETS

The HARP unit was in position. There were eight men waiting for the order to hit the Emporium, jammed into an unmarked van a half mile west on Rocky Lake Drive, in an empty rest stop. Bored stiff. They had had many false alarms like this, and honestly, a plant store? Who could possibly need their help in a plant store? A group of endangered orchids? They had seen McGregor's rental car go past a few minutes earlier but hadn't reacted. Lots of cars were going by. They were informed on the radio that there were four friendlies just outside the Emporium, two in uniform, and two in plain clothes.

Hicks and Donnie heard the call on the radio in the RCMP car. Donnie thought it was pretty cool to be identified as a "friendly in plain clothes on site." He couldn't contact his parents. But Fong had sent a message through the RCMP, and O'Byrne replied in kind, informing him that his mom had been briefed that he was busy assisting on the case at his own request.

Hicks was tense and worried about Rafuse. They sat for most of the time in silence, waiting for instructions. Hicks was in the front seat; Donnie was in the back. There was a wire screen separating the front and back seats.

"You got a girl, don't you Donnie?" asked Hicks, maybe just to quell their nerves.

"Yes, her name is Heidi. She's originally from here but lived the last six years in Liverpool. Her birthday is a week from this Monday."

"Oh yeah? Did you get her anything yet?" Hicks asked.

"No. I'm not really good at this kind of thing. Any suggestions?"

"Hmm. Can't go wrong with a pair of pearls."

"With pearls?" Donnie asked.

"Pearl earrings, my scrawny friend. The girls go crazy for them."

"Yeah? Maybe. But that's a pretty serious gift for someone who's still bringing in Family Allowance money to the household!"

"Ha. Maybe Donnie, but you have to grow up some —"

"All Units, All Units, 10-60, I repeat 10-60, Officer and civilians in imminent danger at the Lake William Plant Emporium, 1828 Rocky Lake Road."

"All Units, All Units, 10-60, I repeat 10-60, Officer and civilians in imminent danger at the Lake William Plant Emporium, 1828 Rocky Lake Road."

"All units respond code 3. All units respond code 3."

The Mounties had left the keys in the car for any emergency. Hicks started the cruiser and took off down the dirt road onto Rocky Lake Drive for the short spin to the Emporium. He parked the car over on the left side shoulder of the road about two hundred feet short of the turnoff to the Emporium. He pulled out his revolver, checked the load and turned to Donnie. "I have to break my promise, Donnie. I told you in Burnside you'd stay with me till I saw you in your home tonight. But I have to go and find MacKay and help Rafuse. You'll be safe here, so stay put! Help is right around the corner, but it's best if you don't leave this car for any reason! Got it?"

This was a different kind of Hicks. "Yes sir!" Donnie said.

Hicks got out and started jogging towards the Emporium but skidded to a stop. He turned around, looked at Donnie in the back seat for a few seconds, then jogged back.

"I was just thinking Donnie, with that metal wire dividing screen between the front and back seats, you're more or less trapped in the back there. Try the door handles."

He did and they wouldn't budge. And the window crank handles were missing as well, so Donnie couldn't roll them down.

Hicks opened the front door, looked for a switch and found it. There was an audible click and when Donnie tried the door, it opened.

"Okay, you're good to go." And then off the officer went to join the fray.

What he had just done would be the difference between life and death.

THE GANG'S ALL HERE

Madeline drove up Rocky Lake Road. About a quarter mile north of the Emporium entrance, she slowed down. There was a car parked on the wrong side of the road, just before the turn off.

"Hey man, that's a cop car," said Natty.

Madeline nodded and pulled her car over to the right side of the road under a thick copse of low hanging trees. She stopped about two hundred feet behind the police car, shut off the lights, and killed the engine. She rolled the window down, but couldn't hear anything.

"Yup, Mountie car," said Clip, jammed into the back seat. "Shouldn't we drive into the Emporium and see what's happening?"

Madeline's intuition was screaming *no* at her, not just because of Heidi missing or the empty police car parked on the wrong side of the road, but the air itself hinted that there was something big happening right now and they should stay put.

Natty felt it too. He looked at Madeline and said, "Naw, I'm happy right here for now."

Clip stared a little harder at the back of the police car. It was dark but with the headlights out, their eyes were adjusting to the gloom. "There's somebody in that car."

"Yes, there is," said Madeline. They could all see the vague silhouette of a person. "Let's stay put for now and keep an eye open from here. We don't want to be in the middle of something that we don't belong."

SHE'S MINE

Heidi flew out the back door and hit the cold ground running. She was sure the gravel beneath her socks was cutting her feet, but she barely noticed. She was terrified and almost panicking, but still had time to see two men fumbling past the greenhouses in answer to Erik's scream of "Girl!"

Tiptoeing along the shore of the lake was now out of the question. Heidi reasoned she could outrun them to the little wooden dock. Then just get lost in the lake, if the cold water didn't kill her. She remembered the train tracks at the last second and brought her feet up high to avoid tripping over the rails, then ran the fifty feet down to the dock.

She hid behind the dock shed to catch her breath and was gratified to hear a yelp and crashing in the bushes. Erik had apparently tripped over the rails and gone sprawling. His two buddies helped him up as he was cursing and sputtering.

"Get her, get her!" he roared.

Heidi knew what she had to do. She took three or four deep breaths, ran down the dock, and dived straight into the cold, dark water of Lake William.

When they reach the end of the dock, Erik and his goons watched her swim straight out into the lake. One of the men pointed a gun at her but Erik pushed his hand down and said, "No way man, she's mine and I'm going make that bitch sorry she was born."

He ran over to Norberg's twelve-foot boat moored on the side of the dock, jumped in, fired up the outboard motor, and took off after his quarry.

THE CAVALRY ARRIVES

Everyone in the Emporium had rushed to see what was going on in the office.

Mr. Norberg followed the group who were milling about and all speaking at once. He noticed that the phone receiver was sitting on the desk. He put it to his ear and listened.

"Ma'am? Are you still there, ma'am? We have units on the way."

Norberg slammed the phone back on its base and stared at MacGregor. He didn't have to say who had been on the line.

"Who saw what?" Norberg asked.

"I was right behind Jorgen, as he came down this hall. She was on that phone," said one of the men, pointing to it.

"Who is 'she'?" asked Norberg.

"Can't be sure but it looked like Erik's girlfriend."

"Heidi Freeman." Norberg cursed himself for not taking Madeline's earlier phone call more seriously.

"Who is she?" asked McGregor.

"Just one of our summer students. But if she talks ..."

"Call your people back. I can get rid of her later, before she testifies," said McGregor ominously. "Is this place clean?"

"Yes. All product has been moved to a safe location, the packaging and storage rooms hosed down," said Norberg.

"Well, you could probably walk away clean tonight except for two problems." McGregor climbed up and stood on a desk. "Now listen up. The first cops will be arriving within five minutes. I want every single gun in that box right there. Now! I promise you'll get them back tomorrow or the next day, tops. And the cops will be setting up roadblocks in every direction, so don't even think of trying to drive away. And the cops will be searching everyone. If you have an illegal handgun on you, you're looking at ten to fifteen in Dorchester. Just play mum and remember, you were all hired as temporary workers during the busiest time of the year. Don't say anything else, and Mr. Norberg here will get you lawyered-up if you do have problems."

He jumped off the desk and walked over to Norberg. "The other problem is the people in the van. I'll risk getting them away from here. I assume the keys are in that van? Good. I'll try for Enfield, hide the guns, and take care of the people in the back of the van. Also, get your people to stop chasing that girl. It won't look good when the authorities arrive. If she has gotten away, she can be dealt with at a later date. Cheer up Mr. Norberg, you just might get out of this completely unscathed."

"How will you get through the roadblocks?" asked Bradley.

"If I leave this very minute, I should be able to get away before the roadblocks are set up. I have experience with this kind of thing."

"What about Rafuse? Taking a cop out is a big no-no," asked Bradley.

"I may still do a car accident, but the more complicated a job, the more chance of failure, so perhaps I will simply make the detective 'disappear'. I'll just have to do it at a different location and time. Good luck gentlemen." He looked at the box full of handguns and motioned to one of the workers, "You, grab that box and come with me." Surprisingly, most of the men had complied, though a few had to be convinced to give up their firearms.

McGregor ordered the worker to put the box full of firearms on the van's passenger seat, and then instructed him to close the van's rear cargo door. Moving briskly, he went to his rental, got his satchel from the back seat, and brought it back to the van. He threw it onto the box on the passenger seat of the van, walked around and jumped into the driver's seat. McGregor nodded to Norberg and pulled away through the gates, past two the Mounties hidden in the trees on the west side of the Emporium.

Mackay made note of the van's description and licence plate and cursed the fact they had no portable radios.

"Shouldn't we have stopped and searched the van?" Hassan asked.

"You know better than that, Ali. We would need a warrant and you wouldn't want to screw up a case for the Crown with an illegal search."

The van continued down the road, toward Hicks, who was

running to the Mounties. Hicks attempted to flag it down but the driver swerved around him, at a relaxed speed. As the two men were looking at each other face to face, the driver nodded to him.

Hicks watched as it passed another car down the road parked under a copse of trees. "Who the hell was that?"

Frustrated, he continued on his path and found the two Mounties in the bushes.

"We just got an imminent danger call on your radio. The cavalry's coming," Hicks explained.

"Damn! I could have stopped the van as he left."

"Where's Donnie?" asked Hassan.

"I left him in the back seat, but I unlocked the back doors."

"Is that wise?" asked MacKay. "With the doors locked, it stops anyone from getting access to him."

"Yeah, but I wanted him to be able to run if he has to."

Hicks then looked through the trees at the Emporium. "Hold on Rick, we're coming!"

A single siren was whooping in the distance.

In Madeline's car, Clip said "I think we're going to have company any minute now." Seconds later two RCMP cars flew past the parked Chevelle. Then two Dartmouth Police cars. And suddenly sirens were everywhere.

HUNTED

Heidi swam like a machine. Starting off she felt fine, but this early in the summer the lake water had not had enough hot days to warm up and she was getting chilled. She headed to the shore about sixty yards to the right of the Emporium's border fence, having seen the faint flashes of emergency lights and heard the sirens. If she could get through the woods and back up to Rocky Lake Road to find a police car, she'd be safe. But she could hear the little buzz of the engine from whoever was following her in the boat. Probably the same guy who chased her out of the building. She aimed for the darkest part of the forest that came right down to the lake, and swam in under the trees. She realized she was only twenty feet to the right of the boat following her.

To get up the forest slope to Rocky Lake Road, Heidi needed to get through the rough spruce and fir trees packed close together, and she had to do so in soaking wet sock feet, already numb with cold and bruised from her run. She pulled herself out of the water and started picking her way through the sharp thick brush. But she was making so much noise! Heidi had to get as far from her pursuer as possible while his engine was running. Then the engine died, and Heidi dropped behind a tree, breathing deeply through her nose in order to make less sound, while she caught her breath.

A waxing gibbous moon spread its half-hearted light through clouds and amongst the labyrinth of trees, both a good thing and a bad thing when you were being followed. She could hear her pursuer beach his boat to her left and behind her. Heidi risked a quick look and saw a figure tying the mooring rope to a low hanging tree branch. Then he stepped up into the forest and crept between the trees trying to find her.

Heidi's first impulse was to get away as quickly and quietly as possible. Maybe head parallel to the lake with the trees as cover. But she could barely see where she was stepping, which could result in a lot of noise if she tried that. The best place to be when being chased was where your pursuer has already been. Heidi decided to be the follower, not the followed. She patiently waited crouching behind her tree, darting a glance every so often at the figure, passing her quietly just twenty feet to her left. Her heart leaped in her chest as she saw the tall figure with blond hair — *oh my God. Is it ... Erik? Dear Jesus, it is! Will I never be free of this horrible person? And was that a gun in his hand?*

She watched Erik as closely as she could. He had a pattern. He would walk a few steps, then stop to listen. Then he would repeat. Each time he paused, she had to control her breathing and remain motionless — not easy when you are shivering. *You are strong, you'll get through this.*

At last, he had moved past her. Heidi rose up and walked when he walked and stopped when he stopped. He was heading for the road, assuming, correctly, that's where she was headed. Heidi kept up with him, about twenty feet behind and to the right. She had sticky tree sap on her fingers, her feet were torn, and her face had scrapes and scratches everywhere. Heidi was worried about her eyes and was extra careful not to run into any poking branches, which were so hard to see in the dark. She was amazed that her feet didn't feel cold.

NOTHING TO SEE HERE

The chief finally arrived at the Emporium. They had spent too much time trying to find Jennifer Horn, and he was late, arriving close behind the cars that had responded to the emergency call. Since Fong and O'Byrne were on site at the Commercial Street warehouse, he left his sergeant in the station to man his phone and relay any messages to his radio. He and an RCMP staff sergeant took charge of the scene.

The HARP team had gone in first, strategically positioning two snipers on either side of the Emporium main building. The remaining six men did a sweep of the entire property. Every person found was led out into the front parking area, sitting on the asphalt, their hands tied behind them with plastic ties. There were nine suspects, including Norberg, and seventeen police officers from three different departments in front of the building. Two officers had been dispatched from Halifax to assist.

Hicks had searched everywhere for Rafuse. He feared the worst and was getting angrier by the minute. Finally, he grabbed the suspect named Bradley and threw him down on the floor, grabbing and shaking him, until he was restrained by another RCMP officer.

Despite the general search, no guns were found, no drugs were found, and Norberg gave an Oscar-winning performance for his 'confused and abused' display.

"These eight men? Why do you care? This is our busiest time of year, and I am going to hire them tomorrow for extra work. I do this every year."

"Rafuse? Yes, he came, we talked, he wanted a tour. Then he left."

"Well, he asked me about our shipping company, DIK. I knew them from my time in Europe. They have an excellent reputation. That's why we use them and not a North American courier."

"Guns? I used to have a shotgun for a while, behind the door in my office. I liked to go partridge hunting, in season of course. Why?"

"I'm sorry, who? The Meijers? No, no, can't say as I saw them here today. But we do have a display area where you can buy from us directly. Maybe they were here then? Meijer. That's a Dutch name, isn't it?"

"A van is missing? I hope it's not stolen, we're very slack here in keeping an eye on the front of the building, and we do leave the keys in the ignitions. Oh, can you and I not mention what just said? You know, for the insurance claim of course."

And each of his eight men clammed up. Wouldn't say a word without a lawyer present.

But Norberg's performance didn't make a bit of difference. Because at that same time, crime scene experts from the Nova Scotia Drug Task Force had joined Fong and O'Byrne, and were swarming over the Plant Emporium's Commercial Street warehouse, armed with a legal search warrant from the Crown. The warrant was granted due to the evidence and eyewitness information given to the RCMP by an employee of the said Emporium. Now a former employee.

A NEW TARGET

In the brush nearby, Erik was still looking for Heidi. He had made numerous stops, staring in every direction and straining to hear or see something, to no avail. Each time he stopped, Heidi ducked down, fearing she had been heard.

Now he was stopped, staring at something in front of him. He started walking again, this time at a forty-five-degree angle to his right. About fifty feet in front of him was the street. Heidi had been concentrating on Erik in front of her, moving as he moved, then stopping when he stopped. She took a glance at the road up ahead and her heart leaped. There was a police car parked on this side of the road. It was empty save for someone in the back seat, but he or she was sitting on the far side of the car, in darkness.

When Erik reached the road, about sixty feet behind the police car, he looked all around him, maybe to see if it was an ambush of some sort. Heidi slipped behind a tree to stay out of his view. The woods were thinner away from the lake, which made walking easier but hiding harder. The treetops of the woods further down the road shimmered red from the lights of the emergency vehicles that had arrived. Erik started walking *towards* the police car. Maybe he wanted to give himself up? *Not Erik, not with that ego!* Maybe he was rescuing someone caught by the police and put in the car?

Heidi grew more worried. Erik had stepped out on the road such that he was thirty feet behind the police car. Who was in the car? She increased her speed. She reached a dangerous position where she was just thirty feet behind Erik. And a single twelve-inch-thick spruce tree for cover. With the moon's growing brightness between clouds, coupled with a streetlight on the road next to the Emporium, she caught a glimpse of the lad in the back seat as he was looking out a side window.

She thought her heart would stop. That wonderful head of curly brown hair. It couldn't be. He was dead, Bradley said so. But there was no mistaking who was in the car.

Oh my God! Erik was raising the gun and pointing it at Donnie.

Madeline, sitting in the Chevelle parked in sight of the police car, saw a thin male figure dressed in Emporium work clothes and a black jacket emerging from the woods between her car and the police car. The blond hair suggested Erik, but in the dull light and distance it was hard to tell.

"Is that a gun in his hand?" asked Madeline.

"Jesus, he's going to shoot the cop!" said Clip.

A second person crashed out of the woods, closer to the police car, running onto the gravel edge of the road.

"That's Heidi!" Natty exclaimed. She was soaked to the bone, Emporium work clothes torn up, hair dishevelled. And she screamed.

She screamed as long as her lungs had air, as loud as her vocal cords could possibly make it, as desperately as any woman in history. A primeval scream of fear and anger. A scream of warning and terror that slapped Madeline into action, and she started the Chevelle, threw the Hurst shifter into first, and popping the clutch, hit the gas pedal.

Heidi screamed so loud that the cops in the Emporium parking area heard her clearly and started running towards the source. And then they were running even faster when they heard a gunshot. And leading them was Hicks. Because he knew the gunshot came from Donnie's location.

MIND NUMBING

The scream had almost no effect on Donnie, sitting in the car with the windows rolled up. It did affect Erik, who pressed the trigger a split second after the scream hit his ears and made him flinch. The bullet punched through the back window of the RCMP car, blowing glass fragments all over the back of Donnie's head. Pieces of glass sliced his left ear, the bullet missing it by an inch.

He knew what it was before the glass settled. He half turned his head and saw a figure with blond hair. More peripheral vision. Erik had the gun pointed right at him and Donnie ducked as a second bullet flew over him, spraying more glass. He reached over and flung open the right rear door of the car.

Erik, seeing that door swing open, lunged right, and fired another shot where he expected Donnie to be. But he wasn't there. Donnie had launched himself the other way across the back seat. His hands, now bloodied by the window glass, flung open the left rear door and he bailed out, dropping three feet down into a dry ditch. He landed on his bruised thigh but didn't feel a thing.

He sprang up and dove into the thick woods, hiding behind a tree for a moment, then dropped down into a gully running to his left as quietly as he could. He dared a glance back the way he came. Erik wasn't following him. He was walking toward Heidi, gun pointed right at her. Donnie's heart was in his mouth because he knew he didn't have a chance to do a damn thing. Then he heard a roar, unsure what it was, and out of nowhere came the Chevelle, wheels spitting up shoulder gravel, aimed straight at Erik. It must be Madeline, and Donnie was absolutely certain she would have run him over if she could have. But he dived out of the way, firing a shot blindly which went over the top of the car.

Madeline stopped, about a hundred feet past where Erik had been standing. She, Natty, and Clip all looked back. They couldn't see Donnie or Heidi, and assumed they had both run into the wood. Erik, in a ditch on the side of the road, was getting to his feet, gun still in hand, and Madeline was sure a bullet would reach them from that distance. There was nothing more she could do, except get help, and she stomped the gas pedal, racing down in the road.

INTO THE WOODS

Donnie, hidden in the trees, watched as Erik got to his feet. The Chevelle had taken off with squealing tires and was far up the road. Heidi was nowhere to be seen. Erik turned to walk into the woods, and Donnie thought he might be after Heidi. He had to do something to stop him.

"Erik!" he yelled. "You're such a pussy. I know what you did at the Commercial warehouse, you gutless ass. I saw you and your buddy steal all those bottles of coke from your boss. I can't wait to tell Norberg." That got his attention. Erik stopped, but instead of coming after him, Erik scampered back to the RCMP car, rooted around in the front of the car, and ran back along the shoulder towards Donnie, looking for him in the woods.

Donnie knew there were no guns left in the car, so he yelled, "Erik you're such a loser —" and was promptly blinded in the face by a bright light. The bastard had found a flashlight in the RCMP car! Erik fired a shot, and it whipped over Donnie's head. The boy dropped into the thick brush around him, cursing himself for being so stupid. The only thing that saved his life was the tendency of people on higher ground to overshoot when aiming at a target below them.

Donnie took off through the bush like the scared rabbit he was. He had discovered that having someone shooting at you is no picnic, and after three misses, his luck was running out.

He had to get away from Erik and his damn flashlight. He knew the heavy brush and trees were thickest along the lake front, and if he could get there, he might find a place to hide until help arrived. Also, if he had to, he could always jump in and swim, but it wasn't the best option as Erik could stand on the bank taking his time to aim at him. At least Heidi had been able to get away, thanks to Madeline. Maybe she even made it to the Chevelle.

Donnie heard engines and voices getting closer, and flashing red lights strobed through the forest, bouncing off trees, leaves, and branches. Help had arrived, but Erik was between him and the road, the flashlight swinging in his direction. Donnie moved closer to the lake.

Then he heard Heidi. She must have been in the wood, then doubled back to the road while Erik was chasing Donnie. She was yelling to the cops not to fire. "He's chasing my boyfriend!" And Hicks booming voice: "Hold your fire, hold your fire! We have a friendly in the woods!" Donnie was relieved Heidi was safe, and the cops wouldn't be shooting into the woods, but he still had to evade Erik. As he plunged further down the slope, the emergency lights were fainter, and he couldn't make out anything else said.

The HARP team plunged into the thick forest. They had trained hard, and lived for this kind of thing. They were going to find Donnie and Erik and sort things out. They each had a flashlight attached to the barrels of their rifles but kept them turned off. Heidi had told Hicks and the HARP team, "The guy with the flashlight, you have to get the guy with the flashlight! I don't think my boyfriend has one."

They knew it would be a close thing. This was a race, and the results, good or bad, would come down to who would find who first. They searched for the fellow using the flashlight beam, which they could see occasionally in the deep woods in front of them.

INTO THE LAKE

Donnie knew the police must be in the woods. He could hear them occasionally calling out to each other. But Erik was between him and the officers, and if Donnie made his presence know, Erik would find him first. He caught glimpses of a flashlight, mostly low on the ground but occasionally sweeping higher, and it was getting closer. He didn't know if it belonged to Erik or a cop, and couldn't risk assuming the latter. Donnie kept heading toward the lake to keep a distance between himself and his nemesis.

Heidi must have run into the woods as well. Donnie could hear Hicks sputtering and cursing and calling her to come back. Then everyone was quiet again. All he could hear was his heart pounding, his breath gushing in his lungs, and bushes and branches rustling and snapping under foot in every direction. It seemed everyone was headed for the lake.

Donnie spent several desperate minutes of stop and go running in a zig-zag pattern through thick, horrible brush. His curly hair was filled with spruce tree needles. He was praying he wouldn't snap an ankle on a downed tree or branch. He kept his work boots at the Emporium, and he was wearing the sneakers he had put on that morning, not ideal for crawling through bush. Better than work boots if he had to go in the lake, but he really didn't want to get into that cold water.

He reached the edge of the lake. Despite the cool evening, sweat was pouring down his face. His heart was pounding in his ears, but at least he couldn't hear Erik following him. That meant the HARP guys weren't nearby either. No scrunching sounds in the bush. The moon had gone behind clouds, making it darker at the lake than it had been at the road. Donnie decided he would stay put here in the dark heavy woods on the lake's edge, catch his breath, and figure out what to do. After a few minutes, he took a chance and peered around the tree he was hunkered behind.

Crack! The branch next to Donnie's ear exploded in bits of bark and tree wood! Erik was much closer than he realized, and he had no choice but to swim for it. He ran three steps and flung himself into the water. As he did, he heard a bang from the woods behind him. It was louder than the pistol, so he figured one of the HARP guys took a shot at Erik. But he didn't hit him. "Hold your fire!" boomed an official sounding voice, just as Donnie hit the water.

It took him several minutes to swim out to the middle of the narrow lake, and by then he could hear an outboard motor. Erik came racing out of a thicket of trees and brush, just thirty yards away, headed straight for Donnie. *A boat? Where did he get a friggin' boat? What's next, a damn airplane?* Terror fuelled his sarcasm. Then Erik stood in the boat, and pointed his gun at Donnie, and all semblance of levity deserted him.

He wondered why the cops wouldn't take another shot at Erik. But what they could see, and Donnie couldn't, was the string of houses along the other side of the lake. There were BBQs and children playing. People were out on their back decks, patios and yards, attracted not just by the pleasant evening but the flashing red lights at the Emporium on the other side of the lake. Some of them thought the gunshots were firecrackers or fireworks. In several places people were lining the shore, watching the show. All of them were in the line of fire.

Erik apparently figured out the police wouldn't shoot at him, because he took the time to aim before he fired again. The bullet flew over Donnie's head, and he ducked under water and swam to his left. As he did, a second bullet whizzed past where his head had been seconds before. He kept changing position, popping up, grabbing a gasp of air, going under, then changing position and back for up more air, before going under again. Disoriented, in his most recent dive he swam towards Erik.

Donnie hadn't been hit, *yet*. The swimming and diving was tiring, and he wondered how many bullets were in Erik's gun. He couldn't count on Erik running out before hitting him. But with police gathering on the shore, Erik wasn't paying as much attention to him.

There was a pause. Donnie realized Erik was torn between getting away and killing him. But then his enemy decided, and damn if he didn't turn his boat in Donnie's direction to get closer for a coup-de-grace. As Erik was repositioning the boat, Donnie had only seconds to think of something. And something did jump into his mind. It came from a movie or something he had read or whatever. He hoped it was true. A 9 mm bullet fired from a handgun was only lethal to a distance of eight feet once it entered the water ... or was it ten ... to hell with it!

Donnie took a huge breath and dived, swimming down and away at a 45-degree angle from the approaching boat. He doubted he made eight feet because what must have been a bullet struck the sole of his left sneaker, knocking his whole leg forward and screwing up his motion. Then, after a couple more downward swim strokes, what felt like a sledgehammer hit him square in the back and knocked the air right out of his lungs. He started choking immediately. Which meant he had to surface *now!* He kicked hard with everything he had. It was either that or drown.

He burst up into the night air coughing, up water and gasping, exhausted and expecting a gun shot. But there was no gun shot. The wheezing noise he was making subsided and as it did, he could hear the outboard engine getting quieter. His vision cleared and he could see Erik's boat speeding across the lake, almost to the other side. After a few minutes it beached, and he could see Erik limping through someone's backyard past the startled owners, sitting next to their open bonfire. He had hurt his leg somehow. Despite his obvious desperation to escape, Erik paused and looked in Donnie's direction. Apparently, he couldn't see the boy he'd been shooting at moments earlier. He turned away and ambled past the astonished residents toward the front of their home and Waverley Road.

Donnie was exhausted beyond exhausted. He didn't have the energy to call for help. He couldn't see people on the shore he'd come from, and wasn't sure exactly where that was. He needed to rest. When his breathing settled, he took a deep breath to prepare for drownproofing. He relaxed as his head slightly submerged. After a few seconds, he stuck his head above water grabbed a deep breath and relaxed again underwater. The third time he surfaced, he heard two faint voices.

"Donnie?" A heart-breaking plea from Heidi.

"Donnie, can you hear me?" He heard a crack in Hick's voice as he called out. Or was it his imagination?

Underwater again, Donnie realized that no one could see him this far out in the dark water. He was thinking he should have worn a white T-shirt, or maybe his Habs white road jersey. It had number 20 on the back for his favourite player, Pete Mahovlich. His red home jersey still had number 4 for his idol, Jean Beliveau, but he retired two years ago ... Donnie shook his head to get his thoughts back on track. *Better stop babbling to myself and answer I suppose!* He tried to push back to the surface but his back ached and his left leg wouldn't move. He leaned back and floated on the surface.

God, he was tired, but with his wind somewhat restored, he called out, "Over here!" It came out as a croak, so he tried again, a little louder. "I'm over here!" And he feebly splashed his hands in the water to make a noise. He could barely lift his arms, and it was hard to breath. He heard a welcome voice, though.

"I heard him, he's out in that direction, halfway to the other side," said Hicks, then "hold on, Heidi you can't do that." Donnie heard a splash from the water's edge.

"It's alright, I'll go with her," said an unfamiliar voice, and another splash.

Donnie floated in complete relaxation. He wasn't cold, he wasn't in pain. He was drifting off to sleep. A minute went by, or it might have been an hour. Then there was something soft on the right side of his face and he heard a kiss and caught a glimpse of Heidi. He tried to smile at her and say something, but nothing would come out. Someone grabbed his left arm. Donnie looked in that direction and saw a young fellow not much older than him. He was swimming one-handed while holding on to Donnie's arm. *I didn't know Peter could swim this well ...*

The young fellow saw Donnie staring and said, between strokes,

"Donald, I'm Constable Harper, RCMP." After a few more swim strokes, "Heidi and I'll have you high and dry in no time."

Call me Donnie. He was too exhausted to say anything.

Donnie figured if everyone else was swimming, the least he could do was kick his legs to help. When he tried, his left leg wouldn't budge. His right leg worked, but he only had the strength for a couple of weak kicks. He tried to lift his left arm to look at his watch, but Harper was holding that arm tightly. He couldn't see his new gift. He hoped it didn't get smashed or lost, and that was his last thought for a while.

ENFIELD, NOVA SCOTIA

Rafuse noted that for a fellow making a getaway, his driving was neither fast nor in any way panicked. McGregor seemed to be making the turns and corners as flat as he could, and he accelerated and decelerated gently. There are only two reasons to drive like that: You don't want to bruise the basket of apples in the back of your truck, or in this case, the hostages in the back of your van. On the other hand, you'd drive this way if you don't want to attract police attention.

Rafuse also noticed McGregor had slowed down and come to a stop at one point, apparently right in the middle of the road they were on. Rafuse heard muffled voices. Roadblock? Friend or foe?

One thought gave Rafuse hope. He had seen this McGregor fellow embarrass the hell out of Erik, as well as intimidate the entire group in the Emporium. First, McGregor looked much too well trained and polished, and too smooth at removing the guns, to be anything but an undercover cop. And secondly, when McGregor had been initially confronted by Erik at gun point, he had moved his adversary's line of fire away from the hostages in the van. No hitman would bother to protect the lives of people he was contracted to eliminate.

But he couldn't let himself count on that. This whole thing might end up with his wife being a widow and his son, if it was a boy, not having a father, in the next five minutes or whenever McGregor stopped driving.

Peter, propped up against the sidewall, had noticed the van stop as well. His youth and his position closer to the driver, and his not having a concussion, meant his hearing was better than the detective's. As far as he could tell, McGregor said *"Pretty sure she's in serious trouble."*

It was another fifteen minutes before they finally stopped. No one in the van had spoken during the drive. Then Peter said, to no one in particular. "I hope Clip meets Erik someday."

Rafuse tried to remember who Clip was. The van moved again, turning onto a gravel road, which scared the hell out of him. A quarry? The van stopped, then backed up for a distance. Was that a good sign? The engine stopped, and the only sound was Mrs. Meijer murmuring a prayer, crying softly.

Footsteps in the gravel, and then the back door of the van went up.

McGregor was standing there, bathed in an unexpected light. Too much light for a quarry. He was smiling.

Relief flooded through Rafuse as his eyes squinted in the light. "Which agency?" he asked.

"I work for Her Majesty Queen Elizabeth, buddy," said McGregor in a telltale accent.

Rafuse smiled. "So, you're a Mountie AND a Newfoundlander."

"Ahh, they said you were a good detective!"

The two of them shared a chuckle, but the pain in Rafuse's head turn it into a grimace. McGregor said, "Come on b'y, let's get you to a hospital."

Other uniformed Mounties had appeared and shook hands with Rafuse as he was strapped into a gurney. One of them was a towering fellow with a handlebar moustache and three stripes on his arm.

"Sergeant, have you heard anything from one of my men, Officer Hicks?" asked Rafuse.

"Yes, indeed we have. Last we heard, he and another young fellow were safe and sound with two of our men."

Relief flooded through Rafuse' body, soul, and spirit. Guilt at having let Donnie walk off on his own had been in the back of his mind all day, and if anything had ever happened to the boy ... At least he could now go to his dismissal hearing with peace of mind.

The Meijers walked out on their own, supported by the officers, though Mrs. Meijer swooned and officers and medics tended to her.

McGregor walked back over. "Sorry it took so long to drive here to Enfield. I had to make sure none of the buggers were following me."

They came to an ambulance. "What's your real name?" Rafuse asked.

"Well, I like the name McGregor, think I'll keep it for a while."

Rafuse smiled. "Roger that."

Just before the ambulance left, Peter came to the back door. They were bandaging Rafuse's head, though he had long since stopped bleeding. They shook hands. Rafuse noted that Peter's hand was trembling, but his voice was strong.

"Thank you, Detective," said Peter with tears flowing down his cheeks.

"For what son?"

"For being there. For being with us."

He looked at the boy. *Something familiar there, like seeing myself at that age.* Rafuse leaned back into the stretcher and said, "You're welcome, Peter. Come see me when you're ready to join the police force, I'll personally put in a good word for you."

THURSDAY

THE VICTORIA GENERAL HOSPITAL

The next day, feeling much better but still prone to the occasional headache, Rafuse sat in his hospital bed entertaining a constant stream of friends, colleagues, and the press, all asking questions. Normally reticent, Rafuse used his concussion to have most visitors shooed away.

A phone call from the chief informed him that the FBI had, a few days earlier, broken a code name for the real McGregor. He was on their top ten wanted list. Armed with this information, the RCMP traced his whereabouts to Moncton. Through information supplied by a deep-cover agent they had in Jerry LaChance's group, they discovered details of McGregor's trip to the Emporium. They intercepted him in Truro and substituted their own undercover operative, who did his job magnificently. All involved realized they were lucky, because LaChance and any of his people who could have identified the real McGregor had left the Emporium before their operative arrived.

Police had arrested everyone at the Emporium last night, on a variety of charges. However, there was no sign of the escaped Erik Jorgen or a certain Paul Delaney.

Rafuse had also heard what happened to the two kids, Donnie and Heidi. Donnie had been rescued, and ended up in danger again. As for Heidi, under duress, she had managed to call the police with verification of his and the hostages' location, escape armed criminals in her sock feet, swim a cold lake to safety, then follow an armed murderer through the woods, and save her boyfriend's life — twice. All with very little regard to her own safety. Jesus, he thought, she's just a kid.

But enough of that. After the most stressful day of my life, here I am surrounded by family and friends. I'm just so damn lucky.

As for Donnie, he was resting comfortably in his hospital bed, his parents and friends coming and going. He was delirious by the time they brought him into the Victoria General Wednesday night. He barely remembered the emergency room where they patched up his left foot and assessed the nasty bruise on his back. He remembered them encouraging him to cough.

Afterwards, in his room, he remembered seeing glimpses of his parents, as well as Clip, Natty, Madeline, and all their folks. He had asked for Heidi and was assured she was here in the hospital and doing well. He remembered he started crying when he asked about the Meijers' whereabouts. No one knew where they were. After that he slipped off to a deep, black, restorative fourteen hours of slumber, waking up just after noon.

Ironically, the first thought he had was where's my watch? He felt sore in many places, but his mind was working perfectly. The people who were around him when he was brought into the hospital the night before were back the next day and Donnie started tearing up again when they told him that the Meijers were safe and healthy, except for Peter's black eye. They would come to see him later in the afternoon.

Heidi was in another room, on a different floor, getting treatment. Her feet were cut and needed several stitches after thorough cleaning. She was wearing only wool socks on her feet, and had raced across rocks, gravel, splintered wood, railway tracks, and heavy boulders on the shoreline. But most of the damage to her feet was caused by the thick, brambly Nova Scotia woods, as well as the very dangerous tree limbs and heavy brush she had crossed in darkness twice last evening, trying to help Donnie. Aunt Matilda was there and never left her side until she was discharged.

Donnie's parents were by Donnie's side as he slept Wednesday night and Thursday morning. And they were furious with the Dartmouth Police. But after apologizing profusely, the chief sat down with his parents and explained why the officers involved had kept him with them last night. He also explained that the actions of the two Mounties, Hicks, and Donnie saved at least six lives yesterday and perhaps many more.

Soon after he woke up, Donnie talked to his sister Anita on the phone. He tried to play down any dangers from yesterday, and told her he was being discharged Friday, but she wasn't fooled and was flying down in a few days.

When he tried to put eight feet of water between himself and Erik, Donnie must have almost made it, because Erik's first shot, which hit his left foot, actually went right through the sneaker, and lodged a quarter inch into the ball of the foot. It hurt a lot but wasn't serious enough to warrant a longer stay in hospital. When Erik fired the second bullet, Donnie must have made the eight foot distance because it hit just to the left of his spine, right in the middle of his left lung. The bullet had lost its lethality but not its force, so there was no penetration. The doctor said it was like getting hit with a hammer. It left a large, deep bruise and would take a lot longer to heal.

Donnie also had a large painful bruise on his left thigh where he had fallen off the couch while trying to escape his cage yesterday. From the point in time that Hicks and the Mounties rescued him until this morning in hospital, Donnie hadn't felt it at all, not once. Now it hurt as much as his back. The adrenalin had worn off, he supposed.

And another important fact, maybe *the* most important fact. One of the HARP officers, they wouldn't tell Donnie his name, climbed up a wholly unclimbable tree to see if he could get a better down angle shot at Erik, a shot that wouldn't pose a threat to nearby civilians in the line of fire. Apparently, it still looked iffy even eighteen feet up. But when the officer saw that Erik had altered course to try and finish Donnie off, he said he just couldn't let him do that. When Donnie felt a hammer knock the wind out of him, the cop in the tree had fired a single bullet. Erik, who had been standing up by the outboard motor, shifted, presumably to get a better angle to shoot at Donnie. As a result, the sniper's bullet struck him in the leg or thigh instead of a vital area. He collapsed in the boat, fumbling his gun over the side and into the lake — thus ensuring Donnie's safety.

The HARP officer's hope that his downward angle shot would make it less likely to hit someone on the opposite shore was correct. It worked. But Erik hunched down behind the outboard motor for cover, sped across the lake, and made his escape. The HARP commander had radioed for units to be dispatched as soon as he could see where Erik was headed, but Erik must have caught a ride with someone because there was no sign of him, and despite roadblocks and man hunts, no one knew what happened to him.

FINGERPRINTS

Chief Daweson came back in to see Donnie Thursday afternoon. He had another long talk with Donnie's parents out in the hall. They still weren't fond of the police but, whatever he said, it seemed to do the trick. He came in and sat down next to Donnie's bed, his parents on the other side.

"How are you feeling, son?" he asked.

"I'm fine, sir," he answered, to which the chief raised an eyebrow. Donnie re-evaluated. "Okay, I hurt all over." In terms of physical damage, he was a mixed bag. Psychologically, he was fine ... for now.

Daweson smiled. "I'm not surprised. You know you're going to be okay, right?"

"Yes sir. I feel kind of sad and happy at the same time. Like I could laugh and cry at any minute. It's frigging weird."

"Yes Donnie, that happens when you've been through a trauma. You'll be fine, just give it a little time."

"Yes sir. Thank you. Has anyone caught Erik Jorgen sir?"

"No sign of him as yet, Donnie. Hospital security will be keeping an eye on your room while you are here, but we imagine he has left the province and possibly even the country."

Where have I heard that before?

"Several people who were arrested at the Emporium on Wednesday night have stated that they heard him bragging about 'killing a shopkeeper last week'. So, all police forces in North America and Interpol are to arrest him on sight under suspicion of murder — which is one reason I am here. We need to place him in Mr. Martin's store. And we've been trying to find a fingerprint match for the courier slip. Which we have in several places in the Emporium, but we have no witnesses attesting to who made those fingerprints."

"He wiped his room clean at the Norberg home. Wore gloves at work this past week. I think he was preparing for a getaway at least two days prior to yesterday. The Norberg's are refusing to attest to what he might have touched that would prove to us it was his fingerprints. My question for you is this: Is there anything you can remember seeing him touch in the Emporium with his bare hand to an extent that you would feel confident enough to swear to, in a court of law?"

"I don't think so." Then he remembered. "Wait! Yes, I might be able to help. And there's a guy from work named Graham, sorry don't know the last name, who can confirm he saw Erik handle it as well. It'll have my prints on it too, but hopefully you'll find a second set of prints. It's not in the Emporium though."

The chief leaned forward. "No? Where is it, son?"

"It's at home in my backpack. And it's an empty root beer can."

Hicks came in to visit right after the chief left. Donnie figured the two policemen came together and Hicks was waiting outside the door for the chief to finish. He was in full uniform, and holding his hat in his hands, apologized to his parents and then to Donnie.

He said he never should have left Donnie alone in the car outside the Emporium. Donnie reminded him, and made sure his parents heard, that Donnie was in the car because Hicks had rescued him in Burnside from certain death at the hands of Louis Ryan. He reminded his parents that there was literally no safer place he could have been yesterday than with three cops with three guns, and one in the trunk. As for leaving him in the back seat of the police car, he couldn't very well take Donnie along to a gun fight. And he reminded Hicks that his simple move of coming back to unlock the back door of the police car was the only reason he was still in the world of the living.

"Yes, that's all well and good officer, but as you said, you should never have left him alone in that car in the first place," Donnie's mother said, in an exhausted voice.

"No, Mrs. Langille, I sure shouldn't have. And that's something I'll have to live with and learn from. Your son is quite a fellow and I, well, all of us at times, forget he's only fifteen."

The room was quiet for a moment. Donnie said indignantly, "Sixteen!"

Donnie had a nap later that afternoon and woke up to the voice of the duty doctor talking to his parents. "We want to keep an eye on Donnie for another night because of two other reasons. One, he probably had more stress on him on Wednesday than most people will ever have anytime for the rest of their lives." The doc noticed he was awake. "Unless Donnie here decides to become a doctor." He grinned, then addressed himself to the whole family but looked at Donnie. "As a consequence of that stress, you went into shock last night Donnie, and add to that, total exhaustion. A one-two punch. Very serious conditions, but luckily, you're young and people your age often come through this kind of thing with no long-term problems. Right now, this seems to be the way you're trending."

"Two, there was some water in your lungs. Your chest is sore right? Well, that was you last night, doing some deep coughing here in the hospital." Donnie had a vague recollection of that. "Our biggest concern in a situation like that would be pneumonia, but again, I would say from your vitals, you're out of the woods. So, we're going to send you home tomorrow but you're going to stay in bed there for a few days to rest and relax. Your parents will keep an eye on you and report if anything unusual should appear."

"And I'm sure some or perhaps all of his friends will be keeping an eye on him," said Robert.

"His friends?"

"They're a very tight-knit group, believe me."

The doc raised an eyebrow. "Really?"

Donnie smiled thinking of them fondly and said to him, "Trust me, I'll never get near the front door!"

"There's nothing like friends, is there. Alright, good luck and take care Donnie, and don't take this the wrong way, but I hope I never see you again."

"The feeling is mutual, Doc!" He paused. "Ahhh, one more thing, has anyone seen my wristwatch?"

"Your watch?" the Doctor replied, "Just a minute." He went out into the hall and conferred with one of the nurses. "It's in the bottom drawer of your night table, son."

Donnie didn't wait for help. He stretched painfully downward and opened the drawer and there was his gift from Heidi. He inspected the treasure and found it didn't have a scratch on it. Just like Donnie, the watch had taken a lickin' and kept on tickin'.

COMPANY

Visitor hours were over at eight, and his parents reluctantly left him alone that night. Both his parents kissed him on the forehead and told Donnie how much they loved him. That hadn't happened in a while. Dad paused at the door to told him to get a good night's sleep. And then, "I'm very proud of you son. Good night."

"Thanks Dad, good night," he answered.

A few minutes later, one of the nurses-in-training entered his room to check on him. "Hello there. Donald Langille, is it? My name is Catherine. The other girls warned me that you're always getting in trouble, so I'll be keeping his eye on you, thank you very much." She said all this in a brogue as deep as an Irish mist and then she gave a small chuckle and continued, "Is there anything you need, love?"

Catherine was on the short side, about five-foot four. She looked very young to Donnie, maybe just two or three years older than himself. She had bright brown eyes and jet-black straight hair in a ponytail. She'd be what his mother would call 'Black Irish' — not a trace of red hair or blue eyes.

"No, I'm great thanks."

"Well, I'll be here till midnight, Donald. If you need anything at all, just press the button."

"Call me Donnie. Nice to meet you too. And that's a great accent!" he said. "How long have you been living here?"

"I moved here to live with a friend of the family in '71 and finished me schoolin' at St. Pat's High last year. I went straight into the student nursing program —it's what I've always wanted to do. And as such, I'll be having your temperature now if ya don't mind."

She took his temperature with a thermometer, orally, to his relief, checked his pulse rate and blood pressure, and checked his meds. Then she asked if he wanted any help going to the bathroom.

"No, the walker gets me there and back," he said.

She went to the bathroom and checked the graded container he was supposed to pee in to make sure it was the right colour and to verify the amount of urine to match his intake. They were being very careful with him.

He loved how her accent kicked in occasionally. He also noticed she had an old injury to her left arm, an accident or possibly a fire, which ran from elbow to wrist. But whichever, she still had full use of it.

"So, you don't have any family here? You must miss them back home," he remarked.

Catherine had a bit of a far away look on her face for a second and said, "Yes I must." Then she looked at Donnie and smiled. "Well, I better continue on my rounds. Donnie, do you want me to leave the door open tonight, or should I pull it to?"

"Thanks Catherine, could you pull it to, please?"

"Call me Katie." She winked at him, "I'll check back on you before I leave at midnight."

Donnie was in a semi-private room, but there was no one in the second bed. There was a guard stationed outside his door due to the fact that Erik and the elusive Louis Ryan were still on the loose. It was quiet, and he hovered on the edge sleep for a half hour, before he saw the door swing open. The guard was holding it for a small figure, Heidi. She had stopped by to see Donnie in a wheelchair earlier, but he was surrounded by people, and they couldn't talk. And they both felt they needed to be alone with each other after the events on Wednesday. She must have hobbled up the stairs because he could see no wheelchair in the hall. The guard pulled the door to, as she limped over to his bedside and stood looking at him for a few seconds. He pulled himself up into a sitting position as she sat on the edge of the bed and took his hand. Then her eyes started to water, and she pulled her legs up onto the bed and tucked herself into his side. She cried softly and so did he, and they held each other tightly. He felt closer to her than anyone ever in his life, before or since.

They must have fallen asleep, because near midnight they were awakened by Katie. She was well aware of what happened to the two of them these past two days, and she gave them a smile lit by her romantic Irish heart. Then she helped Heidi off the bed and guided her back down to her room on the second floor.

LINGERING DREAMS

Four days later, Donnie was home, and he felt amazing. He felt stronger or more excited, euphoric even, about the future. His back was hurting much less the past two days. His foot hurt worse now, but he had no trouble walking.

This past weekend, there had been a steady stream of relatives and friends visiting the Langille house. They all wanted to hear the story. He kept it short and to the point. *I got caught up in the Martin affair by accident, was taken by the bad guys and locked away, only to be saved by the good guys in the nick of time.* When pressed to elaborate, he just shrugged. He was in a restrained mood. Heidi, who was with him constantly those days, described it best, "Donnie, you were taciturn at every turn!"

The Crown had informed the press that several local area teenagers had been instrumental in unveiling the nefarious activities being perpetrated by the Lake William Plant Emporium, which included kidnapping, attempted murder, illegal narcotic distribution and money laundering. Their identities were not released as they were underage. But it was a small city.

Jennifer had vanished. She walked out the door of the police station last Wednesday evening and hadn't been seen since. Also missing was Harold MacLeod, a technician at the RCMP crime lab where all the evidence for the Martin case was stored, including any items that may have contained fingerprint evidence. Conditions at his residence indicated he had left in a hurry for an unknown location.

Although arrest warrants had been issued for Erik Jorgen and Paul Delaney in Canada, the United States, and Mexico, they seemed to have disappeared. There had been reports of two men matching their description crossing into the U.S. at Houlton, Maine, a few hours after Erik had escaped, but nothing after that.

And these same police forces and agencies across the continent were told to immediately apprehend and detain an individual using the name Louis Ryan, as a 'person of interest' in these same crimes.

THE OLD FORT

The following week, Donnie stood on top of the Old Fort, staring at the blue shimmering harbour waters in the distance. The weather was incredible. Already 72 degrees, early Monday morning. Beautiful white cumulous clouds at random in the cobalt-coloured sky produced fascinating shaded patterns on the surrounding landscape. It was great to be alive. Heidi was meeting him here in twenty minutes and life was good.

"Hello, Donald," came from behind him. Donnie knew the voice.

But he wasn't afraid of him, not anymore. *The only thing he can do is kill me, after all.* He turned and looked at him. Ryan was dressed similarly to the last time he'd seen him, even down to the Beretta in his left hand.

"I see you survived last Wednesday," said Ryan.

"Why didn't you kill me at the Meijer's place on Wednesday afternoon? Why stick me in that building in the first place?"

"I told you that day that I'm not going to kill you. Besides, I needed time, Donald. The entire situation was out of control by that point, and contrary to what you may believe, I do not believe in hurting people unnecessarily. So, I decided to store you in the building in Burnside because at that point I didn't know who to trust. Later, I drove out to the warehouse to pick you up and passed an industrious police officer with his ladder. I thought about intervening, but that would create even more chaos. Then the Mounties arrived and made the decision for me. My, my, always riding to the rescue, aren't they? I'd never been to the Plant Emporium, and with things spiralling out of control that evening, I had no desire to start."

"So why are you here? Going to finish the job."

"My, aren't you straightforward."

"Sorry." Donnie had no idea why he said sorry, he felt exhausted from the whole process. "I just lived through the worst week of my life."

He could tell he surprised Ryan, the way the man did a double take. After a long pause, "Donald, I have a request."

"What do you mean?"

"I need you to do me a favour and, by the way, I have already done one for you."

"You've done me a favour, like what?" he asked.

"Well, let me just say, you don't have to worry about Erik. He'll no longer be gunning for you, so to speak."

"You got rid of Erik? For me?"

"No, no, not you, personally. I did it for the people I work for. He was completely talentless, and psychotic. And a danger to the organization."

"So, LaChance ordered you to do it?"

"LaChance? Good God no, he is what you might call small peanuts? Just a minor sub-client of ours. I work for a rather ubiquitous group that goes by the name Materie über Geist – Matter over Mind in English. I take orders only from them, and my coat hangs over very many hooks, I assure you. We were supplying LaChance with high grade product and I had been sent here to keep an eye on things. Help where necessary, so to speak," said Ryan.

They were silent for a moment. "No," Donnie said.

"Pardon me?" asked Ryan.

"Whatever you did to Erik, you did it for yourself. I want no part in a murder or any other horrible thing you might have done. I am not interested in doing you any favours. This acquaintance ends here and now. And I have no plans to help you with anything anymore. Now I am going to sit on the edge of that roof and enjoy the rest of my life, whether it's fifty seconds or fifty years." Donnie turned and walked over to the roof's edge; his defiant exit marred as he had to bend down on his right leg. He was still in a lot of pain from the left one. Then he rolled onto his right side to sit up straight. All of it mixed with grunts of pain cause by the injuries in his back and that damn foot. He enjoyed the view for a minute or so before Ryan spoke again.

"I am impressed with you, Donald. And I have been, ever since I first met you. I have threatened you and terrified you more than anyone or anything ever has in your life, I'm sure. But you are refusing to be cowed by me. Out of pride perhaps? And you walked away from me now with your head held high. You have gained dignity for yourself in a situation that you consider might be hopeless, and I can appreciate that effort in anyone. I truly can. I have an example of that in my own family. You see, my parents were in Treblinka in 1943."

Donnie knew Treblinka and he knew that date. He turned his

head to the right and said, "Your parents are Polish." It was a statement, not a question.

Ryan smiled. "They were, yes."

"And 1943 ... so, were they part of the revolt?" he asked.

"Yes, they were. My father killed one of the SS guards. Strangled him with his own belt." Ryan said it with pride.

"Good for him," Donnie said, turning his head back to look at the harbour. "And did your parents make it through the war? I hope they did."

Ryan looked at Donnie's back, the gun in his left hand now pointing down at the roof. And then Donnie spoke while looking out over the shimmering harbour. *"Because life, no matter what it is like, must be lived, and because to live is not merely to survive; it is to laugh, to think, to write."*

Louis Ryan shook his head in amazement and smiled at this boy. *Steiner? He's read Steiner? My God, the intelligence and genuineness in this young man. He's no real threat to me. And to think I almost broke his neck in Mr. Martin's store two weeks ago.* He thought back to that moment. He had followed Donald closely to grab him from behind, but saw the policeman on the opposite side of the street, and decided he could not settle the matter. And now, as far as Ryan could see, the matter *was* settled ... and for the better! "Yes, my parents did survive the war, Donald. So have you."

It didn't quite register. *So have you.* What did that mean? Donnie sat there waiting for an explanation from Ryan but there was only the breeze in his ears. After a couple of minutes, he turned around, and Louis Ryan was gone.

Tears flooded his eyes but for the first time in ten days, they were tears of relief and joy because he understood what Ryan meant. *So have you* ... SURVIVED. Donnie was not a superstitious person by nature, but he knew he had just dodged the biggest bullet he would ever see in his life. Literally.

With tears still in his eyes, he staggered back to his feet, climbed down from the Old Fort, hobbled over to the water pipe, and had a big drink of the water. He looked up at the sky and yelled to no one in particular, "God Bless the City of Lakes!"

"What are you doing?" Heidi walked out of the bushes a few yards away.

He limped over to her and hugged her tightly. "I'm just thankful for Dartmouth bringing us together."

"Dartmouth? Bringing us together?" She giggled and kissed him, "You're weird." And then she saw the tears running down his cheeks, "Hey what's wrong? Are you okay?"

"I'm just so happy to be alive."

Donnie knew he would never see Louis Ryan again. He was technically correct.

EPILOGUE

ALONG THE NORTH-WEST ARM

Two weeks later, on a hot sunny Monday morning, Donnie and Heidi were visiting an old haunt from six years ago, the Dingle beach in Sir Sanford Fleming Park. It was the Dominion Day holiday, and the beach was packed with people.

Heidi was wearing a one-piece black bathing suit and Donnie had on the basic seventies style swimming trunks, red with blue stripes down the side. They found a spot in the sand to flatten out their beach towels and stake a precious, albeit temporary claim.

Donnie had decided to do Louis Ryan a favour after all. He hadn't told anyone about that last incident at the Old Fort, and didn't plan to. He still didn't know Ryan's real name. Something Polish, he supposed. If the cops knew, they never told him. He hadn't been found, and wouldn't go to court, but Donnie believed him when he said he hadn't killed Mr. Martin. But then again Ryan had apparently killed Mr. Martin's killer, so there was justice of a sort.

The court case against Norberg and his henchmen was scheduled for the fall or possibly next spring. Heidi and Donnie were two of the main witnesses along with Rafuse and the Meijers. He was both nervous and excited by it all, his first experience at a trial. They had summoned Madeline for some reason as well. Donnie figured maybe the prosecutors called her because, if they ever caught Erik, she could testify to his murder attempt. But if what Ryan said was true, she wouldn't be needed.

Jerry LaChance had fled the country and at that moment was in the Venice of the Middle East, Beirut, in Lebanon, a country with no extradition treaty with Canada. Jennifer had apparently gone with him. Donnie tried to reconcile their conversation in the Dartmouth Police Station, including Jennifer's excitement to become a police officer, with what they told him she had done and for whom she had done it. *Another life lesson, people will surprise you both good and bad.* As far as anyone knew, they stayed in Lebanon at least until the civil war broke out in 1975 and ruined that stunningly beautiful country.

The two teenagers sat on their beach towels, among the kids playing, the gorgeous girls sauntering by and the handsome hunks swaggering past. But Heidi and Donnie only had eyes for each other.

"Hey, we're in the shade, you can take off your sunglasses now, Mr. Cool." She giggled.

"It's still pretty bright out on the water," he answered.

"I like looking at your eyes."

Donnie smiled and, blushing slightly, pulled them off. They lay on their sides looking at each other, enjoying the moment. He ran his fingers lightly on her cheek. Her scrapes and scratches were healing nicely. Donnie was still limping, but that was more from his back than his foot. He was slowly returning to the person he used to be physically, but psychologically it was a different story.

He had experienced true love and sheer terror for the first times in his young life. He had been forced to contemplate his own mortality, especially during his captivity. He'd been coerced into performing an illegal act. He was confused on how he felt about Louise Ryan, the man who had threatened and yet spared his life.

It had been a life changing week. And surreal; lying on the peaceful beach, it was hard to believe it even happened. Donnie looked at the beautiful girl in front of him and decided that the future was bright for both of them. How could it not be?

After what he had gone through, Donnie knew he was changed, whether for better and for worse remained to be seen. He was slowly getting used to not having to look over his shoulder, and not jumping at the sound of every loud noise was his next goal. In later years he had nightmares. In those dreams he was always the guilty one doing horrible things. Thank God for mental health professionals who helped rid him of those nightmares. Mostly.

Donnie's mom and dad were different people after that week in June. Nearly losing their son was a wake-up call for them and it re-arranged the priorities in their lives. They were still going to go their separate ways, but they were much more civil to each other and, Donnie would say, even friends again. And that was a relief to both him and Anita.

His parents and Aunt Tillie also decided that Heidi and Donnie should have the summer off to recuperate. They weren't going to argue. No more summer job, especially not in the Emporium!

Last week, Donnie took Constable Hick's advice and gave Heidi a pair of pearl earrings for her sixteenth birthday. His parents had to buy them for him, but he was determined to pay them back. He'd have to get an after-school job in the fall. Maybe at another plant nursery. After all, he had three days experience!

Clip was taking his driver's test this week and hopefully, counting Madeline, there were two people the group of friends could rely on for rides. Donnie would start his drivers-ed course in August.

Heidi sat up and reached into her beach bag, "I need some suntan lotion on my ugly freckled back." As she rooted around, she frowned and pulled out an envelope. She looked at it and passed it to Donnie. "It's addressed to you."

His name was hand-written on the front. No address and no return address which meant someone had slipped this envelope into his girlfriend's beach bag. He knew who wrote it before he read it.

Donald,

I want you to be aware that our dealings are finished. I have no more interest in you.

But as I said previously, I am very impressed by your words and actions. And as a favour to you and in admiration for your knowledge and kind words regarding my parents and their whereabouts after the Treblinka Uprising, I would like to offer you the following gift.

If you ever need my services or influence in any way, just run an ad in the Miami Herald personals with this title: DNSL Actions International. In the body of the ad, put any ridiculous gibberish you want, it won't matter. The title will tell me that you need my assistance and I'll contact you and do whatever I can.

But please note, call on me only if you are in desperate need, because anything I do for you comes with a small price. You may have to do a favour for me in return. Nothing dangerous of course but I do tend to collect all debts owed to me.

Nice to have met you,

LR

Wow, Donnie said to himself, putting the note in the envelope and tucking it back in Heidi's bag.

Heidi handed him the lotion and as he rubbed it into her back, he mused over the point that, despite the fact that she saved his life twice two weeks ago ... she also saved it a third time. And she did it six years ago when she befriended the bashful, lonely creature he was then and singlehandedly did what no teacher ever could. She gave him a gift — *the love of reading.*

Two years ago, he had to read *The Diary of Anne Frank* for a book report in grade nine. He was floored by Anne's bravery, and her joy of life regardless of her circumstances. It gave him the impetus to find out more about that period of history. He tried approaching his uncles, one of whom had survived D-day and Juno beach, and fought the Nazis in Holland. He wanted to know what they saw and experienced. But they never wanted to say much. *We went over there because it was a job that needed doing.*

His parents were kids at the time, but his mother was more specific. She said to Donnie that out of all the wars throughout history, almost all could have been solved by negotiations or something similar. But World War Two was the only war that, in her opinion, *had* to be fought and *needed* to be won. And she adamantly stated that the Nazis with their death camps were one of the most vile, evil organizations there ever was.

His mother's passion piqued his interest, so he went to the library to find out more and chose two books about the holocaust. *Night* by Elie Wiesel and *Treblinka* by Jean-Francois Steiner.

They were well-written and heart-wrenching books. And his mother was absolutely correct, Nazi fascism was a horrible evil. Of the two books, the Steiner book had a strong effect on Donnie. Its message of hope and resistance in the face of annihilation inspired him. That the prisoners in Treblinka staged a successful uprising considering all that was against them was amazing. Donnie was so impressed, he had memorized one of Steiner's lines, the one he had quoted to Ryan fourteen days ago, on the roof of the Old Fort.

Was it fate, or was it coincidence, that the book *Treblinka* would stay in his mind? That is a mystery for higher powers to keep. All Donnie knew was that the book may have saved his life two weeks ago. And the mere fact he had read that book was due to his love of reading, a gift from the beautiful person sitting on the sand with her freckled back facing him. He put the cap on the bottle of lotion, tucked it back into her bag and kissed her shoulder.

Heidi turned to face Donnie with an inquiring smile, "What did the note say?" He leaned in then, and kissed her on the lips, "I'll tell you later, let's go swimming!"

AUTHOR'S NOTE

This book is a work of fiction. The background is loosely based on my life in my early teens in Dartmouth, Nova Scotia, Canada. All characters are fiction, and though their physical traits may have been inspired by actual people, their characters in the book bear no resemblance to, and are not meant to represent, any persons living or dead.

For the purpose of this fiction, I have changed certain historical dates to suit this story. Also, I have played free with geography, buildings, and infrastructure but only to the extent of what 'might have been'. For example, I re-designed the interior of the Dartmouth Police Station to better suit this story. And I introduced HARP into the world about a half-dozen years too early!

I hope you enjoy the book.

DJ Watt

ABOUT THE AUTHOR

DJ Watt was born in New Glasgow, Nova Scotia and has lived in many towns in Nova Scotia, and beyond, including a ten-year period in Dartmouth during his school years. An avid reader, Doug always enjoys historical fiction with occasional side trips into the dystopian world. He attended Dalhousie on scholarships but became disillusioned and left the university after two years. Taking the next year off to save money, he worked at various jobs including warehouseman and mixer operator at Ben's Bakery. DJ then obtained a Drafting Diploma and began a 42-year career, working on major engineering projects in the United States and Canada. During this time, he found the love of his life at a New Years eve party in St. John's, Newfoundland. He retired in 2022.

Contact DJ Watt through the Somewhat Grumpy Press web site: SomewhatGrumpyPress.com

Help independent authors and small presses by leaving a review at your favourite online retailer or review site, or sharing on social media.